LOVE
OUT OF
SEASON

Books by Ella Leffland

LOVE
OUT OF
SEASON

Ella Leffland

PERENNIAL LIBRARY
Harper & Row, Publishers
New York, Cambridge, Philadelphia, San Francisco
London, Mexico City, São Paulo, Singapore, Sydney

Grateful acknowledgment is made to the publishers of the following material for use of excerpts:

"The Awaking," copyright 1948 by Theodore Roethke, from *The Collected Poems of Theodore Roethke*. Reprinted by permission of Doubleday & Company, Inc.

"On Houses," copyright 1923 by Kahlil Gibran, from *The Prophet*. Reprinted by permission of Alfred A. Knopf, Inc.

"In the Desert," from *The Poems of Stephen Crane*, Alfred A. Knopf, Inc.

"Little Boxes," words and music by Malvina Reynolds, copyright © 1962 by Schroder Music Company (ASCAP). Used by permission.

A hardcover edition of this book was originally published by Atheneum Publishers. It is here reprinted by arrangement with the author.

First PERENNIAL LIBRARY edition published 1985.

Library of Congress Cataloging-in-Publication Data

Leffland, Ella.
  Love out of season.

  I. Title.
[PS3562.E375L6 1985]   813'.54   85-42832
ISBN 0-06-09130-9 (pbk.)

85 86 87 88 89 MPC 10 9 8 7 6 5 4 3 2 1

LOVE
OUT OF
SEASON

1

"The world's lasted too long . . . there've been too many combs and rings and wars shoveled under since the Sumerians . . . not to mention billions of cats and dogs without names . . ."

"Whoever you're quoting's a sick man," Morris Levinsky remarked with half his attention, looking around the cocktail lounge for a waitress.

"I'm quoting myself," his companion said, surprised that she had given voice to these private thoughts. It must be because she was exhausted, light-headed.

"Well, Joanne—" he said, snapping his fingers for service.

"Johanna."

"Well, Johanna, you've got a way of turning a phrase."

She grimaced. Simultaneously, his face hardened, as it always did when he sensed he had spoken glibly.

She was offended by the glibness, but held it in abeyance, involving herself with his face. Now, with its breeziness sloughed off, it was incised to something harsh and imposing. An air pocket of excitement rose in her chest—surprising. Her eyes flicked away from him.

He felt dismissed; and he leaned forward like a kindly family doctor. "You know," he said, "you'd probably be passable if you fixed yourself up," and waited uncertainly, for, though remarkably messy and very drawn, she was brazenly well favored and her voice was as intimidatingly classical as a harpsichord. But he had hit the mark. She was hurt; it showed in her eyes.

At once he felt better disposed toward her.

But she was getting decisively to her feet. "I'm tired; I don't want a drink."

She realized she was a stale and shabby figure. All week she had slept badly, losing the energy to change her clothes—faded green pedal pushers and an oversize gray sweatshirt hanging low in the front and shrunk high in the back—or to wash her hair, which now hung greasily around her face. She had smoked too much and eaten too little and sat immobile in a corner brooding over Philip. But tonight she had at least taken her wash to the laundromat.

"This is the first time I ever went out for a drink with

a man I met for three minutes in a laundromat," she informed him coldly, "and it will be the last."

Superior bitch, he thought as they stepped outside. It was early November, hot in the daytime, warm at night; the evening sky was hazed, like a cloudily erased blackboard. As he roared off in his battered Datsun, following her cool directions to her address, he knew he should drop the little enterprise and try another laundromat, or a coffee house or a bar; but it was past seven and he had a dinner engagement at eight thirty. Therefore, when they drew up before the dingy brick building where she lived, he stated in a tone brooking no contradiction that he would carry her laundry in for her, and when she attempted to take the bag from him he tightened his grip with a smile of severe courtesy. The bag had a red donkey stenciled on it, and it gave him an encouraging sense of dealing with a child.

In the dim foyer as they waited for the elevator she studied him from the corner of her eye. He had strolled into the barren apple-green laundromat and flopped down in a chair, a man in his late thirties, heavyset, thick-haired, wearing chocolate-colored slacks, an unbuttoned brown tweed jacket, and loosened tie. He had picked up a torn magazine, but made no pretense of reading it. His eyes had impaled, and then denuded her. She had not wanted to go with him, but she had felt empty of will. Now she should go to the building manager and have him thrown out. And she would have if his face had been different—the nose less grandiose, the mouth less sensual, the heavy-lidded eyes less ignited and direct.

They rode up to the fourth floor and walked down a narrow hall as dimly lit as the foyer. She stopped before her door, which displayed a homemade sign—POSITIVELY NO ADMITTANCE, DO NOT DISTURB UNDER ANY CONDITIONS—and took a key from her pocket with deeply nicotined fingers.

"What's the sign for?" he asked.

"I like my privacy," she said, reaching again for the laundry bag and adding a firm "Good night." But instead of giving her the bag he drew the key from her fingers and turned it in the lock, stepped inside with a cavalier gesture for her to follow, and switched on a lamp with a shabby paper Tiffany shade.

She hung back in the threshold. He was a man who took care of everything. He insulted you, he invited you into your own room, he would rape you as soon as possible. Still, when you were so exhausted, it was a comfort to have someone guide you, even if it was toward a mistake. Closing the door, she brought out uncertainly, as though in defense of her compliance: "I want to tell you I like your face."

"Sit down, make yourself at home!" he told her jovially, confidence exploding inside him.

He doesn't know where to draw the line, she thought; if he makes a fool of me in my own room I'll be forced to kick him out.

But he did know where to draw the line. He said no more, and glanced noncommittally around the room.

The furniture was cheap and mismatched; all over stood overflowing bookshelves. The air was stale with cigarette smoke and unaired bedclothes. In one corner was shoved some painting equipment, but there were no paintings on the walls. The room's single decoration was a curled poster of Venice.

"You paint?" he asked.

"No."

She perched herself on the edge of a footstool. He sat down on an unmade pull-out bed and studied her at his leisure, expansively. About twenty-three, she had a figure obviously slim and well proportioned under the shapeless clothes. The face might have been beautiful—dark Mediterranean complexion, lips generously modeled, nose short and straight with delicate nostrils, eyes long, curved, an unusual pale amber color—but the eyes were dull, with deep circles under them, the skin was toneless, the long dark hair stringy, without gloss.

The lamp threw a pool of light on the wrinkled rug between them, illuminating the girl's shoes—a pair of beat-up sneakers through whose largest rent protruded a toe with a corn.

Suddenly he was overcome by a great sadness, the sadness of never getting the best, in any way.

But at length he stirred himself. "Got a drink around here?" he asked.

"Look, you forced yourself in here. I could call the building manager."

She saw him smile at her. She got emphatically to her feet. "If you want to waste your time, fine, but I've got things to do. I've got to wash my hair." And she marched into the kitchenette, turned on the light, and stuck her head under the faucet.

"Where's your wine cellar?" he shouted over the running water. She kicked out her foot, indicating a cupboard where an old bottle of thirty-seven-cent sherry stood, and knew she would sleep with him.

"Look here, Boris," she began when she had wrapped a towel around her head.

"Morris." He was leaning against the wall, sipping from one of her cracked green plastic tumblers.

"You said your name was Boris." She was angry, nervous, and a flush had crept into her cheeks.

"I said it was Morris."

"It sounded like Boris to me!" she said threateningly.

"Okay." He smiled, shrugging. "It's Boris."

"I don't care what it is. And I don't really know what we've got in common. And I think you'd better leave."

He nodded agreeably, but took his glass into the other room with the brisk heavy stride she already recognized as peculiarly his own, and sat down again on the unmade bed. She followed him, violently rubbing her hair with the towel. "If you think I'm a . . . if you think I'm in the habit of . . ."

Oh God, he thought impatiently.

Sitting down again on the edge of the stool, she dropped the towel to her lap and lit a cigarette with her stained fingers, blowing out a stream of smoke as if to form a barrier between them.

There was a silence.

"There's a medieval legend," she said with sudden aggressive detachment, staring before her. "The souls of the dead keep marching, nowhere, all day and all night. When they drop they crumble to dust . . ."

Oh, God, he thought again, shrinking away from this high seriousness; and he glanced at his watch, feeling the routine project slip from his fingers as she drew in the rays of her simple loneliness and replaced them with this wall of metaphysics. And along with his impatience he felt a familiar pang of self-evaluation as he looked at the solemn face with its background of books.

"I suppose it sounds pointless," she added. "All finalities sound pointless."

He shrugged, setting his glass down on a scarred end table.

"I realize it's bad form to be morose," she murmured with dry self-disparagement.

"Morose? I'd call it sophomoric. How old are you, anyway?" he demanded.

"Thirty-three."

Surprise lifted his voice. "You're kidding."

"I look even younger when I'm up to par," she remarked indifferently, as she laid her cigarette in the overflowing ashtray and felt the ends of her damp hair. He saw with satisfaction that the fingers were shaking.

"Do you pick up women regularly?" she asked. "Or is this your debut?"

He was embarrassed by the naïvety of the question.

"You do it all the time," she prodded.

"When the spirit moves me," he said irritably.

"The spirit comes first, then the woman."

"Why don't you drop it?"

The cigarette burned in the ashtray, sending up a thick plume of smoke. She looked at it, but dared not pick it up with her unsteady fingers.

"There's something of the Cossack about you," she came out with, roughly shy.

"Shit. With the name Morris? I'm a Jew."

"I hate words like that," she said disapprovingly.

"Like what?" he asked. "Shit or Jew?"

"Bathroom nomenclature. But I suppose it doesn't matter. Who are we to each other?" She paused. "But you're from Russia, your family?"

He gave a short nod.

"How nice."

A malaise spread through him, darkening his eyes. She started drying her hair again as scenes from Tolstoy flashed through her mind: harvest festivals, Cossacks on rearing mounts.

"What d'you do for a living?" he asked, as though to insult her, gesturing at the squalid room.

"As of last week, nothing. I was fired for not showing up. I was a file clerk." And she added with a frigid glance: "If it's any business of yours."

She saw him openly check his watch, and her heart gave a lurch.

She began speaking hurriedly. "This man I was going with—Philip—he's English, very proper, almost a caricature. When he wanted to go to bed . . ." She broke off for a moment, then went on with uneasy determination, "He'd stand there like a waiter, very discreet, with lowered eyes. I mean, not really, but the impression . . ." Her eyes fastened on the man sitting opposite her, on his crude high-colored face.

"So?" he said, relishing her discomfort.

"I broke up with him last week."

"So?" he said again.

"Well, I'd never have . . . while we were going together . . . you wouldn't be here . . ."

"Look," he broke in, feeling the moment's ripeness, ".you use a lot of words, but life's simpler than that." And leaning past her, he switched off the lamp.

"Leave me alone," she warned him, scrambling to her feet in the darkness. "Get out of here!'

Grabbing her by the sleeve of her sweatshirt, he pulled her down on the bed, where he pinned her expertly beneath him. In a matter of seconds he had her lower clothes yanked down to her ankles. With her two struggling wrists clamped in one hand, he shot his other hand down to his trousers while his torso tried to avoid the blows of her damp, ferociously lunging head, whose teeth bit him once, painfully, through the cloth of his jacket. But as soon as he had thrust himself home, her outrage dissolved in a wild release that left her mouth limp on his sleeve, her teeth exposed but harmless.

She lay still a long while after he had stopped moving. His arm was around her, he was snoring regularly. She rolled away from the encircling arm—that intimacy was for people who knew each other—and sat reflectively on her knees, looking down at him in the faint light from the window. She felt spent, drowsy, not at all angry.

His hands gave a jerk and joined across his chest. They were blunt hands, rather small. The feet, still in their scuffed brown suede shoes, were also small. But the rest was on a grand scale. Grand scale, she thought with a sardonic smile, he's just overweight. But there was the power of a bull in the broad body. She could picture him laboring with peasant vigor in a field, dancing with fury at a harvest festival. And drawing closer, she saw him also in death. He resembled a figure on a tomb carving, lying straight as a rod, hands crossed over chest, head thrown back. In sleep the features lost their animal confidence and showed a gaunt quality strange in so heavy a face. The lips were drawn pensively down; the soaring nose looked pinched at the nostrils; the eyes with their heavy lids seemed permanently closed; and between the eyes extended a deep, bitter, anxious line.

She put her hand out and touched the dark hair by his ear.

"What time is it?" he asked, sitting bolt upright.

"I don't know," she said, withdrawing her hand and standing up to turn on the lamp. She pulled the pedal pushers around her waist and held them there. He had broken the zipper.

"Almost nine," he said, glancing at his watch; and he swung his legs to the floor, feeling powerful and joyous, as he habitually did after the sex act, *post-coitum tristesse* being a mystery to him. Buttoning up his clothes and running his fingers through his rumpled hair, he looked up at her, relieved to see no quarrel on her face. Her lips held a faint smile. The cheeks were flushed and there were points of light in the eyes. She was beautiful—unequivocally.

He found that he could not take his eyes from the face. Hastily he straightened his jacket and stood up. Confusion swept over him; and at that moment, with an embarrassed, almost pained look, she reached for his hand and brought it quickly to her cheek. He felt a burst of warmth, more than warmth, radiance—completely unexpected.

He pulled his hand back and made for the door, stepping over the laundry bag with its red donkey. "Joanne, it was a ball," he said with a brisk sweeping wave.

She stood where she was, still holding up her pants. "It was okay," she returned coldly, "Boris."

With a wrench she heard his footsteps fading down the hall. She dropped her pedal pushers, stepped out of them, and kicked them across the floor. An upheaval of gonads, insult, abandonment—none of these things she needed; she felt worse now than before she had dragged herself to the laundromat. But the confused emotions poured through some wrenched-open door inside her, and with them she had to acknowledge a rush of fresh air. Even so, it was painful to admit to herself that she had made this final disposal of Philip in such a way, to remember that moment in the laundromat when she had turned to accept the whetted gaze of a stranger. And with an intake of breath she flung him back into the night, catching a glimpse of the sleeping face as it whirled away.

Morris climbed into his car, forcing the girl down into all the faceless one-nighters of his life. Twenty minutes later as he greeted his date, his girl, his mistress, whatever she was —in any case, one of several—and she having waited an elaborate dinner for an hour, he saw that this was finally her breaking point, that they were finished; and he realized for a brilliantly illuminated and somehow comical moment that this was precisely what he had been aiming for all evening. Her bitter eyes made him want to leave her with a comforting embrace, but she slammed the door in his face, and after a moment he sighed, not unhappily, and went on his way.

2 | Morris seldom remembered his dreams, but often woke with an anonymous heaviness of heart. This almost always dissolved under the shower, and he emerged rosy and brisk, his thick hair plastered flat to his head, his blue eyes shining.

On such a morning a few days later, having dripped a path of water to his window, he stood naked surveying the hot fall day—fall was San Francisco's best season—and he stretched his wet thick arms as high as they would reach.

"You'll catch cold, Morrie," came a high-pitched Arkansas drawl.

He turned, almost pained by the intensity of well-being that this new morning brought him—as nearly every morning did—and he clenched and thrust out his fist in mock fury: "Get out of bed! Get in there and make breakfast!"

From under the bedclothes the girl tittered appreciatively.

"No!" he commanded, lowering his head, bull-like. "Stay there, babe, you're gonna get it!"

"Again, Morrie?"

"Price you pay for staying overnight." In three floor-shuddering bounds he was back in bed and had pulled her to him, adding humorously, "A stiff price."

"No, no," she reassured him.

His eyes rolled. If a contest were held for the purest feather-brain in the Western Hemisphere, Zaidee would win head and shoulders above all contenders. But driven by the energy that always made her think he was consumed by desire for her, he plunged into the imperfect being, rolling away afterward and saying in the same breath as his *cri de coeur*, "Come on, get going." She glanced at his eyes, but this time she saw no humor there, and accepting the mood change—always inexplicable, always abrupt—she threw on his big red terry-cloth bathrobe and hurried into the kitchen.

As he was driving her to work he suddenly turned off on a side street, drove down a block, and pulled over to a curb.

"What are you stopping here for?" Zaidee asked.

He was gazing at a shabby brick apartment building, running his blunt thumb over his lips.

11

"What are you stopping here for?" she asked again.

He was distracted by the questioning buzz, but it vanished as he jumped out of the car and strode vigorously across the sunny pavement into the dark foyer. He had expected the girl to stay put with all his pick-ups, and he was surprised to find her troubling him like a speck in the eye. Apprehension made him clear his throat as he took the elevator to the fourth floor. He had no idea what he wanted, what he would say; he experienced the memory of her as a strangely compelling aggravation raying out from a source he couldn't locate. Going down the hall, he looked for the sign, but found only the four tacks. He gave a loud knock and waited. "I don't even like her," he said to himself.

He knocked again, taking a few steps back and forth and drumming his fingers on his thigh. "Open up, damn it!" he muttered, giving the door a series of blows as he reached some peak of obscure expectation. Still, only silence. He turned heavily on his heel and walked back down the hall, which was lit by a begrimed milk-glass light in the shape of a lily; he paused and looked up at it, bitterly sorry for this dim unsung fixture; and all passion, hope, life fizzled away inside him.

As he got back into the car and started the motor, the questioning buzz assaulted him again. He turned and registered Zaidee.

"What did you stop there for?" she was asking him.

"Guy I had to see on business."

"Getting a simple answer out of you is practically impossible. I asked you three times!"

He gave her a look that stopped her voice, which, even when she was angry, came out in a slow drawl.

Driving with expert intimidation through the heavy morning traffic, he said impersonally: "How did you get this way?"

"What way?" she asked cautiously.

"The way you are."

She did not answer.

"How did you get the way you are, Zaidee?"

"I don't know what you mean, Morrie."

"The way you are," he enunciated roundly, yet preoccupied.

" . . . You mean that I'm in love with you?"

He made no response. He knew exactly what she was. A lonely simple-minded child who had held on to him for over eight months now, despite the unbelievable crap he had laid on her . . . but why had he allowed her to hang on? Was he— he, so heavily freighted with social conscience: professional worker among public school children, English tutor to confused foreigners, Suicide Prevention volunteer, fervent distributor of leaflets announcing the upcoming peace march— was he in actuality so inhuman, not to mention prosaic, as to use this poor dim thing as a sexual convenience? Could sexual convenience be that important, even to him? Or did he at bottom find her quality, fifth-rate, his natural niche?

Double-parking before her office building, he leaned over and threw her door open, resting a pair of heavy eyes on her face. It was a very young, meager face attached to an exceptionally long neck that soared displeasingly, idiotically, from the narrow shoulders. The mouth was too wide for the narrow face, a mobile tremulous mouth, like a child's. She wore her hair in a ponytail. A huge impatience took hold of him, a physical need to shudder, as a horse shudders to be rid of a fly.

She stared back nervously. "We'll go on the peace march Saturday?" she asked. "Like we planned?"

"What do I get from you? Nothing!" He slammed her door shut and drove off. An anguish had seized his whole being, an anguish so deep, so unbearable, that he was forced to nose the car into an alley and switch off the engine. Throwing his head back, he began rapidly to count the holes in the perforated ceiling, but broke off and sat forward with his lower lip clamped between his teeth. With one stroke he had been grabbed deep inside his body and turned inside out, and all his darkly nestling nerves, organs, veins now hung free, exposed excruciatingly to the air.

". . . Pity!" he whispered, not even aware that he was speaking until he heard the word, which came out "Phity!" because his lip was caught between his teeth; and there was something ludicrous, horribly unfitting, about this sound that made his terror ludicrous too, completely loathsome.

Something touched his shoulder through the open window and he swung around to find a man in a gray business suit squinting at him. "You're blocking traffic," the man said; and it seemed to Morris that this creature, whose suit caught the morning sunlight in a thin gold wash and whose hand was covered with golden hairs, had had his interior removed, as an egg's contents are sucked out through a tiny hole without disturbing the exterior. The sunlight, so delicate that each tiny bump in the gray sleeve cast a long, precise, transparent shadow; the vast number of individual hairs on the hand, each busily glinting under the great orb of the sun; these things were horrendous, lying as they did over an empty, lofty, body-shaped hangar.

"Move it, will you?" the shell asked. "I'm trying to get through."

His lip still anchored between his teeth, Morris switched on the engine with a shaking hand and drove into the street.

By the time he reached his office he had gained some control, but he still felt hollow, detached from the earth. He opened the door cautiously. It was an office of the candidly unprepossessing variety—no thick rugs or sleek desks here; you knew at a glance that you were in one of the lesser cells of the State Board of Education. It was, in fact, a converted chemistry lab, the building itself once having been Commerce High, taken over in its old age by the Board of Education. This room, the Bureau of Research, bore decades of spilled experiments on its floor, was still outfitted with blackboards, Peale's portrait of George Washington, and varnished yellow school chairs. Four big battered desks were visible. Two more stood behind the filing cabinet and were used at various hours by the eight psychometrists, of whom Morris was one. Here he labored over his reports, labored not to fall asleep, wondering if he was more bored in this musty room or in the school broom closets and nurses' offices where he administered his tests. He felt about the Board of Education as he might have felt about a huge fossil, wired, cemented, and screwed into erectness. Each time he opened the door with its frosted glass window, he knew the exact amount of dandruff to be found on the secretary's shoulders, the exact quantity of ancient dust, chalk, and sulfide hanging in the air. Each time was like the last time, yet as he stepped inside this morning he found himself terrified.

Leaning over her desk, the secretary was spearing the steno pad again and again with her knifeblade eyes, while somewhere else her sharp little fingers stabbed at the typewriter keys without rest. Far away from all this, in another hemisphere, his boss could be seen from the back, sitting in absolute immobility as puffs of smoke detached themselves from his bald head and rose ominously to the ceiling. Suddenly there was a hurried sound at Morris' side as the water dispenser, glaring all over with highlights from the window, gave a deep solitary gulp and relapsed into deathly silence. The secretary had stopped typing.

"Good morning, Rhonda," he said, testing his voice.

"Him's late today," the great powdered thing warbled, holding up a forefinger, "and him's got a hangover."

He regarded the finger, which was shaped like a small, very hard white carrot. With lowered head he made for his cubicle behind the filing cabinet. He flung his briefcase down, picked up the phone, and dialed a number as the fingers of his other hand nervously pinched the crease of his lapel. "Hey, Zaidee, forget all that jazz in the car . . . pick you up after work . . ." He listened briefly, his eyes closed. "Whose birthday? Your mother's? Tonight? . . . Maybe you mentioned it, I don't remember . . . Well, get out of it, can't you?" He opened his eyes and dropped his hand from the lapel. "*Yes,* ten o'clock's too late . . . Forget it, forget it, no sweat . . . Ah, Jesus, don't *cry* . . . I just said skip it."

He pulled out his address book, but instead of going through it, suddenly squeezed it into a cylinder and sat down heavily at the desk. Other people's pens, papers, balls of Kleenex. Not even a desk to himself. And he must sit here and work for four long hours in this condition of anxiety, and then go to Jackson Elementary and administer a test—playing blocks of different colors, flashcards of animals, and some vacant-eyed ten-year-old refusing to look at them, refusing to connect. Hours of that before the day ended.

"Coffee, lover?" came Rhonda's voice as she stepped into the cubicle. "Oh, it's a *bad* one, a lulu, poor babydoll—he must have been up all night."

And again everything that was moronic, puling, and pointless seemed to discolor his torment and increase it. He would rather she had come rushing in with all her pointed white fingers fixed like bayonets and killed him. Instead, she leaned over his desk and beamed at him, the powdered folds of her cheeks falling forward.

"What are you doing after work, Rhonda?" he asked, looking at the dandruff on her shoulders.

"Oh, then he can't be as sick as all that. Him's putting on."

"I feel fine."

"Which one did he break up with this time, that he wants to kill a couple hours with Rhonda?"

He shook his head.

"Anyway, Rhonda's got her ceramic class tonight, sorry, hon. You want coffee?"

"Yes," he said in a low tone. "Thank you. I would like some coffee."

"Him's so *formal* this morning," she smiled, straightening up with a flourish that shook every gelid pound of flesh. He had even slept with that.

3 | Seven hours later he climbed into his car outside Jackson Elementary, tossed his briefcase beside him, and drove off. Where, he didn't know, didn't care, but found himself parking at Ocean Beach twenty minutes later. Ordinarily, the salt air would have sent him pulling off his shoes and wading through the surf, but today he sat behind the wheel and stared at the lengthening shadow of a beached log until his eyes ached. Then, abruptly, he drove back to the city. The sun was setting, leaving a soft ashy light in which all movement seemed hushed. The streets were touched by a simplicity, a forlornness underlined by the windows standing open to the fading light. His eye was caught by a sill where the white pages of an open book gleamed. Like a small stage, it seemed to invite his audience. But he could not stop and stare into open windows, so he drove on, glimpsing here a vase of yellow flowers, there a cat licking itself. Now and then someone stood looking out, and there was a stillness about these figures that calmed him. But as he turned a corner he saw a young couple leaning against a wall, laughing in paroxysms, as though nothing in the universe existed but their pointed laughter and his pointed exclusion. It was too theatrical a juxtaposition, and he gave the moment a wry objective smile, but behind the intelligent smile his heart pounded raggedly.

He turned up a steep street lined with narrow Victorian houses rising like towers from the hill. Looking upward, he noticed, dizzyingly high and alone, in a little cupola, someone —he could not tell if it was a man or a woman—leaning out with crossed arms, gazing over the city in the direction of the darkening ocean. A pang went through his heart. As though he had heard the figure call down to him, he stopped and put his head out the window, and simultaneously the figure looked down. Morris hesitated, then lifted his arm high in a wave. A moment passed, then without responding, the figure turned in a different direction. He pulled his head back in through the window and drove on, unaccountably ashamed.

Now lights were beginning to appear, each one making his hands tighten on the wheel, as though dusk had been only a breathing space between the persecution of the day and the persecution of the night.

* * *

Johanna's apartment had stood empty only a day after she moved, then an elderly pensioner had taken it. He set up his parakeet cage in a corner, arranged a few plates in the pantry, and gave an accepting nod to the poster of Venice and the colorful if shabby lampshade. Then the excitement of moving was over and he lowered himself to a chair and fell asleep upright.

In the evenings he sat down to a dinner of frankfurters and canned string beans and then cleared the table to face a night of solitaire. Tonight he had just laid the cards on the oilcloth when there was a knock at the door. There had been a knock this morning, too, but he had been too slow in getting out of bed and answering. Now he rose hurriedly as his mind blundered back and forth between two possibilities: a new neighbor or an old acquaintance.

A thickset, thick-haired man of thirty-five or forty stood there. Because of the hair he looked like one of those musicians who played the accordion at the Hofbrau down the street. The old man himself had played the accordion in his youth, and his lips parted under the impact of this coincidence. He waited as in a turbulent dream for a connection to be made.

"I must have the wrong room," the man said with a frown.

"No, McClintock's the name," the old man said.

"I thought a girl lived here." There was an accusation in the voice, a sharpness that made the old man turn his head a little away.

"McClintock's the name," he said again.

Ignoring the baggy figure, the man stepped over the threshold. He saw the poster of Venice, the cheap imitation Tiffany lampshade. The books, the painting equipment were gone. He stepped back into the hall. "When did you move in?"

"Couple days ago," the old man answered and began closing the door, not because he wished to return to his solitaire but because he felt a quivering in his chest, a sensation so long departed from his experience that he did not even recognize it as fury. But without lifting his heel from the floor the stranger pivoted his foot so that it obstructed the door's progress. "You know the girl who lived here?"

The old man refused to answer. He stared past the face as the quivering in his chest grew into a flapping like the wings of an enormous bird. Then all at once the man went away and he found himself alone again. He closed the door and stood in the middle of the room for a full minute. Then he sat down at the table and laid a red two on a red three.

No one responded to the manager's doorbell downstairs, and going back to his car, Morris felt that it was just as well. What did he want with her? With anyone? He pulled away from the curb as a delayed image of the old man's perplexed face floated through his busy, despairing mind, striking a gong of blurred remorse and passing on, leaving him halfheartedly scanning laundromats for girls. But there was only a bent woman in a babushka. Anyway, he didn't want to be with a girl. Or with an old man, or a bent woman in a babushka, or a person up in a cupola, or anyone. He realized that now, at last, he would drive home and close the garage door and sit there with the motor running until the carbon monoxide overcame him.

He had reached this point more than once in his life, but only once had he actually tried it. This was during his marriage. But he had been so worried that his wife would come into the garage and discover him before he had died that the attempt had lasted only a moment, after which he had turned the motor off, collected himself, and gone inside. His wife had commented on his pallor and suggested an aspirin. Talk about different wavelengths. Her idea, for instance, of a hike in the wilds was to flop down under a tree with a basket of sandwiches and the *Saturday Review* Double-Crostic. Sedentary, pedantic, hysterical. Given to flashing psychological insights—at least, she thought they flashed. Never once, never for an instant, had she grasped him.

Oh God, those smug, fruitless forays of hers into his psyche —now as he drove along the dark streets to his death, their recollection opened veins of anger into his despair. For all her probing, she had never known more than a bare outline of his soul. Which she had written down toward the end of the marriage—a short biography of a man whom she called Zero—and left, as though accidentally, where he could find it.

It was a memory that thudded onto his back only when he was already staggering; he gave a wild shake of his whole spine, and without slowing the car, without even realizing it, he veered off his path to extinction and made for a bar known for its crowds and noise. Once there, he slammed the car door shut and, dragging all ten fingers through his hair like rake prongs, hurried toward the action.

At the age of thirteen Zero read Turgenev's Virgin Soil,

*expecting a racy book. He was disappointed, but before tossing
it aside he must have been impressed by references to the
landed gentry, because he felt sure that he should have belonged to that class. Land would have been his, a manor house,
an old name, serfs. In an age of exploitation it would have
remained to him to treat his ten thousand subjects with en-
lightenment, and to receive with deepest modesty their deepest
love. As the years rolled by he would set them free one by one
and present each with a thousand roubles and a thousand
acres, dying at last an old man, freed of possessions, in a blaze
of great and simple goodness.*

Bursting into the hubbub, he went directly to the bar, where
he wedged into the crowd and shouted an order for tomato
juice. He disliked liquor, and drank it only when the occasion
called for it.

Someone was flattened against him just below his chin.
He saw a young female face, upturned. She was talking to him.

*It did not trouble him that his vision of renunciation oc-
curred only at the tail end of a long life, for he realized that
to be done with power you must first have it, and certainly
you should have it in abundance if you were to understand
its sacrifice.*

"Bloody Mary?" the girl yelled as he was handed the sloshing drink.

"Tomato juice."

"It's so crowded here!" Her gaze jumped from his eyes to a
nearby table being vacated.

*But he was born heir only to a tailor's thimble, and only
partial heir at that, being the last of eight sons. His mother's
long disappointment culminated in his birth and she was
struck down by a nervous ailment, after which she called him
Saralah and dressed him as a girl . . .*

They grabbed the table—she grabbed, he dimly extended
a hand—and she plumped herself down with an out-of-breath
grin. He asked her her name, forgot it, and turned his eyes on
the roaring fireplace.

*He grew husky, energetic, and clownish; when knocked
down in play, he rolled over like a trained seal under his class-
mates' amused eyes, but their interest was never sustained,
nor was his mother's, for whom he had grown too coarse, loud,
and unladylike. She swung her attention back to her older
sons, from whom she requisitioned hours and grandchildren.*

20

*As for Zero's father, he was gray as pavement, and stepped
on like pavement.*

"I was supposed to meet my girlfriend here, but she didn't
show up."

He nodded from the border of his thoughts. At the dart-
board a youth in suntans and a white T-shirt hit the bull's-eye
three times in a row. A cheer burst inside the din like an under-
water detonation.

*Puberty sneaks sideways into the lives of many children,
but to Zero it came as a bolt of lightning, electrifying him
from crown to sole. As Moses was commanded by the voice
in the tabernacle, so Zero was smitten by a booming pronun-
ciamento: Fornicate. Aided by circumstances, in the form of
a retarded neighbor girl, he was able to know the confidence
denied the miserable young onanist; and when the girl was
institutionalized and he began looking for other conquests, he
discovered that he possessed the one thing essential to his
calling: animal magnetism . . .*

"Would you like to play darts?" he asked, still looking at
the fire.

"Uh-uh."

An orange log fell down with a thud, sending up a shower
of sparks.

*In the meantime he was growing into a stocky young man
with a crude face mercifully aided by glossy dark curls.
Drafted at eighteen, he left Brooklyn never to return, and
ate his first piece of bacon. Nausea hung heavy in his chest all
day, but a month later he was eating pork, a citizen of the
world. The war was over too soon for him to see action, but he
had seen action of another sort in several states with a staggering variety of women, and, armed with new dimensions of
confidence that touched every corner of his disparate personality, he determined to become a psychiatrist. Not an obscure shrink, but a renowned name in the field, the name.
Levinsky. Not to be forgotten. The combination of rewards
that the profession offered was exquisite: wealth, prestige, and
also the opportunity to do endless good. With GI Bill in hand,
he began his labor. Such energy, such enthusiasm his professors had never seen. Nor did he lack intelligence. Zero at
the age of twenty had the world in his palm.*

"So what's *your* name?" the girl asked.

He put his face in his hands. "Levinsky."

That was fifteen years ago. What can be said of him now except that he is hopeless?

She had called him Zero, dismissed his ethnic break with a reference to indigestion, reduced his father to one line of indifference, turned his sexual stirrings into a slapstick comedy, commercialized his desire to help people, branded him hopeless. No one in his thirties had reached his peak yet, no one that age could be called hopeless. After two years of marriage she could only produce that sarcastic piece of drivel. She had not found him. No one had found him yet.

"You don't talk much."

He saw that the girl across from him was not complaining. Cheerful. Mildly drunk. A deep velvety tan, strawy hair, well-filled blouse. He had no interest in her, felt no desire. She took his hand where it lay beside his tomato juice. He observed his hand being touched, and the corners of his mouth pulled down, fighting a surge of tears.

Ashamed, he got to his feet, but she would not release his hand. Pushing through the crowd, with the girl still clutching his hand, he hurried outside and got into his car—the girl pressing close to him as he switched on the motor—and drove back to the brick apartment building he had just come from.

He copied down the manager's name from the card over the doorbell, and as soon as they were in his apartment he flopped down on the rumpled bed with the telephone book and anxiously riffled through the pages. He dialed, his sorrowful face hardening with purpose. "Hello! Hello, Mr. Schuster! You're finally in! Sorry to bother you. Morris Levinsky's the name. I'm a friend of one of your tenants. Ex-tenant. Fourth floor. She moved out a few days ago, I need her forwarding address . . . ah, Joanne, Joan . . . Joanna? I don't remember the last name . . . I'm a friend, I told you! . . . Why not? . . . Okay, okay, no sweat . . ."

He sat back and closed his eyes. She had swum into the anonymity of the city. She might even have gone to another city. Reaching for the lamp, he plunged the room into darkness as a deep, moiling grief took him, an utter ecstasy of pain compared to the estrangement of the morning. He felt the blonde girl sitting down next to him on the bed, and he found her hand and pressed it to his face, the hand of all suffering creatures on this earth . . . After a while the phone rang from between them. He answered it quietly. ". . . What?

No, don't tear yourself away, it's your mother's birthday . . . No, it's too late . . . I know it's only nine, but I was sound asleep . . . Look, I have to go back to sleep.'' He hung up gently and put the phone on the floor.

In the morning the blonde girl flatly refused to leave the bed and began to tell him about a terrible man she had been in love with, and there was a look in her eye that he diagnosed as schizy; also, her velvety tan belonged to Helena Rubinstein and had come off all over him and his sheets. He pried her out of bed along with the sheets and blankets she clung to, helped her dress, popped her into his car, and drove to Mendel's bakery down the street. He bought her two cheese bagels, advised her to seek professional help, and deposited her among the crowds, pigeons, and sunny breezes of Market Street.

He knew exactly what he had done as he drove off. He had given a disturbed young girl back to the streets simply because in his mood, the irritable mood that followed an anxiety attack, he could not be bothered. The most he was willing to do was to feel guilty, but that fitted in very well with his mood.

He knew exactly of what his anxiety attack had consisted. Absence of authentic feeling, fragmented drives, sexual obsessiveness—and he was sorry that as soon as he felt better he would cease to worry about any of it. He knew he caught himself only in passing; arbitrary lights were beamed into his soul, he looked, they went out. So that even as he sat behind the wheel keenly absorbed in the structure of his unfortunate character, he was aware of an equally keen urge to forget it all and throw himself into the first pleasurable pursuit that struck him.

He knew exactly what he would do. He would take tomorrow off—Friday—and drive to Reno or Tahoe if the roads weren't snowbound. He would return Monday with a good three-day weekend under his belt, and some money in his pocket from the blackjack table, and his seared mood gone, and then he would face everything fresh, he would start a new life.

Even as he planned all this, he knew he was hopeless, yet at the same time he scoffed at that point of view and felt increasingly cheerful.

4 Johanna, too, felt increasingly cheerful. She was going to be interviewed for a new job, and she had moved into another apartment. This was located between the Fillmore district and Pacific Heights, in a section where several blocks of Victorian slum buildings had a year or so before been torn down in a haphazard way that left a few standing, like random teeth in a broken comb. Going north, the same species of building continued along the street, but in a shining row, restored and painted olive, deep gold, chocolate, and fitted out with brass knockers and French shutters, gradually metamorphosing into mansions of various foreign styles which increased in size and grandeur as they climbed the top of Pacific Heights. To the south the street proceeded into the Fillmore, the black ghetto, an ulcerated grayness webbed overhead by turn-of-the-century black telephone cables, its air sweetsour with barbecued ribs, garbage, and dog excrement.

It was to the demolished section in between that Johanna finally went after a day of fruitless apartment hunting—the day following her encounter with Morris. The few remaining buildings were three-storied, the white paint of their fronts grimed black among the curlicues of the gingerbread, the sides a sheer raw brown where other buildings had stood against them. All through the rubbled lots dry grass and brambles and geraniums grew in unchecked profusion, shaded here and there by unpruned black-walnut trees—the buildings incidental to the overgrowth, forgotten. The apartment was on the third floor of one of these buildings, in miserable condition, filthy, but very large and relatively cheap, though not so cheap as it should have been. As soon as she had paid the deposit Johanna went around to see her friend Wanda.

They sat down with sweet vermouth—no longer in jelly glasses but in proper goblets—surrounded by splashy gold-and-green furnishings, the pleasant flat of a young career woman beginning to make good money. Wanda had pinched and scraped her way to a Master's in Public Administration, and now at the youthful age of twenty-five had started a job as assistant city manager of an industrial town across the bay. Tall and large-boned, she had a Scandinavian farmgirl's face, ruddy and round featured, the teeth strong, the blue eyes set deep under an already vigorously lined brow. Her hair was a rough gold, curling close to her brainy skull. She sat in a new chiffon dressing gown and a pair of slippers with pink pompoms—she felt uneasy in the outfit—looking out the window that streamed with the last light, and considered Johanna's move.

"I suppose that means you're getting your things out of storage," she said.

"Yes, it does."

"Do you think you should? I don't think you should."

"I think it's the only thing to do."

"I'm sorry to hear it."

"You saw what happened without them. I couldn't paint, I couldn't do anything. I stored them as an experiment, and the experiment failed."

"I don't think you gave yourself enough time."

"Five months is enough time."

"What made you decide all of a sudden, today?"

Johanna was silent a moment before speaking. "I let a man pick me up last night. At the laundromat. We went to bed."

"Oh? Why'd you do that?"

"I liked his face. I never liked Philip's face especially."

"You just liked his face?"

"Oh, there was more. There was something vital about him; I was feeling low, I was depressed about breaking off with Philip. I wanted to get Philip out of my system."

"How did you feel afterwards?" Wanda asked with curiosity.

"Horrible. But much better. I stopped being depressed about Philip. I don't know why I was in the first place—I suppose it wasn't him so much, it was ending an affair again."

"You're always fine until they start getting serious; then you kick them out and feel guilty." After a pause, she said, "This man of vitality, are you going to see him again?"

"No." And she added: "Maybe that's partly why I moved out, in case he got it into his head to come back."

Wanda gave a shake of her head. "I don't understand you, I really don't. You meet somebody who gets to you, and all you can think of is running in the opposite direction."

"It's not as simple as that. He's crude, he's a sexual fascist—"

"But you liked him—"

"I didn't say I liked him." She swirled the vermouth around in her glass. She had thought of him all day, her blood running alternately hot and cold.

"Well, we all mature at different rates of speed," Wanda remarked.

"Oh, don't take that donnish tone. You were stuck in Academia too long—it leads to condescension based on the theory of the ideal. If you have to condescend, do it from your personal basis, you won't find it so easy."

"I've always admired your rudeness; when you're rude you always make good sense."

"Well, I'll be ruder. I've come to borrow money. I'll have to have my things moved from storage. I'll pay you back as soon as I can, I've decided to take that gallery job Conrad told me about."

"What d'you mean, take it? What if they don't give it to you?"

"They will," Johanna said indifferently.

Of course they would, Wanda thought. If men were hiring, Johanna would get the job. With a decent night's sleep and the smallest attention to her appearance, she had only to present herself. She might have become a model, but she drifted from one undemanding low-paid job to another, easily hired by impressionable males, then doing the work with boredom and inefficiency until she was fired; ad infinitum, but having to eat, while she faced her real demands in another realm.

"I know the place," Johanna was saying. "Op, pop, slop. But Conrad says the hours are short and the pay's good. And it will be a change from filing."

"Conrad's always there when you need him." Wanda involuntarily underlined the word "you"; and there was a note of wistfulness that crept in whenever she talked about him, which annoyed her.

"He's there when *you* need him, too," Johanna said.

"Oh, I suppose," Wanda said with a shrug, hoping to end the conversation.

But Johanna went right on. "You underestimate his feelings about you. I think he's in love with you and doesn't realize it yet."

"Oh, stop it."

"No, really, I think he's hanging in the balance. He's carried a torch for me for four years, that's a long time, you can't expect him to douse it just like that. But more and more I sense him going over to you—I think he's fonder of you than anyone else in the world."

"Oh, you sound so patronizing," Wanda muttered, putting her glass down.

"I do?"

"You never know how you sound when you talk."

"I'm only being honest. We both know that for four years—"

"That's you, all right; your scrupulous candor. Saint Verity. Everything sacrificed on the altar of truth."

"What's being sacrificed?"

She wanted to say: My feelings. But it sounded too whining. Besides, she generally shared (though no one could equal) Johanna's enthusiasm for frankness. "Do you want some more wine?" she asked, ruffled.

"No, thanks, I've got to leave. I've got a million things to do. Thirty would do if you could spare it."

Wanda took out her checkbook, thinking, as she filled it out, of how she and Johanna had met—brought together by a drunk in a filthy coat to his ankles, shoelaces dragging, hair on end. He was stumbling along the street behind a pin-up type in a pair of shorts and a sleeveless blouse, and as Wanda came abreast of them he flung his arms around the girl. A comical shuffle ensued, the girl as embarrassed as she was unnerved, the drunk so fomented that he slurpingly kissed his own arm. "Stop!" Wanda cried at the drunk, who threw her a glance that ended in a coat-flapping gallop in the opposite direction. There followed thanks from the girl, then a coincidence: each had with her a pocketbook edition of Huizinga's *The Waning of the Middle Ages*, Wanda's under her arm like a billy club, Johanna's on the ground. "As compared to Durant?" Wanda asked without prelude, juicily expecting a blank "Huh?" because the girl looked the type who would carry a book strictly for purposes of ostentation. "Huizinga's more specialized," came an immediate reply, "but in my opinion with deeper insights." They had gone to a coffee house and talked for two hours. Within a month they were close friends. But Wanda could never forget that she had first appeared to Johanna in the form of a savior. She wondered if any of Johanna's friends had not, despite the prickly impression she gave of needing no one and nothing.

The check was taken, her hand was warmly pressed, and

Johanna was gone, hair flying, a book sticking out of her bag, the picture of a young coed, she who was more than ten years past that time. But, Wanda reflected, time was Johanna's confusion; she didn't know where she stood in it, which year of her span, or, for that matter, which century of the world's.

Half an hour later Johanna stood in the basement of the building where her possessions were stored. The light bulb by the door cast a weak illumination toward the canvas-covered bulk, which she approached like someone returning to a sorely missed friend.

5

Johanna could never reduce her early life to less than the dozen memories it consisted of. Government camps. Outhouses. Tin plates. Bare feet. A floundering truck piled high with belongings. Her parents: his blue jaw and wine breath, a foul mouth competing with the burning brakes. Her mother's round coppery face and black hair crimped up in a perm, out of place among the wispy buns of the other women, like her red nails. She was city, at least town; Johanna remembered, even earlier, the rundown outskirts of a town: auto camps, one-pump Esso stations, clapboard bungalows in dirt yards strewn with junk. The blue-jawed man, a dustbowl farmer, wasn't necessarily her father. He had probably been latched on to just before the big Depression drift to California.

These two people called her Fayette. It was her name. Fayette Coombs. As ugly a name as had ever been put together—and who did the "Coombs" belong to, the mother or the man? There was no way of knowing. Both had dissolved early, the mother more rapidly than the man. Johanna's most distinct memory was of a county hospital, in Stockton, or Sacramento, or maybe somewhere else. Behind a screen lay her mother with her round face wasted away. Her eyes had fastened on her child's and brimmed, and Johanna had never seen her again.

After that came foster homes, and when she was seven or eight, a return of Blue Jaw, bringing with him a very fat elderly woman who smelled of kerosene and owned a turkey farm high in the Napa hills. His breath was no longer sour with wine, but he looked crazy, like someone bound from head to foot with ropes, teeth clenched and ears trying to grow into wings. Clarrie, the old woman, had religion. When her convert broke loose and escaped to a flophouse down by the Napa River and then into oblivion, she poured her learning into his daughter, ward, whatever Fayette was to him, pasting a red star into a thumb-smudged notebook each time the girl correctly repeated a passage from a magazine called *The Light of Christ*. These passages went in one ear and out the other as Fayette fastened on the importances: a waterfall a mile away with the skeleton of an animal (a hunting dog, Clarrie told her) stuck in the limbs of a tree growing halfway down the cliff; Clarrie's scruffy, dispirited cow and goat, unnamed, unpetted, sometimes unfed; and the farm's nearest neighbors, the von Kaulbachs, whom Clarrie loved with narrowed eyes and trembling lips. The von Kaulbachs were unnatural aliens. "They filled the trenches with blood thirty years ago," declaimed Clarrie, "and they're out to do it again, sweet patient Jesus on the cross. France has fell, and the aliens, they're dancing in the streets! But we don't hate our enemies!" So Clarrie loved them.

Mrs. von Kaulbach was Fayette's teacher in the country school, a woman in her late fifties with marmalade braids piled on her head and silver chains attached to her glasses. She spoke like no one on earth (it was a German accent, she said), grinding up the words in her throat; but she was as soft as a peeled fig not only in her looks but in her ways, always smiling, always allowing her pupils to do as they pleased, and sometimes standing corrected by the smarter ones. It was not easy to picture this lady "giving the lowdown to the Huns" over her shortwave set, or to believe that she had crammed her water tank with people who'd snooped, or to believe that she was married to a man one hundred and ten years old ("That's what they say, people who've ever seen him!"). It was hard to believe that Mrs. von Kaulbach carried in her soft white hands the seeds of impetigo that plagued the schoolchildren ("Who else?"), and that her one hope was to see the golden city of San Francisco bombed off the map. It was not easy, and Fayette failed so badly that she became the von Kaulbachs'.

It began with her loitering around their house and ended with an invitation inside. She sustained the shock of a floor covered not with linoleum, but a rug; then she lifted her eyes for the rest: tables with thin curved legs, row upon row of big gleaming books with gold titles pressed into the leather, curtains like an old wedding dress she had once found in a trunk, with masses of raised yellowish flower shapes darned into them, and set off on either side by looped and tasseled dark drapes; candles in twisted silver holders, and hanging from the ceiling a sparkling collection of icicles topped with light bulbs. "Come along, then," her teacher said and took her into another room, where someone sat in the depths of a large black chair like a throne. His skin was pale and tight except where there were big gray pockets under his eyes. Over the eyes were glasses without stems, clamped tightly to the bridge of his nose. Under the nose sat a square gray mustache, and on the chin sat a square gray beard. His hair, gray too, lay in two long strands combed straight back across a bumpy polished skull. All over his sunken cheeks were broken red veins that gave his white skin a raw look, as if he had just come in from the cold. He wore a spotless white suit, and there were cloth covers with tiny buttons on his shoes. For the first time in her life Fayette was deeply, unpleasantly aware of her rundown shoes, her hair matted under its outer layer, her arms and legs covered with scabs from hikes and impetigo. A loud voice broke through the room: "Kindly introduce us, Maria."

"This is Fayette Coombs. Fayette, please be known to mine father-in-law, Herr von Kaulbach."

He lit a cigarette with trembling fingers and blew the smoke out powerfully. "From the window I have seen you standing about. I am pleased to make your acquaintance. Kindly sit down." She sat in a soft chair the color of a ripe plum. Maria stood behind the old man's chair with her vague smile, turning a little aside whenever his smoke drifted up to her nostrils. He twisted around. "You may leave us if you wish, Maria." She gave a bow of the head and padded from the room. "You smell of kerosene," the loud voice informed Fayette. "It's for the lice," she explained uneasily, touching her hair. "Have you something more cheerful to talk about?" he asked. She shook her head. "Of course you have. Speak up. Tell me about these mountains we live in, I like a bat in its cave." She told him that the one they lived on was called Mount George. "Yes, I know that," he said. She told him there was a waterfall a mile away. "That I did not know," he said, smoking away and glaring at her from under his nose-pinching glasses.

"There's a skeleton of a dog stuck in a tree halfways down the cliff."

"That is not imagination?"

"Uh-uh."

"How did it come to be there?"

"Nobody knows. Anyways, that's what Clarrie says."

"What is your opinion?"

"I think he was a dog who jumped off that cliff because his master died."

"I suppose it is within the realm of possibility."

His response relaxed her. She swung her feet up under her on the chair and leaned back. "Remove your feet from that chair, young woman. Sit properly. How old are you?" She put her feet back on the floor. "Eight," she said. He stubbed out his cigarette with his shaking fingers and leaned forward. "Your manners are in a sad condition. What is your background?" "Huh?" she asked. He shook his head at her. "One does not say 'huh.' One says 'I beg your pardon.' Can you say that?" She said: "No" and got up to leave. "I believe I have offended you. I am sorry. Please sit down again. We will talk about something pleasant. I will tell you about Germany. Do you know where Germany is located?" "Near France," she said, "it's where the Huns are from. Clarrie said you and Mrs. von Kaulbach were alien Huns, but I didn't believe her." "Not von—fon. And not Callback— Kaulbach! One must be correct. You were correct not to believe this deplorable person. I am a citizen of Rostock in the north, near the Baltic Sea . . ." Twining his bony fingers, he described the city as she listened, not daring to scratch an itch on her leg. ". . . When I was young I had no idea I loved Rostock. I left it. Now I am in that peculiar position of all old exiles—cherishing every memory of their homeland with a depth of feeling not to be understood by those who remained. They would find my sentimentality strange." He had removed his eyes from his listener and was looking into the air before him. "After this second great war, the ruins will be cleared away and history will take a direction that seems new. Yet it will not be new. If one lives in the past, this is what he learns." He stood up. He was tall, and seemed more real to Fayette standing. "I will show you through my rooms, which are furnished, item for item, from my family home in Rostock. Kindly take my hand. You will steady me, and I shall guide you."

Clarrie accused her of moving in with the aliens. Fayette spent as long as two or three days at a time with the von Kaulbachs, sleeping in their well-appointed little guest room. Her speech and manners underwent a change that offended Clarrie, and twice she plodded up to the von Kaulbach house to demand the girl back, filling the rooms with the reek of turpentine and gorging her eyes on the monstrous pair. She was treated courteously and given coffee, which she complained was too bitter. There was no third visit—not because of the bitter coffee, but because she had come up with a new protégé, a stringy little ranch hand from St. Helena who shared her absorption in *The Light of Christ* and fed the turkeys. Her life was bloatedly happy as they sang mission songs late into the night; and she forgot about the increasingly absent Fayette.

When Clarrie died suddenly, Fayette disappeared for a week. Every day the search party plowed up and down the steep, thickly wooded green-blue mountains and found nothing. At night they turned back, and the moon rose high and shed its light across a vastness of uniformly dark, silent peaks and valleys. One night there was a knock on the von Kaulbachs' front door. "Have they buried her?" Fayette asked as the door was swung open. She was dirty, and dragged a burlap sack behind her.

Herr von Kaulbach was speechless. Maria broke into tears of relief.

"Have they buried Clarrie?" she asked again.

"Yes, of course they have, that is the thing to do," said Maria, beaming, and she threw her plump arms around her.

"I knew if I stayed, her kin would take me, or that old fellow she got a hold of, or my father. I thought if I disappeared and she got buried and everything, they'd forget about me. Do you think I stayed away long enough?"

"Where did you go!" Herr von Kaulbach demanded.

"I just walked around. I hid when I saw them looking for me. I brought food along." She indicated the burlap bag. "I had a good time."

"My God!" he said.

"And you were not frightened of the rattlesnakes?" asked Maria, leading her into the front room as the old man followed.

"Rattlesnakes don't scare me. Nothing scares me."

The atmosphere that had been punctuated by turkeys, red stars, and the milling classroom now closed its gaps. She awoke to the sight of Johann Wolfgang von Goethe staring at her from a gilt frame; she "made her toilet"—Maria's term— with disciplined thoroughness; and ate her breakfast in a starched dress, her hair clean and well brushed, her finger-nails immaculate as she took the rolled linen serviette from its silver holder and said grace in German ("But it's you who's giving me the bread, not God,'' she protested when they translated the words for her, to which the old man replied, "You would embarrass us with thanks, but God is never embarrassed,'' and Maria crossed herself, though she too was a fully lapsed Lutheran and only plucked the gesture from a treasury of superstition). Herr von Kaulbach had undertaken to tutor Fayette himself, and after breakfast he led her with a quickened step to a round marble-topped table by the bookcases, adjusted his pince-nez, and gave flesh to Weimar's glory, to the soaring Schiller and tormented Kleist —ancestors of an illustrious modern named Mann whom they would arrive at presently—brought the smell of smoke and blood to Wallenstein's battles, spread the flames to Marengo and Austerlitz and thence to Metz, striding down the ages with side excursions into the religious leanings of Queen Christina, the stag hunts of Louis XV, the cloistered days of L'Aiglon, sometimes shooting wildly ahead (from the Wrangel of the Thirty Years' War to a descendant who befriended Dostoevski in Siberia), swinging through the intersecting corridors of art, music, philosophy, until his Teutonic sense of order came to the fore and he cut short his heady plunge and went back to start at the beginning, with the Stone Age.

In the summers they took their books into the yard, where Fayette had planted a garden. One warm morning as they paused in their work to observe the promising flowers, Fayette said suddenly: "Herr von Kaulbach."

"Yes?"

"The last time I saw my mother, she was laying behind a—"

"Lying."

"Lying behind a screen in a hospital. She died that night. She didn't look happy.'' She watched him intently, overcome by an urgent desire to feel his hand pat her head, to hear him say: "Never fear, your mother was happy.'' She waited as he tapped the ash from his cigarette with his trembling finger.

"Few people are happy the day of their death."

She was silent. The face behind the hospital screen, the dead hunting dog in the tree, Clarrie's mistreated cow and goat—nobody would ever fix them up for her; unless Mrs. von Kaulbach did, someone like her; and she glanced at the porch, where that plump, vaguely smiling little lady was serenely watering the potted plants. Her eyes turned back to the old man's terrible face—it seemed terrible to her at that moment, and she seemed small to herself and unfairly treated. She wanted to protest against him, to break into tears, to run off, yet something held her back. At last she put her hands on the table and looked him straight in the eyes, patiently, like a student unconditionally prepared to learn. It was then that he patted her head.

It was art that struck the deepest chord in her. Melodramatic scenes of towering cliffs, flying armies with Mephistophelean wings, great stag-like dogs flailing in the crystal icicles of chandeliers flowed onto her paper. When on her fourteenth birthday she was asked what she would like, she said paints and canvas, and after a small bout with the memory-stirring turpentine, she slashed a color—viridian—on the rough taut canvas and realized that her name no longer fitted her. Herr von Kaulbach had had a daughter named Johanna who was born in 1888 and died the same year. The name had hardly been used.

Johanna, like Fayette, enraged the old man in one respect. She disappeared into the mountains overnight every now and then, returning hungry, scratched, and deeply out of touch. He roared the dangers at her, but she paid no heed, and eventually when she returned from a nocturnal climb he would only glance up from his black chair and tighten his lips. She would eat ravenously, her hands dirtied to a solid cinnamon color and filigreed with red-jeweled scratches. There was a look of the animal to her at these times, and this she realized. She would turn and say in a low voice, "I'm sorry." Then it was over until the next time.

Except for this, they had an accord so deep that sometimes she lay awake at night agonizing over the certainty that it must end. He was eighty-five, Maria over sixty.

He did not alter; he had gotten too old to look older. But Maria began to stoop and her marmalade hair was graying. Sometimes Johanna overheard references to money, and she gathered that Herr von Kaulbach's savings had gone to finance his late son in a business venture that failed. Refusing to sell a stick of his cherished possessions, the old man had, after some years of dogged survival in boardinghouses, taken his furnishings out of storage and moved with his daughter-in-law to this secluded spot where rents were cheap and not too fine a point was put on Maria's faded teaching credentials. "We are doing well," he would state at intervals. Their food was not the best, but it was served with elegance. Their entertainments cost nothing: old books and phonograph records. Their clothes were fastidiously darned, and their shoes never wore out, for Herr von Kaulbach kept to his chair and Maria walked to school and back with her shoes in a bag and her feet in a pair of commando-like boots that also served to foil snakes.

Maria contended that she would die of a snakebite, but she was never approached by a snake. She died of heart trouble the year Johanna turned seventeen, having been so characteristically vague about her pains and palpitations, so unwilling to make the effort to trace and tend them, so sure that life would roll along as always, that her death came to Herr von Kaulbach as a shock he never recovered from.

He began Johanna in a study course for the university, but his mind had blurred. He murmured over and over, "At least my poor Maria never went to the poorhouse. I will refuse to go to the poorhouse. I will refuse!"

"You mustn't worry about that," Johanna told him, "it won't happen. I'm here with you."

"You shouldn't have to be a nurse for an invalid . . . You're leading a life unnatural for your years . . . and to the age. Perhaps I've turned you into something useless for the age. Useless . . ." Then with a return of his old clarity, he said: "No, I've tried to show you what is of importance in any age. The world has always been less than it could be, but that is bearable as long as one is as much as he can be; if he holds steady a sense of beauty, a sense of order, and a sense of honor." And he looked at her with dry, affectionate humor. "At seventeen you are not embarrassed to hear such grand sentiments, are you? There is a thrill to their sound. But when you grow older you will find it increasingly easy to be embarrassed, and you will then begin to hear new sounds at the gate, small sounds that can embarrass no one, the sounds of compliance and expedience. That is where the battle of life is pitched."

One night when he fell asleep in his chair he did not wake when Johanna tried to rouse him. The hollows and pockets of his face had smoothed, giving it a calm, finely chiseled look of great beauty. His pince-nez were still in place, one hand still rested on a book in his lap.

Johanna stayed on in the house after the funeral, walking in a desolate circle marked by the black chair, the bookcase, and the closet where Herr von Kaulbach's clothes hung. After a month she took herself in hand. Armed with nine years of *Kultur* and a battery of white scars from her nocturnal hikes, she took the Greyhound bus to Berkeley and presented herself at the University of California. Herr von Kaulbach had left her everything. She had sold the larger pieces; everything else was shipped to Berkeley, where she crammed it all into the room she rented near campus, hanging the heavy yellowed curtains between her and the street outside.

6 Although San Francisco has its sunny days, they link together only in autumn, when they may form a sweltering heat wave. In early November not a breeze stirred through the Bay Area; the hotter days were crushing, tropical. Saturday, the day of the first peace march, was one.

Ten thousand people gathered in Berkeley as the leaves overhead oozed oil into the dusty air. There was a sense of tolerance among them all—university students in T-shirts and suntans, middle-aged suburban women, gnarled Socialists, the new tribe of youngsters in long gowns, bedspread togas, and fringed shawls—and when the columns finally got under way, a flow of unity was communicated all the way down the line.

Zaidee was one of the first arrivals. She had not heard from Morrie for two days, not since the night of her mother's birthday. She was sure she would find him here. But after marching a mile in the heat she stepped out of line and sat down on the curb under the shade of a palm tree, scanning the faces as they passed.

At six o'clock that morning Morris had sat slumped at a half-deserted blackjack table at Lake Tahoe, a hundred and sixty dollars in the hole. It was then that he suddenly remembered the march. He would leave.

Except for a dash to the snack bar, where he swallowed three hotdogs, he had been playing steadily for twenty hours. Now his weariness caught up with him and he was heavily aware of his bristled cheeks and the sour smell wafting up from his clothes. Finishing the cold coffee at his side, he looked around the casino, a place he always felt at home in, not because of its alluring atmosphere—plush carpets, low intimate ceiling, everything bathed in the rosiest of lights—but because of its raucous excitement, its explosive aura of purpose and drive. But at this dead hour half the tables were cordoned off by red velvet ropes and the rest boasted only a handful of haggard players who sat with their elbows spread out in the unaccustomed space. Staring vacantly across the room between games stood the dealers, women of all ages dressed in black skirts and white blouses. As a neophyte he had been astonished by the agility of their hands, which shuffled, dealt, paid out, raked in with such swiftness that his own swift mind boggled. It was a long time before he had noticed their faces above their hands, and then he began taking pleasure in cracking these faces, which were like jawbreakers. With tips and zestful jokes he made them smile, talk, even laugh, and eventually they came to know him, and a flicker went up in their eyes when they saw him.

But at this hour he was uninterested in them. An old lanky Negro in a white jacket creaked over the deserted red carpet sweeping debris into a long-handled dustpan, while through the plate glass windows the sky began to pale behind the black mass of the mountains. Usually at this point Morris grabbed some sleep in the back seat of his car, but this time he would leave, because it had been a twenty-hour standstill.

He had lost the hundred sixty at the very start, and from that minute on had been hogtied by the meager forty-five he had left. You could survive on little, but you couldn't live. To live you had to take chances, and forty-five dollars wouldn't last three days unless you played tightly. But now that he remembered he had a march to go on and needn't sit here enjoying himself for three long days, he pushed forward his forty-five dollars' worth of chips and slid off the stool, ready to depart with a clean loss.

He won, and the forty-five was doubled. Not touching the ninety, still ready to leave, he played again. Again it was doubled. And now a cynical coldness filled him, because he knew that if he left the hundred eighty there it would be snatched from under his nose. He looked down at his hand lying on the green felt and willed it to draw in the chips, but it did not move. Two tiny Filipinos in orange baseball caps stopped to watch, and the pit boss wandered over with a yawn. Morris compressed his lips and nodded. He was dealt his two cards, and turned them over. Blackjack.

More people drifted up to the table, but now he was mindless of his surroundings, of the dealer's rare look of minor interest, or of any sound. He felt immersed in water. Deaf. Very cold.

The dealer was looking at him.

"Leave it," he said.

She began dealing.

He would be wiped out. Without lifting his hand from the green felt, he flipped the cards over with two fingers. Seventeen—the worst possible. His whole body trembling, he watched the dealer as she kept hitting herself with small cards until she reached sixteen, then came up with a king of hearts. He had seven hundred and twenty dollars.

Now he smashed up and out of his numbness into a state of ecstasy. He put his whole arm down on the table and drew in his squat columns of green chips, ordered another cup of coffee, and threw a grin into the crowd around him. The march had disappeared from his mind. His insides melted with a radiant warmth, and there was a sharp tingle in his finger-tips, his loins, and down his spine. All around him was the sound of congratulations and admiration. He felt that if he wished, he could influence anyone in the little crowd to do whatever he wanted, or that he could twist the dealer's flat face into the most unbelievable embodiment of passion, that he could lose fifty pounds of flesh in a week, that he could go back to the university and get his Doctorate. He had a strange feeling that the people around him had come to a stop, as if they had been derailed from their own tracks and had slipped onto his, where they stood rooted to the spot while he sped into the horizon. He felt a strong sympathy for them, a love.

Now that he had a solid basis to fall back on, he could take all the risks he wanted. In control, canny and strategic, he began.

By seven o'clock he was a thousand to the good. By eight o'clock he had fourteen hundred. Then he began losing until he was down to eight hundred.

He knew what would happen. His winnings would go back to the house in chunks or driblets and he would stagger out into the daylight feeling like shit. These thoughts always assailed him when he had reached a peak and begun to lose. They came in little stabs of illumination in which he could see himself standing aside from his sweating body and shaking a fist at it.

Then all at once the march came back to him with shattering immediacy. What was he doing a hundred and eighty miles away when the march would be starting at ten o'clock? Why should he miss the march and lose his money, too?

"That's it," he barked. "Give me hundred-dollar chips."

As the dealer counted out the chips, Morris' victory was clouded by the knowledge that he had remembered the march only as a lever to get him out of the casino before he lost more money. And yet the march embodied his deepest convictions; he had passed out announcements all over the city; he argued the war passionately; there were nights when he could not sleep for thinking of it. Then how could he have forgotten it for a gambling spree? Staring at the green felt, he envisioned his mind as a shabby box crammed with fragments of intention.

Plunging through the crowd to the cashier's window, he speculated that if the roads had dried in the sun and he could drive at his usual high speed he might make it in two and a half hours. Then, stuffing the bills into his wallet, he did something he had long considered doing. He applied for a casino credit card. He had always held back from doing this because he was afraid he would wipe out his whole checking account if he were free to draw on it. But now he felt lucky and prosperous enough to take the step, and as he filled out the application blank he was relieved to know that he would never again have to bear the restrictions of playing with cash on hand.

He pushed out through the swinging doors. The cold air ripped through his sweaty shirt and trousers as though they were paper, and sent a razored shudder down his back. The silence was no less jarring, nor the sight of the mountains looming before him a blinding white against the bright blue sky. But all this seemed cut off from life, which still spun on in the packed din behind him; he always had this sense of strangeness when he stepped out of the casino. He began the walk back to the parking lot, and as he walked the strangeness wore off and he stopped and breathed in the fresh scent of pine needles and snow, giving vent to a cavernous yawn that left his whole being dazed with satisfaction. He went on leisurely, savoring the chill mountain-blown silence, awed by it, and thinking with desire of the outdoors, of summer hikes and camping trips, of the hooting of hunched owls in the evening, and of dawns as long as whole days. How good all that was, how good the summer would be.

And here was his car waiting for him, mud-spattered, dented, reliable. He gave it a hearty slap on the hood and threw himself into the proper frame of mind for a breakneck trip to Berkeley. As he drove into the sparkling snowbanked street, a cry broke from his throat: "Eight hundred!" and his heart banged like the clap of a bell. And then, whistling with frantic exuberance, he tried not to think of the bulging wallet in his pocket. He wanted to feel good because the sky was blue.

7

"What do we want?"
"*Peace!*"
"When?"
"*Now!*"
"When?"
"*Now!*"
"When?"
"*Now!*"

Whenever Johanna blinked the sweat from her eyes, the stinging liquid shattered in magnificent revolving lights. She looked through them up into the sky, which was pulsing, boundless, tropical.

(*"Do you know that you will die someday?" Tolstoy once asked his young sister-in-law.*

"Me, die? Never!")

"Tolstoy's sister-in-law has been dead for fifty years," she said.

The column was moving from Berkeley through West Oakland, down a street of dusty palm trees and gray garage-size houses where black figures sprawled on the rotting steps.

"What'd you say?" Wanda asked over the noise.

"Nothing. There's Philip."

He was standing on the curb with a television crew, wearing a dark suit in the heat. His face was pale in the sunlight, lined with middle age. He held a microphone in his hand and stopped talking into it as the chant went up again. Johanna felt his existence fade from her mind as they marched by him, past him; far more interesting were two figures in front of her, a young girl whose hair hung to her waist like an undone scouring pad, and a being of whom nothing at all could be seen under a majestic black cape.

"What do you make of them?" she asked Conrad.

"What should I make of them?" he replied with his usual shrug. "What should surprise me, a battered old-time North Beach bohemian, forgive the passé term."

"I want to kick them."

"Why?"

"Exhibitionists. What do they know about dying?"

42

"Whereas you, of course," Wanda put in, "have fought in the trenches of fifteen major wars."

"No, but I understand history, I understand the meaning of war, the chopping off of individual lives . . . "

"Why should you know better than anyone else?" Wanda asked irritably.

"I don't say I do; most people do, I'm sure. But *these* idiots—"

"You're just assuming—"

"Wanda," said Conrad, "you look hot. Johanna looks hot. And I feel like my head's coming to a point. Let's get in the shade for a while."

"What I mean is this," Johanna continued as they threaded their way out of the column. "In themselves they're fine, that bag of fuzz growing from that girl's head is a fine shriek at the usual thing, and that cape's a blessed wonder—who's usually given a chance to watch a cape trailing across the ground? They're like two gifts to the world, walking along. But I think they weaken the effectiveness of the march."

"Do you ever stop thinking and thinking?" asked Wanda impatiently. She realized that her irritability sprang from the three of them being together, and tried to amend by putting her hand on Johanna's arm.

Zaidee looked up from under her palm tree as three figures stepped out of line and approached the curb. An uncertain smile hovered on her lips, then widened.

"Oh Lord," said Wanda, "there's that thing from my old office. What's she doing here?"

"Wanda! Wanda! It's me, Zaidee!" she called, and just then her jaw went slack as she glanced back at the column and looked directly at Morris' face. Stubble covered his heavy jaws, his suntans and maroon shirt were crumpled, and he walked with the jerkiness that always marked his gait when he was exhausted. Calling his name, she waved excitedly, though half afraid he wouldn't acknowledge her.

He looked in her direction, shaded his eyes with his hand, and stepped out of line. A moment later he appeared at the curb but, ignoring Zaidee, he went directly to the girl with Wanda. Abruptly the girl walked away. He followed her.

"Joan . . . wait now, Joanne?"

"No," she said, keeping her back to him.

"Well. But you remember me." His head still spun under

a rain of images: a Tiffany lampshade, a poster of Venice, an old man in a doorway.

"No, I can't say that I do." In the few nights since she had met him, she had hosted him repeatedly in the dark corners of her mind.

"Sure you do. How've you been?"

"Fine," she said after a silence.

"You're looking great."

The strained look had vanished, her dark hair was shining, she wore a yellow summer dress, and her exposed arms and legs were tanned even darker than their natural tawny shade. He could not reconcile her with the girl in the dismal room, except for the eyes; almond-shaped eyes the color of cider, but rested now, clearer. He saw how finely delineated those eyes were, creations of a high order—the lashes forming a dark curve over the gold irises, which were sharply edged by black; the whites gleaming with a blue sheen, like porcelain.

"Looks like you've been out in the sun," he ventured.

She gave a nod.

"The beach?"

She shook her head, staring straight ahead. Then she said, "The fire escape. I use it as a sun porch. I've moved."

He would not confess that he knew she'd moved, that he had come back to her apartment hunting for her. It would give her an edge over him.

She looked at him with a reluctant smile. It was as if he drew it from her.

Immediately confident, he yanked a pen from his pocket. "What's the address?"

"Screw yourself," she said. The words sounded forced, ludicrous, but there was such a metallic bite to them that he held his pen in mid-air a moment before sauntering off.

She continued to stare straight ahead for several moments, then gave in to the temptation to glance sideways.

He was standing talking with the little group at the curb with his legs apart, one hand on his hip. Next to him Conrad looked tepid, inconsequential, peeled down by reflection. She could not hear what they said.

"I'm not sure," Conrad was saying, "the death count's over twenty thousand, I don't know the number of casualties."

"Her brother was just killed over there," Morris said, indicating Zaidee.

Wanda turned to the girl. "Not your younger brother?" she exclaimed abruptly, taking her hand. "Not Ollie? Oh, Zaidee, I'm so awfully sorry. I didn't know."

"It's okay, it's nothing," the girl drawled, lowering her eyes. Sympathy made her speak stupidly; even now, though it had happened three months ago. She felt the muscles around her mouth begin to work.

Conrad looked at the columns of marchers plodding down the torpid street. They gave an impression of great number, but they were skimmed from a population whose vast bulk was not even aware of this tissue-thin layer gone. He had been part of that bulk twenty years ago in Salerno; part, and yet apart enough to send a short yowl into the air after having subdued his first representative of the enemy, who in repose, pulp-headed, appeared to be someone of his own height, weight, and years.

The group began leaving the curb. Zaidee's chest tightened with the fear of being left behind, and she stepped closer to Morrie. But hardly aware of her, he fell in behind the girl in the yellow dress as she rejoined the column.

Another hour passed before the column reached its destination, a dusty tree-filled park with a clearing where a speakers' stand had been set up. The sun shed a steady glare on the marchers as they poured through the entrance and made for the trees, where they threw themselves down in the shade and watched the rest spill in. Though the majority was unremarkable, the keynote of the march was one of ebullient eccentricity, as though the column were a long plain board mounted with a scattering of bizarre knobs that caught all the light. Once in the park, they thronged together in a rich clot of ancient wedding gowns, net undershirts, velvet breeches, Indian headbands, and long webs of beads. Here and there a star or moon was painted on a bearded cheek, or a line was enigmatically drawn down the middle of a face. These people had been multiplying for months, perhaps for years, but this was the first time they had massed in such numbers—only a fraction of the crowd, to be sure, but a few hundred was enough to give the effect of a new constellation bursting into existence. Balloons were released into the air, and the sound of the bongo drum was heard.

"It's like a vaudeville show," Johanna said.

"Why add more darkness to life?" Wanda murmured, plucking a grass stalk. Conrad had stretched out between them and lay with his arm over his eyes, sweat trickling from his lined brow to his fringe of hair, which was spattered with blue paint.

"You need to step under a nice cool shower of turpentine," she said, drawing the stalk across his chin.

"I don't mean that it should be like a funeral cortege," Johanna went on, "but these masqueraders provide just the right feeling of indignation for nine tenths of the voters in this country to plug up their ears."

"They'd plug up their ears anyway," said Wanda. "Do you really think they care what *they*"—she gestured at the speakers' stand—"come up with? The usual bunch of liberals?"

"That sounds odd, coming from you. They're your sort; you and your enlightened Poly Sci Unitarian friends."

"They may be my sort, but I don't necessarily have faith in them any more."

"Well, I don't either. But a movement won't get anywhere if it's used as a hitching post for a crowd of kids who would have swallowed goldfish a generation ago. A movement must have high purpose, it must have organization and sacrifice."

"My poor young idealist," Conrad sighed.

"Young!" exclaimed Wanda, and she could have bitten her tongue.

"Well, younger than I am. More idealistic than I am."

"Everybody's younger than you are, and more idealistic. Even Cato."

He reached over and patted her hand and was silent.

"What are you thinking of?" she asked at length.

"Nothing. That timid little girl's brother."

"Who?" asked Johanna.

"The little girl on the curb," Conrad told her. "Her brother's been killed over there."

They watched as the speakers mounted the stand and the microphone was tested. The television cameras were set up alongside it. A speck of Philip's dark suit could be seen through the crowd.

"How's your moving coming along?" Wanda asked Johanna.

"It's all done. Everything is cleaned up and put in order."

46

"Your Prussian thoroughness."

"It's great having my things around me again."

"I think it's a pity. I think you should have sold them. They're like an incubus."

"I'm going to wander around," Johanna said shortly, getting to her feet.

She stopped a few yards away to take off her sandals, her eyes searching for the badly wrinkled maroon shirt. He must sleep in his clothes, she thought with opprobrium.

The sun was low, its rays as they grew more oblique carrying more heat and absorbing more dust. The speakers had long since departed, the park was almost empty. She came to the glade where the bongo drummers were crouched, surrounded by youths in headbands and girls with frizzed hair and long gowns. Dancing alone, oblivious, was the creature in the great cloak.

Morris stood under the trees looking on. He saw her emerge from the other side of the glade, and she, catching sight of the maroon shirt, turned instinctively on her heel, only to complete a full circle as casually as she could. Swinging her sandals, she directed her attention back to the glade, where the cloaked figure dipped and weaved over the dry grass, untutored, graceless, yet compelling in its intensity. Now and then a long, medievally pointed cloth shoe was revealed. She tried to see the face, but the stiff collar stood high, and the head, covered by an animal-hide skullcap, remained bent.

Morris studied her as she stood in a pool of dusty sunlight, swinging her sandals back and forth, innocuous as a schoolgirl. I'll give it another try, he thought.

"It's nice here!" she greeted him with, nervously, and shot her hand out toward the glade as though to draw his attention away from herself.

"The war's over?" he asked, relaxing, and ran his eyes down the golden outstretched arm.

"The war?" She saw in a flare the timid little girl's timid little brother formally arranged somewhere under the solid earth. She shook her head.

"I wish you'd let me in on it."

"Oh, you mean *our* war. That's an odd thing, our war." She felt suspended, no longer nervous, nor at ease, either, but as though the crest of a wave were rising. She stopped swinging the sandals. His thick hair was rimmed red by the sun, and all his big, slightly crowded teeth shone in a smile. "Got a ride back?" he asked.

". . . Yes. With my friends."

"Ditch 'em." But seeing a line of resentment form between her eyes, he amended the sentence. "I'd like to drive you back. It would be a pleasure." And he was moved for some reason to shake her hand, which he did slowly and candidly, a little abashed.

She gave a nod, feeling unexpectedly light-hearted, and she looked at his face, and at the shafts of gold that slanted into the glade, and at the cloaked figure flinging itself among them.

Morris rubbed his eyes with his fingers, their nails lined with green from the felt of the gambling tables. The beaded sweat along his hairline cooled as a small breeze slapped it. His fatigue was receding, he felt recharged, and a growl issued from his sturdy stomach just as a red spark of desire shot through his loins.

"It must be an Arab, not to suffocate under that outfit," she remarked of the dancer. "I'd like to get a look at him— it—whatever."

"You never will, baby," he said, grabbing back the hand he had just released. "It'll remain one of the great unsolved mysteries of life, because we're going now." And he started off, pulling her along.

Her hand in his was a fist. It was the absence of simple prelude in him that jarred her—not only because it was crude and proprietary and offended her pride, but because it made him seem like a man condemned to death who, for lack of time, rips to the center of each thing and out the other side without knowing it. She pictured herself being ripped out like the pages of a book. And yet the very crudeness of his approach, the nakedness of his interest, the vitality that poured through his fingers exercised a powerful curb on her tendency to retreat.

As he led her along the path his spirits climbed steadily. She was better than he remembered, better-looking, better groomed, better disposed. But he did not want to acknowledge the wild pull that had twice deposited him on her doorstep. Now that he had found her again, he insisted to himself that their first encounter and this one were ordinary. In an hour or less they would be in bed, that was all. But this anticipation, ordinary as it was, always put him in the best of humors. It was the best way to end the best of days—he slapped the wallet in his back pocket, popped a stick of gum into his mouth, and threw his arm around her shoulder.

She removed the arm as they approached Wanda and Conrad, lying asleep side by side.

"What about that girl you were with?" she asked, suddenly remembering her.

"An acquaintance. She's gone." He had spent a full half hour scaring up a ride for Zaidee, who never minded being shuffled around—all the while, he realized now, laying the groundwork to drive this one back alone, even though she had frozen him solid with her silence every time he edged up to her on the march.

Suddenly he felt with a chill click of certainty that some irresistible force had brought them together; there was nothing ordinary about it. He was electrified by the urge to flee.

"I've got a ride back," Johanna told Wanda, who had awakened and was rubbing her eyes with her big hands and looking around her. The park was empty. The furnace of the setting sun burned through the foliage in gashes. "I'll call you tomorrow," Johanna threw over her shoulder.

Wanda watched the pair walk away, then looked at Conrad's sleeping face. They would drive back together alone and she would ask him in for dinner. She looked once more at the diminishing figures, then gave a growl of duty, got to her feet, and yelled after them.

"What is it?" Johanna shouted back.

"Come on back. I have to talk to you!"

"I'll phone you tomorrow."

She sat down again. Through months of Zaidee's sad stories she knew this man wasn't the kind to get mixed up with. If Johanna had come back, she would have warned her not to ride off with him. But if Johanna wouldn't come back, there was nothing she could do about it.

Morris stopped at the park entrance and looked back. Debris littered the ground, the shadows lay long and desolate. He thought of Zaidee's brother. He thought of the military cemetery in the Presidio where he used to park with Zaidee (not since her brother's death), the markers stretching as far as the eye could see. He thought of the fervor with which

49

he had handed out leaflets and tacked up posters about the march. Now it was over, the park was empty, the war ground on, everything ground on as before, he ground on as before. An excruciating loneliness filled him as he looked at the darkening scene. If it had been any other girl at his side he would have crushed her to him in a massive embrace, but his urge to flee this one had not abated, nor could he act on it.

"Come on," he said abruptly.

"I'm putting my shoes on." There was the same quality of distance in her voice as in his.

They caught a bus back to his car in Berkeley, keeping a mutual silence.

8

He stood in the middle of her front room. It was a replica of some long-dead way of life. His grandparents in Odessa would have lived in a room like this if they had been rich. Although the apartment itself was in worse condition than the other one—the dark wainscoting battered, the high ceiling stained, the door flaked and outfitted with an ugly collection of tarnished bolts and chains—its commanding quality was a tasteful, mellow self-assurance. He stood on a rug of superb workmanship, in claret and blue, worn to the fiber in spots, which only enhanced its beauty. From floor to ceiling one wall was covered with framed etchings of landscapes and villages, brown with age and impressively dotted with white mildew. Throughout the commonplace furniture—a threadbare sofa and its spawn of threadbare chairs, which probably came with the place—stood the real thing, antiques of value even to the untutored eye: a delicate walnut escritoire; a heavy round marble-topped table; an elegant chair upholstered in plum-colored velvet, and a carved black throne-like chair; old mahogany bookcases; tomes bound in gleaming leather, pressed with Gothic letters; an elaborate crystal chandelier, apparently unwired, hanging from a shiny new hook in the ceiling; needlepoint pillows and throw rugs, blood red and black, gold and maroon, ivory and deep blue; lace curtains, heavy auburn drapes.

He stood with his hands on his hips, attracted against his will, and repelled. "What is all this?"

"It belonged to my family." She gestured at some small framed photographs of dated figures, faded as the sketches on the wall. "I had it all stored. It's a long story."

"The rug's okay," he said sourly, "but the rest—what d'you want all this junk around for? It's 1965."

"Junk? It belonged to my family."

"So?" He faced her irritably. "You know what I've got from my home? From the House of Levinsky? A—" He broke off and tightened his lips.

"A what?"

"A possession. But I don't keep it in the middle of the room and make a shrine out of it. I don't go in for this crap of hanging on to the past."

51

"Who's asking you to?"

"Let's see the other rooms."

The bedroom put him at his ease with its nondescript shabbiness, its mattress flush on the floor, walls Scotch-taped where the wallpaper had buckled, its rug cheap, shaggy, tan, dotted with hardened gobs of fingernail polish and white spots of Clorox and giving off a faint odor of powder and perfume —the kind of rug his feet had trod, bare, a thousand times. On the door peg hung the laundry bag with its red donkey, and a pair of blue filmy babydoll pajamas. He turned to her, but she went out of the room and opened another door.

This was a studio, actually a glassed-in back porch, holding rolled and stretched canvases, two strapped-up paint boxes, easels of different sizes, and spattered Mason jars crammed with brushes. Everything bore evidence of long hard use, yet nothing seemed to be in use at the moment. He tipped a canvas forward and, in the second before she pushed it back, looked at the picture upside down, seeing something vaguely mythical, like a winged horse rearing through the cosmos. He felt an odd panic, which he squeezed into a frown.

"And this is my fire escape," she said, returning to the front room and pointing through a window at the usual metal encumbrance. She had fixed it up with potted plants and a bamboo mat. "The last tenant left all those beautiful plants, can you imagine that?" she was saying, as he pictured her stretched naked on the mat, a rivulet of sweat running gracefully from between her breasts to her navel. He glanced at the plants, dusty geraniums stuck in rusty coffee cans. "I'd leave 'em behind, too," he said, and then, abruptly, with a tinge of humor, "Let's have another look at the bedroom."

Her response was so immediate—"I didn't want you here in the first place!"—that he received it with the twist of humor still on his lips. Then she was gone, striding, not gracefully but noisily, to the bedroom. He followed cautiously. "I wish I'd never gotten mixed up with you!" she said, struggling out of her dress, glowering steadily at him through her movements. She unclipped her bra with a yank and threw it on the floor.

Running his eyes over her body, he came up to her and put his hand under her hair at the back of her neck. Her eyes were wide, with a deep frown between them, giving her an unholy look of dread.

52

"I was all right before. I don't want you," she said.

"You haven't got me, don't worry."

"This is just a romp, a nothing."

"What d'you think *I've* got in mind? Jesus, what's with you, anyway?"

"Then all right," she said, drawing his hand down along her arm; and again, in a barely audible voice, "Then all right."

Up until the moment she went under, like a swimmer gathered high by a breaker and thrown deep into soundlessness, she told herself he was a passing taste, a perversion, an antidote to so many months of mealy Philip-love . . .

"Johanna . . . I think we could be something to each other." They lay in a dim cocoon, cut off from the sound of their own voices, which would have struck them as shocking earlier, and would strike them as shocking soon. "I think so, too," she whispered back. "This is nothing ordinary," he said. "No, it's not . . ." "We'd have kinks to iron out . . ." "I'd be willing to try . . ." She put her face to his hair, its aroma was fresh, like wind and sun. And at that moment the conversation rebounded baldly in their ears. She sat up and lit a cigarette. He threw a covert glance at her. The panic invaded him again. Her eyes were clear, intelligent; there was nothing whatsoever in them to pity. Everything about her— her furnishings, her paintings, her age, her whole aura— represented weight. Purpose, tradition. No blurred edges, no promise of casualness, of the endless reprieve of casualness.

He got up and began to dress. "Shit," he muttered, tightening his belt around his broad middle.

"Don't use that word here. I don't like it."

He gave a long descending whistle to take in the whole disoriented and failed evening, and left.

9 At two in the morning, unable to sleep, Johanna picked up the phone and dialed a number, remembering only then that the phone was not yet connected. Throwing her trench coat over her pajamas and thrusting her feet into her sandals, she walked down the street until she found a phone booth.

"Wanda?" she said when she got the number. "I wouldn't call you so late, but—"

"Are you lucky! Are you lucky! If I'd been asleep I'd have killed you!" Her voice was uneven with gaiety.

"Why are you up so late?"

"I'm not . . . I mean, we were in bed, but I wasn't asleep. I mean, Conrad stayed. I'm in the kitchen, I took the phone in the kitchen. I'm wide awake, don't worry. I ought to take a nerve pill or something."

"You mean you and he—? I don't know what to say. You must be absolutely— I'm so pleased for you."

"I don't know what to say either." Her voice sparkled with pleasure; it seemed to go in all directions at once. "Hey, what are you calling about this late?"

"Listen, I'm standing in my pajamas in a puddle of urine in a phone booth in the middle of the Fillmore at two in the morning, surrounded by rapists and dope addicts in porkpie hats . . ." She gave a laugh at the description, and pushed down the rising despair she heard in the sound. "So it's urgent, I suppose. It's about this Morris person. Do you know him at all? You worked with that girl he knew, the one whose brother was killed."

"I have an apology to make, Johanna. I should have told you not to go off with him, but I wanted to drive back with Conrad alone."

"That doesn't matter. Why shouldn't I go off with him?"

"Maybe it doesn't matter to you, but it matters to me. It's all right to commit a *crime passionel*, but there's no excuse for petty deviousness—go ahead and murder a rival, but don't indulge in a cheap lie of omission. Really, our values are all screwed up, but here I am feeling guilty just the same. It sounds Edwardian, doesn't it? That's in your line, absolve me, Johanna."

"You sound drunk."

"I am, I am."

"Can you tell me anything about Morris?"

"Only bad things."

"Fire away."

"Well, it's all from the mouth of that little cretin—I mean, I'm fond of Zaidee, I'm sorry for her, but there's no denying she's dim. Anyway, you get a straight story from an unimaginative mind. He's just a womanizer, that's all. But on a grand scale, compulsive, exploitative. He's totally unstable. Undependable. Un-everything you'd ever want. I'm sorry."

"No. I wanted to know."

She hung up and squeezed out of the booth and walked back up the street, ignoring figures loitering in doorways, cruising Cadillacs. No longer involved with Morris, she allowed herself to indulge in their whispered conversation. Now that their union was lost, it seemed of incalculable promise. But it would remain as unplumbed as the cloaked figure she had seen in the glade.

At that moment Morris was finally falling asleep before his television set, where the late movie had just ended. The American flag rippled across the screen as "The Star Spangled Banner" was sung; then the screen went gray.

Earlier, pulling off his shirt in the night heat, he had wandered restlessly through his rooms. He felt not only fatigued by his long blackjack stint, but wearied by his encounter with Johanna. "I'm getting old," he said thoughtfully, and swung open the closet door, where a full-length mirror was attached. Just a few pounds off, that was all. He pulled his stomach in. As for the face, nothing wrong with that, the color was good, the eyes were clear. And he'd never have to worry about going bald. In need of a haircut, though. And he should get some new clothes. And clean up this mess of an apartment. And take home the stuff he was behind in at work. Put some direction in his life. He looked at his littered desk and picked up a letter. It was from a girl in Denver he had had a brief affair with when she was here on vacation. The letter was two months old. He picked up another, an illiterate item from his oldest brother in Brooklyn. "My oldest brother is sixty years old," he said aloud, as though offended. He had scrutinized his bookshelves—psychology, sociology, politics. He yanked out two, three, six books and began reading the top one, a history of modern China. In an hour he had advanced only to page thirty-one. "I never have enough time," he muttered, flipping through the remaining four hundred pages. He threw the book down, went to the refrigerator, got out a carton of tutti-frutti ice cream, picked up a spoon, and settled down before the television set. And as he sat, he forgot the busy screen and sank into the deepest chambers of his mind.

He wore rich vestments, yet there was a solemnity about him, carried out in a black skullcap. People sat around him, he poured out wisdom, he touched them and made them healthy. In gratitude they pointed somewhere in the distance, and he went there. The sun poured down in abundance, a woman was splashing in a stream, she came to him and gave herself, afterward slipping back into the stream. As he walked along the bank with the sun drawing him on, different women came out of the water and joined him, this time a frightened girl, the next an amazon, or a sophisticate, or an animal. At night they lay at his side, and disappeared at dawn as another group of people gathered around him, and the sun rose in all its power, and the new day began.

It was a fantasy that shamed him, but he had had it for years, it was at the very core of his life.

My life, he thought with a stillness. A giver of IQ tests in elementary schools. He would quit. He had never held a job longer than two years, why make this one an exception? He would live frugally for the next six months and save his money, and then he would quit, go back for his Doctorate, even if he was pushing forty. It would mean the whole med-school bit, years and years out of his life. But he must do it. And thinking of this, he fell back into his fantasy, and finally into sleep.

10

Another sunny week went by. He turned his attention to a recently divorced elementary-school teacher who seemed in need of solace, finally getting her up to his place only to find a frigid hysteric. He washed the event away with a blowsy pick-up from an all-night laundromat on Polk Street and the following evening, with two empty hours on his hands and another tumescence on the way, drove to Zaidee's house in the Mission.

Zaidee's mother answered the door. She stood silently, with lowered eyes.

"Zaidee here?" he asked.

She turned and walked down the hall. "It's M," she said. There was a clatter as Zaidee burst into the hall.

"C'mon, I'll take you out to dinner."

"I was making our dinner," the mother said, still averting her eyes from him.

"Maybe Morrie could eat with us?" Zaidee suggested without confidence. She hovered between the two, then said with a look of contrition, "I'll be back early, Ma."

"Your mother bugs me," Morris complained as they got in the car. "How come she won't look at me? How come she calls me by my initial? What's with her?"

"She's got her funny ways. Especially since Ollie." She glanced at him apologetically. "But the real thing is that she don't like you, Morrie. She says you've made me unhappy."

The ill-favored face looked very young and very sad to him. And it was a pity, because she was so good. She was a good, sweet girl. "I'm sorry," he said, and a resolution burst inside him. "I'll make it up to you, I mean it." What could make him happier than to make her happy? He wanted to make someone happy. "I mean it," he repeated, pulling her head onto his chest.

"I want my dinner!" she exclaimed an hour later as they lay on his bed.

He stretched deeply, with a long sigh. "I've got to get you on home, baby. I've got a class to teach tonight."

"But you said we'd eat . . ."

"I know, I forgot."

"You're always going off in a hundred different directions, Morrie," she said in a small voice.

"Anyway, you ought to eat with your mother. Think of her alone in that house."

Guiltily, she began to dress. "Someday when I'm married she'll be all alone," she reflected aloud.

"That's life, baby, the old get squeezed out of the picture. Gather ye rosebuds."

In front of her house, as she got out of the car, she said anxiously: "When will I see you?"

"Give you a buzz Friday. We'll do something over the weekend."

At her door she turned and waved, and for a moment he felt toward himself all the bitterness she should have felt.

"Our vocabulary for tonight's lesson," he said, raising his pointer to a list of chalked words on the blackboard. "The first word is 'hobby.' H-o-b-b-y. Can anyone give me a definition?" Most of the students were Chinese, not recent arrivals from Hong Kong, but native-born San Franciscans, old women who came primarily for the tea and cake served afterward. "Mrs. Lung?" Silence. "Mrs. Wu?" Silence. "Mrs. Kee?" Mrs. Kee thought for a while, her eyes darting around their crinkled slots. His best pupil. "Do you have a hobby, Mrs. Kee? Can you tell us what it is?" She continued to think, grimacing. At last she said shrilly, "My hobby. Smoke cigarettes." And she waved her streaming cigarette before the others like a baton. Mrs. Wu pointed to the cigarette: "Hobby."

He clicked the stem of his stopwatch down. The child with whom he sat in the school's storeroom—a boy of eight with round blue eyes, his upper lip tucked under his lower incisors, his forefinger up one nostril—looked sideways at the sunny window. "The man, Christopher, he has something missing. What is it?" The boy glanced at the picture before him. "Pick up your pencil, Chris, draw in what's missing." The boy removed his finger from his nose, took the pencil, and looked out the window again. "Draw what's missing, Chris." Chris circled the air with his pencil and finally brought it to bear on a nick in the table.

Putting the receiver to his other ear, he switched on the tape recorder and snapped his finger at another Suicide Prevention volunteer, who picked up the emergency phone. "I'm thinking very seriously of killing myself," the slurred voice repeated. Morris said quietly, "I understand, I understand. What's your name? I think it's always more friendly . . ." "I'm thinking very seriously of killing myself." "Have you taken any pills? Are you at home? Are you calling from home?" "Yeah . . ." "Whereabouts do you live, would you like to tell me?" "Why are people against me? I don't know, I don't know, but I've had enough . . . when she died, and they all turned against me . . . and then today . . . I don't know, I'm thinking very seriously of killing myself . . ." "I'm listening, I understand. Tell me what happened." "I know I'm crazy . . ." "Why? Why do you say that?" "Oh, because of the things I do, because I'm mentally unbalanced." "Have you done anything, have you taken any pills?" "Nope . . . just boozing . . ." Morris switched off the tape recorder and the other volunteer put the emergency phone down. Morris leaned back in his chair with the receiver. "Just say whatever you feel like saying. Cry if you want to. I'm here, I'm listening . . ." But at the other end of the line, after several clumsy attempts, the receiver was replaced.

"Nothing connects," he said through clenched teeth as he drove home after midnight. "Puny, pointless." As soon as he stepped inside the apartment he leaned heavily against the door. Every hour of the week had been crammed with activity, now it was already Friday and the weekend loomed before him empty. He scribbled a letter to the girl in Denver and asked her down for the Thanksgiving holiday. He picked up the book on modern China and, holding it unopened, paced back and forth. "Hell," he said, tossing it down; and he went back outside and got into his car.

There was an assortment of rusty buzzers by the door of Johanna's building, some with names in splotched scripts taped above them, but there was no Johanna, and he didn't remember her last name. He pressed a buzzer at random. Several minutes passed, then a young black woman in a hastily thrown-on pink chenille bathrobe opened the door.

She rubbed an eye sleepily. "Hey, I don' know you, man. What you want?"

"Sorry, must've rung the wrong bell," he said, starting to brush past her.

"Yere, just a minute!" she demanded, blocking his way; and she pointed her finger through the open door. "That bell, it read Aquiline F. Adams! Aquiline F. Adams—that me, and you woke me up, woke my kids up! You take a good look at that bell, man, and you remember it, 'cause you ever punch it again in the middle of the night jus' to get inside—"

"Sorry," he said again, pressing around her and hurrying on, "it's my cousin upstairs, she's got an appendicitis."

He heard her slam the front door shut with an oath.

Arriving out of breath on Johanna's floor, he was greeted by a male voice coming from behind the door, and he stood stock still as his heart pounded with an anger that astonished him. It was a resonant deliberate voice, speaking German, and it went on and on without pause as he stood breathing in and out furiously, until he realized with piercing relief that it must be a radio. He rapped sharply on the door.

"Listen, how could I phone you, I don't know your number," he blurted, showing a grin, a frown, a blankness, one after the other, unaware of what he was doing, yet sensing that he must look a fool. The majestic voice droned on. The girl's face had gone bright red. Her hand dropped away from the doorknob. "Hello, Boris," she said.

An enormous jollity invaded him, a flush he felt to his fingertips. He picked her up and swung her in circles, rumpling throwrugs and knocking books from table to floor, at last sinking into a chair with her, his head resting on hers. The drapes were drawn, only one lamp was lit, its light shedding down on a table covered with papers, inkpots, and pens. It was a quiet scene, yet it had a disturbing quality, its solitude was like a heavy presence. The measured voice drew to a close, the room was silent.

"What was that?" he asked.

"A record. Thomas Mann, reading from *Tonio Kröger*." She wondered, idly, if he had ever read Mann. The crown of her head was pressed into the warm arc of his throat, her eyes saw in a magnified blur the short hairs of his neck, the creases of his rough tweed jacket.

His wife had read Thomas Mann. Nothing but. Thomas

Mann in English, Thomas Mann in German; analyses, dissections, critiques of Thomas Mann. Before that it was someone else—who? Oh, yes, Dante. A whole year of Dante with an Italian dictionary at her side. She was too intense. She was theatrical. She would pounce on him with one line of urgency and expect him to respond. Once, shortly after she had left her ugly little Biography of Zero on the bureau for him to find, she came to him and said: "A catastrophe is in store for you." "Oh? What kind of catastrophe?" he asked. She sat down opposite him. Three or four minutes passed; a long time, he had thought uneasily, for a silence to last between two people sitting face to face. As he waited he observed how upset she looked, how uneven her breathing was. "A divorce?" he asked, curious. Her breathing grew more uneven. He had no idea in the world if he wanted a divorce, but since she was working so acoustically toward a decision, he would let her make it. Whatever it was, it could always be altered later, decisions never being final. "Yes, a divorce," she said, and divorced him. It was a surprise, but not a catastrophe. Unless it was a catastrophe not to feel that it was a catastrophe. Many times since, he had realized this was possible.

"It's a balmy night, baby! Let's go for a ride!"

"Now?"

"Why not? Where d'you want to go? Anywhere."

She answered quickly. "A mountain."

He got to his feet, setting her on hers. "Mount Tam. We'll watch the sunrise." While she went for her coat he glanced at the paper-strewn tabletop. Sketches of hands in various attitudes, rearing horses, a marine scape, a cloaked figure hanging in a pocket of dark space, arms lifted and toes pointed like Nijinsky frozen high above the footlights. His scalp prickled; he walked to the door and waited there for her.

As they drove away from the house, he remarked, "Never been married?"

"The matrimonial state has never enticed me."

"Why not?"

"I like my privacy. And you? Have you been married?"

"Yeah, once."

"What was your wife like?"

"She was a kook."

"What a shame."

"Why?"

"Kookism is to eccentricity as Kool-Aid is to wine. Add a quart of water and stir. Your wife was a sign of the times."

"You presume a lot. As a matter of fact, my wife was a bona fide crackpot."

"Really? And you were attracted to her. Is that why you're attracted to me?"

He glanced sideways at her. "Why do you say that? You look pretty sane to me. A little Weltschmerzy at times, but—very sane." He smiled. "And your attitude toward marriage is sound."

It was an intelligent, reasonable attitude, and one he endorsed—although for a moment his blood beat with a mad impulse to drive non-stop to a Reno justice of the peace (but he had had that short-lived urge on several occasions; once even, God help him, with Zaidee). He began to whistle, filling up the girl's silence and wondering if she was one of the moody types you had to cater to. He had no time for such types, yet he sensed he would make time for this one, and he stopped whistling and blew hard through his nostrils. "What's the matter?" he asked. "Is something the matter?"

"No. I don't have anything to say."

"Think of something."

"The moon. There's a ring around it."

"More."

"That's all," she said with a finality.

He stopped at a traffic light in a well-lit, middle-class neighborhood. "This section's going to be the new North Beach," he remarked, "home of the vital spirit. It's going to be here." He pointed to a darkened handicraft shop; to a metaphysical bookstore, still open; to another store with a big daisy painted on its window.

"Oh?" she said.

"It's just a feeling."

"What is it, what district?"

"The Haight."

11

He parked at the summit of Mount Tamalpais and turned the motor off. The wind battered the car, first from one direction, then from another, with deep intervals of silence, as overhead the night clouds eclipsed and released the moon. All around, the moonlight lay in a white sheen broken by shadows like splattered ink. He felt the triviality of his day evaporating. Flinging his door open, he stamped his feet on the ground in the biting cold. Johanna got out the other door and disappeared from sight.

"Where are you?" he yelled, then he caught sight of her walking through the trees at the edge of the clearing, bending now and then as though patting the trunks. Shivering, he turned back to the car and switched on the radio. "Let's dance! I'm freezing!" he yelled. A faint breath of music seeped into the night air, quickly soaring into an ear-splitting waltz, its tempo mounting in a fury. A shout rang from the trees: "Masquerade ball!" and to his surprise she came running to him and grabbed his hand. He plunged them into a furious impromptu dance, they laughed through their gyrations until tears rolled down their cheeks, then all at once the music ended and the mountain silence rolled back in. Under the windy dome of the sky they climbed inside the car again and huddled under a blanket to wait for the dawn. Morris finally fell asleep, but Johanna smoked and shivered and yawned, and at last she slipped back outside and disappeared into the trees.

"Where the hell are you now?" he shouted, waking to find the sky paling.

She walked into sight, her shoes sopping wet, her clothes caught with twigs. She seemed disinclined to talk, and started abruptly up the sandy path to the peak. A single raindrop bit into the sand, followed by a gapped patter.

At the top they leaned over the stone parapet and looked into a gray landscape as the sun rose up from the horizon. The flashing needles turned gold, dissolving on their heads and shoulders. In every direction, as far as the eye could see, hills, forests, and meadows spread out before them in nuances of mauve and sea green. Slowly the drizzle slackened off and steam rose from the parapet.

* * *

The noon sun sparkled through the treetops. They could hear the rippling of the stream they had parked by, and the creaking of an old gate in the wind. Taking off her coat, Johanna rolled away from Morris' blanket and breathed in the grass and dirt. She pulled her blouse off. "I don't want my clothes on," she said, "there's no one around."

"Go ahead."

Her body produced a soft catch in his throat; his arms went up in an arc of invitation and she slid her head onto his chest as the arms returned in a solid clasp. The old gate creaked back and forth, a mellow warm sound.

The sun was already at an angle when they started to hike down to the ocean, and it was low in the sky when they stumbled onto the glassy, sweeping expanse of green water, sweat streaming under their clothes, the sting of dry brush in their nostrils. Taking off their shoes, they walked through the surf, aching in all their bones from want of sleep, as the cliffs and rocks turned a flat matted lilac in the softening light. Round and burning, the sun was almost gone. They stood still, watching, and it sank quickly into the water, leaving a red glow across the horizon. When they turned around, the moon had risen behind them, as though the sun had gone around the globe, cooling its fire in the sea, and emerged clear and silver on the other side. They began the long hike back.

She looked around his apartment, her eyes heavy with fatigue. The floor was haphazardly covered with raveled mats, on which stood an oversize bed whose coarse bedspread was twisted through the sheets and blankets. Tables and shelves were strewn with dusty driftwood, seashells, rocks, household tools. Except for an aerial photograph of San Francisco, the walls were decorated exclusively with bamboo-framed scenes from the life of Lincoln, probably hanging there when he moved in. On a severely modern divan was tossed a fringed, moth-eaten pillow embroidered with the sentiment: *Friendship is God's loveliest garden.* Large windows without shades or curtains gave onto the sky. It was the room of a nomad, a place to sleep.

"Where's that possession of yours, the one you don't turn into a shrine?" she asked.

"What possession? I don't know," he said, throwing off his clothes.

64

She followed his plunge under the blankets, pressing close to him. His body radiated such heat that she kicked off her half of the blankets, and with a deep, carnal grinding starting up in her bones, she touched his chest, his forearm, his throat; but he was already snoring; and a few moments later she too was asleep.

The doorbell split the air. Morris jerked his head up. He looked at the clock. It was almost one A.M.

"What is it?" Johanna asked.

"Ssh."

Whoever it was had not taken their finger from the bell since first pressing it.

"Ignore it," he whispered, lying down again.

"But who is it?" she whispered back.

He closed his eyes without answering.

"It's that Zelma, Zulu, whatever her name is," she accused him. "That office girl, that friend of my friend."

Friend of a friend, he thought bitterly, all women had a friend, they always knew everything, it was like a fifth column. "Her? We broke up months ago," he said, and he bristled with the unfairness of having to lie, and felt a fury building up in him. Five minutes passed as the ringing continued while Johanna looked at him in the dark.

Suddenly it stopped. "Morrie," came a faint voice, "please open the door."

He gave Johanna's hand a stiff pat. She pulled the hand away."

"It's Zaidee, Morrie. Please, honey, open the door."

Johanna scrambled to her knees with an explosive breath.

"Shut up!" he shouted at both of them and tore out of bed. Pulling on his pants, he stepped out into the hall and shut the door behind him.

The long face was screwed up with apprehension. "Don't get mad, honey . . ."

He pulled her away from the door. "What's the matter with you!" he hissed.

"My mother kicked me out of the house," she snuffled. "We had a fight."

"Your mother'd never kick you out of the house, you lying little crud."

She stepped back and said defensively, "I stayed home all night last night waiting for you to call, and all day today and all night tonight. When I left, she said if I left she'd lock the door on me.''

''So why'd you come, for Christ sake?''

She stared at the floor, the lips of her wide mouth parted.

''I've forgotten to call before and you didn't come barging in at one in the morning.''

''But you said we'd do something this weekend.''

''So I forgot.''

''I had to walk part of the way,'' she told him, as though to soften him. ''Men kept following me, it scared me.''

''It was a stupid-ass thing to do.''

''I know. I saw your car outside, I knew you were home. I thought maybe you were sick. Couldn't we go inside?''

He stepped in front of her.

''Oh, I see,'' she said with a nod, smiling idiotically.

''Go back downstairs, I'll call a cab for you.'' But he lingered, running his fingers agitatedly through his hair. ''Wait here, I'll drive you back.''

He dressed in the dark, saying briskly to Johanna, ''I'll be back in a minute, it's nothing, one of those freak things.''

''Zaidee.''

''Who? Yeah, more or less. Look, I'll explain later. I'll be right back.''

As soon as he was gone she dressed and walked out of the apartment, banging the door wide open.

12 In a dingy paint-encrusted bathrobe, a paint-brush stuck behind his ear, Conrad had just fallen asleep in his chair, the lights on, the radio playing, his cat, Closeto, kneading its claws on his thigh. Canvases stood against the walls of the room, which was so small that you could cross it in two paces, and more were stacked on chairs and on the floor and on the cot. The washstand in the corner was a rainbow of color, even his cup and plate were spattered. He had put water on for coffee, but it had boiled away hours ago without his notice. The gas ring still burned, and the room was very hot.

Through his sleep he sensed a commotion at the door and he stirred. Gently putting the cat down, he turned the radio off and opened the door to a crack. Johanna stood there, her face raw with sunburn and dark with fatigue under the eyes. "I haven't slept for two nights!" she cried at him as she pushed into the room. "I came here because it was closer, I couldn't walk thirty blocks. A man followed me, he called me a— There're degenerates in the streets, Conrad! What kind of a world is this?"

"You need some hot wine," he said without a sign of perturbance, and he poured wine into the blackened pan on the gas ring, humming softly but looking at Johanna from the corner of his eye: she was walking around the room distractedly.

"Collect yourself. Sit down; you'll put your foot through a canvas."

Silence, as he stirred the wine with a bent spoon. The cat jumped into Johanna's lap. "How are you, Closeto?" she asked in quieter tones, looking at the gray sober catface; and she said to Conrad, "I think I first realized I loved you when you told me you named him Closeto because he was born in a closet."

"I've asked you not to say you love me."

"Oh, don't carp when I feel so rotten. You know how I mean."

"I know how you mean." His face, knobby and seamed, with its long nose and bald dome, looked at her with an ex-

67

pression of confessed vulnerability, amused at itself, and wistful.

"I wish I could tell you what happened," she said suddenly.

"Yes?"

"But it wouldn't be fair to you. It would be callous."

He poured the steaming wine into a mug and handed it to her. "But you *are* callous, Johanna, we both know that. Not cruel by design, just callous in passing. Too far inside your own head to notice other people."

She threw him a pained look.

"Go ahead," he said, "tell me what happened."

"It's like an oven in here, could you open the window?" While he was at the window she said swiftly, "I think I've— it's a matter of love." She put the wine aside without tasting it. Her fingers pulled at each other on Closeto's back.

"What's wrong with that?" he asked as casually as he could.

"It's the one from the peace march. You saw him."

He nodded.

"We had a wonderful time yesterday," she went on, "really wonderful. But tonight everything suddenly fell apart. We keep coming together—by chance, it seems—and flying apart, maybe by chance, too. I don't know if I want him. I don't think he knows if he wants me. But in the meantime my stomach's a disaster."

"Well, what's so great about this guy?"

She searched her mind. "I like his face."

"Didn't look like such a face."

"Really?" she said, surprised.

"Crude. High color. A kosher butcher."

"No, I think of a Cossack. A fur-lined cape slung over one shoulder."

"Very romantic."

"Yes, but I don't like him. I don't like his manner. And there's more. Things Wanda's told me. But still, I don't know, he's taken hold of me—" And making a fist, she struck her chest, hard, in the area of the heart.

He looked at her wordlessly.

"I wish you could tell me what to do."

"God, you make me impatient. A sixteen-year-old could ask that, but you're past thirty. You tell me you were raised in some crazy ivory tower, and I believe it." He picked up a drawing pad and a pencil and glared at her. "Well, you're going to have a rough time with this jerk." Lighting a cigarette, he began rapidly to sketch her as she sat with the cat. "Just keep it in mind. From what Wanda's told me, he's a nut. And you're a nut for sure."

"Well, I don't think I'll see him again."

"Just drift till the tides wash you up."

"First you say I shouldn't, then you say I should—"

"I only say you'll drift—"

"I'm no drifter! I've got roots into the past! How can you say I'm a drifter!"

"Don't get mad about it, it was just a remark."

"And remarks, as opposed to statements, are licensed to mean nothing and can be retracted at will. Shit!"

He glanced up from the sketch pad. Her cheeks were burning. "You always look so ashamed when you've said something vulgar," he commented. She continued to blush, her lips set with self-opprobrium. "It's an interesting thing," he went on, the cigarette dangling from his lips as he drew her, "if I looked at your work without knowing who'd done it, I'd say it was painted by a diabolist, a fanatic. Decorum is not a factor in it. Your psyche is infinitely contradictory, my love, infinitely weird."

"And what about your own weird psyche?" she asked, as though suddenly wishing to turn the conversation away from herself.

"Don't be patronizing. What does my psyche matter? I paint like Renoir, which was quite a step a hundred years ago. You're a different kettle of fish."

"Huh!" she said glumly, stroking Closeto's back. "We're all in the same kettle. The age of easel painting is finished."

"Ah, well," he murmured, sketching away, "it's no use gnashing your teeth over the fate of art."

"No?" she flashed at him. "*You* should sit in that gallery every day with a lacquered tennis ball mounted on a shoebox on one side of you and what looks like a mammoth pink earplug on the other." She threw her eyes up angrily at the ceiling. "I tell you, the age disgusts me. Stump-end discrimination!"

"But don't you see," he countered with humor, narrowing his baggy eyes against his cigarette smoke, "that big earplug is meant to jolt you into new patterns of thought."

69

"Jolt me! How dare that imbecile lump presume to jolt me!"

"I don't know, I don't care," he yawned, clearly not up to a discussion of art; and he added with a sigh, "I'm a simple person." Then he was silent, sitting back as ashes spilled down his robe front, and studying what he had done.

She sighed in her turn.

"Here," he said after a while, and handed her the sketch.

"It's very good. It's very serene. I must look better than I feel."

"Those are my good wishes for you." He stood up and stretched. "Are you ready to sleep? I'll clear off the cot."

"You use the cot. I'll take the chair. I can't sleep anyway."

"Because of him? It's really bad?"

She nodded.

"Congratulations," he said with a smile.

"Don't laugh."

"I'm only human. In spite of all my good wishes, I admit it's pleasant to see the obsession suffer."

"You're honest," she said briefly.

"But you're not. You want to dump these feelings because they upset you."

"Because they're just an infatuation!"

"Oh, sure, you write it off as infatuation, as if that took care of it. Well, I know infatuation's going out of style—passion, obsession. They're all ego—when you feel your knees shake because of the turn of a lip, it's just some sick vanity in yourself, it won't result in personal growth or community good, only in dark nights of the soul. Jealousy. Ecstasy. God help us, how juvenile. And what right do we have to be jealous? How dare we impinge on the freedom of another person? Neurotic possessiveness, with some itch and schmaltz thrown in. So find a proper object to love, who you could leave forever without falling apart—that's the test of maturity. Bunkum! Loving kindness and mental health are great, but they don't cover all the points by a long shot."

"I don't say they do, but—"

"All I'm saying is, don't pull back just because that's your pattern when something gets close to you. Make a choice. A real choice. Get behind the steering wheel."

"Except," she said with a sharp smile, "I don't have a driver's license."

"Well, it's time you got one." He bent down and picked up Closeto gently. "I've got to get some sleep, Johanna, it's past three. You sure you don't want the cot? I sleep all right in the chair."

"No. Thanks. May I keep the sketch?"

"It's yours."

He dragged the canvases off the cot, put out the light, and lay down. With deep thought, Closeto turned round and round at his side, finally settled, tucked his paws under his chest, and closed his eyes. Johanna tried to sleep, but couldn't; she sat looking at the dim figure of her friend on the cot with the little form at his side, her stomach churning, a sour taste of fatigue coating her palate. She lit a cigarette and drank some of the cold wine. Framed by the window, the sky was a deep carbon blue. The room grew very cold.

After a long while a soft ashy light gradually filled the room. She was surrounded by ladies in long pastel gowns and wide-brimmed straw hats, sitting and standing in dappled shade; by round-faced girls languidly drying themselves after their baths; by children with plump red cheeks and glossy bangs playing with tops and hoops in deep green parks. The beauty of these figures, their grace and innocence and their radiant pleasure in life, grew richer as the room lightened; their eyes looked at the brightening window in a glowing certainty of life's goodness.

Johanna got abruptly to her feet.

"Are you leaving?" Conrad asked, striking a match and lighting a cigarette as Closeto stretched at his side.

"Haven't you slept?" she asked.

"Not much. Did you?"

"No. I'm going now."

"Hang on, I'll give you some breakfast."

"I can't." She was already at the door. A moment later she hurried down the gray deserted street in search of a phone booth.

The phone rang twelve times before it was answered.

"It's me," she said, clearing her throat, "Johanna."

His voice came across the wire dull with sleep. "You all right? . . . What happened to you?"

"I left."

"Where'd you go? . . . Drove to your place, but I couldn't get in . . ."

"I stayed with a friend."

"Look," he said sleepily, "I want to see you . . . What time is it, anyway? . . . I'm shot . . ."

There was a momentary silence; the wire hummed in her ear.

"I'm choosing you," she stated. "I don't know if you're choosing me, but I've made my choice. I'm choosing you." She exhaled shakily.

"I'll come over later . . ." he said in a drowsy murmur.

"In the afternoon," she told him. "I'm going home to bed now. It was a long night."

13

He came to her house that afternoon. She dug her fingers into his back, loving the broad sweating expanse and all the secret parts inside him —heart, lungs, sheaths of muscle—and the closed eyes above her, lids fluttering like insect wings and then wildly tightening—my God, he could make noise, her neighbors would come to know him by his pleasure—and then the eyes once more, open now, blue flaring and pouring from them.

They rolled apart, then back together. Then he rolled away and jumped to his feet, not one to float like a water lily after making love.

"Hey, this is you," he said, seeing Conrad's sketch. He picked it up and looked at it. "It's your way of sitting."

She was exorbitantly pleased. "Would you like it?"

He accepted with pleasure, rolling it up and holding it aloft like a torch, his fingers making a sharp dent in the cylinder. "I will cherish it forever," he said with a gracious, naked bow, his body still shining with sweat. "This place is an oven."

"We could go up on the roof," she suggested.

They spread a blanket on the tarpaper, which glittered like ground glass in the sun. She had put her bathing suit on; he lay in his shorts. She sat next to him, looking down at the back of his dark head. At length she spoke. "I . . . I've been waiting for you to mention what I said on the phone this morning."

There was no response.

"I said I've—"

"What d'you want me to say?" he asked without turning.

She felt herself sliced deep by the tone, surprisingly deep; she sensed an alien world laid bare inside her, a world of finely interlocked susceptibilities. "By God," she whispered, standing up, "if that's what he's doing to me, he'd better be doing it with good reason."

He turned over on his back and looked up at her standing stiffly over him in her faded blue bikini. "What's wrong?" he asked, shading his eyes.

"I want you to say something about my phone call. I told

you how I stood. I want to know how you stand. Are you involved with that Zaidee?"

"No," he lied, with a smile at the directness of her words, as if words could be seen, weighed, as if they had actual substance.

"Or anyone else," she continued. "If there's anyone else. Do you want just me? Am I the only one?"

"I can't believe this conversation," he said, sitting up. "How old did you say you were, twelve? You want a pledge of eternal love signed in blood? Life's a risk, don't take all the risk out of it, that's its beauty."

"I don't think you've ever risked anything. I think everything you do is calculated to leave you exactly as you are."

"Shit!" He rose and walked to the edge of the roof. Below were faded geraniums, choked brambles, patches of bald earth littered with broken glass. "All this intellectualizing," he said heavily, feeling her presence beside him. "Why not enjoy what we've got—the sky—the grass—"

"What's that got to do with us!"

"What are you so *mad* about?"

"Because I can't play—if you're going to play, I want to know so I can cut you off now—because you've got a hook into me, and I can't play, I don't know how, with a hook—I'd want you to leave if you don't feel even the slightest hook in you—but I can't tell—you're either facetious or elusive—it's like slapping at a mist—and I refuse to match that with —what I feel—"

"You're whipping yourself up into a froth," he murmured, his head beginning to ache.

"A froth!" she said contemptuously.

"A storm?" he suggested uneasily, with a shrug.

"You shrug! You stand and shrug!"

"What would you like me to do?"

"Dive down three stories on your head!"

He broke into a relieved smile at her sudden spurt of humor.

"I mean that."

"Send me over," he said, ruffling her hair.

Her hand shot out and brutally caught the unsuspecting jaw, flinging him off balance so that he saw a reel of blue that ended with a thud—body sprawling on the tarpaper, head hanging over the edge into the air—as seventy feet below bim the scattered red of the geraniums flared and shimmered and came to a standstill from which a word burst into his head like a comet—*signify, signify*—leaving him dazzled as he got to his feet. Terrified, enraged, and elated, he slapped her face and embraced her. That was what he had come back for the first time, each time—the end of play.

14

The hot weather broke soon after. A damp mole-gray winter nosed into every corner of the city.

Each evening Wanda drove back from work across the foggy Bay Bridge to Conrad's room. She spread out her work on his cardtable while he painted or did his menus and postcards, which was how he earned the little money he needed. Closeto chased a ping-pong ball through the room, banging into the wall with a look of utter astonishment (he also had a cigarette package tied into a ball with string, and a marble which he carried around in his mouth, but Conrad refused to buy cat toys because of their offensive fluorescent colors); or the animal would sit on the edge of the cot, his eyes closed with the wisdom of the ages, motionless except to scratch his ear with his back foot and give his head a violent shake, the ears making a noise like snapped leather. Later he was gently removed to a chair and Conrad and Wanda lay down on the cot. Usually Wanda left by midnight, but sometimes she stayed overnight. Conrad was a light, erratic sleeper. His eyes would suddenly open, he would fold his hands across his stomach and stare into the darkness looking wise and content. Then his eyes would close again and a faint smile come to his lips. He always smiled in his sleep. She watched him in the dark, reluctant to close her eyes on him.

One morning when she dropped by her flat before going on to work she found a letter addressed in a childish penciled hand. She opened it and saw that it was from Zaidee and that the i's were dotted with loops, which annoyed her. After meeting Zaidee on the march she had sent her a sympathy note about her brother. She had been Zaidee's reluctant confidante while working part-time in an insurance office, and she knew all about the silent widowed mother, and the older brother, progenitor of a welfare-supported brood, and the younger brother, Ollie, similar to Zaidee in mental prowess, whose touchingly outdated goal was to become a tapdancer, and the boyfriend, Morrie, often absent from Zaidee's life but never from her conversation. When Wanda quit the job she was glad to get away from the girl, yet her thoughts often returned to her. She read the letter in her hand.

Dear Wanda,

It was really nice to hear from you I really enjoyed seeing you at the march, I am still hear filing Sandy got married and Mrs. Bowman retired. That was Morrie you saw on the march I didnt get a chance to talk to you what do you think of him? We are still going together my mother took what happened to Ollie very hard she wants to move back to Arkansas to the farm, I dont want to. I really wish you could drop by the office and we could visit some time you were really a good freind when we worked together, well by for now Wanda thank you very much for your kind letter of sympathy about Ollie.

Your Friend Zaidee Dawson

Impulsively, she found Zaidee's number in the phone book and called her. She was just on her way to work and she would be happy to come to Wanda's for Thanksgiving. Her mother wasn't going to celebrate.

By one o'clock on Thanksgiving Day, Wanda had everything under control. The turkey was in the oven, three leaves were in the dining-room table, which was set for ten and decorated with a centerpiece of carnations and red candles. The phonograph was playing *My Fair Lady* and the bathwater was pounding into the tub. The doorbell rang. It was Zaidee, forty-five minutes early, dressed in a bright aquamarine coat which, when she removed it, revealed an even brighter aquamarine dress with violet collar, belt, and pocket patches.

"Oh, Zaidee," Wanda said feelingly over her shoulder, running back to the bath, "I want everybody to be happy today—" but caught herself before finishing with: and you can't be happy in that color.

The bathroom door slammed shut. Zaidee folded her coat over her arm and stood where she was in the hall. Fifteen minutes later Wanda emerged. "Why didn't you sit down, for goodness' sake? No, don't sit down. Come with me, I want to try something. I want everybody to be happy."

When Johanna arrived the other guests were all present. Wanda had mentioned to her that Zaidee had been invited, and she looked around for the thin little girl she had seen on the march and concluded with frustration that she hadn't come. She knew most of the guests, a mixture of Poly Sci grad students and Unitarians. The atmosphere would be topical and humane; they would discuss the Poverty Program, the peace march, and the Yugoslavian folk dancers that had appeared at the Community Center. They were the conscience of the world, yet she found them somehow bland and lacking.

"How's the big earplug?" Conrad asked, coming over to her.

"I kick it at intervals. If my boss weren't in love with me I'd be fired by now." She spoke without archness, as if her boss were incomprehensible.

"You watch out for Josh," Conrad said as Wanda joined them.

"And wouldn't you know his name would be Josh," said Johanna. "It couldn't be George or Charlie."

It was odd to see Conrad put his arm around Wanda, to know that they were sleeping together. Four years ago she, Johanna, had met him in Flack's art-supply store, where she was waiting for a roll of canvas. He had come in and asked the clerk for some stretchers. His baggy eyes had widened at the sight of her, he had fumbled with his wallet and spilled coins across the counter, and he had followed her outside without his stretchers. Now his faithful and restrained arm had come to rest on someone else's shoulder. She was relieved. He was going to be happy.

In the kitchen with Wanda, she squeezed her friend's arm. "Are you going to get married or something?" she asked.

Wanda threw her hands into the air as if astonished by the idea. There was something light and girlish about her, a quality totally new in her. "Johanna," she said, "I forbid you to moon because Morris wasn't invited. I want you to be happy. I want everyone to be happy."

"I *am*. I know it would have been awkward to have him and Zaidee here together. And it's worked out fine, he had to go to his brother's in San Jose for Thanksgiving. But I'm sorry she didn't come; I was curious to have a look at her."

"Oh, she *is* here—didn't you see her?"

"No, I looked."

"Oh Lord, maybe I went too far. I sort of made her over."

"Well then, off I go, I must have a look at her."

"Johanna?"

Johanna turned around.

"I don't want to be in the middle of anything just because I know her. Don't pump me about her—I'm strictly neutral."

"What's to pump? She's out of the picture."

Wanda nodded briefly and turned to the oven.

It was some time before Johanna singled out the creature by the fireplace as Zaidee. She was wearing something between a robe and a toga made of claret velvet; gone was the pony-tail, her hair was parted in the center and hung down her narrow face to her waist; and her eyes were made up with theatrical boldness, sweeping in two black wings to her temples, like an opera star's.

Zaidee had been listening to a young man in horn-rim glasses and a corduroy jacket talking about soul food, whatever that was; and when she mentioned the kind of food her mother made—good plain country food, Jerusalem artichokes and cattail pancakes—he grew fascinated. She smiled uncertainly. It was then that she saw the girl in the yellow dress. She remembered the yellow dress from the march, and she remembered the face, and for some reason she felt in her bones that this was the girl Morrie had had in his room that night. Maybe because the girl was looking at her so hard.

Aware of the two women's mutual interest, the young man went off to replenish his drink.

"I think we met on the peace march," Johanna said, wishing she had walked away, yet magnetized by curiosity.

The girl nodded. The expression in her sooty exotic eyes was one of worried receptivity.

"Your gown is unusual," Johanna said, feeling stilted.

"Wanda made it, she just threw it down on the sewing machine and made it in a minute, she's very nice," the girl said nervously. Johanna heard a thick Southern drawl.

A silence descended.

"Just took some old drapes and seamed them together," Zaidee said.

"Wanda's handy," Johanna agreed.

There was another silence. Johanna looked at the girl's empty glass. "Would you like another drink?"

"Oh, no thank you." She put her finger down the glass to the ice. "I guess you know Morrie?"

". . . More or less." She was suddenly deeply angry that this girl had been made unhappy.

"I thought maybe you did. He was talking to you on the

march.'' She pursed her lips, taking on the look of an old woman. ''I guess you've seen him since?''

Johanna didn't answer, overcome by a sense of criminal guilt.

''Would you know where he is today?'' the girl went on, looking at Johanna with bald humility.

''Oh, I wouldn't know—I think someone said he was with his brother in San Jose.''

''Oh, Morrie doesn't have any brother out here. They're all in Brooklyn.''

Despite the fog, the flight from Denver was on the dot. Morris stood in the brightly lit waiting room and couldn't pick out the girl until she walked up to him, and then he remembered not her face but her round calves.

''Morrie!'' she cried.

He draped an arm around her and started down the hall.

''I can't walk so fast, Morrie, please.''

''How was your flight?''

''It was fine. Do you mind taking my suitcase? Are you glad to see me?''

''Would I invite you down here if I wouldn't be glad to see you?''

''Aren't you going to kiss me hello?''

Without slowing his pace, he smacked a kiss sideways on her lips.

There was a sheen of sweat on Zaidee's brow as she ate. Her eyes peered anxiously up from the plate. People were asking her questions. Someone had just asked where she came from.

''From the Ouachita Mountains,'' she said, ceasing to chew.

''There's some sort of sect there?''

''. . . A sect?''

''A religious sect?''

She was silent for a moment. ''Like the praying mantis?''

''I haven't heard of that one.''

''It's the only one I can think of,'' she murmured.

''But you're not a member?''

She shook her head. Wanda guided the conversation in a different direction, and Zaidee resumed her chewing with relief. Now and then her eyes crept to the girl in yellow. She was very attractive, very cool. The men were aware of her. Zaidee stopped chewing again, unable to swallow.

Wanda, too, was looking at Johanna, wondering why she appeared less cheerful than when she had arrived. She had eaten little and was leaning back in her chair with her arms crossed, distant and unapproachable. The women were put off, but the men were not, their glances including her in their conversation as if she were the key listener, though she gave no indication that she heard them—nor, Wanda thought, would they want her to. Their double inequity—reducing a woman to a dinner-table figurehead and withholding the supposedly coveted office from the plain—annoyed Wanda even in her happy frame of mind. She hoped Johanna would throw a wrench into the conversation, but it was so intelligent and enlightened that it would seem to offer no opportunity. Johanna's table partner, a local journalist, grizzled and tweedy, was describing the sorry state of the Fillmore, its ancient rotting housing, its drug traffic, knifings, and diseases, the gathering hatred of whites, which you could smell on the streets along with the overturned garbage cans . . .

"Good," said Johanna, staring at her plate, thinking of the black figures she had seen on the march, sprawled with monstrous lassitude on their decayed stairs, and of the Negro woman downstairs from her, Aquiline, with four children under the age of seven, no husband, and an imbecile belief in the pale Christ of her storefront church. "Good," she said again, "I hope it explodes."

"Good, sure, what d'you think I'm *saying?*" the journalist responded, swinging around in his chair. "But don't think because you're sympathetic you won't be brained along with the Birchers." He turned to the others. "That's the price of revolution, and we'd better damn well accept it."

"We deserve it," a young girl put in darkly.

"Right on!" someone else cheered.

"If a Negro tried to brain me," Johanna stated, "I'd kill him."

There was a silence around the table.

"That's the price *they* pay for revolution," she went on. "If you think you're all going to remain so moved by the Negroes' plight that when your own sympathetic middle-class head is cracked on the street you're going to accept it and not bash heads in return, you're wrong. Wait around a few years. The price of revolution isn't that we get brained along with the Birchers, but that we'll retaliate like the Birchers. It's the Negroes who'll pay.''

"They prefer to be called blacks," the journalist said, picking up his fork with a cool glance at her.

Wanda gave her friend, now *persona non grata* at the table, a reassuring smile. What she said was true, but, like the subject of death, it was only tacitly acknowledged; to articulate it was somehow to court it, to honor it. Trust Johanna to refute the role of figurehead not with a gentle tap but a hammerblow.

Morris planted salami, crackers, and a bottle of root beer before his guest.

"I thought we'd go to a restaurant," she said, "it's Thanksgiving."

"We'll eat out tomorrow."

"Why did you take so long to answer my letter?"

"I was snowed by work."

She chewed heartlessly on a cracker and looked around the messy room. "At least you've got a decent picture on your wall at last," she remarked. "It's beautiful."

Morris sprang up, pried the tack out with his fingernail, and dropped Conrad's sketch of Johanna face down in a chair.

"Why'd you do that?"

"How would you like to go to bed, my little jewel?" he asked suddenly, crouching before her with an impatient smile.

"I'd like to make your bed first. I hate a rumpled bed."

"The dumps are overflowing," a girl with a hoarse voice, hair like a boy's, and big ceramic earrings was telling Zaidee. Dinner was over, the guests milled around the living room talking above the strains of *Rigoletto,* with which *My Fair Lady* had been replaced.

"I know," said Zaidee, no longer fazed by the things these people talked about, "I went out there yesterday." She had driven there with her mother, the back seat and trunk of the car stuffed with trash.

"Most people wouldn't bother to go out and see for themselves," the girl endorsed her zealously.

"My mother's moving," Zaidee explained.

"I don't doubt it. People are leaving the cities. In five years it'll be a national problem."

"It's a problem now," said Zaidee, thinking of her mother and Arkansas.

"But no one is angry enough," the girl announced angrily.

Zaidee looked at her nervously.

"That's how I feel," the girl said, dropping her hoarse voice. "Under the anger, fear. I'm frightened. What's going to happen to this planet?"

Zaidee shook her head, more bemused by her popularity than by the fate of the planet. People kept singling her out and talking to her, and though she couldn't follow their words, whatever answer she gave seemed to sit well with them. This had never happened before. She was usually a flop at parties. Morrie wouldn't even take her to parties.

"Your gown is absolutely smashing," the girl stated suddenly. "I think you people may have the answer. You're totally outside the deadly rigidities of the Establishment. I think you might just have the answer."

"I hope so," murmured Zaidee, wondering who the girl was referring to, but pleased to be numbered among them. Someone cut off *Rigoletto* and put on a Beatles record. The girl pricked up her ears. "Excuse me," she said, walking off, "I'm doing a paper on them."

When toward evening people began to leave, Johanna went to Zaidee to say goodbye. "I'm sorry," she told her, and she was not sure if she was sorrier because she had taken Morrie away from this poor little creature or because Morrie had lied to her about San Jose.

Zaidee stared at her for a moment. "Oh, you mean because of Morrie? Oh, listen, thanks, it's not your fault. I always know when he's seeing somebody else. He does it all the time. It's not your fault."

"You're still going with him?" leaped from the girl.

"Well, sure," said Zaidee with a shrug; sad, enduring.

The girl grew tall and remote, as if a physical change had taken place in her. "Good night," she said, extending her hand. It seemed odd to shake hands, especially with a woman. Zaidee watched as the girl shook hands with the others. Morrie couldn't have much in common with her. She was like somebody from a different country.

"What d'you say we drive up to Tahoe?" Morris asked from his pillow. "We could make it by midnight."

"I just got in from a three-hour plane trip!"

"You can sleep in the car on the way up."

"But it's all snow and ice up there, isn't it? That's just what I got away from."

"You'll love it, baby. Come on, let's move."

15

Thirty-six hours later Morris gathered up his now white-faced and furious guest, who had spent most of the time sitting in the ladies' lounge of the casino, and put her on a bus for Reno and a plane home. "I'm sorry, baby," he said, pressing the bus fare into her hand. She dropped the bills to the snow, her teeth chattering and her eyes wet. When the bus had gone he picked up the bills and went back to the table, where they quickly joined the rest he had lost. He spun away from the table empty-handed. "That's the last time you see my face up here!" he said outside, throwing his haggard face up into the falling mist of snow. As he got into his car he remembered the girl's face through the bus window —pale, rigid, red-nosed. She must have wanted to see him badly to come so far, at such expense. He would send her a letter of apology. His life from now on would be one single reparation for all his past crimes. This last crime—the elaborate lie to Johanna, the thoughtless abuse of the Denver girl, the total erasure of his checking account—had been as necessary as the last smoke or the last drink before quitting. A last fling; and on that final foul-smelling mass of self-indulgence he would plant his boot and make his leap up.

"That's true," he sighed, standing in Johanna's room that night and trying to sharpen his sleep-starved mind. "I don't have any brother out here. I made Thanksgiving plans before I even met you . . . with this co-worker at the office . . . and her family. They live in San Jose. I couldn't get out of it. I didn't think you'd understand . . ."

"What about Zaidee? You don't say anything about her. I'm telling you that it was Zaidee who told me."

"Zaidee," he murmured, his mind elsewhere. He was thinking of the money he had lost.

"She says you're still going together!" Johanna accused.

Johanna's face reminded him of the girl's in the bus window. Only there was a smoldering fuse behind Johanna's, a promise of attack, of significance. It stimulated his mind, and roused a sexual heat in his blood. "Zaidee wants to believe I'm still seeing her," he said, "so she believes it. She's got a low IQ."

"Did you give her one of your tests?" she asked bitterly. She found his lie about his brother contemptible, she found his involvement with poor little Zaidee—whether still in progress or finished—unworthy of a man his age, and she found the frankly sexual pouching of his lips insulting to the seriousness of the conversation. She hated him for all that and she hated him because in spite of it she was overjoyed to see him.

She looked at the blue, heavy-lidded, not especially large eyes; at the oversized nose; at the thick, carelessly combed hair already scattered with gray at the temples; at the sensual, not particularly well formed lips; dazzled by this constellation of commonplace features, moved to an idolatry that compressed her throat and sent streaks of adrenalin through her arm veins.

"It's more than I expected," she told him in a low voice, resentfully.

"What is?"

Words rose and fell back in her throat. She remembered Conrad's impassioned defense of love that night in his room, and it belatedly occurred to her that he had not stuck to his own fine counsel but had chosen the opposite course, companionship with Wanda; and she felt conned, thrown alone and without weapons on a dangerous isle.

Renewing his snow-blessed resolution, believing each word because he was now prepared to make them true, he said: "I haven't seen Zaidee since that night she rang the doorbell. And I spent Thanksgiving with this very kind but nowhere co-worker and her family in San Jose and was bored stiff."

It gave him a thrill of self-denial to humble himself like this, to taste the demanding commitment of the future. He had discussed his plans with Johanna—a move to a cheaper apartment so he could begin saving money; a trip to Berkeley to get the Doctorate rolling. Since that moment when he had hung over the edge of her roof, he had seen his horizon glowing with promise, and now, as all his plans rolled tumultuously through his head, including a brutal cutoff from all women except Johanna, he saw his future burst into triumphant light.

She was still looking at him balefully.

"I've said all I can say," he stated in a final tone, running his hands through his hair. Then he cleared up one last possible point. "I caught a cold down there, I couldn't sleep. I feel lousy." It would explain the bloodshot eyes and fatigue; it would end the argument and bring them back together. And he believed every word as he spoke, because all that he said was a valid dimension of himself: the dimension of wish, which was no less real for its relationship to fact.

Her eyes bored into his bloodshot ones, trying to see through them and failing. The only tool she had at hand was faith, and as she took hold of it, covering the short distance between them with one step, she felt a shifting and blurring of all that was familiar and dependable in her, and sensed the map of her character dimming.

16 The next week Morris took an afternoon off from work and drove to the University of California in Berkeley to check into the steps he must take to apply to medical school; but he got no farther than Sather Gate. This campus entrance, the bone of contention during the free-speech sit-ins of a year before, now looked like a corner of Hyde Park, with its competing haranguers and its cardtables surrounded by posters and heaped with leaflets and petitions. What had begun as an act of civil disobedience against the teaching methods of a multiversity seemed now to have exploded into a rebellion against nothing less than the entire status quo of modern existence. He felt suddenly impatient with the purpose that had brought him here; and with the same whirr of excitement in his bones as when he had tacked up the peace-march notices, he sat down on the steps of the Student Union with a crowd of young onlookers, non-students for the most part, an endemic band of wanderers; the same kind he had seen on the march and in the Haight, in wild Salvation Army clothes, Buffalo Bill hair whipping in the winter wind. He felt ill at ease in his good old suede shoes, his roomy slacks and shapeless tweed jacket, an outfit which till now had satisfied him as an expression of his contempt for the gray flannel uniform of the American professional man. His tie seemed to burn around his neck. He took it off and stuffed it into his pocket.

He sat there all afternoon and into the dusk. The commingled exhortations—mostly about black power and sexual freedom—brought him a dawning realization that some new ideology had finally put its hands to the stale epoch, that all the seemingly unconnected fragments—the peace march, the mushrooming metaphysical bookshops, the Freedom Riders of the South, the strange costumes, the nude beach he had heard of, the happenings he read about where people were sprinkled with water and bombarded with flowers, the appearance of the bongo drum and the rediscovery of the guitar—all these things were jewels strung closely together on the same strong catgut of disenchantment. He felt poetic and resolute, a heady combination that left him still sitting when the cardtables had been cleared and the cold sky was dotting with stars. He got up, stiff and enthused, and walked back to his car.

When he got home he did not call Johanna as he had promised. He felt cast adrift.

"Why does it have to be one thing or another?" he asked himself, walking around the room. "Why can't I see her like I'd see anybody and lead my own life as I see fit? Why should it matter to me that she'd disapprove if I went back on my plans?" And he felt his old anxiety buzzing close. The crowd at Sather Gate began growing smaller, becoming static and soundless, and with equal rapidity Johanna was contracting into a miniature of herself, as though seen through the wrong end of a telescope. The old anguish had shot through him, coring him like an apple. Everything in the room possessed a smallness, a coldness, and a kind of silly sheen. The phone rang. He stared at it, then picked up the receiver as if afraid it would dissolve in his hand.

"Boris?" Her voice startled him. "I had the phone put away. Have you been trying to get me for hours?"

"Yeah," he said, wiping his forehead.

"I'm sorry. How did it go today?"

"Ah, red tape," he said, bridging his desire for her and his fear of her disapproval with procrastination. "You know what it's like over there. I have to go back." The room began to look more normal. "You feel like a visitor?" he asked.

"As a matter of fact, yes."

"Okay, out of your clothes, baby, I'm on my way."

The universe was coming back to life and tingling down his spine.

When he returned later he was able to think more rationally. He realized that he saw Johanna symbolized by a sheet of rain and fifty cents.

She had jumped out of the car one rainy night to buy cigarettes and milk at a Fillmore grocery store, hurrying back through the downpour with the paper bag in one hand and her change in the other. She discovered as they drove off that she had accidentally been given a half dollar too much, and when he refused to drive back, she opened the door at a stoplight and jumped out. He made a U turn and followed her back through the rain, and felt a strange fear when she came out of the store and told him, sopping: "There are moral obligations."

It reminded him of her problem with the potato plant. She had rearranged its vines, which were crawling among her books, but when she was finished she stood there frowning. Then she draped the vines back in their original position. "They have their rights."

Climbing into bed, he thought, not for the first time, of her name, Kaulbach: the Prussian fanaticism, the obsession with principle. "We're at opposite ends of the human spectrum," he said, staring at the dark ceiling. And yet he had never felt so drawn to any other woman—certainly not his ex-wife. But Rachel had been thickset, bumpy-featured. Could the difference in his feelings for her and Johanna really boil down to the difference between plain and lovely flesh? "Knowing me," he sighed, "it probably could."

Hadn't he stood before the sketch on his wall and felt desire bloom and quiver in him at the sight of Johanna's penciled arm? Such a thing had never happened to him before. With *Playboy* centerfolds, maybe, but a few penciled lines depicting a fully clothed figure holding a cat? It was because the figure was hers. And digging his head into the pillow, he felt with explosive certainty that he must not see her again.

Instead, he cut his testing short the next day and went to the gallery where she worked.

"I vould like to haf a look at the Rape of the Sabine Goils," he said.

She glanced up. A smile broke over her face and she replied conspiratorially, "I'm afraid we don't handle Rubens, sir. It *is* the Rubens you mean?"

"It is the *rape* I mean," he whispered intensely.

"How about the rape of art instead?" she asked, waving her hand at the walls.

"I vill haf a look." He glanced around, and swung his eyes back to her. "I vill haf *you!*"

She left with him on the spot, bursting into uncontrollable laughter outside.

He didn't know what to do. If she saw him renege on the plans he had given so much lip service to, something would be spoiled at the center of their relationship. But he had not yet applied for med school, and he was no longer sure he wanted to. All he had done so far was to borrow a university library card from a fellow psychometrist doing grad work;

with Sather Gate within short walking distance, he began doing some rereading of Freud and Jung in the stacks.

And there he spied a plump little redhead yawning over a pile of books. He tested himself to see if he could feel an attraction in spite of his sexual immersion in Johanna, and when he found that he could, it seemed natural to act upon it. He took her out for coffee.

Michelle, it turned out, was a drama major, and when within a very short while she began flying into jealous rages he was able to enjoy them without having to believe them.

He enjoyed the campus atmosphere, too. Electricity had been released into the air. Gone was the calm of his own college days, the conventional attire, the obedience to scheduled classes and automatic respect for professors. But he was a product of that age and he understood the reason for the academic tradition. It provided a unity of culture, a sense of time, a network of causal relationships; nor could the half-baked, the gimmicky, the random, crack a system in which standards had been compared, argued, and shaped over the centuries. But he knew, too—or at least felt—that the past centuries were no longer quite relevant. The humanities had not humanized. And it was also possible that their check system excluded originality as much as it excluded the spurious. It was time that the academic tradition, as part of the status quo, was questioned; time that the campus rang as it did with breakthroughs.

He began spending weekends there, staying with Michelle in her studio apartment with its Beatles poster, its small tarnished Buddha holding a triangle of smoking incense, its scattering of clothes and upflung issues of *Vogue* and *Theatre Arts*. He told Johanna he was attending a series of weekend seminars on disturbed children.

Most of his evenings were spent there too. He gave up teaching his English class, parting from his Chinese ladies with the hurried counsel to keep their noses clean, and forgot his occasional volleyball nights at the Community Center. He carried a change of clothes in his car so that he could throw off his suit and tie after work and wander around campus in a pair of old Levi's and a gray workman's shirt. He forgot about looking for a cheaper apartment, and stopped going to the stacks entirely. The only thing he remained committed to was his volunteer work at the Suicide Prevention Bureau.

Christmas Eve he went to a party with Michelle. The

dawning era was reflected only in a poster of Che Guevara, pinned mindlessly alongside a sorority group photograph, and in one couple who excitedly exhibited a brownie someone had baked with marijuana, which, when gingerly nibbled, produced no effect. Everyone was in neat clothes and a short hair style; they drank Scotch and danced the Frug. The party was no isolated pocket from the Fifties, but still the general texture of the times, and Morris marveled to find it so close to Sather Gate. Bored, he drank more than his usual glass and reeled caressingly from girl to girl until Michelle presented him with a brilliant performance of Sophia Loren-type outrage. Sick and lucid the next day, he vowed to do penance by spending New Year's Eve at the Suicide Prevention Bureau. He could have the calls relayed to his apartment, but somehow he preferred the idea of sitting in the empty, darkened office while the festive sounds of the New Year seeped in from the street. He would buy a bottle of champagne and ask Johanna to accompany him; he could make up for his negligence and at the same time demonstrate to her his commitment to the Bureau, the one thing he was proud of. And who knew, maybe he would wind up breaking with her, since the exhaustion of a sleepless night might easily fray their tempers.

"It's grotesque, spending New Year's Eve here," she complained as he led her through the door.

"Balls," he said, sitting down at his desk and switching a lamp on. "Somebody's got to do it."

Outside it was raining. He had forgotten the champagne.

"It's cold," she said.

"Leave your coat on."

She sat down on the leather couch by the desk. She had seen so little of him lately that often when she took the bus home from work she rode past her stop and got off in his neighborhood. It was dark by then and his building seemed to beckon to her like a lighthouse. She would loiter in the doorway, studying the MORRIS LEVINSKY in the slot above his buzzer, looking at the mosaic tile his feet traveled across every day, then hurry away, humiliated by nosing around his life like a stranger.

"You've been busy lately," she ventured.

He did not reply. He had picked up a pencil and now he tapped it thoughtfully on the desktop.

Her heart began racing.

The phone rang. For forty-five minutes he soothed some lonely creature calling from a furnished room in the Mission. "Yes, I know . . . a furnished room isn't the same as a home . . . Yes, I'm sure you had a home once . . . Sixty-seven? That's not so old, there are good days left . . . Believe that . . . Yes, go ahead, I have all night . . . Sure . . . I know . . . There's a first time for everything, don't feel embarrassed, I'm here to help you . . ."

The gentleness in his voice soothed her; she felt comforted, like the old soul in the furnished room. But when he hung up and swung around to her in the swivel chair, the tenderness, the concern had evaporated.

"You're a rare one, Morris," she said with a spark of hatred.

"What's wrong?" he asked, not looking her in the face. "Is it that I've been busy lately?"

She felt the spark of hatred ignite, not at his words but at his expression, which, illuminated by the harsh white glare of the lamp, was insolently closed, while the texture and contours of the face remained deeply compelling.

"I don't think you've been busy!" she said suddenly, scrambling to her feet and throwing her husbanded patience to the winds. "I think I'm just low on your list of social priorities. Which is your privilege. As long as you admit it. Then I'll have the freedom to remove myself from your life!"

His eyes swung to her angry face; the ultimatum burned into him, melting his vacillation; he felt alive with her intensity, his eyes heating with it.

"You're reading things in," he protested. "Every weekend it's been that damn seminar; and weeknights—weeknights there's the English class, there's the reading I have to do in the stacks; and I've been doing double duty here. You call that a social life?"

As always, her need to believe him rose like a tidal wave. She took a few steps away.

"You make me sound like—I don't know—some nagging wife!"

"No, I'm just saying—"

"I know, I don't *want* to sound—" She turned around and faced him.

"No, it's my fault, I've got too many things going. After the New Year I'm cutting down."

"It *is* the New Year."

He glanced at his watch, and his fingers passed over his face. "Already." And he stared past his desk into the darkness. Then he brightened. "We'd better begin celebrating," he said, getting up and going to her with his arms open.

At eight o'clock in the morning of the New Year, having made love twice on the leather couch between phone calls, they opened the door to the bright rainwashed morning and stepped tiredly into it.

He hung in limbo, wandering around Sather Gate and up and down Telegraph Avenue with his hands in his pockets, drifting to meetings on draft-card burning, on sexual freedom and black power, held in barren lofts plastered with posters of Malcolm X or the Kama Sutra positions, and though he believed in it all he could not find the singleness of purpose to throw himself headlong into the activities. Always in the background hung the specter of his ambition, the knowledge that if he didn't soon buckle down and get on with it he would be into his forties and the remainder of his life would be too short to undertake such a longterm struggle. The thought of the grinding years of med school stunned him—life would sweep around him as he sat into the small hours over his books; and afterward it would be years before he could build up a clientele; he would be fifty. But the thought of being anything else at fifty stunned him more.

This was a breathing space before the academic plunge, he told himself as he drew on a roach held in a pair of tweezers, and pasted a bumper strip on his car saying MAKE LOVE, NOT WAR, and climbed into sleeping bags with young girls with long uncombed hair, in dirty sweet-smelling rooms. But if it was a breathing space, his breath grew more labored as the new year progressed. Spring was always the real beginning.

94

17

The day after Wanda's Thanksgiving party Zaidee summoned up the courage to tell her mother she didn't want to go back to Arkansas with her. She stood long-faced and sorry, smudges of black eye makeup still evident on her lids. After a long blank look, her mother nodded her head. It was weird, Zaidee thought, that some bullet thousands of miles away had paralyzed her mother sitting right here in this kitchen.

"I guess you'll wind up marrying that M," her mother said tonelessly.

"He'd never marry me," Zaidee reassured her dejectedly. She had seen very little of Morris in the past few weeks.

"You promise me you'll write every week, Zaidee."

She kept her promise. At first there was little to write about, but she wrote it. Then there was a great deal to write about, but she didn't write it.

She took a room at the YWCA residence club downtown, as she had promised her mother, and she went to work in the morning and came back at night and waited by the phone on the wall for Morrie to call, but he never did. Finally she began calling him. He would listen to her unhappy voice and agree to pick her up outside the residence club, and they would spend a few hours together, and sometimes he slept with her—but only from habit, she was afraid.

One Saturday afternoon she went with some girls from the Y to the Haight—a wilderness of costumed youths and girls, leaping dogs, yawning babies carried on backs, guitars, bongos, beaded doorways, drifts of incense and some other sweet smell, and throughout it all, like a warm wind, smiles of welcome. None of this had been there a few months ago; it had sprung up overnight, a dazzling carnival. She found strangers saying hello to her; someone gave her a yellow daisy, someone else a string of wooden beads. She began stooping to pet the heads of the smaller dogs, but she didn't have the courage to respond to anyone else, and when she lost her friends in the crowd she grew uneasy and took the bus home.

But she went back the next day, this time feeling conspicuous in her aquamarine coat with its little rhinestone poodle on the lapel. When she returned the next evening after work she wore the claret robe Wanda had made for her, and the wooden beads, and her hair was released from its red rubber band. As she rode the Haight Street bus to her destination she was uncomfortably aware of the stares of the other passengers, who all looked like the people in her office, and she kept her eyes glued to the floor. But as soon as she stepped off the bus into the crowds she felt like an old-timer. With her hair as long as or longer than anyone else's and her robe as striking, who was to say she didn't belong? Strolling through the milling figures, she caught glimpses of sightseers dressed as she had been the day before, and she realized with a rush of pleasure that she was now one of the sights.

She wondered why she had never worn her hair loose before —she guessed it was because nobody else had. It was nice having her long neck covered by hair. It was warmer that way. All her life her neck had felt chilly. She began saying hello to people. She felt she was in the middle of a big birthday party, and the good thing was that she didn't have to converse with anybody or worry about the proper time to leave. All she had to do was to be herself and stroll and smile and say hello.

Somewhere along the way she found a boy of about fourteen walking with her. He seemed very open and pleasant, he had a handsome rosy face under a mop of golden curls, and he wore a threadbare duffle coat, bell-bottom jeans that were ripped or cut in long shreds right up to his knees, big scuffed boots with a green question mark painted on each toe, and a rucksack on his back. His name was Thor. "Not the god," he explained (What god? Zaidee wondered), "just short for Thorwald." She liked having him walk with her because he didn't say much and he seemed cheerful and it was nice to have somebody with you, especially somebody who knew everybody on the street. She felt more of an old-timer than ever, right at the very center of the action. People complimented her on her gown; it pleased them, it was right. She began to feel mysterious, as if there were a secret part of her she hadn't known about, where all this rightness came from. And she wondered what Morrie would think if he could see her standing in a long gown in the middle of the Haight-Ashbury with a real Haight-Ashbury hippie at her side.

Then it began to rain and she thought of the bus ride back with all the passengers staring at her, and her bare room at the Y, and standing at the files the next morning with her hair in a ponytail and her long neck chilly. But the boy grabbed her hand and began to dash down the street in the rain, running for blocks until he stopped at a house the color of uncooked liver with its lower windows broken and stuffed with rags. A minute later she stood in a dark room that smelled sweet and Thor was handing her a thin blanket and pointing to an empty spot on the floor where people were sleeping. She would have turned and fled except that there were children sleeping, too, and they made her feel safe.

She was cold and wet and the floor was hard, and there was a dog that kept getting up and sniffing around, but she tried to make the best of things. But in spite of the children, something terrifying happened: two people a few feet away started making love, stark naked and powerfully noisy. She had never thought of how people looked and sounded when they made love—in fact, she had never really thought of anybody doing it but Morrie and her—and now she was jarred by it, so disgusted and frightened that she shot her head under the blanket and put her fingers in her mouth. After the lovemaking had stopped, someone started moaning in his sleep, then some people burst through the door and stood arguing in the hallway, and when they settled down, God knew where on the crowded floor, a child began to cry. When the room was finally quiet Zaidee felt an urgent need to empty her bladder, but she was too nervous to move, so she crossed her legs tightly, as cold and miserable and worried as she had ever been in her life.

Finally she dozed off a little, and she dreamed of Ollie; she often dreamed of Ollie. He was tapdancing. Ollie wanted to be a great tapdancer. He was tapdancing like anything in the middle of her mother's kitchen, only there was no sound. And when she woke up from the dream she felt so heavy with sadness that it was almost unbearable.

But in the morning she felt better. After dashing to the bathroom, she returned to find the dark room of the night before filled with the harmless friendly types that thronged the street. The room smelled of oldness, of damp plaster and dank corners, but it wasn't too bad. There were some bright posters on the wall, and some candles in bottles and flowers in jars. A boy with a pointed beard picked up a guitar and began to sing in a low careless voice. Then Thor woke up and introduced her all around: Sally, Pickles, Bob, Linda, Jumbo. She always grew confused when she was the center of attention, but she had the courage to correct Thor when he told them her name. "Zai-*dee*," she said, accenting the second syllable. It sounded better that way, more interesting. There was welcome in their faces.

A week later she had given notice at work and moved out of her room at the Y. At first the dampness of the house bothered her and she had one cold after another, then she began wearing slacks and sweaters under her soiled robe, and sleeping on an old fur rug she bought. She spent the nice days wandering around the street, and on rainy days she stayed indoors and made jewelry to sell, or helped take care of the children.

At night she was no longer bothered by the sporadic bouts of lovemaking, but she herself did not participate. The others respected her attitude—for some reason they thought she was a virgin—and although Thor got into the habit of snuggling up to her in his sleeping bag, he never tried anything. He was like a younger brother, though he was very smart and old in some ways; she had an unhappy suspicion he went downtown during the day and picked pockets.

She didn't dare call Morrie; she was sure that he would yank her out of this damp pleasant house and send her back to the office where she would be safe—and then forget her again. Sometimes on his Suicide Prevention night she went to a phone booth and called the hotline and listened to his familiar voice, which urged her to speak, to tell him her problems. Then, her throat so tight she couldn't have spoken even if she'd dared, she hung up.

One afternoon she hitchhiked over to Berkeley with some others from the house. For hours they went from street corner to street corner and from pad to pad talking with people, and finally some bargain was struck and everybody seemed happy, and they wandered down Telegraph Avenue to thumb a ride back. And suddenly, as they passed Sather Gate, she saw only a few feet away from her, sitting on the steps of a building, Morrie.

Her apprehensions were forgotten in a flash. Lifting her dirty hem, she ran to him, and when he looked up his eyes popped out of his head. She had finally captured his full attention, and stood there in her robe, her long hair uncombed and five or six exotic rings on her fingers, and she smiled broadly, disclosing white even teeth that he had never noticed before because she had never smiled so widely before.

"Jesus," he said, "what's happened to you?"

She shrugged languidly.

"What do you think you are, a flower child?"

She winced for him—it was so out-of-it to actually use the term. But he didn't look out-of-it: his clothes were old and he wore sandals. Suddenly she felt a new bond between them —they were both part of a new and loving world. But he didn't seem to know it, there was no love in his eyes, only surprise and criticism.

"Your mother moves away and, first thing, you go off the deep end," he exclaimed, getting to his feet. "You're on something, aren't you?"

"No I'm not."

"Come on, don't play around."

He stared at her as if she were important and difficult, and a great thrill shook her from head to foot.

"Who're you hanging around with?" he demanded.

"Don't make trouble for me, Morrie."

"I'll make trouble for you," he muttered, staring with narrowed eyes at her friends, who were waving for her to hurry as they climbed into a car that had stopped for them. "Scroungy bastards," he said, taking her by the arm and leading her to the car. "Zaidee's got business with me," he told them brusquely, "she'll see you later."

Thor stuck his head out the window and looked at her questioningly. She nodded.

"Who's that little creep?" Morris asked as the car drove off.

"He's not a little creep. He happens to be a very groovy cat."

"You're priceless, Zaidee."

"Look," she pouted happily, "you're going to have to drive me home because you made me miss my ride."

In the car she forgot her friends, and she knew she would give up her new life in a minute if he would only ask her to marry him—and maybe he would, to save her. When he stopped in front of the Y and she told him she had moved to the Haight, she was deeply encouraged by his concern.

"You mean you're not fooling around?" he asked incredulously. "You mean you've moved *in* with that crowd, lock, stock, and barrel?"

"I guess I have."

"What's the address?" he said shortly. "We'll go pick your things up."

"And then what?" she asked hopefully.

"We'll move you back to the Y."

"Nuh-uh. I'd move in with you, but I wouldn't move back to the Y."

"Well, you're not moving in with me," he said, tapping his fingers on the steering wheel.

"Well then, I'll probably starve to death," she told him tragically.

"What do you live on, anyway?"

She shrugged, looking at him from the corner of her eye.

"What're you doing this to me for?" he suddenly exploded. "You know I'll worry myself to death every time I think of you wandering around that circus."

"Then you're not going to take me home with you?" she asked with wrenching disappointment.

"What am I supposed to do—open my place up to every down-and-outer who comes along?"

"I'm not just anybody, I'm Zaidee, and we've been going together for over a year . . ."

"Look, Zaidee," he threatened, "I'm going to drive you to where you live, and you're going to get your things and—"

"Why? You don't want me to be happy! I'm happy there! At least *they're* nice to me!"

"Yeah, look, I think they're great, I think they're wild, but I *know* them—"

"You know Sally and Pickles and . . . ?"

"I know the *scene*. You don't have the sense to come in out of the rain, and you're going to get messed up. It's no place for you!"

"The only place for me is with *you!*" she said, her eyes big and tearful.

"Why's that the only alternative?" he sighed. "Why can't you make it on your own?" And he stated flatly: "We're driving to your place for your things."

"I won't tell you the address. You'll drive around all night."

He was silent.

"Okay, you win," he said at last.

He stopped the car at the corner of Haight and Ashbury. It was dark now; the skies had opened up and the street stood half empty, pounding with rain.

"I'm going to write your mother a letter," he told her sternly.

"Shit, you don't even know where she's at."

"You're getting snotty, Zaidee." He compressed his lips, feeling sorry for her, looking at the dirty velvet robe and the still hopeful face—barely hopeful. He took three ten-dollar bills from his wallet and put them in her lap. For a moment she looked offended, then she picked them up and stuffed them into the fringed bag she carried.

He rolled down his window as she hurried across the rainy street. "I'll come back and make you see sense!" he shouted. "I'll be back to look for you, Zaidee!"

"You'd never find the *time* to look for me!" she shouted back, feeling her boiling tears mix with the rain. The car started slowly down the street, and then, gaining the speed she always admired and feared in Morris, it was gone. "Morrie," she whimpered, standing on the deserted corner. Then, shielding her head with her bag, she began making her way back to the house through the downpour.

18 Every morning except Sunday Johanna's alarm clock went off at four forty-five, awakening her to a dark, bitterly cold room whose windows streamed with rain and echoed with the gurgling and splashing of the old building's broken gutters. She filled the bathtub with cold water and immersed herself with a sharp gasp, furiously rubbing her body dry afterward and drawing on a pair of paint-stiffened Levi's and two sweatshirts. Resetting the alarm for noon, she went quickly to the glassed-in porch and flicked on an electric heater, hurried to the kitchen and put water on the stove for coffee. While it heated she walked up and down the living room, gazing at everything in the dark sheen from the window —the chairs and tables and rugs and books all existing in a hush. There were no sounds from the building or the street. She poured her coffee and took it into the studio, lit a cigarette, and began to paint.

From a great height she looked down on a mass of buildings, cramped, half-timbered, ancient, whose chimneys poured out smoke in such profusion that the whole night-shrouded town seemed to lie in the smoking aftermath of a battle. Around the buildings ran a city wall, beyond that lay flat fields. The height vanished. Inside one of the buildings a heap of turf glowed in a grate. A pair of feet stretched from the shadows to the warmth, clad in stiff slate-colored shoes with long tapering dented toes. She could see each fissure in the material— skin? cloth?—and she could make out the form of the bony foot inside. There was an overpowering smell of sweat and cured meat in the room. She was near a table where she could see the rims of wooden bowls outlined in the glow from the fire. There were figures eating, one wore a cross, one was a child, two were old and had white hands. A man in a cloak stood by a window. Hounds lay in a corner, snapping and flinching in their sleep. She heard the child whine. The alarm clock rang.

She stepped back from the canvas and looked at it; laid her brushes down and walked slowly from the studio. She combed her hair and put on her yellow dress, returning to the studio to clean her brushes; then with time running short she threw on her trenchcoat, grabbed her umbrella, and ran downstairs to catch the bus to the gallery.

There she chain-smoked, read the newspaper or a book, spoke abruptly into the phone, and refused to smile at the customers. She was asking to be fired; but Josh would not fire her, he would not even complain about the tiny return she gave for her salary. Carrying a white rat named Antigone on his shoulder, driving a London taxicab circa 1931, and pressing money into the hands of every struggling artist who happened by, he admitted to being a strange sort. He was, in fact, beginning to figure in the gossip columns as a San Francisco character, a kook, but he was very open in his resentment of the rubbernecks that this notoriety brought into the gallery. He admired intensity and conviction. It was this quality in his receptionist that he responded to. A pile of fecal matter was her opinion of the gallery, given without hesitation during the job interview. Since then he had come to realize that she hated him, and he realized that he had never been hated before. Dressed in black chinos and a black turtleneck sweater, with Antigone crouched on his left shoulder, he watched her come to work a little later every day, never changing from her scuffed sandals and faded yellow summer dress, only adding a shapeless sweater now that it was cold, never expressing less than contempt on her face; and he said nothing. With his face open and gentle under its monkish fringe of blond hair, he only gave his slow half-smile when friends urged him to get rid of her.

She waited daily to be fired, though she dreaded the thought of returning to the pale green lunchroom, the lunchroom that had figured in every job she had ever held the past ten years, as file clerk, messenger girl, saleswoman; a room always painted the coldest, palest green in the spectrum, its tables wet with puddles of milk and coffee and strewn with back issues of the *Reader's Digest;* by the sink a clutter of mugs with Mary or Flo or Bev written on pieces of adhesive tape, throwaway Handi-Kups for the less particular, yellow plastic spoons, a jar of Pream, an electric coffeepot, and at the foot of the waste receptacle, a scattering of cigarette butts and balled-up wax paper. Paper bags rustled as their owners busily opened them in a cheerful matter-of-fact atmosphere, a predominantly female atmosphere, since most of the male employees went out for lunch, with the exception of the sixty-year-old elevator operator, Herman, hands dry and gnarled, back rounded, feet in square-toed black boots, whose days were spent from eight till five in his shuddering cubicle, where beneath a dim light he pulled open and shut a grudgingly sliding door, a big padded glove on one hand to minimize blisters, chipper enough in the morning but by noon emptied of greetings and small talk, and eating in silence, deaf to the sporadic chatter about meatloaf recipes, dull or promising dates, and *I Love Lucy,* holding a sandwich of dry brown bread in his hand, or a square of store-bought cake with wavy yellow frosting that could be peeled back like a strip of rubber, or spooning up an apricot from a plastic margarine container, chewing with deliberation and sometimes lapsing into immobility, his eye caught by some crumb or reflection of light on the table.

Once at lunch she heard him say that he didn't know what he'd do when elevators were all self-operating, and she understood that he needed and wanted the stifling cubicle, the pale green lunchroom, that he had no choice. She looked around the room with its chatting women and girls drinking from their name-tagged mugs, glancing into the mirror with a pat of their bouffants, or turning the newspaper to the crossword puzzle, making the most of their forty-five minutes away from their typewriters and file cases. She was lucky enough to float from one job to another with periods of freedom between, but some of the older women had been here for thirty years and some of the younger ones would be. She took a pencil from her purse and figured something out, and turned to the woman sitting next to her, the chief file clerk, who had received her twenty-five-year pin the week before, a woman in her fifties with gray hair set in symmetrical rows like stone waves, and said: "You've eaten in this lunchroom six thousand, two hundred and fifty times."

The woman glanced at her with surprise; then with a neighborly smile she said, "I guess that's about right, at that."

"And you—" said Johanna, shyly—"you don't mind?"

"Mind?" she said, clearly not understanding.

Johanna had put her pencil away chilled to the bone and more than ever anxious to be fired.

Sometimes she thought of trying to sell her paintings, setting herself financially free from these jobs; but she worked in such an absolute state of privacy, almost an unconscious state, that the idea of exposing the results to the eyes of strangers was somehow impossible. And the idea of marketing, the whole commercial system, went absolutely against her grain.

Since she had moved into the Fillmore apartment she had returned to her painting, but now in the evenings, instead of picking up her brush and continuing her work, she felt a restlessness. She never put her NO ADMITTANCE sign on the door at night. She anticipated the tiny vibrations that were set off in the old floorboards when somebody started up the stairs, hopefully to be followed by Morris' impatient rap of the knuckles. In Morris, she thought, walking around unable to work, trying to pinpoint his quality, was a pith, an essence, an itness of the same compelling density as certain paintings or views or pieces of music that were immediately yours by some inexplicable affinity; something that pulled you into their center, that fed you even as it made you hungrier for more, something that quickened your blood and made your heart ache. The difference was that when the music ended or she turned away from the painting or the view, she felt good. But when Morris left she felt only a clutch of painfully heightened sensibilities that could not be satisfied until his return.

But when he did come, he burst in and they would topple onto the mattress, or they would speed to a downtown movie, or if it was a Sunday they would go hiking in the rain, their shoes stained with grass and mud, stopping to make love standing up in a litter-strewn cave or under a dripping eucalyptus tree. When he was gone she felt as if a glass of wine had been snatched from her lips before she had been able to take more than a sip. There was no leisure in their few hours together, no sense of time gathering and deepening. Time seemed madly and emptily onrushing.

She knew he was keeping her in an antechamber of his emotions. It wounded and insulted her; but though she had made the decision to take him, she apparently could not make the decision to leave him. She felt caught in a wind-tunnel where all her old signposts were gone. Montaigne on love, de Rougemont or Stendhal or Dostoevski on love—they seemed irrelevant to a psychology like Morris'; if she tried to fit him into their depths, he would be rejected as an alien transplant. Instead, on the bus she found herself eavesdropping on girls' conversations about trying lovers, she listened to movie dialogue on the subject, and looked over the advice-to-the-lovelorn columns in the newspaper, as if only the immediate could bear upon the immediate, or, perhaps, only the shoddy could bear upon the shoddy.

On the days that he didn't see fit to call or drop by she went to his apartment building to see if his lights were on; but even if they were, her pride would not allow her to ring the buzzer; she remembered what Zaidee had found when she came there unexpectedly. And so she would walk away, wondering what she had accomplished. Whenever she saw a white Datsun a nail bored through her heart, when she saw a man carrying a worn briefcase like Morris' her breath caught in her throat; she was even affected by the sight of a red package of Dentyne gum, his brand.

"As if I loved someone who hadn't even noticed me yet, or someone who had died," she explained to Wanda, who no longer showed much sign of analyzing or judging. Wanda was gentler these days. Conrad had moved in with her. The flat bore enormous evidence of his presence, which Wanda seemed never to tire of gazing at: his painting equipment was relievedly spread out in the dining room after so many years of cramped quarters; his apple-cheeked children and joyous nudes hung on every inch of wall; Closeto played wildly on the big gold-and-green rug and ran up and down the hall, celebrating his new freedom. Wanda smiled like someone digesting a large meal. "It's unbearable," Johanna prodded, looking in vain for the hard light of analysis to flash in her friend's eyes.

"Well," said Wanda at last, with a grudging sigh, as if loath to give up her sense of elysium, "I warned you. I told you what he was like."

"You told me what he was like with Zaidee," Johanna returned quickly, stung. "Don't think for a minute that we've got the same kind of relationship."

"Well then, what's your problem?"

"I can't put it into words."

"Because you don't want to. The fact is that he *is* shallow, and he *is* probably playing around, and he *doesn't* know what he wants but doesn't want to give any of it up."

"Oh, you're very wise!"

"I don't know why you ask me—"

"I don't know either!" said Johanna, staring with a kind

of passionate blankness at the floor.

"Anyway, you don't love Morris."

"No?" asked Johanna with a bitter look.

"There's tenderness in love. You lack that completely. You talk about him as if he were a bad infection of the gonads, that's all."

19

In the patio behind the gallery Josh had been building something for a long time. When the rainy season began, the work had already grown too large to be moved inside, so he had a glass roof erected at great expense. There he spent most of his time, building a great shape from paper-mâché. Now and then mention of his enigmatic work-in-progress reached the gossip columns, and eventually a cluster of onlookers could be seen hovering around him as he labored. He did not shut the door of the patio on them, but he did maintain a monastic silence and sometimes scratched his crotch as if he were alone. All through February and March he worked as the rain pounded like a waterfall on the glass roof. In the afternoon he would shoo out his audience, put his tools away, and return to his duties in the gallery. Miss Kaulbach, he noticed (she would not let him call her by her first name), was coming in later and later, and talking more and more unpleasantly into the phone. For a while a burly big-nosed character with a loud voice had been in the habit of dropping by, and his visits seemed to put her in a better frame of mind, but now he hadn't been around for weeks and her old attitude had returned with a vengeance. Josh was afraid she would quit.

One afternoon as he was talking with a painter, looking at one of his canvases, he heard the door slam. It was Miss Kaulbach.

"So I'm forty minutes late!" she said, closing her umbrella with a belligerent yank. She glanced at the painting between the two men, and Josh saw on her face an explosive frown, as if whatever demons had been nipping her heels had now sprung on her in a pack. She strode up to the canvas, her eyes riveted on it—a flat Van Dyck brown, with three equidistant strings glued to its center, each dyed a lighter shade of brown. She leveled her umbrella like a saber.

"This painting is a trivial declension of color. Its design is so static that it falls outside the definition of design into that of trim—it catches the eye for a second, the way a stenciled old tune catches the ear for a second. My belief is that one second is too little to pay even a dollar for, much less the five hundred you'll probably have the gall to ask."

She saw Antigone staring at her with its beady red eyes. Josh's face had pinkened, but he said pleasantly, "Miss Kaulbach is a conscientious echo from the Royal Academy," and the artist nodded.

"Don't fire me, I'm quitting!" And she walked directly to her desk for her things, calling over her shoulder, "I leave you to your oversize earplug and Niagara Falls."

He broke away from the artist. "Niagara Falls?" he whispered. "Is that what it looks like to you?"

"That thing you're making? That's what it looks like to me."

"Why? And lower your voice, please, Miss Kaulbach."

"How should I know? A bad Niagara Falls. Without the water. I'd like my week's pay."

"No one else has ever said that it looks like Niagara Falls."

"Is that what it's supposed to be?"

He looked at her with a worried frown.

"I won't tell," she said, rummaging around the desk drawer. "I don't know anyone who'd be interested in knowing. May I have my pay?"

"Stay, Miss Kaulbach. I'll double your salary."

Antigone hopped excitedly around on his shoulder.

"Are you joking?" she asked.

"I'll triple it. I'm not joking."

She was silent, tempted. She shook her head. "You're not normal."

"I've never pretended to be," he said, as Antigone stared into his ear.

"No. Send me my pay." She strode to the door and opened it on the rain.

"Think it over!" he cried after her. "Take a week and think it over!" He went back to the artist, but it was a long while before he was aware of anything but her escape.

She walked all the way home in the rain with her umbrella closed, her hair plastering itself to her head. There was the smell of ocean in the air, and the air was silver and gray, icy, shredded, lifting itself high as umbrellas snapped and hats went flying, then pounding straight down again, hissing and exploding underfoot, battering the puddles into foam. She stopped at the corner of Sutter and Van Ness as the traffic rumbled by, windshield wipers persevering against the torrent, smoke shooting from exhaust pipes only to be soaked up at once; and took off her sandals and proceeded across the street barefoot. She would have to go back to the pale green lunchrooms, but she felt that for the first time in months she had done something that was absolutely right. When she got home her face stung and water trickled down her body inside her clothes. Throwing off her coat, she went immediately into the studio.

An army with pikes and banners rode over an arched stone bridge. They rode on plump gray rats like the rats from nursery tales. The lake they crossed was coppery, and the rats' eyes were the same. A black fortress or cliff, punctured with great holes like a black Swiss cheese, was half obscured by tawny smoke, and from the holes poured beams of light like searchlights, at all angles. There was a mountain, and strung between the high peaks were ropes with ant-like figures crossing them, holding poles for balance, some of the figures falling through the smoke and light beams to the coppery lake.

She put her brush down at a sound from the door. It was past midnight. "Morris?" she called, and at the sound of his voice let him in.

His mouth was set in a melancholy line. For weeks he had had a bitter, wandering look; he was still filled with activity and drive, but they struck her as hollow.

"It's late, I wasn't expecting you," she said with a touch of coolness. "You come whenever it suits you."

"I'll go."

"Don't be silly," she said hastily, "sit down."

He sat, looking reflectively around the room as though he had never been there before.

"What is it?" she asked.

He turned his face ominously to the windows. "Do you realize it's stopped raining?"

She listened. The pounding had ceased. There was a vast silence, softly punctuated by drops falling from the eaves to the ground.

"Do you realize it's almost spring?" he asked, his face dark with apprehension.

"Well, Despairovitch, so it is."

He put his hands together in his lap like an old man.

"What is it?" she asked again, sitting down on the arm of the chair.

110

"Nothing," he murmured. "Spring."

After a while she said: "I quit my job today."

"Why?" he asked with a trace of life. "You shouldn't have. You needed that job."

"I just got fed up. Besides, I have some money saved. And listen to how crazy Josh is, he offered to triple my salary if I stayed."

"He offered to triple your salary and you walked away?" he asked mournfully.

"Ah, Morris, all the life's gone out of you."

His eyes flicked to her face. Then he closed them, as if no sight was of any help. She sat watching him as the minutes went by, resentful that he had taken her away from her work for nothing more than this willful absence of communication. Still, it was different. He had never before dropped by without some activity in mind—bed, a movie, a snack. Silence was something she had never shared with him. But he looked like a dead man. She thought of the tomb carving that first night, how she had been moved to touch the hair by his ear; and since then he had never stayed still long enough to be looked at in his sleep; and even if he had, his refusal to connect had stifled the possibility of her making that gesture again.

She said reflectively, "I still think of that figure we saw dancing in Oakland."

There was no response; he obviously didn't remember.

"On the peace march. In a black cloak. You couldn't see what was in it, just the cloak; it looked from the Dark Ages."

"So?" he asked.

"Oh, it's always reminded me of—how it is with us."

"Why?" he asked, opening his eyes without any real interest.

"I can't explain it; it's something between us that we don't understand."

"Ah, sweet mystery of life," he murmured.

"You really are banal!" she said disgustedly, and stood up.

"If it was a hundred years ago," he said, looking again at the silent window, "I could go to war."

The non sequitur depressed her.

"When your life got to be a stupid snarl, you found some glorious cause and went into the battlefield and you either killed or died for it. It was a simple thing."

He had closed his eyes again, with a look of inward

suffering she could not begin to fathom. She found herself looking at the closed eyes helplessly, and suddenly, stooping, she touched his face softly with her hand. He grabbed her wrist like a drowning man and pressed it against his cheek.

A terrifying happiness whipped through her as she heard herself say, "I want you to come with me," and she took him by the hand and led him into the studio. She lined the canvases against the wall.

"You've never shown me your work," he said hesitantly.

"It takes me a long time to change habits. But I think I want you to see them—I know I want you to see them."

"I don't know anything about art," he warned her.

"It doesn't matter."

He looked at the unfinished painting on the easel, then at the canvases standing against the walls; then he went through the rest, carefully tipping each one out and studying it. His first sensation was one of relief; he liked them. The subject matter didn't bore him, there was nothing like an apple on a plate or a tree on a hill. And the style was sophisticated, there was nothing of the Sunday painter in it. But to take it from there? Once he had gone through a heavy Jung phase and had come to know great works of art, but they were symbols to him, not things-in-themselves. He didn't know how to respond to a painting as a painting. Crossing his arms, he stood back and searched his mind for the names that seemed to come closest to her work: Kokoschka, Brueghel, Vermeer, Soutine—but they all seemed to contradict each other, and, besides, they would sound pretentious on his lips, and, besides, comparisons were odious. To give himself more time, he made a second tour. He liked her colors; they were intense, they looked glazed and deep: jewels, keen-edged slashes, rich flat planes, holes that seemed to go through the canvas. Unsettling; strange. Her drawing was always clear, yet you had to look twice before things jelled; a funny structure, you could get lost in it; it seemed to go deep into the canvas, everything dovetailing, distance and close-up mingled. Lots of finely wrought detail. A medieval city seen from a distance, and somehow behind it, above it, in it, a dark corner holding a cloaked man; embers gleaming from a grate; a pair of feet in shoes with long pointed toes. Another canvas, an animal, a stag, thrashing in what looked like a huge chandelier, the whole picture shivering in cold-white light. The scene on the easel, a mouse battalion, child-like in a way, yet ominous; shades and hues and intensities of copper burning in large flat pieces, forming a design of almost palpable tension. She could sell stuff as good as this. Portraits, too; simpler; an old man in a pair of pince-nez looking up over a book, his face pale, keen against a background of rich rose; looked ready to rise up from his chair, eyes followed you. A black woman wearing a crown of thorns, white blood oozing from under it, a halo around the face, covering the eyes.

What to say about so much? Where to begin, and how to make it sound considered and weighty when he had no terms at his disposal? And obscuring all his critical attempts was the full realization of the discipline she brought to her private world—it panicked him, yet stung him to admiration, and moved him; the hopefulness of it, the idea that it was worth doing.

"Thank you, baby," he said, taking her hand and kissing the palm.

She turned out the light. They went back into the other room.

"I think they're tremendous," he said. "My opinion doesn't count for anything, but if you want it anyway—I think they're tremendous. You ought to have an exhibit."

"No."

"Why not?"

"Just no."

"You ought to hang them up, anyway."

"I've tried, but the wall's no good, you can't get a nail in."

"I've got some tools at home, I'll do it for you."

But when they sat down he was silent again, and looked at the window for a long time.

"I've got at home, in my desk, this box—this matchbox," he said at last. "I've had it since I was eleven years old. I mean, not the matchbox, but this thing that's inside, a thimble."

"A thimble?" she asked, when he did not go on.

"It's old, it's black now."

His father had sat in his shop with his legs crossed and a piece of material over his lap, something you never saw anymore. His hands had been small and square. He was humble, obscure, truly represented by the tool that was now all that remained of him. He was old by the time Morris was born,

tongue-lashed by his wife and abandoned in his shop by his
sons, who had no wish to become tailors. Jews, Morris discovered, were supposed to be intelligent, and if not intelligent
then shrewd, but his father was neither; he had no special
understanding of anything, not of religion or human nature
or even of his work; he was a competent tailor because he was
diligent, but he knew no specialties, no shortcuts, he had no
sense of bargaining, no smalltalk. His customers, his neighbors and family thought he was a nebbish, and he probably
was. Morris, as round and rambunctious as his father was
thin and quiet, helped him in the shop. His father liked the
boy around, and Morris felt safe with him. They seemed to
melt into each other and take from each other. In the house
Morris was his father's champion, but he was too young to
be listened to, and his yells of protest were swallowed up by
the others' yells at his father. His father's temper, when
finally aroused, was mild and useless. He was at ease in his
shop, where he sat among several stray cats which he fed
and whose litters he always found homes for, usually by going
up and down the street ringing doorbells and doffing his hat
with Morris at his side. In silence, broken now and then by
the yawn of a cat, he sewed pants and dresses and coats, his
needle and thimble flashing, and it seemed to Morris, working
at his side, that his father was a good man and deserved some
honor. But even when the family celebrated his father's
birthday, he was not the center of attention but seemed only
to serve as an excuse for a party. Yet he stood on the sidelines with a festive smile.

Sometimes in later life Morris pondered: what if a voice
told him that if he were to crawl on his bare hands and knees
over a mile of rocky terrain every night for a year, and by
doing this he would see his father again long enough to embrace him—would he do it? And he knew he would; somewhere inside him he cherished the vague expectation that he
would be given this opportunity. Only when he took the
thimble out did he realize he would really never see his father
again. Then the thought of joining him was overpowering,
simply going into the darkness where his father's bones lay,
being at least part of that. But he did not do that. His life
went on; and when he thought of his life it rose up like a
dirty wave and splashed over him, leaving him sticky and
foul-smelling and desecrating the memory of his father. He

knew that almost every night he dreamed of the long-dead face.

"We'll go to my place," he told Johanna, taking a deep breath.

In Johanna's palm, under the light of the desk lamp, the tarnished thimble's every row of tiny dots was illuminated; the scratches down its side, the dent at its base. She turned it in her fingers, moved by Morris' possession of it, and by his willingness to share it with her. She returned it silently, and he put it back in its matchbox.

"I think," he said heavily, looking her in the eyes and slowly taking her two hands, "we should move in together."

20 Morris' landlady made a great scene when she discovered him moving out without notice one morning. As a prospective tenant, he had delivered her his most moist, heavy-lidded gaze, and she had meltingly agreed to waive not only the cleaning deposit but advance payment of the last month's rent. Now, with her cocked-up bosom heaving in its tight sweater and her cheeks burning under an old facelift, she realized that the boy's every caressing glance and comment over the last year had been leading to this betrayal. "Leave that junk where it is!" she screamed at the Good Will men who were carting off his straw mats; and running after Morris, laboriously pulling his heavy desk down the hall, she stopped and slapped the top with her speckled hand. "I took you at your word! I'll sue you, you bastard!"

"You're beautiful when you're mad, baby," he puffed at her with a smile, and even in the teeth of her fury she felt herself melting again. She drew back with a stricken look.

"Get the elevator for me?" he asked.

Forcing down a gush of tears with an obscene gesture, she turned on her Cuban heels and hurried, bent, back to her own apartment.

Morris parked in front of Johanna's building with the U-Haul trailer he had rented and started unloading his belongings. The sky was cold, white, clear, the sharp air pierced by the smell of new grass. He saw Johanna at her window and waved vigorously.

She put her hand over her mouth with sheer exhilaration, then crossed herself as Maria had used to do, and ran down to help him. Though he didn't know Morris, Aquiline's boyfriend, Charles, was already pitching in, a tall good-looking reverend in a clerical collar. He and Morris carried in the heavy desk and Johanna followed with a box of seashells and driftwood. Aquiline lounged in her doorway in her pink chenille bathrobe, eating a banana.

"You tell me why Charles he rush out and lend his hand to every mortal that's movin'," she said to Johanna as the men staggered up the inside stairs; and she answered herself, " 'Cause Charles he always lookin' to do the work of Jesus. Like he give to beggars and all, and he move people."

She took a bite of her banana. "That guy, he movin' in with you?"

"That's right," Johanna answered.

"Yeah, he ring my bell one night when I sound asleep and when I complain he tell me you' his cousin with a busted appendix. He lie too fast to suit my taste. What you want with him?"

Johanna turned away, offended.

"I bet you get took every day."

"I beg your pardon?" she asked, turning around.

"You don' know nothin' from nothin'. Man," she said, looking at Johanna's knitted brows, "life too short to stand around talkin' polite. I cut through the shit and give my view." A thud echoed from upstairs as the men gained the top floor and set the desk down. She finished her banana and bounced the peel in her hand. "Charles he move 'em into houses and he move 'em out of houses, he lift big furniture and he lift little furniture. Anybody movin' inside three miles and Charles he sniff the air, and he *there* to do his good work." She paused. " 'Cause Charles dumb."

"Dumb?" Johanna said, astonished. "You're saying that about a man of the cloth?"

"What cloth you speakin' of?"

"A man of the cloth is a man of God. Like Charles."

"Yeah. They all dumb."

"But—I always understood you to be a sincere churchgoer."

Aquiline leaned against the doorjamb and gave a long smile.

"I think you've been putting me on," Johanna said slowly.

"Who know?" the other said lazily.

"Why? All that colored kowtowing-to-the-system talk?"

The woman's eyes lifted, narrowed. "You jus' said somethin' could get you' throat cut by certain parties."

"You purposely made yourself sound ignorant, obsequious."

"Ob-shit. What language you speaking? All I know, you drunk it up like it was the gospel, and that a sight; I don't get much entertainment with four kids on my tail."

"I hate put-ons. What's your purpose?" Johanna asked, confused and angry.

A clatter of descending footsteps drew their eyes to the stairs.

"Here he come again!" Aquiline called out. "All fired

up an' glorified with his movin'. Hey, baby! Charles!" And she swatted the seat of his trousers as he passed.

"You put him on too," said Johanna accusingly. "You *really* put *him* on."

Aquiline protruded her lower lip reflectively. "It ain't the same," she said, and looked up as Morris came bounding down the stairs two at a time. "An' here Cousin Appendix! Hi yere, Cousin Appendix!"

Morris flashed her a smile, not remembering her or the appendix.

"Now, he have nice teeth, I give you my view on that," she said as he went out the front door. "He have good big teeth good as any black man. But he no beauty, honey, he look like a toad."

Johanna's eyes stabbed her.

Aquiline put her hands together prayerfully. "Oh, I is *truly* sorry to offend," she intoned, closing her eyes. "If you could *fo'give* my unkind trespass . . ."

"Oh, for God's sake, why can't you just act like a normal person?"

She opened one eye. "Don' look a gift horse in the mouth, honey. Otherways it the end of a beautiful acquaintance." She opened the other eye, gave her long smile, and wandered out to the splintered front porch to watch her children playing in the grass.

Going up the stairs, Johanna felt fiercely protective toward Morris, as if he had been physically slapped by Aquiline's jibe. The driftwood and seashells she carried intensified the feeling, made him seem terribly vulnerable. She put the box down on a table and saw with a twinge that the apartment was no longer hers.

Going back downstairs, she brought up an armload of clothes and began putting them away, enjoying a sense of secret discovery. His handkerchiefs, his socks. A gold suede vest, not his taste—gift from an old girlfriend, probably. His own taste ran to the utilitarian: tweed jackets, brown or tan slacks; suntans and solid-colored sports shirts. She hung the unsuitable vest at the far end of the closet. Of headgear, she noticed, he had none. And she pictured him in a Russian fur hat.

"That's it, Reverend," came Morris' voice from the other room. "Put it there, thanks a hell of a lot. A heck of a lot."

"Plenty to do still," Charles said in his hollow tone. "That desk—seems to me better off on the other side of the room."

"No thanks, it's fine."

"She don't want anything moved out? Seems it's more crowded now, she want to move some stuff down to the basement?"

"No thanks. Listen, thanks again, man—I mean, Reverend."

Charles reluctantly took his leave, and before doing anything else, Morris wrote out a check for a month's rent to the old coquette. It wrenched—he needed money; but he even added a note in pencil that he was sorry he'd been in such a rush and warmest regards to her. Then he went into the bedroom, where Johanna was putting his clothes away. He took her face between his hands, feeling a new life open before him, a bestowal of time, recharged and boundless.

The next day he began writing letters, making phone calls, and setting up appointments, and the following week he took an afternoon off from work and drove to Berkeley for a conference at the Psychology Department. He parked near Telegraph Avenue, and in his brown slacks and tweed jacket strode down the street to the campus. Only a couple of weeks had passed since he had last been here—he had sloshed through the night rain into coffee houses and milling record shops resounding with rock, picked up a bushy-haired girl in torn jeans and a halter, and spent the night smoking hash and making simultaneous love to her and her roommate, an immensely fat, mute creature who bit his ears—but now he felt like a stranger from a different generation, and nostalgia stirred in him, a bitter craving for youth; it grew as he crossed the campus with its deep green lawns, its cool air sweet with cut grass. He pushed the feeling down and hurried up the steps to his appointment.

He returned to Johanna with good news. He need make up only one course, a year of organic chemistry, which the university was offering in one concentrated summer session. In the meantime he could apply for admission to med school, take the entrance exam next month, in May, and if he passed, be given a conditional acceptance dependent upon the results of the makeup course. If all went well, he would begin med school in September. He was dazzled by this smooth sailing; one of the reasons he had procrastinated (the only concrete step he had taken in all these months was to send East for his transcripts) was that he might have to put in a whole year or more of makeup work.

"And to cap it," he told her, his hands on her shoulders, "they're giving the chemistry course at night, I won't even have to take off from my summer job." And he released her and began divesting himself of his shirt and trousers. His blood ran hotter than most people's and he always kicked off his clothes once inside his door. Johanna was growing used to the sight of him sitting around in his BVDs.

"Didn't you know any of this before?" she asked, puzzled. "I thought you said you applied months ago."

"Red tape—red tape, baby, you know how it is." He stretched his naked arms into the air.

"All this time while you've been studying at the library over there, I thought it was in preparation for a specific course."

"That's right, the chemistry course."

"But you said you were reading psychology."

He was silent for a moment. One of the good things about Johanna had been that she never asked questions about his outside life. But now that they were living together, her attitude had apparently changed. He didn't really mind; his outside life would be an open book from now on; but it irked him that she was taking him to task for something he had already given up.

"I read all sorts of things," he said irritably, "I went off in all directions. I'd been away from books for a long time." And he had been away from them a long time since; he had gone to the library exactly twice.

"And another thing," she said, as a nervousness ran down her spine. "You mentioned the other day that you hadn't been teaching your English class for months. But only a while back you said you couldn't see me because of it."

"I did drop it—but they ask me to fill in once in a while," he answered, forcing himself to look steadily into her eyes.

She looked back at him, on the brink of pushing him farther. But he was here now, his seashells were in her drawer, his sketch was on her wall, and he was ardent, jolly, companionable, and there was a contagion in his high spirits that made the whole world seem newly rinsed and polished.

She gave a nod and dropped the subject, feeling a brief strong hatred for him.

It was as if he had the powers of an alchemist, was able to turn every ordinary, even annoying characteristic into something of fascination and allure. At night his harsh snores captivated her with their timbre, their rhythm. That these sounds came from inside him was somehow a fascinating thing, a deep secret revealed. Sometimes she turned the lamp on and scrutinized his face, and was moved by his whiskers, each growing from its own pore; by the hairline creases in the parted lips; by the motionless eyelashes whose tips the lamplight gilded. She would turn off the light and whisper, "Morris" into his ear, and he, from within his heavy sleep, would stir slightly, move his hand out, and she would take it and sink down at his side, pressing herself against the warmth of his flesh, where she felt the steady heartbeat under his breastbone. His skin always smelled of sunlight and wind.

Rhonda said she saw a big change in him. He still blew in like a hurricane and joked around, but he no longer flirted, dozed, and brooded. "Him's found Miss Right," she told him maternally.

"I'm going back for my Doctorate, that's my 'Miss Right,' " he informed her sharply.

All day her remark and his response rankled in him. He sat in the storage room at Lincoln Elementary and tested a small girl with frightened eyes, and his mind wandered, his hands got the flash cards mixed up. Dead-end domesticity, that's how the remark had struck him. And he was appalled by the fury it worked up in him. Some of the flash cards dropped to the floor. He bent over and picked them up and turned gently back to the child. Testing was repetitious, frustrating, but he liked the children; one look at their unformed groping faces restored his patience when he felt it crumbling.

"Go ahead, Susan," he said, holding a card up for her to see.

The other day he had overheard Aquiline and Johanna talking in the hall. "Oh my," Aquiline had told her, "you is all revved up and flyin' since he move in." And realizing this, he had been touched and awed by Johanna's capacity to be so affected by another human being.

"Come on now, look at the card, what do you see?"

He was considered an excellent psychometrist, good with his little subjects, always earning their affection. It was the paperwork afterward, the boring grading and categorizing, where he fell down, procrastinating until he had to catch up in one night with strong coffee and NoDoz. He wondered if he could really endure the years and years of bookwork ahead of him before he would be ready to sit down with flesh-and-blood clients.

And those years were inextricably woven into Johanna, and he loved her body, admired her soul, and enjoyed her company, and yet, and yet—

He gave the child an encouraging smile. "Just tell me what you see, Susan; there's nothing to be afraid of," and leaned forward to catch her whisper.

When he got home that night he said at once, before he could change his mind, "I'd like you to come down to the office and meet the people I work with." Johanna responded with a look of pleasure, as if she understood that he had never before introduced a girl into the private world of his work.

He was dazzled by her as he took her through the office. Removing her ratty trenchcoat (in the hall, at his suggestion), she stood in her old yellow dress—it seemed to be the only dress she owned, but she had carefully washed and ironed it and she wore it well. Her sandals had fallen apart during the rainy season and she was in a pair of high heels that made the most of her long legs. Her hair was combed straight back from her face and smoothed behind her ears, and her fine cheekbones and yellow eyes were strikingly set off. She never used jewelry, but on this occasion she wore a pair of gold loop earrings, and they gave her a look of sensual elegance. The formality which sometimes tried his patience seemed transmuted into a warm intelligent graciousness as she shook hands with Rhonda, his boss, and the others. Rhonda, with the generous self-abnegation you sometimes found in unattractive women, fawned over her and shot him melting looks of congratulation, and he found himself thinking: At least she knows I'm not stuck on some broad who leads to suburbia; and he wondered why he should care what Rhonda thought, what anyone thought. Yet he was delighted to see the hastiness with which his boss rose to greet Johanna, to see the slight flicker of intimidation and arousal in his usually impassive eyes; and he pictured with a wince what the office's reaction to Zaidee would have been.

"We'll miss our Morrie when he leaves," Rhonda was

telling Johanna. "He's just more fun than a barrelful of monkeys. What do you do, sweetie? I bet you're not a teacher."

"Nothing at the moment," Johanna said. "I'm between jobs."

"She's a painter," said Morris, cringing at the bragging note in his voice, the voice of a man whose private life in no way paralleled the small stale lives of his co-workers.

By the time Johanna left, Rhonda had promised to send her a recipe for ambrosia chiffon pie, and Johanna, with a charm rare for her, assured her that she would be delighted to try her hand at an ambrosia chiffon pie. More handshakes all around, a hum of pleasantries, and she and Morris walked back down the hall together. She turned her face to him, buoyantly, and it came as a blow to him that he had the best, he had somehow got hold of the best.

When he left her at the entrance, he went back with a sick feeling in his stomach, as if he had eaten something too rich.

"I know, I know," he said impatiently to Rhonda, who overflowed with compliments as she followed him to his desk. He spread out his work and stared at it. He began totaling up Johanna's detractions. She might be good-looking, but she made no use of her appearance; she might appear youthful, but she was in her mid-thirties; she might be talented, but she had never sold a painting; she might be intelligent, but where had her brains gotten her? He took out his pen and began to work, feeling somewhat better.

Because if you did have the best, there was no farther to go.

Johanna was impressed by Morris' intense study habits. He spent every night except Friday, when he went to the Suicide Prevention Bureau as usual, over his books. Monday night was devoted to verbal composition and Tuesday night to math (they would weigh heavily in the med-school exam next month), Wednesday and Thursday nights to organic chemistry, and Saturday night to general reading in psychology. She lay stretched out on the floor with her own books—she was rereading Stendhal—or with her pen and sketch pad, and the silence was absolute.

As he had anticipated, it was a good room to study in. The paintings—he had hung them up, using screws and putty— were the only things he enjoyed looking at. The medieval scene, the Mouse Battalion with the weird lights, the stag

123

thrashing in the chandelier (she had not allowed him to hang the two portraits) provided him with a vaguely inspired feeling, while the rest of the room, with its booklined walls and musty air of the past, sealed off all tempting images of the contemporary world. And then there was Johanna herself, in the center of the hushed room; she brought him coffee, she asked him the questions at the end of each chapter, and if sexual thoughts came to him he no longer had to rush to his car.

There were aspects of their life that he was not entirely happy about. She insisted on getting up at a quarter to five every morning to paint, which meant not only that she didn't make love in the morning and she didn't sit next to him at breakfast (much less make breakfast), but that she was dead to the world by ten o'clock at night, while he never went to bed until one. Another problem was her cooking. Although she tried hard, her dinners were either as bland as wafers or they burned your palate with spices, they either steamed like a gutted building or were cold as her silver-plated cutlery. He decided to make the most of this failure and use it as a reason to go on a diet. This worked out very well; the pressure was removed from her efforts and he lost ten pounds in three weeks.

But the business of her rigid schedule remained. She could mold her hours any way—she had no job to report to—and her explanation that she painted best in the gray early hours rather than in the full flood of morning struck him as the self-indulgence of a prima donna. It aggravated him that she sacrificed a relaxed routine for something that would never bear fruit, something no better, really, than a hobby; and whenever he thought of her tiptoeing to her studio before dawn in her paint-stiffened clothes, her body still damp from its icy immersion, her eyes puffed and intense, he thought also of money.

He paid half of the unbelievably low rent (forty-five dollars apiece), he had cut down drastically on food costs with his diet, he no longer spent money on movies or other women or trips to Tahoe and Reno, he still had some money in his savings account, and he would have his salary until he quit work in September. All of which meant he could get through seven or eight months of med school without worry. But then he would have to find a part-time job, apply for a loan, something.

"Look," he said one night as he pondered these things, "I've got to make one thing clear. I can't carry you if you run out of money. I'll have to live like a scarecrow just to see myself through."

"I don't expect you to carry me."

"You haven't started looking for work yet—you can't have much money left."

"I've got enough for another month, maybe longer," she said, thinking of the pale green lunchrooms with distaste. "Sharing the rent helps. Anyway, you know how frugal I can be."

"I know how frugal you can be," he murmured, thinking of her one dress. And he said impatiently, "I can't understand why you sacrifice so much for nothing. I mean, you don't get anything in return for what you paint. You've got a good salable talent and you keep it inside these four walls."

"That's how it is."

"Why?"

"I can't explain it. I'm a private person. And I hate the idea of marketing, middlemen, all that."

"But you've got all sorts of contacts now—Josh, all those people he knows—"

"Josh," she said contemptuously.

"What have you got against him, anyway? He seems like an okay guy."

"I loathe him. He's empty. He plays with art. He plays with people."

"Oh, come on, he's a very giving guy."

"What he gives me is the shivers. He's subhuman."

"You're crazy."

"Well, you asked me."

"Well, you're crazy to let your feelings stand in your way. Look, I'll tell you what I think. I think you ought to at least go back there and take him up on that triple-salary offer."

"I'd see myself dead first," she said with a finality that ended the discussion.

The obdurateness of her character appealed to him in the abstract and drove him up the walls in its particulars. The havoc her schedule wreaked on their lovemaking seemed ruthless to him, and he told her that.

"But it never bothered you before you moved in," she said.

He could not very well tell her that he had had other outlets then. "Doesn't it bother you, too?" he said instead.

"Yes," she said truthfully.

"And the mornings are the best times."

"But we do have the nights."

"And I have to break into my studying."

"But I can't stay awake until one."

"You could if you got up later in the morning."

They always got stuck at this point, having gone around in a circle. She hated this argument about her schedule; it drained the energy she had to conserve for her work.

He tried to appeal to her humor, and perhaps to something deeper. "Where's your feminine magnanimity?" he asked with a smile.

But she received the smile coldly. "What's that?" she asked.

"No, you wouldn't know," he said with a sigh, "you wouldn't know."

"No, I'm ruthless," she said sarcastically, angrily.

"You are," he agreed.

"A woman shouldn't be ruthless about anything but keeping her man. I know."

"Let's just drop it."

"Gladly!"

Gradually she began to sense a change in him, a withdrawal, which frightened her. And she thought, finally, looking at him from across the room as he studied: After all, he does have a schedule imposed from the outside. And one morning, for the first time in years, except on Sundays, she stayed in bed past five o'clock, aching for the smell of turpentine. At seven Morrie awoke, delighted to find her beside him, and they turned to each other. From then on the sun rose without her. She felt a difference when she stepped into the studio at eight o'clock; the exhilaration was gone, the sense of existing alone in the universe. But their habits were adjusted, the friction ceased, their life together ran smoothly.

Yet this very contentment gave Morris pause. They were so different, their combined imperfections were enormous, yet they seemed to be overcoming all this and there was no reason why they shouldn't go on together forever. And he found his thoughts twisting and nosing into odd crevices, into the fact of her name, for instance, Kaulbach—not just

Gentile, but German, despite her Mediterranean coloring. Ever since he had moved to the coast his Jewishness had been a thing of the past; people out here were largely free of Eastern prejudices, and though occasionally his old sensitivity broke through, he was generally unaware of a heritage any different from that of the other rootless newcomers around him, and was very glad of it; background, races, nationalities —they were stumbling blocks to human fellowship, created by past generations. But now he gradually found himself dwelling on blood lines and raising up an atavistic barrier between him and Johanna which both repelled him with its emotional falseness and soothed him with its factual legitimacy. He saw their unlike ethnic sources as the one possible irremedial flaw in their relationship.

21 He need not have looked so hard for irremedial flaws; by May their differences were making headway again. No more trips to Tahoe, no more drives around town, no girl-hunting or movies or television (his television set had been stored in the closet), not even any treks to the refrigerator. He tried to be entertained by the small social activities of their lives—an evening with Conrad and Wanda, or with Aquiline and Charles.

Charles was always with Aquiline. His eyes—black, ponderous, with dusky yellow eyeballs—filled up with an uneasy radiance at her glance. She was a handsome woman, darker than Charles, almost coal black, with a neat heart-shaped face, long fine-boned hands, a supple carriage. Her voice was slow, yet sinewy, like her walk.

She lived in an apartment as battered as Johanna's, painted a shocking peacock blue and deep purple—some early flower child's taste. Aquiline had made the place aggressively bald. The lofty, cracked, and buckling blue walls and the wide purple floors were bare. The living-room furniture, secondhand chrome and white plastic reminiscent of a bankrupt dentist's office, was lined against the walls, leaving the floor empty. Rusty Venetian blinds hung at the long turn-of-the-century windows. On the television set stood a vase holding a single branch of pale bluish eucalyptus leaves. It was a room of strangely pleasing severity and spaciousness.

"You don't get that with most welfare cases," Morris told Johanna. "You get a big mess of hopeless belongings."

"She makes me think of someone pacing around in a vacuum, not knowing which way to go. Waiting for something."

"Well, you don't do much to bring her out. Whenever we go down there you sit like a lump."

"I don't like the way she talks. Everything is always loaded with double meanings."

"Sure, as long as you play her straight man she'll put you on. Get rid of your starch and joke around."

"I don't joke."

"*You* don't joke. *You* shouldn't change, *she* should change."

"The world won't end because Aquiline and I can't communicate."

"That's where you're wrong. That's what whites have been saying about blacks too long. Look, make an effort, because I like what I'm getting from Charles and I want to keep going down there."

"You said Charles was a jerk."

"Sure, he's a kindhearted, upright, well-meaning Tom. But he represents an attitude, and I want to get a good look at it."

"You make him sound like a textbook example."

"What d'you mean? I *like* him."

To make her silence more acceptable, Johanna would bring her drawing pad down with her and sketch the children as they played on the floor. Morris and Charles discussed jobs and religion. Aquiline painted her fingernails or darned.

"You' so bored," she yawned one night.

"I was listening to them," Johanna said, indicating the two men.

Aquiline cast them a critical look. "You' Cousin Appendix, he really try. He sound more colored than Charles."

"People have begun taking on black speech mannerisms," Johanna said, defending him. "Black culture is being popularized on a vast scale."

"Do tell."

"I've said the wrong thing, as usual."

"There ain't no thing for you to say but the wrong thing."

"That's why I don't say anything."

Aquiline smiled her long smile. "Don't give up so easy." After a silence, she asked without smiling, "You know what honky mean?"

"Of course, a white person."

"Yeah, that is white hide filled with shit." She looked at the girl with inexpressive eyes.

Johanna's hand stopped sketching. "That's how I appear to you."

"It ain't *you* that 'pear," Aquiline explained, "the word, it 'pear. No word, really, just *is*. Like in the eyeball." And she began painting her fingernails again.

With every page Morris read, his memory had rekindled. Life had sprung back into view as a pattern, a mosaic of art, history, philosophy, science. He had been away from books for a long time.

"Where have you been keeping all this?" Johanna asked one night, impressed.

"I don't know," he said with an odd feeling of apprehension.

"You really know so much!"

"Knowledge. What's knowledge but a foundation to be built on?" And in that instant, for the first time, his whole project swayed in his mind; and he repeated worriedly, "Just the bare foundation."

"No one would deny that," she said with a complacency that infuriated him.

"It's not like art," he said. "All *you* build on is your private emotions."

"Of course, art is just a pastime, a frill."

"I believe in doing!" He closed his book and stared around the room, seeing the dust of the past. And outside the window the world was clamoring for a huge surge of mass intent, not for the tiny piecemeal efforts of individuals bent over books and sketch pads, building on the mistakes of the past. Maybe he hadn't accomplished much individually, passing out anti-war pamphlets and tacking up peace-march posters, but he had been part of a movement and the movement counted.

And she, as his head swarmed with these thoughts, she was going on and on about art.

". . . What do you think art is, anyway?" she was demanding. "I'll tell you what it is. It's the deepening, the honor and betterment of the human race!"

"The human race!" he crowed. "You don't give a damn about the human race. You don't even show your paintings!"

"So what?" she said angrily, trying to think of a logical reply. "So what!" she said again.

"You're just a lot of empty tradition. Principle!" he said contemptuously. "Form!"

"Life is nothing without form!" she protested, but she noticed a growing habit in herself, that of listening with his ears to her own voice, of feeling his response even before he expressed it, and somehow absorbing and housing it even as she pushed her point. It made her words seem hollow to her.

"Form is dead!" he insisted. "All that rigid tradition-bound crap. You and your schedules and discipline—I'm sick of it. You're so damn punctual, so damn well-mannered, so damn formal." He knifed his finger at her cigarette. "Every time you stub out a butt I expect you to say, 'Thank you very much, and God bless you.' Shit!''

"Oh, really! Oh, really!" she breathed at him. "You know why you hate formality? Because it's final, it ends one thing and starts another. Casualness makes everything the same, it blurs outlines. And that's why you're casual!"

"Flexible," he countered, but without heat. He seemed oddly satisfied with her argument, as if he had wanted her to win the quarrel, and he sat down to his books again with a severe and challenging look. Whereas her neck trembled with the tension between her convictions and her fear of alienating him.

Sometimes on a Sunday they drove over the Golden Gate Bridge to the Marin coast, where the hills were already fading from their brief greenness to a biscuit brown, and where costumed youngsters could be seen thumbing rides on roads where once only hikers and an odd tramp had walked. Once Morris was sure he saw Zaidee shivering by the roadside with her hair blowing in the wind—but then, they all looked alike. If he was in the mood he screeched to a stop and gave them a lift, annoyed by Johanna's constraint, a mixture of cool reserve with strangers and jealousy that he should want more company than hers. He slipped effortlessly into their argot, sometimes he slipped them a couple of dollars; and when they got out, his eyes followed them enviously into their fluid future. But he threw his book-filled rucksack over his shoulders, found a spot high above the water, and grew easier in the sun and wind. He forced himself to put in at least an hour of study while Johanna wandered around the hills alone; then he pushed the books aside, their pages snapping in the salty wind, and with a yell went after her. Sometimes they played a game he had invented. One would blindfold himself with a handkerchief and start walking over the rough steep terrain, trusting the other to call "Halt!" just before a tree was plowed into or a ridge stumbled over. You lost if you paused to feel ahead with your foot, or if your hand went up to the blindfold. "Where am I going?" the blind one would shout, stumbling in darkness. And only silence from the other, and the ocean booming below.

Once a week they spent an evening with Conrad and Wanda.

"Conrad and Wanda and Closeto," Morris would mutter as they rang the bell.

And then Johanna would smile inwardly as Conrad, with a barely perceptible nod at the cat, somehow drew it into the bosom of the company.

"How are you, Closeto?" she would ask out of habit.

"He's nuts about his new place," Conrad would say, looking fondly at the cat, who lifted his neat mouse-gray head attentively. "You know how he hated that room of mine, he always wanted to stretch his legs . . ."

"He always tried to make a dash through the door," Wanda put in, who was almost as fond of Closeto as Conrad was.

"But he never knew any other place," Conrad explained to Morris. "I felt so damn guilty I finally gave him to a friend in the country. But he wasted away without me."

Johanna saw Morris fight down a smile.

"I remember," she said loyally. "He was skin and bones when you got him back."

"He loves it here," Wanda said. "He's too timid to go over the fence, thank God. He's vincible, is our Closeto. He just stays in the backyard and rolls around in the dirt like a mad thing."

"Well, he's young, he's only two and a half," Conrad said indulgently.

"Do you know Connie's planted a garden?" Wanda asked.

Conrad shrugged. "I don't know anything about flowers, they probably won't come up. What I really like to do is just poke around the shrubs—I feel like I'm out in the country."

"You're the ones in the country," Wanda said. "All those trees and bushes. How do you like it there?" she asked Morris.

"It's all right." He felt uncomfortable when people pinpointed his ménage—not its location, but its existence.

But at least they were off the subject of their pet. And they were good hosts, breaking out imported beer or good wine and unbelievably succulent pastries that Wanda had baked. He greedily went off his diet, partly out of nervousness.

It was not Wanda who made him nervous. He could categorize her: brainy but domestic, plain but amorous; found her niche with a congenial mate that no one would want to steal; basically cutting, but softened for the time being. Even her judgment of him, colored as it must be by the things Zaidee had told her, did not bother him. It was Conrad. The odd calm of the man, the detachment, or not really detachment, but a kind of glowing omniscience. His small blue eyes, half lost between overhanging eyebrows and sagging pockets of flesh, seemed to penetrate and light up the depths of everything they rested on. He was impressive; oddly; despite his joke of a face, his catfuss, his passé and unsalable paintings. He could even sit tailor-fashion on the floor with a glass of wine, stroking his cat and reading from an old book of poems, without embarrassment. He would look up now and then with his small warm eyes, and read on in a slightly softened, workaday voice.

> Come, Sleep, and with thy sweet deceiving
> Lock me in delight awhile;
> Let some pleasing dreams beguile
> All my fancies; that from thence
> I may feel an influence,
> All my powers of care bereaving!
>
> Tho' but a shadow, but a sliding,
> Let me know some little joy!
> We that suffer long annoy
> Are contented with a thought
> Through an idle fancy wrought:
> O let my joys have some abiding!

He smiled reflectively at his listeners, as if all of them, himself included, carried the seeds or scars of such need; a fact of life, but not necessarily the final fact, not necessarily a tragedy.

Johanna smiled back and felt the essence of this room— its warm splashy colors, its smell of cut flowers and linseed oil and burning firewood. He and Wanda were happy. As if by some magnanimous coincidence, their gears meshed perfectly.

But for a horrible moment Morris met Conrad's eyes with a glaze of tears. He shot his legs out, rumpling the rug, and bit into the cream puff he held, scattering powdered sugar down his shirtfront. "Shall we now proceed into the parlor for the Sunday night hymnfest?"

"Ah, Morrie," Johanna protested softly.

"I'm a functionalist." He brushed off the sugar, leaving white streaks across his navy-blue shirt.

Conrad followed the exchange with interest. He was sorry

133

for the graying china-shop bull with the nervous eyes. He was sorry, too, for Johanna, with that unmarked cameo face which still sent a stitch through his chest. And he thought back to the part he had played in bringing them together, yet he could not be sorry for that.

Morris picked up another cream puff and crammed it into his mouth. The archaically phrased verse had spoken to him as Johanna's heavy, dated apartment did; it said that the generations go down, the crest of the wave is never eternal, joy is never abiding, the individual is snuffed out like a candle, leaving only a musty poem, some yellowed curtains, a tarnished thimble . . .

"What's your definition of a functionalist?" Wanda was asking.

He felt himself surrounded by alien spirits. His studies rushed into his brain like an arsenal of weapons and he picked a phrase by an author they probably all respected.

" 'I have no use for the introvert's anguish over the impenetrability of ultimates, the absurdity of man's place in the universe, the discrepancy between our ideals and attainments.' One of your boys, Montaigne. I go along with that. I get things done. A million dusty old poems won't stop somebody from killing themselves. I *do* stop them. A painting of a kid rolling a hoop won't get you any closer to understanding a real kid with problems. My tests do."

"But after that?" Johanna queried. "After you find out that a child is a genius or a moron or has an aptitude for carpentry. After you persuade the voice on the phone to flush the sleeping pills down the toilet. After that?"

"At least there *is* an after that," he said shortly, stung by her disloyalty.

"But then what?" she pursued. "It's like the parable of the Good Samaritan. Why didn't he take the poor man home to rest up? And find a job for him? And bring his family out from Damascus or wherever? How did he know where to stop, and how do we know he was right in stopping where he did?"

"Jesus, I should bring home all my would-be suicides and kids with a low IQ. Your first responsibility is to yourself."

But now his arsenal sank back into darkness. Who but himself did the quote from Montaigne describe? No wonder it had stuck in his mind. All the fine talk about his work—the phone-callers killed themselves some other day; the kids he tested went on to junior high school and drugs. And if he became a psychiatrist, his clients would come into his office, one at a time, for years on end, and with this tiny handful of the earth's multitudinous imperfect souls, he would probably have the same paltry percentage of success as he had with his phone-callers and kids. He felt a rush of despairing impatience, and was further depressed by the fact that it was not even directed honestly at himself, but at that symbol of persever-ance, Johanna.

But as Conrad led the conversation away from personal exposés, Morris' emotions subsided. The grate crackled in the cold spring night, the ashtrays smoldered, the glasses and bottles gleamed in the firelight. He slid down in his chair, closed his eyes halfway, and warmed himself in the scene, a vignette of peace and friendship.

"They're okay," he said as he and Johanna got into the car, "even if they are two old maids."

"They're not two old maids."

"Sure they are. And we are too. Sitting up in your attic reading and studying. Our big night out is a visit to some-body's house."

"Do you regret it?" she asked, with such intensity that he threw his eyes at her. He wanted to take fire from that intensity, he wanted to burn with all his lights.

"Don't be crazy!" he told her with a burst of feeling.

But they both thought he needed a break from his work. They decided that he should plead illness at work and they would spend a whole week camping in the Sierras. Beyond the cool environs of San Francisco, the weather was superb.

22

The campsite, lying alongside the Yuba River in a gorge, was deserted except for one other early-season party. After choosing a spot and unloading, they changed into their bathing suits and walked over to the river, feeling buoyant and unpeeled in the May air, which was filled with the fresh smell of water on stone. They stood on a low cliff and looked down to a deep, pale green glassy pool, the submerged boulders on its floor as clear as those on the shore. On the other side of the river was a strip of grassland, then the wooded mountains, rising almost vertically, hazed at their peaks with afternoon heat and lazily circled by hawks.

Lowering themselves over the cliff, they began working their way down the rough lichen-stubbled stone. Suddenly Morris saw Johanna fall, a smile on her face.

With her arms held high above her upstreaming hair, she felt an explosive ice-raw roar, then the heavy closing-in pressure of deafness as she sank. She opened her eyes on a lost motionless world, sank to her knees on the sandy bottom, and shot back up, soaring toward the green glass ceiling, and shattered through it in a shock of vividness: white boulders, green grass, among them lakes of bluebells; then turning—Morris, powerful chest and shoulders, thighs flexed against the cliff; he was spread-eagled, his face sharply etched by the sun.

He was looking at the mountaintop. He felt that he could fly. The warm air with its rifts of breeze, the green water, the mountain soaring into the steadfast blue, all beat through his veins with such joy that he didn't know if he wanted to savor it or to crown it with a leap.

His arms moved away from the cliff as his body tipped slowly forward. With a grace that caught Johanna's breath, he dove off in a long dazzling arc and cut cleanly through the water.

A moment later she felt her ankles grabbed, and she was pulled under. They wrestled in slow motion, skin ivory in the water, hair fanning up; then they lost sight of each other as they swam apart to explore. Pulling off her suit, Johanna returned to the secluded world at its deepest point, where not a breath of current could be felt, and finger-walked over the drowned boulders. Small fish darted out from them, and skimmed over orange pebbles lying on the floor. She scraped a handful of the pebbles for Morris' collection and swam to the shallows on the other side, where sun reflections floated under the water like loose gold nets.

Drifting, she heard voices and lifted her head. The other camping party stood on the cliff, a man and a woman and three children. As they caught sight of her naked body their voices stopped. The mother moved first, casually, as if not wanting to seem embarrassed; then the father turned away, taking the hands of two of the children; the third child remained, staring, until he was called sharply. The cliff was empty.

"And stay away!" she shouted, climbing up on the boulder where Morris lay.

"Sh," he said, wondering if there was a park attendant around this early in the season. She never thought of consequences when she was in the outdoors.

"Get your suit," he said.

"It's floating downstream." She spilled the pebbles onto the boulder. "I brought you these rocks for your collection."

"Go get your suit."

He followed her with his eyes. She ran, jumping from boulder to boulder with her hand shading her eyes. There seemed no touch of exhibitionism in this disregard for possible onlookers; it was as if she felt sanctioned by her surroundings, as if she were part of the river: sexless, natural, beyond human judgment. He was stirred by this abandon, yet it made him uneasy, as if she had disappeared into an uncharted dimension.

But the sun was hot and his blood ran salty. He swam vigorously upstream to a path and hurried wet and libidinous through the camp, checking out tire tracks, campfires, garbage pails. Definitely the place had not been used for months: no reason for an attendant yet. And the other party would now keep its distance. He rushed back to the cliff and jumped off into the water, plowed back to the boulder, and ripped off his trunks just as Johanna returned with her bathing suit flung over her shoulder.

They made love on the rock as the sun sank behind the mountain, leaving the gorge filled with amber light. Slowly, evening crept in with a cool pungent smell of earth, and the water ran darkened around the boulder. They put on their bathing suits and made their way downstream to a footbridge. Walking back along the dirt road, they passed the family, which was sitting before a large elaborate tent looking at a portable television set. They had strung up clotheslines; they had even brought a playpen for their toddler. Morris waved, curious to see their reaction. The father lifted his hand peremptorily. Tame, domestic, plodding, weighted down by children; they were old, old, futureless. "Do you realize that couple back there's probably younger than we are?" Morris asked, delighted, and he felt a searing love for Johanna, for her unmarked face, for her abandonment, for her marginal place in society.

He was asleep. Johanna lay next to him in the double sleeping bag and listened. Now and then a plop echoed from the black river—a fish, a falling stone. From the other camp came a faint sporadic sound of clinking pots and pans, and the thin notes of children's voices. Then they died away. She closed her eyes.

When she opened them the gorge was awash with light, the moon had risen, white and blazing. She climbed from Morris' side, shivering in her clothes in the cold, put her old tennis shoes on, and hurried away. At the dirt road she ran, very fast, on the balls of her feet, until she reached the footbridge, where she slowed down to a walk and crossed noiselessly. The boulders lay chalk-white in the powerful moon. She began running across them, leaping from one to the next with all the speed she could summon, until she reached the meadow, then running thigh-deep in grass that whipped her pants legs. At the foot of the mountain she stopped to get her breath. Then, tightening her shoelaces and clamping her hair behind her ears, she began to climb.

The bushes were wet with dew, but the steep ground was dry, slippery with fallen pine needles and unpierced by the moon. She climbed crouched, using her toes for leverage and her fingers as antennae. The speed of her ascent exhilarated her, as the race over the boulders had, when she had had only a split second to exercise judgment, to twist around in the air and land at the right spot on the next boulder and to land with the balance and renewed spring to propel her on without a break, all the humps and crevices rushing toward her like

138

an express train. Now, rushing up the dark hill with only her fingertips to guide her around obstacles—sometimes reeling back in a slide of pine needles and plunging on without a pause—she felt possessed by the good demon which was herself peeled to its core: swift, free. She was no longer cold. Sweat stood out on her face, her spine tingled, her hands stung brightly with scratches.

After a long time, when a pain grew sharp in her chest, she dropped flat to rest with her cheek pressed against the earth. There was a grainy quality to the soil now, a hardness under it, first token of the peak. She climbed on in the shadows of the dense trees, but gradually she began passing through moonlit clearings, and at last the trees thinned and were left behind.

The rest of the climb was over gravel and ribbings of stone, laid bare as bones by the moon's illumination. Looking upward as she mounted, she saw a tall outcropping of rock rising from the summit in the shape of a two-finger salute, and as soon as she reached its base she began climbing again, quickly scaling its rough spine and hovering on all fours for an instant before standing up in the wind.

Below, the river lay smooth and black as oil, curving through the tumbled moonscape of boulders. Everything else was mountains, some smaller than the one she stood on, some larger, dark at the bottom, grading into a ghostly blue-white as they rose, etched with the configurations of firs, a numberless sweep of upturned V's.

Three hours might have passed since she had left camp. The moon was already in its descent. There were no stars. The sky looked as though the stars had been beaten together and poured through it. She lay down on her back on the outcropping with an arm and a leg hanging over the edge into the air. The wind soughed through the trees below, but up here it snapped like laundry on the line, sometimes gathering itself together to torpedo the base of the rock in a single mad attack, after which it dissipated into momentary silence.

She crawled into a crevice of the rock and slept lightly until the cold woke her. Stiff and sore, she climbed down and began walking around the summit, hitting her body with her fists to get warm. From the gravel grew wildflowers, possibly pink or blue in the daylight, but white in the sinking moon. She crouched and brought her face to bear on theirs, magnetized by their perfection—each stem opening into a pronged cup to hold its blossom, the smooth dropleted petals growing from a faultless circle, the leaves intricately veined and gently uplifted at their tips. They had no smell except the freshness of water. From one of them she splashed the drops onto her finger and put them to her lips.

The moon was almost gone, mist floated below. She started back, slipping in the rock-ribbed gravel, picking herself up as a streak of pain shot through her thigh, and took the rest of the descent sideways, one leg extended downward, the other bent behind her acting as a brake. Through the long raking skid she heard the first birdcalls, gapped and tentative, and when she penetrated the foothill, where the mist hung in white wreaths from branch to branch, a great hollow croaking of frogs met her ears. She emerged into the meadow and walked slowly through the sopping grass toward the footbridge. The croaking stopped as she crossed over, and the sound of the river came muted and contemplative.

When she arrived where she had started from, she glanced with surprise at the fluorescent orange MAKE LOVE, NOT WAR bumper strip in the mist, at the damp green sleeping bag with a thatch of dark hair protruding from it.

She awoke to the smell of frying bacon.

Morris sat by the fire in his swim trunks. He looked at her as she stood up. Her trousers lay wet on the ground. Her hands and ankles were red with welts and scratches, and her thigh bore a nasty gouge.

"I took a walk last night," she said. Her words sounded distant.

"What'd you do, fall into a thornbush? You're nuts to walk around at night." She deserted him in the middle of the night to fall into thornbushes, and only woke when snared by the smell of food.

She was silent as they ate. Afterward he pulled the sleeping bag behind the car and made love to her, but she was remote and he went to the end alone.

"It was like the first night we met, when you raped me," she remarked, without rancor.

"Raped you? I've never raped anybody. You wanted it."

"I know, I needed to be raped that night, that's why I wasn't angry afterwards. But you didn't seduce me, you raped me pure and simple."

140

"You can't rape anybody who wants it."

"Well then, you raped me now."

"It's different now."

"I suppose you think I belong to you now."

"I don't like the word 'belong.'"

"You don't like it for yourself, but I think you like it for me."

They took a hike upstream and discovered a tumultuous rapids, a hawk soaring up from the ground, a deer sprinting away. The strangeness, the remoteness in Johanna had worn away by the time they came back to the pool under the cliff to swim. As she climbed up on the boulder to dry off, her eyes rested on the cliff.

"There was a waterfall in the mountains where I grew up. There was a skeleton of a dog stuck in a tree halfway down the cliff."

"Yeah, where was that?" he asked, climbing up beside her.

"In the Napa Mountains. I've mentioned them before."

He caught the annoyance in her voice. "How'd that rarefied family of yours wind up there?" he asked with a show of interest.

"I suppose if you're rarefied, a mountain's the best place for you," she said thoughtfully. She sat up erect, scraping her elbow on the rock. "Morris, I'd like to tell you something."

His eyes were narrowed with concentration. Suddenly he scrambled to his feet. "Okay, baby, we're going into Grass Valley! We need a couple inner tubes. We're gonna shoot the rapids."

She looked at him for a moment, then dropped her eyes. "You go, I don't want to."

"It's twenty miles—I don't want to drive alone."

"The whole day'll be wasted. Why do we have to shoot the rapids? Aren't we enjoying ourselves as we are?"

They shot through the boiling channel in the inner tubes, lifting their buttocks as they skimmed over the submerged rocks and sticking their feet out to repel the rocks that loomed in their onrushing path. At the end of the rapids they floated lazily downstream under the waning sun, then paddled to shore and carried the tubes back for another wild ride, some-

141

times capsizing in a churn of downthrusting forces, battered along the rocky floor until they were caught against a rock they could grab, their heads knifing up from the foam as the black glistening tubes bounced madly into the distance. It was dusk when they returned to camp.

Morris searched the car for a paperback, even for an old newspaper, but found none, and for an envious moment he thought of the camping family around their television set.

"You're bored," Johanna said.

"Bored? Up here?"

He settled for a game of solitaire. Johanna didn't play cards; he could have taught her something simple, like black-jack, but he didn't dare. Even solitaire bothered him, the sight of those rich red-and-yellow face cards with their challenging eyes. He swept the cards together and put them away.

"Let's take a walk," he said.

But it was an aborted stroll. A moment after they started down the dirt road a large shape approached them, dim in the night. It came quickly, was upon them before they could move, and only at the last moment revealed itself as a donkey. Johanna barely had time to pat its rump before it was gone, leaving behind a faint smell of hay and manure. Morris was standing stock still. He felt strangely terrified, like a child, by the monstrosities of the night. "Let's go back," he said, irritated.

They sat by the fire, their backs freezing in the bitter night air, their faces red and stinging from the fire. A whole week more of this, he thought, long nights with nothing at all to do.

"I want to tell you about my family," Johanna said, pinpointing his eyes with hers. "But only if you're interested."

"I'm interested," he said, picking up a piece of charcoal.

"You see—you told me about your father."

He crumbled the charcoal and said nothing.

"Where are my cigarettes?" she asked, but didn't look for them, and began speaking rapidly. "The von Kaulbachs weren't my family. All those furnishings you dislike so much —they didn't come down to me through my family. My parents came out here from Oklahoma during the Depression."

"Okies?" he said, unable to absorb this information. "But those old photographs—"

"The von Kaulbach family. I don't have any pictures of my parents. I hardly remember my mother, she died when I was small. My father—if he was my father—took me to live with him in the Napa Mountains. He lived with a woman up there. Then he drifted away. He was—I guess the word is a wino."

"A wino?" He felt puzzled, cheated, yet vastly relieved.

"The von Kaulbachs were our neighbors. They took me in after the woman died. That's where I got my name. My real name was—" Here she broke off.

"Was what?"

"Fayette."

"Fayette?"

"Coombs," she said distastefully.

"Coombs," he repeated softly. "What difference does it make?" he asked at length, casually.

"You're the only person I've ever told."

"Why? All this crap about background. A big secret because your parents were a couple of bums?"

"I didn't say they were bums."

"Okies. Whatever. Who cares what they were?"

"But I *do* care, even if I shouldn't. And I've told you. Only you."

He put his arm around her shoulder, but she felt that her offering had fallen flat. And there was no way she could retract the confession; its taste lingered alien and unpleasant on her tongue.

When Morris awoke the next morning the face cards were burning into his brain. Five days more, shooting the rapids over and over, going for hikes, having soul-talks in the dragging night—the prospect sent a shiver of restlessness through him and he thought of Tahoe, only forty miles to the east. He ran to the cliff and dove off with a powerful urge to be seduced by the water again—O let my joys have some abiding! —and all day he swam and hiked with a singlemindedness that left Johanna marveling at his vigor. But when evening came and they sat by the fire, she saw boredom hanging from his bones.

Toward dawn she woke in a sweat. What if he stayed bored, and picked up and moved out of the apartment? And she realized that he had left hundreds of times already, in the middle of a sentence, even in the middle of a caress, though his body remained. She pressed her body hard alongside his, fitting into his contours. Something had gotten twisted around in her, some self-feeding vein had been pinched off, her nourishment came only through her ears and eyes and skin and he played upon them. And as she lay there, each of his deep self-contained breaths pushed her deeper into panic.

In the bright light of the morning her fears seemed stupid and lurid. She saw his every action as proof that he loved her: when he insisted she have the last piece of bacon, when he rubbed lotion into her shoulders, when he picked a wildflower for her. They had a good day, though it was cloudy, stifling, and the water dried stickily on their skins. After dinner she suggested he teach her rummy, and the evening passed quickly.

But the next morning, which dawned bell-clear, fragrant, he began to pack.

"You want to leave?" she asked, her heart dropping.

"I can't take so much time off, babe. The exam's next week."

She walked away and looked down at the pool, a cool dark green under the cliff's long morning shadow. The pebbles she had gathered for him the first day still lay on the boulder. A sound of homely activity drifted up from the other camp.

Morris looked away from her when she returned. "Look, I don't *want* to leave. It's just that I'm antsy about the exam."

"You're bored."

"I'm never bored with you," he insisted.

And again she felt the chasm between her intelligence and her need to believe.

The car bounced down the dirt road away from the camp. Their feet were bare, covered with mountain dirt; the morning air, sweet with the smell of clover and pines, flooded through the open windows. At the highway crossing he sat immobile for a full minute, though there were no cars in sight. He was going to turn back, Johanna thought hopefully.

Only forty miles east. They could be there in half an hour. But he could picture her healthy sunburned face as he guided her into the air-conditioned ruckus. She would be thinking of the river they had given up for this. And he could see her look of contempt hours later as he turned away from the tables, sour and empty-handed. On the other hand, why should he turn away sour and empty-handed? Why shouldn't he win?

He clamped his tongue between his teeth, pushed his bare foot down on the gas pedal, and pulled out in the direction of San Francisco.

23

"You ought to sell your paintings!" he exclaimed out of the blue as they drove off the Bay Bridge into the noisy city, which was in the process of being consumed by a bank of gray fog. Why had he chopped off his vacation? The streets were filled with traffic exhaust, tomorrow he'd be back in the office with Rhonda's typewriter clattering in his ear. He said again: "You ought to—"

"I heard you. Among other things, money deforms art." She had assembled her arguments in case he brought up the subject again.

"What about the pleasure you could bring people? The edification?"

"Huh. The Age of Democracy. People buy pictures the way they buy furniture. And the galleries play into it—with them it's a money proposition pure and simple. Back in the Twenties, Lhote was asked which way art was going. The way of commerce, he said. And time's borne him out."

"Okay, but he probably wanted to sell anyway. They all did. How come you're more fastidious than they were?"

"I don't know. It's worse now. Everybody's in it for money."

"So you paint in a vacuum."

"I don't call my own appreciation a vacuum. Or yours."

"I call it a dead end. Look at Conrad. You *could* sell if you wanted to. He'd give his eyeteeth to be in your place."

"That's Conrad. He's not me."

"You seem to think because you're you you're right."

"Of course. Don't you feel that way?"

He pulled up before their building and turned the motor off. "Josh would give you an exhibit, or arrange for one somewhere."

"Josh!" she said with disgust.

"And in the meantime you could be working there, at three times your old salary. Unless he was joking."

"His whole life's a joke. But he lives .t scrupulously. He'd do it, all right, but I won't."

"Christ, everything's cut out for you if you'd just take advantage of it."

Aquiline sat on a towel on the front steps in a red one-piece

145

bathing suit, calling in her children, who were running around the front yard in shorts and bathing suits. Apparently they had had a brief broiling afternoon, and then in one swoop the fog had enveloped them.

"You don't have the guts," he said, squinting at Johanna's stubborn face. "You stick yourself in a vacuum so you can pretend nothing's changed for a hundred years. If you let that gallery really get to you, it'd be like a shot of adrenalin, you wouldn't know what to do with it."

"I won't even answer anything as stupid as that," she said, getting out of the car.

They unloaded in silence and went barefoot up the broken pavement of the front walk.

"How you' trip?" Aquiline asked.

"Great," Morris said.

"How you like my tan, think it gettin' there?" she asked.

"Beautiful, baby," he said, stepping past her long bare legs.

"What you think?" she asked Johanna.

Johanna looked at the black skin. "I think it's a pointless question."

Aquiline broke into a laugh and rubbed her arms in the chill fog.

"You sound like a goddam Lutheran minister," Morris condemned Johanna as they went up the inside stairs. "Or a moron. What's the matter with you you can't get on anybody else's wavelength?"

"I don't like Aquiline's wavelength. She knows it."

"Yeah? Why don't you like her wavelength!" They were in the room. The Room. Stuffy, already filmed with a layer of dust. "Who're you not to like? What makes you so special?" He looked at the morass of books and papers on his desk, at the flat, permanently creased cushion on his chair. "You forgot you said you weren't so special? Your big confession?" The gray light from the window swirled with dust motes as he began pacing up and down the rug. "You don't come from anything better than she does—a DP from the dustbowl."

He saw her lips tighten with shame, for him.

"Okay," he snapped, "I'm unfair. Forget it. You've got me thinking about the same stupid things you think about. I don't give a shit where you come from or anybody else comes from." He paced more resoundingly, annoyed by the tripping throw rugs, by the little tables with their trembling piles of leatherbound books, by the tinkling chandelier. "Only you're here. Now. A black ghetto. You get that? Not the Baltic coast a hundred years ago. 1966. You get that? 1966, here and now. So get with it, or, God damn it, I'm splitting." He struck his fist stingingly into his hand.

The breath was belted out of her as she saw his desk removed, his side of the bed empty, the first long hour, the first long month, the first long year. Her fingers flew out, and with a grimace that shook her face, she rammed into him, going for the eyes.

"Watch it!" he cried, grabbing her wrists and holding her at arms' length as her bare feet flailed his ankles. The fury of her foot blows, her loud breathing and shaking face set his blood pounding with a sense of heightened reality, yet through it he felt one corner of his mouth lift with a smile of embarrassment. He was unfitted to the moment, ludicrous, an outsider with an embarrased smile.

He bit the smile off and pushed her away.

And pulled himself back into normal workaday shape; it was no time for a set-to, he was sorry he had started it; but there were times when her inflexibility drove him out of his mind. "Look," he said gruffly, "forget the junk I said. We both are what we are. I go off the deep end sometimes when I criticize you, but I guess I like you for what you are."

Simultaneously she shriveled at the word "like" and closed her eyes with relief to know that he was staying.

He came over to her and took the hands that had a moment ago tried to put out his eyes; they shook slightly and pressed his own tenderly. "You're crazy, you know that?" he asked.

She nodded, and released a long shaky breath.

"You're crazy. You're my Johanna. Only I still think—"

Her eyes shot to his face. She waited.

"I think you ought to go back to work at the gallery."

A while later he snapped on his gooseneck lamp and settled down to study. Johanna sat in the black chair and tried to read *The Lonely Crowd,* a book he had recommended, but she was restless and lowered the book. The room was dark, a dusky wine-chocolate color except for the pool of amber lamplight at her side and the white glare from Morrie's desk. Sheets of newspaper, crumpled notepaper, red gum wrappers, coffee cups, and socks lay scattered. The Thomas Mann record stood mutely against the phonograph in its dogeared album.

("Do you have to play that thing all the time?" Morris had asked when he first moved in.

"Yes, I love it."

"Why?"

"Because, I suppose, it embodies everything that's—" and she faltered under his waiting eyes, embarrassed by what she was going to say, knowing that it would sound overblown and pedantic to him—"everything that's accomplished, profound, enduring," she finished quickly.

"To me it's a lot of noise."

So she had not played it except when she was alone. His complaint was reasonable, the sound of a foreign language was probably tiresome. But lately she had not felt like playing it at all.)

She got up and walked around the dark part of the room, thoughts breaking half-formed into her mind and dissolving. Morris' broad naked back—he had pulled off his shirt—was bent over the cluttered desk. His fingers toyed with a paper clip while he read. She wandered into the bedroom, turned on the light, and, stooping, pulled open the bottom drawer of the dresser which held her sweaters and underclothes. Pushing these things aside, she carefully uncovered a neatly folded square of closely woven material, once white but now yellow with age, lined with small pearl buttons—Herr von Kaulbach's spats. She touched them with the back of her hand, peering down into the depths of the drawer as though boring, or trying to bore, through time itself.

Conrad was sitting on the receptionist's desk when Johanna came into the gallery. He spent a lot of time wandering around town with his sketch pad under his arm, pausing to dash off a figure on a bench or a pair of strolling lovers, and dropping into galleries along the way to see what was up. The gallery owners liked him because he made no effort to push his work; when he exhibited, it was in a coffee house owned by a friend, or his doctor's waiting room. He was so small-time and so lacking in envy that he established friendships in the art world that were impossible among its more driven practitioners. And he was bright, witty in a dry way, and knowledgeable, so that his personality earned him the respect his paintings didn't. He had known Josh for years, when Josh was a simple, busy man about town, investing part of a colossal inheritance in city real estate that poured out profits whose froth he skimmed off into the purchase of two failing restaurants. Conrad had done the menus—calligraphic gems, he had to admit—and Josh had paid him superabundantly, the same way he had bought out chefs from better places and hired a decorator from London. The man's openhandedness was dazzling, yet in terms of his actual monetary value, almost non-existent. He could be called a prodigal only if he scooped a hole from the center of his fortune, but apparently it was impossible to leave a hole; he was fated to drag his self-regenerating purse behind him forever. His restaurants thrived, his racehorses won, his obscure rock bands took fire, and now his gallery bloomed and boomed under his increasingly monkish gaze. Conrad found him harmless, amusing, and was not offended that Josh found him the same. They discussed art elliptically, with no desire to come to grips. More often they discussed nothing; Conrad had a cup of coffee, and wandered around the gallery with his hands in his pockets. When Johanna had worked there he had dropped by twice a week, but now his visits were rarer.

"I'm seeing things," he said as she came in through the door, and Josh, talking on the receptionist's phone, broke off in mid-sentence. "Call them back later," he told the receptionist, and took Johanna mutely by the hands.

"I see you have a replacement," she said, disengaging his hands.

"My offer still stands, Miss Kaulbach."

"You can't just pull someone off." She indicated the receptionist.

"She's from a temporary agency," he said, and led Johanna into his office and closed the door, Antigone fiddling with his turtleneck as he turned around.

"Why don't you let that poor beast go back to its natural surroundings?" she asked, looking at the nervous paws.

"There are no natural surroundings for a white rat, didn't you know that? Only unnatural."

"You give me heartburn."

"You're really back, Miss Kaulbach, your loving voice fills the air."

"And you're really willing to pay three times my former salary?" she asked, plunging.

"I said so, didn't I?"

She threw herself down in a chair and put her knuckles to her teeth. "You won't get anything in return, you know that."

"No one but myself can put a value on the return," he answered, sitting down opposite her.

"*I* put the value on it. And I say there is none."

"You have no control over your value," he told her gently.

"You swine!" she exploded, jumping up from her chair. "How dare you say that!"

"You've frightened Antigone," he said mildly, touching the rat's trembling flank.

"If you think you're getting something from me without my allowing it—"

"Ah, Miss Kaulbach, you are fantastic. You're from Mars. But don't you have that trouble when you walk down the street? I don't see you putting a bag over your head."

"I don't even know what we're *talking* about!" she said, striking her forehead, and falling into a silence. At last she began again: "Let me speak plainly. I don't like you, but I want to come back. I hope you don't think things will be any different."

"Of course not," he said agreeably.

"Then when shall I start?"

"This afternoon? At one o'clock?"

She nodded.

"Welcome back," he said, offering his hand.

She didn't take it.

With a small triumphant smile he watched her go out of the office.

She walked with Conrad down Sutter Street to Union Square and sat down on the grass in the windy sunshine. Office workers sat around them eating their lunches from paper bags, others were squeezed on benches among old pensioners in heavy coats, while tourists with cameras slung over their shoulders strolled along the walks. Across the street the somber St. Francis Hotel, with its striped black-and-white canopies, stood in deep elegant shadow; everywhere else the cold sun flashed: from store windows, thronged cars, from the grinding machinery of a construction site. Pigeons pecked, strutted, and swooped, a contingent rising with a sudden clapping of wings, hanging suspended for a moment, iridescent against the dark background of the hotel, then fluttered down again and headed as one across the grass, full of hurried aplomb. Conrad was throwing out handfuls of feed. "Come on, lunchtime!"

An old man with a dented bullet-shaped head and rimless spectacles shook his fist at him.

"The world could be divided into pigeon lovers and pigeon haters," Conrad said as the old man stamped passionately through the crowd of birds, sending them flying in every direction.

"I wonder what he does at night. I think he grips the kitchen sink and stares at the wall."

"So tell me, Johanna, what's your reason?"

She looked at him.

"Why did you go back?"

"I've had a change of heart," she said, stretching out on the grass and looking away from him. "I've always over-reacted to things, I think it's hindered me in my personal and artistic growth."

"That doesn't sound like you talking. It sounds like Morris."

"It's me," she said shortly. "Anything I instinctively dis-approve of I close myself off from. I can't learn anything that way, I've got to be open to new experiences. So I want to go back to the gallery with an open mind—I want to really understand what they're trying to do."

"And the tripled salary? You turned it down?"

"Well, no, Josh can afford it."

"But that's not you."

"You're the one who said I should change, don't deny it."

"Change in some ways. But in other ways, no. I never thought I'd see you striking bargains."

"That's just semantics," she said. "What's striking a bargain except making a compromise? You said I didn't know how to live in the world, and that was true because I didn't know how to compromise. You have to compromise unless you live like a hermit the way I did. It's give-and-take, share, learn. That's all I'm doing."

"By accepting a tripled salary."

"I notice you didn't turn down that astronomical sum he gave you for your menus that time."

"Because I don't have any convictions when it comes to

money. Or at least they only go so far as to keep me from taking from someone who can't afford it. That would grate on me, that would make me unhappy. But to accept exorbitant payment from someone as rich as Josh doesn't bother me at all."

"All right. I'm doing the same."

"No, the difference is that it *does* grate on you. It insults something in you not to give what you consider an equal return. That's why you quit in the first place. That's why you always get yourself fired from jobs. It's the way you are."

"But the way I am—I'm self-defeating in so many ways, limited. Maybe the part you're talking about is too. How do I know?"

"You know, Johanna," he said, taking her chin in his hand.

"No, I don't know. I have to explore."

"You may just be an explorer who doesn't come back."

"Stop advising me, please."

"Certainly," he said, taking his hand back and feeding the pigeons again.

"Conrad," she said, pulling on a piece of grass, "you've been talking about convictions. Why did you move in with Wanda?"

"It just got to that point. I wanted to."

"That night in your room—you gave a great speech for the holocausts of the heart, Conrad."

He lifted his baggy eyes to hers. "I feel good with Wanda. We're on the same wavelength. I'm not lonely anymore. Don't look down your nose at those things, Johanna. I had a very long holocaust of the heart, and now it's my time for these things."

"But *she* loves *you.*"

"And she knows I'm too old to start another big bonfire. But she also knows I'd lay down my life for her."

"That *is* nice," she said, smiling at him.

"We're thinking of getting married in the fall. At least, Wanda wants to. I've got some reservations."

"Why?"

"Money. She's got a good job, I sell postcards. Society's a crock. We all get stuck in it."

"Not you."

"A man's ego is flayed if the woman brings in more money than he does."

"Is your ego flayed?"

"You know I have no ego. It's part of my lovableness."

"All right, then."

"I want Wanda to be sure."

Johanna said, suddenly sitting up, "Wouldn't it be something if we both wound up married in the fall?"

"You think you might?" His eyes were fixed on her face.

"Well—it's a possibility. I mean, people get married."

"And you'd want to?" he asked in a hard tone.

"Yes," she said with a defiant ring.

"You would really want to. Marry Morris."

"Do you remember it was once suggested to me that I make a decision about Morris? Well, I made it. And that was the last decision I was capable of, apparently. There's no more choice, only a drive, something that just keeps going on. I have to have him. You know how I feel about marriage, the idea has never appealed to me. But with Morrie—"

"Only if he wanted to marry you would you be sure of his feelings."

She tore a piece of grass in two. "I don't like it, put that way."

"I don't like it either, not that I have any say in the matter."

"I don't have any say in it either. I don't have any control over it."

"And if you did—what would you do?"

She made no answer, shredding the piece of grass.

"Would you leave him?" he prodded.

She shut her lips firmly and looked past his face.

"That's what I thought. You would."

"Why don't you leave me alone?"

He was silent for several minutes. Then he stood up. "When you do get involved, my love, you make a thorough job of it. And now, may God provide." He threw the last of the feed to the pigeons.

They walked across the crowded lawn to the sidewalk.

"I'll leave you here. I have to buy some liver for Closeto. By the way, you've come back just in time for the launching of Josh's paper-mâché thing."

"Oh? What kind of a launching will that be?"

"Nobody knows. But everybody will—the press is invited. Come down early tomorrow if you're interested."

24

Shoots of grass stood before the soldier's face, each stalk blurred white and thick, so close was it to his eyes. The ground was wet, and littered with the ribs and spines of last year's leaves.

He forced himself to consider the field beyond this patch of ground where he had hidden himself, and long shudders of life ran through him as the sound of drums and cannon broke back into his ears. The pale morning sky was blotted with smoke, like spots of black mildew, their edges growing ragged in the breeze. Something was happening to the ground, it had suddenly begun to shake under him. He threw himself frantically on his side, and he noticed that around the epaulets and silver buttons of his blue tunic hung tiny shreds of fibrous earth. An avalanche of hooves bore down on him; there was a deep crunch of skull from inside the clangor, like an isolated note in a symphony. The sky turned instantly black and at that instant all sound ceased.

The alarm clock rang. She put her brushes down.

When she arrived at the gallery, all was confusion. A policeman was trying to unsnarl the traffic behind a double-parked truck and a shabby blue bus, while another truck, equipped with a thirty-foot winch, sat squarely on the sidewalk alongside the gallery, damming the flow of pedestrians. At least forty of Josh's friends and colleagues augmented the crowd, through which a second policeman plunged, shouting commands to disperse while searching for whoever was in charge. Men ran around the gallery roof gesticulating and yelling down directions to the winch operator, and just as Johanna arrived the big paper-mâché object was hoisted into sight from the patio and hung swaying in the fine gray fog.

"I thought Josh was an organizer," she said to Conrad, whom she found flattened against the side of a car with a press sign in the windshield. "Why didn't he arrange things with the police beforehand?"

"And forgo the chaos? You don't know our Josh."

"He'll be paying fines through the nose. Of course, with his golden nose—"

A photographer squeezed them aside for a better shot, but only got the back of a head in a red beret.

"What did they do with the patio roof?" she asked Conrad.

"Tried to dismantle it, but not enough time. So kaput."

"A king-size turd," the photographer said, squeezing around the figure in the red beret.

"Are you reading in literal meaning?" Conrad asked him with lifted brows.

"It's an amphitheater!" shouted the figure in the red beret, a youth in loafers and white gym socks and a long checked overcoat with big padded shoulders. The beret was pulled tightly over his forehead and ears, which gave him a moronic look. "We're taking it up to the outdoor theater on Mount Tam!"

Just then, from the front door of the gallery Josh and Antigone appeared, two solemn figures in the disorder.

"She's had a tranquilizer," Conrad told Johanna. "Actually only a quarter or she'd pass out."

The policeman caught Josh by the elbow and began writing furiously in his notebook, stopping to stab his pen toward the truck parked on the pavement. Josh motioned to an assistant to answer all questions, and began squeezing his way through the crowd to the truck in the street. The winch started again. Its cargo swung through the air until it was over the truck, then it descended in a series of jerks as Josh extended a welcoming hand.

Twenty minutes later, when it had been secured by ropes, Josh climbed in beside the driver and the truck moved down the street, followed by the press car, the bus, and the English taxicab, which was driven by the youth in the beret, who was giving anxious attention to the right-hand steering wheel.

Inside the bus, which was packed mostly with Josh's friends but also with bystanders who had been swept uncertainly aboard by the excitement, Johanna and Conrad sat in the rear, observing.

"That boy should have had Antigone's tranquilizer," Johanna remarked, looking through the back window. The cab's windshield wipers were going, its headlights were on, and the youth's left arm was making hand signals inside the cab. She saw him switch to his right arm, shooting it out the window, only to strike the head of a pedestrian waiting for the light to change. Then the cab stalled, and cars moved between it and the bus. She could barely see it now, the driver crouched behind the wheel like a stone toad.

Across the Golden Gate Bridge, at Mill Valley, the cavalcade stopped dead for half an hour before two white-helmeted motorcycle cops joined it and drove slowly ahead of the wide truck as it began maneuvering the winding road. Suddenly the cab caught up, lights off and windshield wipers at rest, everything apparently under control. The driver had even managed to put a cigarette between his lips, though he hadn't contrived to light it.

In the fuming, grinding bus Josh's friends talked back and forth across the aisle; the others, the street bystanders, sat in uneasy silence, all but an old man in an electric-blue suit and a Panama hat who was talking loudly to himself about kidney stones.

"We've passed the Mount Tam turnoff," Johanna said as they chugged by it.

"Maybe he's taking us to Canada," Conrad said. "I wouldn't put it past him."

But an hour later they reached their destination, a stretch of empty beach with a barge lying at the edge of the surf and a motorboat rising and falling beyond the gray breakers. The bus was emptied of its passengers, except for the street passengers, who stayed where they were. The ropes were undone and the object was carefully lifted down from the truck and carried to the barge, six men on either side, as everyone followed. Suddenly Conrad dashed ahead, argued with Josh for a moment, then plodded back through the sand with something in his hands as Josh stared balefully after him.

"The damn fool, doesn't he know that to a rat the surf's like an atomic explosion?" he said to Johanna, and crouched down in the sand with Antigone, whose pill was wearing off. "He'll be lost without his trademark. But the sun's coming out, it'll cheer him up." The fog had shifted, had heaped up in places and thinned in others, the gaps pouring gold, the masses going a creamy glaring white around bruised centers. "His unfailing luck," he added.

"I think I'll watch alone," Johanna said, stepping away. "There's too much habit between us."

Conrad climbed back inside the bus with Antigone. Johanna saw him sit down by a window and heard a woman's cry as Antigone climbed up his shirtfront into view. His head sank; he was reading from a copy of Vasari's *Lives* that he kept in a back pocket.

A towline ran from the motorboat to the barge. The object

had been set on the barge and was being lashed down. When it was ready Josh walked away from the others and stood motionless. Near the bus, the door of the press car opened and the photographer got out from behind the wheel, stretched, and started down the beach. A figure remained in the back seat, a thin swarthy man whom Johanna recognized from the gallery as Cobbledock, the art critic from the *Herald*. He seemed to be asleep.

Suddenly Josh lifted his hand. A whine broke from the motorboat, and it moved seaward. The towline tautened, then the barge slid down the wet hard-packed sand into the waves, disappeared, and surfaced beyond the breakers. A figure in the boat cut the towline and the boat sped away, leaving the barge rocking in its wake, already sinking.

Maybe the proceedings were over, Johanna thought. It was impossible to tell from Josh's pensive stance if he was satisfied or disappointed, if he had meant the object to float or to sink. He stood like a statue in black, his fingers spread against his thighs, as the photographer jumped around taking pictures. The spectators stood in little clusters, each reflecting Josh's flawless concentration.

She wondered what they were seeing. Certainly more than a mass of paper-mâché lashed to a waterlogged barge. She remembered that she had called it Niagara Falls and Josh had not disagreed. But why had he kept it a secret? Was it the "in" joke carried to its ultimate? The thing was Niagara Falls but it did not matter, and no one but Josh knew that it was Niagara Falls and did not matter?

And yet, these spectators were absorbed in something she was missing. Those six men on either side who had carried it—were they meant to be pallbearers? Was she watching a symbolic funeral, a burial at sea? No, probably not, it was too easy.

Form? Form in action? A big lump metamorphosing as it sank, now just an irregular line above the water?

And now it was gone. The waves rolled over the spot where it had been. Josh turned around and walked slowly back to the vehicles. Suddenly the atmosphere was charged with voices and movement, the sand emptied of everything but a welter of footprints and some cigarette butts.

"Well, did you see it?" she asked Conrad, sitting down beside him in the bus.

"No, but I guess somewhere between Giotto and Titian it sank."

"You're a fast reader."

"I was skipping around. No concentration. I was listening to discussions about kidney stones and the price of artichokes and Lady Bird Johnson."

"Well, what I saw was maybe a burial at sea and maybe a shape becoming less."

"No more valid than kidney stones, I'm afraid."

"I realize that. You're supposed to pass beyond ideas into the act of belief. I didn't pass—"

Josh was suddenly standing over them, lifting Antigone from Conrad's shoulder. "Don't let me interrupt you," he murmured apologetically, moving off, as Johanna called after him: "Who was it that said, 'He isn't great enough to be so humble'?"

He got off and climbed into the press car next to the critic, who was awake and extended his hand cordially. Johanna threw her head back from the window in a fury.

"That's my Johanna," Conrad said. "You look as if you could chew horseshoes."

"This whole thing's a joke. Are you going to joke around too?"

"Why not?—it's my nature. But you're a fanatic. The possessed monk that Josh would like to be—that's right, it's no exaggeration. Nobody can match your certainty. You may be wrong, but what matters is your certainty that you're not."

"But that's what I'm trying to get away from. Don't you understand that yet?"

"I understand, and I'm listening."

"I wish you'd read your Vasari instead," she said as the bus started.

Near the Mount Tamalpais turnoff the bus shuddered to a halt. Johanna looked out the window and saw the tall black taxicab on its side in a ditch, its owner standing nearby, dazed and bloody-nosed.

Josh got out of the press car.

"I'm sorry!" the boy wailed, stumbling up to him.

Josh looked reflectively at the overturned vehicle. "No matter," he said. "We'll call a tow truck from Mill Valley. You'd better get on the bus."

The boy stared shamefacedly at the ground where drops of

158

blood were busily spattering, and began to cry, holding his coatsleeve up to his red-streaming nose. "I lost you in the fog, I started to go up to Mount Tam—that's where you *said*, Josh, didn't I get it right?"

"Don't worry about it," Josh told him gently, stepping back into the press car.

"Poor idiot," said Conrad as the youth lurched aboard and someone pressed a handkerchief into his hand. "Doesn't even get to ride back in the press car."

"I wonder if Josh did tell him Mount Tam," Johanna remarked as the bus started up.

"Sure, he told everybody Mount Tam beforehand. Secrets, false scents, he loves them. Say one place and show up at another. I bet there's people waiting up there right now."

"And what was the point of taking the taxi along in the first place, and having someone drive it who doesn't know how to drive?"

"The point is that there's no point. An action whose beauty lies in its absence of purpose. Except that there just might be a purpose—like everybody wondering why he does what he does. Like carrying Antigone around. And rehiring you. I'd go so far as to say that's what the whole paper-mâché thing was about."

"That leaves him pretty thin."

"As air."

"There must be those of his school who aren't that thin."

"The thing is, there's no way to tell the difference between them."

"I don't know—is it really the emperor's new clothes, or are we missing it? Maybe we're nowhere in sight."

"I know where I am."

"Lucky you. I've even had moments when I've thought of asking Josh for a show. Talk about not knowing where you are. Accompanied by nausea, of course."

"Well, that's something. How much nausea?"

"Like falling into a pile of month-old garbage."

"Bravo, that's my girl."

25

Red-eyed, stubble-chinned, and jumpy with lack of sleep, Morris yanked back the curtain, threw open the window, and filled his lungs with the morning. It was a cold, pure white day, but he wore only his BVDs and a pencil behind his ear. A series of cries rent the air and he saw Aquiline's children throwing themselves face down in the green grass that had surged up everywhere among the rubble and brambles. With a profound yawn he drank in the cool air and watched the children commendingly. He had sat up studying all night—the exam was two days off—and now, at ten o'clock, he had taken a break with coffee and the Sunday papers and was prepared to dig back into his books. His eye was caught by a movement across the street, and he saw a gang of black youths with towering pompadours prowling through the debris where the last remaining house on that side of the street had been torn down. Only a desolate staircase and chimney remained. It came to him that this side of the street would soon be finished off too, probably within the next few months. They would never find a place this cheap. And as he dropped the curtain his exhaustion was hit by a broadside of worry, but, as always, the combination forged itself into a fevered mental energy: he would smash all practical problems, he would arrive at his future with every stop pulled out. Striding across the welter of Sunday papers where Johanna lay stretched out in his red terrycloth robe, reading, he trembled to soar from this preparatory setting into the horizon.

"Ha," she said, "here's the review."

"What review?"

"Cobbledock's, the art critic's. He reviewed Josh's happening."

"What's he say?"

"I don't know," she said, lighting a cigarette. "The usual, I suppose." She threw the sheet of paper aside and picked up another section.

"You never give Josh a chance," he said, scratching his thighs, which always crawled with spiderlegs when he was overwrought.

"Josh is a tenth-rate human being."

"Shit."

"That's exactly what he is. So is Cobbledock."

He picked up the sheet of paper, found the review under a profile shot of Josh standing by the surf, and began to read aloud.

How clearly and well he reads it, thought Johanna, he reads with all the resoluteness of innocence.

"Have you got fleas?" she asked, interrupting him.

"Be quiet and listen," he said, stopping his scratching. " 'Although Joshua Gillingsby of the Antigone Galleries is not given to verbal statement (his one statement being, to define is to defeat), his credo is clear: the creative minority must push its audience to a leap of faith by invalidating accumulated preconceptions. The traditional idea of realistic illusion must be purged from art, for only by destroying the convention of illusion can a state of spiritual anguish be reached—' "

"I knew he'd use the leap of faith, it's vague and inarguable."

" 'Last Thursday, on an isolated stretch of Marin beach, Gillingsby launched a monumental paper-mâché anti-form into the water before a group of some fifty random onlookers. Aggressively absurd, rawly absent of design and symbol, the anti-form spun around—' "

"Spun around? I didn't see it spin around."

" '—spun around in the nexus of pure possibility: to sink, to float, to capsize, to wash back to shore. In a triumph of the aleatory, it chose its course.' "

"He means it sank."

" 'Substance became one with action, the customarily private drama of creation exploded into a collective existentialist experience. In that kinetic moment of truth, the audience was thrown back upon its most inner resources.' "

"Why?"

"Let me go on, dammit! 'Gillingsby's statement is clear. It is no longer enough for art to act as a conveyance. Its validity for modern man, whose patience with interpretation has worn down to the bone, lies in the immediacy of interaction—' "

"Is there more?"

"That's just the beginning."

"I don't have to hear more."

He threw the paper aside with a sharp crackle and furiously

scratched his temples.

"Well, I must say you seem excited about it," she re-marked.

"I'm not excited," he said excitedly. "What do I know about art?"

"Exactly."

"Except this guy sounds alive, and your attitude's dead. Won't do anything with your stuff, won't share it with any-body."

"Are you on to that again?"

"What does it matter if you don't like Josh? What's it got to do with your work? He'll hang it up and that's that!"

"Why is it so important to you!"

"Because"—and he felt himself wobbling wildly on a fence—"because I hate to think of you dividing your time between cruddy office jobs and your real vocation. It's a waste, and it'll always make you unhappy." He was swaying violently now, between gray rational doubt and spiraling venturousness; he leaped. "Because I don't want a wife who's just got some kind of little personal hobby. That kind of marriage is obsolete."

She looked at him intently, her fingers holding the cigarette halfway to her mouth.

"I want to marry someone who's willing to grow," he said, feeling his heart expanding at a tremendous rate of speed. He searched her face for a sign of joy, but there was only tension in it; she was waiting for the final word. "You have any objection to marrying me?" he asked with bursting warmth.

"No," she said, lowering the cigarette. Then the expression he had been waiting for broke in her face like the sun. "I love you more than anything, Morrie," she said in a husky voice, and she shakily ground out the cigarette and got to her feet, like someone standing on a mountaintop overcome by the altitude. Her eyes were wet and shining. She saw him stand-ing there in his BVDs, scratching his thighs, looking at her fondly and excitedly, but with no sign of moving toward her. She wanted him to rise to the moment.

She went to him and put her arms around him. Immediately she felt an erection bloom under his BVDs, but that was not what she wanted at this moment, and she slipped her hips aside. And he, willing to forgo the demands of the flesh this morning, pressed his lips to hers and then gently put his cheek to her temple and stroked her hair tenderly. "I love you," he whispered. "I'm not like you—I've always said things I didn't mean completely, I've told other women I loved them, but with you it's the truth."

He felt a hard breath of air against his neck. "You've got to ruin it."

He was surprised at the very center of his tenderness. "What d'you mean? It's unrealistic not to accept the fact that I've ever been involved with anybody else."

"I don't see why you have to bring it up just now!"

"I'm telling you that you're different."

"Damn it, Morrie."

"I've asked you to marry me, haven't I?"

She wouldn't speak. He tilted her head back and looked into her eyes. "*You,* Johanna Kaulbach, a creature of many and dazzling facets, a painter and philosopher and stunning female, with golden eyes and a rotten temper. *You,* my love, are my woman, now and always."

Two days later he took the med-school exam, and although he would not be notified of the results for several weeks, he felt certain that he had passed with flying colors. His concentrated studies had come to an end. A deep relaxation took hold of him, he felt that he had emerged from a dark cave into life again. Now all he had to do was to attend the organic-chemistry course three nights a week and get a passing grade.

As he walked up the steps of the brightly lit Science Building he felt that everything he had set out to do had gone smoothly and augured well, and when he opened the door of the classroom he smiled with pleasure at the bustle, at all the new faces, particularly those of the women; and it all seemed part of the bountifulness of the brightening world.

He opened his eyes on an orange-and-green-checked cushion which was momentarily unplaceable. Tangerine rug, also unplaceable. Picasso prints on the wall, a bookcase of texts. Light coming out from a bathroom. He yawned and scratched his head. Someone coming out of the bathroom now. Of course, carbon compounds, a clipboard of notes, Miss Dupuy of the creamy skin and black eyes and tight turtleneck sweaters. But in her altogether at the moment, closing the door neatly

163

behind her. She was a neat girl, witty too, but with oceanic things boiling around underneath.

"I've got to go," he said, looking at his watch. It was three A.M.

"Why? You're not married."

"No. But I'm living with someone."

The black eyes were disappointed.

"You want to see me again, Ellen?"

The oceanic business coming out through the eyes, the fingers busy pulling a loose thread from the cushion. Then Miss Dupuy the neat emerged with a dry smile. "I don't think so, actually."

"Right. Wish you'd said yes, but—it was great while it lasted."

As he drove home across the bridge he felt serene. In the past he had been urgent, indiscriminate; and he had exaggerated fleetingly felt emotions and gotten himself into unholy messes. His touch was more honest and direct now, it had more style, more maturity. Johanna had done him good.

He was grateful to her and he loved her, but if they were to marry it would be absolutely essential for him to cultivate some private freedoms. Johanna was one of the great innocents, airily suspended above the temptations and pratfalls of life; but he was not so detached, such rarefied air would kill him. Such rarefied air was good only if you had to cut yourself off from life for some extreme mental stint. But when it was over, and it was over now, you had to deal with life again, and part of life consisted of women, always new women, a long line, stretching into the future like a beam of sunlight. Johanna, being a monolith, could never understand the simple sunnyness of varied sex; summer stood transfixed in the soul when there was a new rendezvous around the corner. Freedom. Excitement. It was one in the eye of old age and the grave. He and Johanna had their own ways of coping with ultimates; she had her painting, and he—an artist without an art, she had once called him that—he had himself.

"I'm knocked out from rapping," he told her as he climbed into bed beside her. "Went to an all-night coffee house after class."

"Oh?" she said. He could not tell from her voice if she was upset and disguising it, or if she believed him. She was facing away from him. The swell of her hip under the blanket and the rim of her small ear, both outlined by moonlight, filled him with guilt, tenderness, and some doubts about philosophy. But she seemed to have fallen back to sleep without any trouble, and slowly all his feelings except his tenderness dissolved in the sanction of her unconcern.

She lay with her eyes open. A section of a continent had cracked off and sunk. She had once had the same sensation when chewing a mouthful of hamburger and suddenly she had heard a crystalline click; with her heart standing still, she had reached in with her fingers and withdrawn almost a whole tooth that had broken off, and it had seemed so astounding, so horrifying and utterly wrong, that she had dropped it and flung her hands to her eyes. Only a mouthful of soft food, to wreak such damage. And only a man tiptoeing home late at night, the stuff of ordinary domestic quarrels. Why was his every action of such earth-shaking moment to her? But she was sure he had risen from another woman's bed to come to hers, and she was not only sick with jealousy, but she felt the shape of death through his defection.

If it was a defection. She was turning into one of those monstrous tight-faced women, sour with suspicion, holding a fistful of chains and locks. He might in fact have sat over a cup of espresso for four hours talking with friends. She dredged up the piece of submerged continent, and with all her strength pushed its raw edge back against the rest of her.

He told her a few days later that in addition to his summer job giving tests at summer schools, he had contracted with a friend, a small taxi-fleet owner, to pick up a few extra dollars by driving a cab on Saturdays and alternate Sundays. She felt he was chastising her, for what she could not be sure, unless it was for not selling her paintings.

"Why should selling my work matter so much to you?" she asked him when he mentioned it the next time.

"It doesn't. Forget it."

But he had never brought up the subject of marriage again.

26

She was still working on the painting of the soldier in the blue tunic, but only altering a line here and there. The picture remained in its first stages. She began to feel starved; it was not only a craving for Morrie, whom she seldom saw, who showed up later and later every night, but some craving of the spirit, which she felt most strongly in the studio. She could satisfy neither craving, and felt a hollowness, as if the heart had been carved out of the world.

Morris sensed this, waxing and waning in his spirits, sometimes bounding in to grab her in his arms, feeling as if the soil of life had been turned over and his future was sprouting like a tree before his eyes; and sometimes mumbling and grousing, unsure of everything. Waxing and waning, he felt her unhappiness, and was sorry for her.

Once he had thought there was nothing at all in her to arouse pity, but she had changed unbelievably. He had wielded an immense power, and this fact both thrilled and disgusted him. He remembered what Rachel, his ex-wife, had written in her Biography of Zero: that he had to have power first, in abundance, before he could be kind. And he wondered if that quivering, pedantic woman had been right; if his Suicide Prevention work, his work with children, his goal to become a psychiatrist—if all this appealed to him and brought out the good in him, the kindness in him, because he was the strong one. And with women, too, all of them; especially Zaidee, and even Johanna. Although it was Johanna's very strength that had attracted him, her look of knowing ultimate things, which he had felt that very first night in her room; no froth, no smalltalk; and that violent sign on her door, the violence of her teeth sinking through his jacket sleeve; and afterward how she had reached up and pressed his hand to her face, an almost pained gesture, but beautiful in its directness. He had not wanted to change any of that, but somehow he had, and he felt a compassion for her that he had never known before.

And yet there was a new frankness in people, a new respect for the instincts; no one went around worshiping monogamy anymore; women were no longer seized with brain fever if their lovers screwed somebody else, they were doing the same thing themselves. And it seemed much healthier than Johanna's wounded heart, her lost eyes. Wouldn't it be better to tell her what he was doing and clear the air? But to tell her would be to lose her. He knew that. Although he didn't yet know if that wasn't what he really wanted.

She painted less and less.

"If you had a show it would revitalize you," he told her.

"Oh, why do you want that so much?"

"It would be good for you. And it would make me happy."

TODAY'S HOROSCOPE
SCORPIO

Do those errands that are important.
Don't overspend or you may regret it.
Stay home and rest tonight.

And because he might come home early tonight to rest, she would feel more cheerful.

She became consciously superstitious, having before been superstitious the way most people are, going around ladders and wishing on the first star. Now she added lore she had never paid any attention to, throwing spilled salt over her shoulder, avoiding cracks in the sidewalk, turning back in her tracks if she saw a black cat. She made up her own superstitions, too, putting her left shoe on first, making a wish if she saw someone walking two dogs, and giving the newel post a tap every time she passed it. She did all these things with worried intensity, repeating a ritualistic phrase, "It will be all right," until she found that she had reduced the phrase to its initials, IWBAR, and that she was saying it under her breath, ubar, ubar, whenever any pain threatened to break to the surface.

The only time the benighted and ignoble phrase was given rest was when they went hiking. The soil was restorative, soothing. But when they passed other hikers, or a farm, or even an empty shack, the salving feeling vanished, as if the hand of man had reached in to remind her of the difference between the self-contained earth and the beings who must find their place on it. Sometimes they came across an abandoned house or shack in the most remote corner of the hills; she would try to circumvent it, but Morris had a streak of curiosity—or of practicality, for he sometimes found a usable item inside—that forced him to explore every empty building they stumbled upon.

Once, having started out late on a Sunday afternoon, they found themselves high on the bald desolate hills of northern Marin County where they had never been before, and where an abandoned warehouse with broken windows stood facing them from the crest of a hill. Johanna stood pulling up handfuls of dry grass and loosing them into the wind. The seeds and stalks drifted away, white against the raisin blue of the sky.

"Listen," he said.

From the warehouse came a wire-thin hum, faint but clear.

He was off; Johanna followed reluctantly. As they approached the warehouse the hum developed into a wild caterwauling of birds, eerie and beautiful. Through a broken window they saw, in a shadowy bluish light, hundreds of small white birds swooping and careening between the floor and the high ceiling, filling the room with deafening warbles and screams, frightening and dazzling in their wild arabesques.

"Are they trapped, do you think?" Johanna asked as they walked away.

"I don't know, they can probably get out when they want to."

"Oh God, I hope so," she said with such intensity that he glanced at her.

"Do you really think they can find their way out again?" she asked, looking back.

"I don't *know*, baby. They got in, they ought to be able to get out."

"But they seem to have gone mad."

He shrugged, lifting the collar of his jacket against the wind.

"We could open the door for them," she said with inspiration, and she ran back to test it, but found it locked.

"Let's go! It's getting dark!" he called.

The sound followed them for a quarter of a mile, until the hills were silent except for the sideswiping boom of the wind.

The summer was uninterruptedly cold and gray. They saw so little of each other that when Johanna went to visit Conrad and Wanda now, she went alone.

"I suppose it'll be five years before Morris and I reach this point," she said, looking at her friends sitting relaxed before the fireplace. "He's got so much work. We hardly ever see each other. I have to consult his horoscope to see what's up with him."

"Do you really?" Wanda asked.

"No, of course not," she laughed.

"Maybe when he starts med school he'll have more time," Conrad said. "At least he'll be free nights."

"I don't see how. Eventually he's going to have to get a night job. Oh, well, maybe I'll get a cat. Do you suppose Closeto will ever father a brood?"

"Our Closeto?" he said, smiling at the animal. "I'm afraid he has the soul of Corot, who was said to have died a virgin."

Closeto luxuriously arched his back in a stretch, as though to show he didn't care. He had grown a little heavier, a little sleeker, like his master. But Wanda was the one who had changed the most. Maybe because she had let her hair grow out —it now fell to her shoulders—but more because she moved and spoke with a certain lightness. But Wanda said it was Johanna who had been transformed.

"You've lost your self-confidence," she told her once when they were alone.

Johanna said, bantering, "According to you, I never had any. You always said I asked too much advice."

"Not advice exactly—aid. There's a big difference. At bottom you were arrogant, you believed completely in yourself."

"I'm trying to broaden my horizons," she said with mock seriousness.

"As long as they're *your* horizons."

"There's an odd thing that's happened, Wanda," she said, dropping her pose. "You told me once that I didn't love Morrie, that I was just suffering a kind of fever. It's not true; at least, it's not true anymore. What I feel is that he's inside me, from head to foot. If you peeled my skin away you'd find Morrie's body inside, like the yolk in an egg. It's as though I'm thinking with his brain and feeling with his heart."

"I suppose that's how it is with me too, in a way. Sometimes I feel that close to Connie."

"Well, it's a good thing, isn't it?" Johanna asked searchingly.

"Well, I suppose it depends on if the other person is a good thing."

Johanna's eyes hardened. "You've never given Morrie half

a chance. You've always kept those Zaidee blinders on. You think he has a subversive effect on me, but I tell you no one's ever been able to lift me higher than Morrie. Even when everything's rotten, there's some force in him, I don't know, that makes me feel it's all worth it.''

''He's good in bed, no doubt.''

''Ah! It's more than that!''

''He hurts you. Maybe that's what you respond to.''

''There's nothing of the masochist in me.''

''I know. That's why it's so odd.''

''I don't understand any of it!'' Johanna said, staring at the floor.

''Speaking of Zaidee, I ran into her the other day in the park. You know that gown I made her? I've got the feeling it set her off in the wrong direction. She's gone hippie. Or maybe it's the right direction. I don't know. She seemed happy. She was expecting a baby.''

''Whose?'' Johanna said quickly.

''Oh, I met him. He must be all of fifteen—a very weird duo.'' She paused. ''You look relieved.''

''Why should I look relieved?''

''You know that you've taken up poses? It doesn't become you.''

Johanna lit a cigarette and blew the smoke out her nostrils. ''I hear Closeto scratching at the back door, you'd better let him in.''

27

Morris was eating breakfast hurriedly, standing up, skimming the front page of the newspaper. Johanna had seen almost nothing of him for the last three weeks except in bed and fleetingly at the breakfast table. Drinking her coffee, she found the back page of the paper.

TODAY'S HOROSCOPE

SCORPIO

You have duties that should be attended to at once. Then consider new romantic interest.

A pain shot through her heart. She crumpled the edge of the paper.

"I'm going to ask Josh to come and look at my work," she said tonelessly.

"You are?" he said, looking up. "Well, I'm damned. Well, that's tremendous, baby." And a blaze of enthusiasm and admiration lit up his face. He gave her a short vital hug and stood back. "Now you're getting off your can and doing something constructive. And Josh'll like them, don't worry."

"Worry. That fool. What does he know?"

"He knows how to hang them in his gallery. Let the buyers bring the aesthetics."

"Yes, I suppose so," she said, stirring her coffee around and around.

A few days later when Josh knocked at her door she had to rearrange her attitude toward him: it would be unthinkable to ask him to her home and treat him like a leper. She gave him a courteous nod and took his threadbare duffel coat, but it set her teeth on edge to have him inside her four walls, and as she looked at the paintings she had displayed through the room she felt a constriction in her chest.

"Whatever became of the boy in the red beret?" she asked conversationally, trying to prolong the moment before he began to study the canvases.

"What boy?" he asked, his eyes on the canvases.

"The one who drove your taxicab into the ditch."

171

"I don't remember him."

"The happening—the barge—he was driving your taxi-cab."

"Oh, yes. I have no idea. He was backward." He had begun walking back and forth in front of the canvases, holding Antigone in his hands and stroking her head as he studied the display. His face was, as always, benign, inscrutable. It did not change when thirty minutes later he finished and turned to her. "They're not at all what I expected. They're more or less in the mainstream."

Her eyes flicked away from him as she asked: "Do you like them?"

"Like? I never *like* a work of art, the word is meaningless unless you're buying a pair of socks."

"You know what I mean," she said impatiently. "Do they stir you, do they reach you?"

"I'm too far from representational work of any sort. Picasso and Braque, for example, reach me weakened by their imagery . . . You understand the difference between imagery and the thing-in-itself, between the attempt at illusion on a flat canvas and the reality of an object taken in its entirety . . ."

"Oh, yes, the tennis ball on the shoebox."

"Exactly. I realize it's a personal response, of course, but shared, I think, by the generating force of the contemporary movement."

"In other words, you don't like my paintings. If they were a pair of socks you wouldn't buy them."

"I'll hang them, Miss Kaulbach," he said decisively.

"But you don't like them."

"What difference—"

"I'd just like to hear you say it."

"All right, I don't."

Thank God, she said to herself.

"But, you see, they're not beyond my range of appreciation. I *appreciate* Braque. I don't appreciate Meissonier."

"I'm surprised you've even heard of him," she said ungraciously.

"To be frank, I'd expected something along the old lines when I came here. Something like your room here." He gestured at the furnishings and paused. "But, you know, you've got some really good things," he said, running his toe along the pattern of the rug as she fought down an urge to strike him.

"What about the financial end of it!" she demanded, and he brought his toe back. "Will I have to be involved?"

"I suppose you'll have to be involved to the extent of putting the money in your pocket," he replied with an amiable smile.

"You suppose they'll sell, then."

"There's always a market for Expressionism. It's not my bag, I prefer to create markets. But I'm not rigid."

"Then it's settled. The discussion is ended."

"Hardly. Which ones are you going to exhibit?"

"Take your pick," she said indifferently. She smoked a cigarette and stared at a blue arabesque in the rug as he made his selection. He chose twenty, among them the Medieval City, the Mouse Battalion, and the portraits of Herr von Kaulbach and the thorn-crowned Aquiline.

"Not that one," she said, putting the portrait of Herr von Kaulbach aside.

"Who is he?"

"It's not for sale," she told him without answering. "Is there anything else to discuss? When do you want them?"

"Wait, wait, slow down. We've got to talk about prices. What prices are you considering?"

"I leave that to you."

"It's not the usual thing," he said, lifting his eyebrows at her insouciance.

"But it doesn't matter, does it? When do you want them?"

"I could possibly give you a month starting the middle of August. But summer's a bad time. October would be better if you preferred it."

"No, the sooner the better."

"Suit yourself. And Miss Kaulbach, as a favor to you, I'll take them down to the gallery and have them framed there. I'll send somebody around with the truck so you won't be bothered with all that."

"I don't want any favors," she said shortly.

"But, my dear girl," he returned with a slow smile, "the whole transaction is a favor, surely you realize that. You're very good. You're remarkably good, in fact. But there are others in this city who are remarkably good, but I don't come to their homes on their request, and then and there promise them space and let them choose the time, especially when I'll have to do some mighty reshuffling to manage it."

"In that case," she said quickly, "maybe you'd rather forget about it."

"No. I just want you to understand the reality of the situation," he said with a steady, glowing look in his eyes, which were fixed on hers.

Her face had gone very red and hot. She looked at Morris' desk, at the flat creased cushion of his chair. "The reality of the situation," she said at last, "is that those other good painters aren't as good as I am. You know quality when you see it."

"Whatever you say," he told her genially. "Have them at the gallery by the tenth of August." He put on his duffel coat and rearranged Antigone on his shoulder.

"Thank you very much," she said at the door, bringing out the words with difficulty. When he was gone she poured herself a straight shot of whiskey to rid her mouth of its bad taste.

But the effort bore miraculous fruit. Morrie's withdrawal faded, he was more cheerful and more amorous, and though his schedule remained full, he managed to squeeze more time in for her. He even took the afternoon off from work the first day of the show. At Johanna's request, there had been no formal opening.

"The price Josh put on them staggers me," she told Morris as they walked from picture to picture. "Fifteen hundred, eighteen hundred, twelve hundred. Eight hundred for two square feet of Aquiline."

"Terrific. Aim high or the buyer won't."

A small shudder ran down her spine.

"What's Josh's cut, anyway?"

"Most dealers take half, he takes only a fourth."

"The guy's a saint!"

"That's his ambition."

"Not many people," he said, glancing around the gallery. "You should have had a regular opening."

"Don't worry, the place will be full after Cobbledock's review. It'll be a glorious review; he and Josh are like blood brothers. I can't stand the thought of what he'll write."

He took her around the waist and beamed at her. "You're just like me before the entrance exam—antsy for no good reason."

He was in such good spirits that she suddenly felt better. Her pictures were hanging for all the world to see, and Morris was proud of her. It didn't matter so much, while she stood in the radius of his approval, that the Medieval City and the big earplug were in the same room.

As she had expected, Cobbledock's review was more than favorable. The paintings were "a brilliant fusion of perspective and mood, a richly personal interpretation of the human condition in which a superlative craftsmanship in no way lessens the effect of a genuinely original vision . . ." What is he *talking* about? she asked herself. And how did he square all this with Josh's happening, about which he had written that the authentically creative artist must purge himself of all realistic illusion? The review only solidified her belief that he believed in nothing. He had slept through the sinking of the sublimely existential barge, and he must have been wheeled out comatose from her superlative craftsmanship. Nevertheless, when she saw him she thanked him, for courtesy's sake.

Her first sale was the one picture she had hoped would not be sold.

She waited until she had received and cashed the check for the picture, then she went to Aquiline's door, where she stood a moment before knocking. Aquiline answered the door in her pink chenille bathrobe.

"There's a complicated thing for me to explain," Johanna said. "May I come inside?"

"But of cou'se," replied the woman with her infuriating smile, pushing the door open.

The blinds were up and the gray afternoon light poured into the purple-and-blue chambers as into a dark aquarium, reminding Johanna of Klee. She forced her mind back to the purpose of her visit.

"You know that I paint," she stated.

"I seen you splattered up on occasion."

"I painted a picture of you once, when I first met you, when I thought you were an Aunt Jemima. I painted you with a crown of thorns on your head and a halo blindfolding your eyes."

Aquiline slowly crossed her arms.

"And I painted white blood oozing out from under the thorns."

Aquiline's face seemed to swell. "Why you do that?"

"To show that the blood had become something that it wasn't. The woman in the picture identified with white, not black."

Her arms uncrossed slowly. Suddenly she pinched her cheek. "White blood. Make me puke. Lemme see that thing, you see me tear it up!"

"That's why I've come," said Johanna uneasily. "The picture was sold."

"To *who?*"

"I don't know, really. Someone with a lot of money."

"White?"

Johanna nodded.

"Shit! That bastard he touch that face and he think he feel me!"

"He doesn't know you exist, Aquiline. To him it's an anonymous face, a symbol."

"My ass. You say it *my* face!"

Johanna chewed despairingly on her lip for a moment. "After I got to know you better I did consider throwing the picture away. The reason I didn't was vanity—it was a good picture. And then when the dealer chose it, I went along with him, I don't know why. I must have suspended my judgment—I really didn't want to sell any of my paintings, at least not through him. But that's a complicated story too."

"You too complicated for you' own good. You better take you' complications out of here."

"The painting sold for eight hundred dollars. My share is six hundred." She took the bills from her purse and laid them on top of the television set.

Aquiline walked over and swept them to the floor.

"You could buy things for your children," Johanna said, flushing. "You could give it to Charles, he works with people who could use it."

"You know I wouldn't touch it when you come down here. You give me a big show to glorify you'self, and still wind up with you' money."

"I don't want it. I couldn't keep it."

"You don't leave it layin' here stinkin' up my house!"

Johanna started to the door, but Aquiline came after her and pulled her back with a grip so crushing that the flesh was bruised blue afterward. She pushed the girl down to the floor and stood over her, and Johanna picked up the scattered bills. She stood up, took a book of matches from her pocket, and set the bills aflame. As they blackened and curled, she laid them in an ashtray, from which a long plume of smoke thickened in the silence. Aquiline was still scowling at her. But when the smoke had evaporated, she said: "Next time you come down here we don't speak no more about this."

Morris was infuriated when she told him. "Six hundred bucks! You're insane!"

"What does it matter to you?" she muttered. "It's my money."

"Of course it's your money, what are you getting at? I don't care. But it was pure egomania, a grand gesture. You could have given it to CARE if you didn't want it, or SNICK, or the Salvation Army, for Christ's sake! But to burn it!"

And so the sale of her first painting was a complete financial and moral failure. But a few days later the medieval painting was sold, for a good deal more, and this time without any guilt attached to it. She telephoned Morrie from the gallery, knowing he wouldn't mind being interrupted at work for news of this kind. His response was one of almost bursting enthusiasm; he said he would even cancel his Suicide Prevention work that night and celebrate with her. "It'll be a double celebration—I passed the entrance exam!"

"Morrie! How great! They called you?"

"No, they send you the results."

"Did it come to the house?" she asked, puzzled.

"The office. I passed, baby!"

"I'm really glad, Morrie—congratulations!"

"I've got to hang up. See you tonight."

She put the receiver down slowly, wondering why he received mail at the office, and how many personal letters went there instead of to the apartment. "Ubar, ubar," she said under her breath, turning and fixing her eyes on the canvas that had just sold for eighteen hundred dollars, to draw confidence from it.

That night they bought champagne and lobsters and asked Wanda and Conrad to join them. Conrad had been disappointed that she had exhibited through Josh, knowing how she felt about the man; but her high spirits were contagious and he promised they would be there.

"You've become a couple of sybarites," he said appreciatively, sucking his fingers at the end of the meal.

"Connie hopes to become a sybarite after we're married," Wanda said, "but I'm going to keep him on a very small allowance."

Morris thought the joke was in bad taste, but Conrad laughed.

"Then you've worked things out," Johanna said, pleased for them.

"I told him every day for six months that it didn't matter to me," said Wanda, "and it finally sank in."

"What sank in," Conrad elaborated, "was the alternative. Facts are facts—with my age and lack of skills I can't find a job. I'm destined to bring in what I've always brought in from the piddling freelance work I do, and that's all there is to it. And Wanda's got a good job that she enjoys, and she's paid well, and that's all there is to *that*. So either we accept this financial set-up and get married anyway, or we take the alternative route and say: This is untraditional, this is an aberration, we can't do it. The alternative was insane. Very sanely, we want to invite you to our wedding on September twenty-fourth."

"We'll drink to that," Morris said, raising his glass. He didn't approve of Conrad airing his and Wanda's financial situation in public, but he appreciated the common sense and teamwork behind the words, and, not least, the optimism. "We'll drink to the joys of marriage," he said, and he put his other hand on Johanna's.

28 Wanda would have been content to be married in the Unitarian chapel, in their own living room, or even at the City Hall, but Conrad felt that the ceremony should be held in a café garden. It was the Renoir in him. He saw an arbor, wooden benches, someone with an accordion. They discussed the growing popularity of outdoor weddings—in Golden Gate Park, on Mount Tamalpais, even at the beach. But though these settings were appealing in their way, they were too staged, too whimsical. "I see something familiar and natural to us," he told Wanda, who was touched by his concern.

"You never know about people," she said to Johanna. "Wouldn't you have thought Connie was the sort to amble down to City Hall with a minimum of fuss? But he wants something very special. It's like a painting he's working up in his mind."

Johanna listened with envy. When—perhaps even if—she and Morrie got married, it would be on the spur of the moment; it would be a breakneck trip to Reno crammed sideways into his schedule, and they would probably have two strangers as witnesses. Still, that shouldn't matter, the important thing was to get married; and this urge of hers made her think back to the men who had wanted to marry her, who had thought marriage would make her love them. They had been in the grip of some desperate credulity which she had never been able to fathom; she thought now with compassion of Philip, whom she had shuffled off with only a week's regret; Philip had thought the wedding ring would somehow make her love him. She understood now that there was a kind of longing for another human being that eclipsed the brain. And with the small light that remained she looked ahead with powerless misgivings, at the same time drawing the keenest joy from the thought of Morris and herself as man and wife.

The prospect of marrying waxed and waned in Morris' mind. At times he withered at the thought of it, and also at the thought of taking a full-fledged professional direction at this point; his old fantasy would flood back into his soul, and forgetting that he had agonized over his future all winter, he would feel that he had plunged without proper reflection. And here he was, stuck in an irreversible situation. There was no way of going back unless he wanted to waste all his months of study and to break off with Johanna; the two things were inextricably interwoven. And anyway, he had to take a stand in life; he would be forty in November (and when he thought of this stark milestone his skin roughened with gooseflesh). And yet, and yet—that haze of golden possibility that surrounded lack of commitment even at its most anguished moments! And yet, and yet—he had chosen the only thinkable course, and inside this course he had carved out a pocket of freedom for himself in the sexual realm. This *modus vivendi* was proving workable—Johanna never questioned him—and there was no reason to believe that it would not continue workable after marriage. And so, why not take a day off and drive up to Reno and truly cement his future? And then the old fantasy seemed a paltry adolescent dream, and he would impatiently wish to be soldered legally to the woman of his choice. If only she would insist on it. But she insisted on nothing. Such an attitude almost precluded the necessity of making a decision. He wondered, with both relief and longing, where her fiery ultimatums had gone.

On Saturdays when Morris moonlighted with his friend's cab, Johanna wandered over to Conrad's and Wanda's and took part in their preparations. She went along with Wanda to shop for a wedding dress, and she watched Conrad hammering benches together in the backyard. They had decided on the backyard. It was small, but could hold a table seating ten people. It consisted mainly of hardy geraniums and a scaly fence; the rest was covered with concrete, and housed a garbage can and a pile of rain-sodden cardboard boxes. Wanda and Johanna were skeptical of the yard's potential, but Conrad was sure that he could turn it into a proper setting. "The great thing," he said, "is that it gets the afternoon sun." A fact attested to by Closeto with all the singlemindedness of a former indoor cat who has discovered the joys of warm earth late in life.

With September, the sun had emerged again, robust and steady. Wanda sunbathed, looking over recipes and planning an exotic smorgasbord, as Conrad whitewashed the fence, propped it upright, cleared away the old boxes, and began making two long benches to go alongside the pushed-together cardtables that would serve as the banquet table. "Chairs won't do," Wanda told Johanna as they watched him, "it's got to be wooden benches. Connie gets bees in his bonnet and he won't be swayed. Like the time he wanted to buy me a hat. I never wear hats, but he insisted I could be very happy if only I had the right hat. I told him I could never be happy with a hat, but he poked around stores for weeks and finally came home with a very funny-looking blue knit cap. But when I put it on, it looked smashing and I fell in love with it. You've seen it—I wore it all winter. That's the kind of bees in the bonnet he gets."

But Conrad wasn't much of a carpenter, and he hit snags that made him put the benches aside and turn to other things until his inspiration returned. He painted the back wall of the house in alternate stripes of yellow and pale blue. He collected all the coffee cans in the house, painted them white, planted them with geraniums, and set them around the concrete floor and down the side of the back-porch stairs. He bought a couple of striped canvas garden chairs and put them in a corner of the yard, and with a stroke of genius painted the concrete floor lawn-green. Statues were the next thing. A friend of his turned out cheap but passable pre-Columbian figures in porous red clay, and he set two of these by the door leading to the alley.

"You're in a frenzy of creativity," Wanda complimented him.

"It's not just for the ceremony, my love. We'll sit out here like landed gentry from now on, sipping lemonade and reading the Sunday papers." And as a final touch he hung a paper lantern from the landing. Then he returned to the benches, spilling nails, banging his fingers, and sending Closeto scurrying off for quiet.

"I don't know where the days have gone," Wanda told Johanna over the phone at one o'clock on the morning before the wedding. "We thought we had so much time, and we haven't accomplished anything. It'll be a complete failure! Why couldn't we have just gone to the City Hall or driven up to Reno?"

"Be glad he wants it this way."

"Glad! If you knew how nervous I am. And him!" But

there was a forlorn note in Johanna's voice that took Wanda out of herself. "What about you, Johanna? When—?"

Johanna hesitated. "Well, Morrie couldn't plan anything until he passed the exam—"

"But he passed a month ago, didn't he?"

"Oh, yes. And he's been in tremendous spirits since, and I'm sure that any day now—"

"Why don't you *tell* him you want to get married? You act as if you're afraid of rocking the boat. What kind of a boat is it if it can't be rocked?"

"Things are never as simple as they seem on the surface—"

"Oh, come on, either take the plunge or break up. And you know which one I'd suggest. What you've got now is a mess; your whole life is going down the drain."

"That's interesting. My life's going down the drain. I've sold all but three of my paintings, I've got a nest egg, I don't have to worry about working. I've got a name. That sounds as if my life is going down the drain."

"But you haven't painted for months. You're depressed, and the only thing you ever talk about is him."

"The trouble with you is that you think of life as a problem to be solved, not a mystery to be enjoyed."

"Well, I leave you to your mystery—but you don't seem to be enjoying it."

"Put it this way; I'd rather have this kind of mystery than not have it. I'd rather be unhappy with him than happy without him."

"God, you sound like an old Helen Morgan torch song. You've turned into a bleeding doormat. The whole mystery is that love has made you a fool."

"I know that."

Wanda was silent for a moment. "Oh, Johanna, I'm sorry. It's just that it's so late and I can't sleep and I'll be a wreck tomorrow and we're leaving right after for three days in Mendocino. I woke you up. You want to go to bed."

"No, it's all right."

"I ought to stop talking. I ought to go back to bed. I ought to take a sleeping pill."

"It might make you groggy tomorrow."

"I suppose everything will turn out all right. It's got to, Connie's put so much work into it."

"I don't know what you're so nervous about. He's doing

it for you—everything else is secondary, if you forget your lines or the food isn't perfect. What does it matter?"

"I know, I know, you're absolutely right. I'll go to bed now."

"Take Henry James with you, you say he puts you to sleep."

"Tonight he'd probably enthrall me. It's that kind of night. I think I'm going crazy."

"But you're happy?"

"Oh God, yes. Oh God, I've got to go to bed. Two thirty sharp tomorrow, Johanna."

29

Conrad snapped awake at dawn, overwhelmed by the number of things to be done by two thirty. In addition to getting a haircut, picking up his trousers from the cleaners and the wedding bouquet from the florist's, he must somehow redeem the two benches, which were fortified by a superabundance of nails, dented all over with the half-circles of hammerblows, yet were still wobbly.

Wanda woke at his side, and he counted on his fingers all the things he had to do.

"Why did you put it all off till the last day?" she asked in the voice of catastrophe, and she listed all that *she* must do: straighten the flat, polish the wineglasses and silverware, set the table in the yard, slice bread, chop pickles, onions, hard-boiled eggs, olives . . .

"You should have done all that earlier!" he snapped, jumping out of bed and rattling the shade up on the red sunrise.

"I happen to go to work every day. Not like some people! Why couldn't you have done something besides knock yourself out over those damn benches?"

"All right! All right! You don't like them, we won't use them."

"No!" she said angrily.

He sat down on the bed next to her. "Look, Wanda, we've got to collect ourselves. Why are we getting upset? We've got hours to spare."

"I know," she said uncertainly, and she counted the hours. "Seven. That should be enough, shouldn't it? But we have to dress, too." Suddenly she asked: "How do I look? Horrible? I hardly slept at all."

"I didn't either," he confessed. "But you look beautiful."

"Really?"

"Really." He leaned over and took her hand. "This old cynic is very happy today."

"Who ever called you that?" she asked softly, and touched his cheek.

The day began. Wanda put *Rigoletto* on the phonograph and hurried to make breakfast. They felt they should eat a large breakfast to fortify themselves, but when it was ready they had no appetite, and instead drank black coffee. Then Conrad pulled on his old clothes and, with Closeto at his heels, hurried down the back stairs for a final attack on the benches. He was still dissatisfied at nine thirty, but broke away to drag the unsightly garbage can into the alley. When he came back, he stared at the benches, unsure if he should leave them as they were or have another go at them. It didn't really matter if they wobbled, but the rest of the yard was perfect and he wanted the benches to be perfect too. But the errands. He ran upstairs and checked with Wanda to see if there was anything she needed, then rushed out to the car.

When he returned, *Rigoletto* was still ringing jubilantly through the rooms, but Wanda was crying. She had broken two dishes in her rush and cut her finger. He bound the finger up for her—"But I can't get married with a bandaged finger," she groaned—and began polishing the silverware as if his life depended on it. Together they cleaned the house and set the banquet table in the backyard, iced the cake, and put the kitchen to rights. The smorgasbord was done, heaped dishes and platters filled the refrigerator and pantry, ready to be taken out after the ceremony. It was not quite noon. He was rocked with desire for her.

The bedroom was bright with sunshine. She watched him pull off his clothes in the alien light. He was a man of evening habit, a responsive but gentle lover. Now she felt his urgency lift all the hairs at the back of her neck. She knew it was the tension of the day that had brought him to this height, yet she wasn't disappointed. She remembered how jealous she had been of Johanna in the past; she had hated his obsessiveness; *she* had wanted to be the object of that intensity. But she knew now that Johanna belonged to an offshoot of his nature, a branch that might endure but would never flower. She, Wanda, belonged to his whole nature. And so this abrupt sunlit nakedness, instead of minimizing his usual gentle lovemaking, seemed merely a happy gratuity. She accepted everything about him, everything about him was somehow right and made her happy. She unbuttoned her robe, forgetting the clock.

Making up for their indulgence afterward, they rushed to shower and dress, bumping into each other, helping each other, and finally emerged from the bedroom, first one, then the other; Conrad in dark blue blazer and gray slacks, his fringe of newly barbered hair glossy with brushing, his seamed jaws splashed with cologne; Wanda in a pale blue dress almost white against her tan, her blond hair long and loose, a vein in her neck pulsing visibly. Spreading her skirt out carefully, she sat down next to him on the sofa. She wore a pair of moonstone earrings which she kept twisting, while he loosened and tightened his necktie. Suddenly he leaped to his feet. "I forgot the bouquet!" he cried, staring at her as if all was lost.

"It doesn't matter," she assured him, lighting a cigarette with bumping fingers.

"Are you crazy? Of course it does!" He squinted at his watch. "One thirty, there's time. Sit tight, my love, I'll be back in ten minutes." Hurrying down the front steps, he noticed that he had begun to perspire, and hoped his shirt wouldn't be limp by the time of the ceremony. Maybe the backyard was the wrong place, it would get *too* much sun, the guests would have sunstroke. "Sunstroke," he muttered as he backed up and nervously acknowledged a grudging quality in the car; suddenly he was certain that, despite the full tank indicated by the gas gauge, the fuel had leaked mysteriously away and the car would come to a dead stop. *Wallet,* he thought simultaneously, and his hand shot to his blazer, where it felt a reassuring bulge. "What else?" he said aloud. "This is impossible," and glancing in the rear-view mirror as he pulled out from the curb, he half expected to see parts of the car littering the street, or the flat going up in flames, but he saw, instead, Closeto.

Why was he asleep there in the gutter? Conrad's shirt was suddenly, amazingly, wringing wet, yet he was cold as a block of ice. He stopped the car and got out and saw with brain-hammering confusion that the open yellow eyes were vacant. Trembling, he swept the animal up in his arms and ran up the front steps, but froze with an inhibition that seemed to come from the outside. Turning around and around before the door, he was aware only of the fact that he could not go inside. Then emptiness filled his head; the street with its cars and figures grew completely silent. He went down the stairs and got back into the car, put it in gear, and drove on, Closeto on the seat beside him. He drove several blocks before he remembered the bouquet, then he turned and headed in the direction of the florist's shop.

The shop was cool and dark and smelled of earth. It was a tiny shop, a hole in the wall, a one-man operation. The florist was a very old man, but Conrad noticed how black his hair still was and how it grew straight up from the forehead with great vitality. A red ballpoint pen was stuck into the hair, behind a long creased ear. His voice was vital, too, and reverberated against the walls. "Just a minute, sir! Got it right here for you! How's that for an old-fashioned nosegay?" There was pride in his eyes as he handed over his small masterwork. The bright buttons of flowers glowed vividly between them. Conrad silently pushed a five-dollar bill across the counter. The cash register was punched in equal silence, and he walked away with the nosegay hanging at his side. But at the door he turned around with an effort at goodwill. "It's very nice," he said tonelessly.

In a while he would have to make normal conversation with the guests. Impossible. Why not tell them? Why not tell Wanda, at least? But he knew he couldn't do that to her, today. The niggardly slice of time he had left for Closeto cut him like a knife. Hurrying back to the car, he threw the nosegay on the dashboard and, for the first time, sank his eyes into the dead animal. He felt something huge crushing his chest, something never to be surmounted. Visions pierced him as he reconstructed the morning: Closeto overlooked in the busy preparations, not even fed, following him when he dragged the garbage can into the alley. That's what must have happened, Closeto locked out in the alley where he had never been before—timid fence-bound Closeto. Finally wandering out to the street and hiding under the car while he and Wanda polished glasses and listened to *Rigoletto* and made love. And then—

His hand smoothed the fur with long trembling strokes. The body was unmarked. There was no blood. He was overwhelmed by the perfection of it, by the delicate striations of the forehead, the whiskers growing from neatly lined bands of tiny puckers along the muzzle, the triangular nose the color of a new eraser, the small cushions of the paws each holding a beautifully curved, translucent claw. And Closeto was young, a young creature still; he had just begun to enjoy the geranium bushes and the dirt, and maybe in time he would have known the joys of mating. "It was too soon," Conrad whispered, and he remembered the days and nights in the small room when Closeto slept by his side on the cot, or sat watching him as he painted. Maybe he had made too much of him; people said so: but there were basic, stubborn things in him that he could not question, and his loyalty to this creature was one. Closeto's company had been a great gift to him. Those long evenings when he sat in the only chair in the room, reading, with Closeto in his lap. He would fall asleep and wake late and Closeto would raise his head, and a look of great intimacy, of deep mutual understanding, passed between them.

He felt if he were to give vent to the pressure in his chest, and cry, he would never stop again, and the pressure turned into one of hatred for everything outside the car, for the world, for the wedding that kept nagging him through his grief. He looked bitterly at his watch. Unbelievable, frightening: twenty-five to three. But a melting, ecstatic relief filled him now; he would give himself five minutes more, and in those five minutes he would make everything right again.

"Closeto," he said softly. "Come back now. Come back now." He sat up, aware that some mental aberration was taking place in him, yet unable to give it up. He looked with hope at the yellow eyes. They had grown glazed; the muzzle had a pinched look. He sat on, incapable of moving, and the sorrow that pierced him the deepest—for he was unable to admit that he himself had driven the wheels over Closeto—was that Closeto had been excluded all morning; that Closeto, who was such a great part of their lives and never doubted it, had been pushed aside; that the last day of his life had had to be spent in abandonment and fear, without love.

It was almost three when he got out and opened the trunk of the car and put Closeto inside. Slamming the lid shut, he forced his grief into a corner deep inside him and drove back to the flat.

All the parking spaces were taken by the guests' cars. Parking three blocks away on a hill, he grabbed the nosegay and ran down the sidewalk, bursting into the crowded living room with a sharp smile and searching for Wanda's face. He took her into the hall.

"Look," he said, holding her elbow tightly, "believe me when I say it was something beyond my control."

"Damn it, Connie! It's three o'clock!"

"I couldn't help it."

188

"But what happened?" she asked, her anger suddenly replaced by a searching look.

"Nothing. An accident—unnerving, but nothing bad. I had to help. I'm sorrier than I can say."

If she looked at him for another minute, the day would fall in ruins. He thrust the nosegay out to her and straightened his blazer. "I'd better say hello to everybody."

"Where's Closeto?" she asked suddenly. "I can't find him anywhere."

"I took him down to a kennel this morning," he threw over his shoulder, starting for the other room, "I'd rather he wasn't alone while we're gone."

"But why? The neighbors said they'd feed him. Why would you do that?"

He shrugged, and threw her a wildly gay smile.

"This wedding's giving you a nervous breakdown," she chaffed, following him.

"I think so," he agreed, and went to greet the guests, shaking hands with such fervor that he was pelted with jokes about the nervousness of grooms. "Sherry?" he asked all around, shakily removing the stopper from the decanter.

"You need it, old man."

"Watch it, Conrad, you're spilling."

He downed the glass in a gulp, feeling not the smallest bud of warmth in his constricted chest. But he had had time to collect himself. He felt strangely abstract now, austere. Wanda came up beside him. He took her hand. He began picking out faces—Reverend Douglas', young, casual, unpriestly; Johanna's, smiling, cheerful; Morris', crude and jolly, almost hectic; the others', all smiling, all in good spirits; his own—he glanced at it in the mirror across the room—colorless, its smile too sharp. It would have to do.

". . . and the benches," Wanda was saying to the others, smoothing over his late arrival, "the trouble we had with the benches. You may wobble a little."

"What's a wedding," said someone, "if everyone doesn't wobble?"

The conversation was so trivial that Conrad looked at the floor. The approaching ceremony made everyone silly; why couldn't it make them great? A stony hunger grew in him for something hallowed, invincible, eternal. He lifted his eyes to Reverend Douglas' blue-striped seersucker suit and red tie, and he wanted to see a black robe and white ruff. And he did not want to go out into the backward, he wanted to stand in a gray stone cathedral whose floor was filled with ancient vaults, he wanted to feel the inevitability of death and the silence that follows it, to grasp the multitudes who lie in it and who will lie in it, he wanted to make death less lonely for his cat and make it meaningful too . . . And he knew that these feelings would sound utterly lugubrious if he spoke them, yet they burnt through him like acid through metal.

30

Reverend Douglas' boyish face creased with a smile as he glanced at his watch and casually extended his hand to the door.

The backyard awaited them in a glare of sunlight. The white tablecloth, the plates and glasses all gleamed, the geraniums blazed, overhead the sky was intensely blue. Silence descended with a minimum of coughs and shuffling feet. Conrad and Wanda stood together. Her pale blue dress was crisp and fresh against her brown skin. He saw the small vein in her throat beat rapidly.

"Friends, here in your presence, we are gathered to allow Conrad and Wanda to express their mutual commitment to each other, their mutual love for each other, and to join them in lawful marriage . . ."

A breeze fluttered through the geranium leaves. Conrad felt the breeze on his neck, then the steady beat of the sun. In one of the back windows of an adjoining building, an old woman sat and watched.

". . . and before the world, this choice to be respected and encouraged by all, knowing that through such respect and encouragement . . ."

He felt Wanda's fingers stretch out to his. He took her hand. In her other hand, its little finger bandaged, she held the nosegay. The small flowers were intensely bright—blue, white, orange. He looked away from them. The words went on. There was a silence, followed by a reading of the poem he and Wanda had chosen.

> I strolled across
> An open field;
> The sun was out;
> Heat was happy.
>
> This way! This way!
> The wren's throat shimmered,
> Either to other
> The blossom sang.
>
> I came to where the river
> Ran over stones:
> My ears knew
> An early joy . . .

His throat tightened. He looked at the sky and concentrated on the silver speck of an airplane whose drone was barely audible over Reverend Douglas' voice.

> And all the waters
> Of all the streams
> Sang in my veins
> That summer day.

Another silence followed.

"Conrad, is it your free choice and sincere desire to take Wanda as your wedded wife?"

He cleared his throat and answered, making ready with the ring. More words—then, "With this ring I thee wed," and he slipped the ring on Wanda's finger. "Let us join in silence," said the reverend, and there was a long emptiness that seemed never to end.

"May these two find happiness in this union . . . may they ever remain in sympathy and understanding, living according to the ways of truth and beauty and love."

It was over. It had been both a wedding and a funeral, neither of which he had been able to respond to because of the other. He kissed his wife, bringing to the embrace the distant sense of apology he felt. But Wanda was radiant, everyone seemed genuinely happy, and he realized that to them all he seemed no more strange than the average tense groom. He turned to the table with new confidence, with a certainty that he would be able to see the day through. But the solemnity of the ceremony had been in accord with his sorrow; when the hired accordionist sent out the first rich burst of music he underwent a deep wrench, and pressed his tongue hard against his palate as the yard swam before his eyes.

He felt himself sitting down on the bench that he had labored over so long, and he no longer understood what he had wanted from these benches, from the yard. He understood death, that was all, and he knew that sorrow was truer than joy. Someone waved at the old woman who was still looking from her window, and she called down some congratulation in Italian. Other people had come to their windows at the sound of the accordion, and a child's head appeared over the alley fence. It was let in through the gate and came shyly, plump and red-cheeked, to the table for a piece of cake, urged on by the guests. As he watched, the thought came to Conrad that someday he and Wanda might have a child, but he was not touched. He looked at Wanda's ring gleaming in the sunlight as she cut the cake, and he felt bitterly impatient with her, as if she symbolized a long unreality that must be borne until reality could be met again, in the trunk of the car with the spare tire and greasy tools.

He watched himself eating and drinking, and he heard his voice coming from him easily, but from the tip of his tongue, not from inside. His only comfort lay in the thought of the end of the festivities. He and Wanda had made reservations at a Mendocino hotel and they were packed and ready to go, but he would find an excuse to get away for a short while —he could say he had to get gas for the car, anything—and he would go somewhere and be alone with Closeto again, and bury him. After that point his thoughts faded.

The soreness of his lungs made him sigh often, covertly, filling his chest with air and releasing it with no sense of having reached the suffocating knot. He took small bites of food, chewed them to a pulp, and swallowed painfully, as if they were sandpaper. The champagne glasses around him were filled time and time again while his remained at the same level. Wanda suggested he loosen his tie, and he did with a startled burst of cooperativeness which he managed to turn into a loud joke about the serenity of brides and the shredded nerves of grooms, but by this time the subject was stale, and he fell silent. He laid his hand on hers and tried to summon the feelings he had had for her that morning, and failed. But Wanda's eyes shone, her voice was soft and vibrant, a film of perspiration shone on her flushed face. He felt the sun burning his skin, but his fingers and feet and the inside of his mouth were cold.

All afternoon his lips and hands continued to move, but his eyes were like stone, and he knew that even when he laughed they remained estranged. From those cold sockets he beheld a vast panorama of time. He saw the world divided into centuries, each one cut off from the one before, and in those centuries he saw lives all cut off from each other, and he saw his own life divided, pushed into isolated groups of years: childhood, youth, his early manhood, his middle years in the small room, now his life with Wanda, each section alone, with its own memories. Everything, everything passed. He looked at the two rows of guests, and his eyes paused at Johanna. That time of his life was over, too. And this day, with its acute loss and gain, would eventually belong to the past. His mind leaped into the future, he saw himself thinking of Closeto calmly, all grief behind him. He longed for that moment, he wanted it now, he wanted to respond to the festivities, and to love Wanda; and suddenly he was engulfed by his love for her, his whole body seemed to break, and at that moment he saw Closeto hurrying bowlegged through the geraniums, his gray fur dappling with sunlight. He stabbed his fork into his food and pressed it between his teeth as the stone stole back through his bones.

The shadows lengthened with excruciating slowness, but it seemed to him that the celebration came to an abrupt stop, with a sudden scraping of chairs, while he was still waiting for it to end. There was a confusion of farewells as they all went up the back stairs and walked down the hall to the door; then the door closed and he was alone with Wanda. He kissed her briefly on the lips, not looking at her, and said, "I'll take the car down and fill the tank," and left her without another word.

He walked the first block, waving to his friends who were getting into their cars, but when he had left them behind he took the last two blocks in a run, pounding up the steep pavement with his fists clenched, his chest stabbed deep with every gasp of his lungs, until sobs tore up through his throat. Slamming the car door shut, he felt the sobs take possession of him, unclenching him in greater and greater spasms, and loosing a scalding flood from his eyes. When the long outburst was at last over he felt weak with fatigue, but still the tears poured steadily from his eyes, running down his cheeks and dripping from his chin. Through the blur he tried to insert the ignition key in its keyhole, and when it finally slid in he realized he didn't know where to go or what to do. He had no shovel, nothing to work with. The car moved slowly down the hill, and after a long pointless traversal of streets, it turned, under its own volition, it seemed, and headed toward a neighborhood park.

The park stood empty in the late afternoon, its lawns a vivid green under the last rays of the sun. He would leave Closeto there on the lawn, where in the morning someone would see him and call the SPCA. He blew his nose with a handkerchief, and wiped his eyes, but still the tears spilled unchecked, and burned down his cheeks. He got out and opened the trunk and looked inside, holding the balled-up handkerchief to his face.

All resilience was gone from the cat's body, it was wooden, the fur like wooden fiber. He took it to the lawn and sat next to it, stroking it with long patient strokes. Closeto's pointed alert ears were transparent in the red sun. Closeto staring at a piece of string with his sober astonished look; then exploding into life, his rear end arching up into the air, his head dropping sideways to the floor as his whole body wriggled in an ecstasy of attack.

He wanted to say something, but he could not produce a sound. The sun disappeared, an evening coolness filled the air. Suddenly he leaned down, took the face in his two hands, and kissed it. Then he walked back to the car.

Wanda was still standing by the door, as if she had not moved.

"You owe me an explanation, Conrad," she said.

"Why 'Conrad'?" he asked with a smile. "Are we going to be on formal terms from now on? The usual assumption is—"

"Oh, shut up, for God's sake! Your face is swollen like a balloon. Are you drunk? Or *what?* You've been gone almost two hours!"

He looked tiredly at her unhappy face, and could feel sorry for it only in a distant way; his deepest pain still sprang from the lawn, now graying in the early evening. He told her in a few words, knowing that from now on her wedding would come back to her as a sad event, and one that they had participated in separately.

He waited for recrimination to join her dismay; instead, she grabbed a sweater and told him to drive back to the park.

Closeto lay where he had been left, alone on the dark lawn. They took him back and, with the aid of a flashlight, buried him under the geraniums.

"Let's sit out here," she said when they were finished. The banquet table stood where it had been left, covered with bottles, empty wineglasses, and clogged ashtrays. From the adjoining buildings, sounds of clinking dishes and television sets drifted down. The windows hung like gold squares, gilding the geranium leaves and Wanda's head and arms. Her hands were soiled with earth. He felt that she must think it grotesque to dig a grave where only a few hours before they had celebrated their wedding.

"Don't you want to go in?" he asked.

"You don't want to, do you?"

For the first time all day he felt a small degree of peace. To know that Closeto was buried here in the yard was comforting, and to sit without having to talk was an almost divine relief.

"No," he said.

It grew chilly after a while.

"We don't have to stay here," he said, but he could not bear to leave yet.

One by one the lights in the surrounding windows went out, until the neighborhood was asleep.

"We should go to bed," he said at last, "we'll have to get up early tomorrow."

"Why?" she asked.

"To go to Mendocino."

"How could we go? We wouldn't enjoy it."

"Maybe we would," he said dutifully.

"No, it would be impossible. We'll go some other time."

He threw her a miserable guilt-racked look, then turned his eyes to the remains of the celebration. "I wanted it to be such a nice day, I am so sorry, so sorry." But he knew that the rough edge in his voice was for his old friend under the geranium bushes, not for his new wife, and he knew that Wanda knew it too. He was too old for her, for her romantic love and her belief in beginnings; he was old and eccentric and a terrifying bungler.

"It's so stupid of you," she said.

"Stupid . . ." he echoed, nodding.

"Why do you think you have to be so fair? Oh, it's stupid, can't you see that? He meant so much to you. I know he's the only thing that's existed for you all day. But you have a right to that. Don't you think I'll keep, Connie?"

She seemed to focus before him, to fill him with her realness: the dirty hands and bandaged finger, the ring, the thick gold hair and deep-set eyes—and for the second time that day he felt himself break with intense love for her, but colored by the sense of death, by the certainty of their smallness in t'e great accident of life, and by a wild gratitude for the knowledge that all he must do to touch her was to reach out his hand.

He took the hand. The paper lantern swung in the night wind, and the edge of the white tablecloth lifted as ashes and crumpled napkins blew along its surface. They cleared everything away, folded the tablecloth and the cardtables, and took them inside.

In the bedroom he stood at the window for a long while, looking down at the geraniums. Then he lay down, falling at once into a blank exhausted sleep. Always after, whenever he felt the smallest annoyance with Wanda, he remembered her infinite graciousness on this day.

31

Morris and Johanna had left the wedding party early. By sunset they were a hundred and seventy miles northeast of San Francisco on their way to Reno.

When she had awakened that morning Johanna saw through the window a flawless sky, the absolute azure of midsummer, and she took it as a sign. No words were exchanged on the subject of marriage when Morris awoke, but his spirits were irrepressible and she felt certain of the day's outcome. She was not surprised when she read his horoscope in the morning paper.

> Get tasks done early in
> the day. Then devote your-
> self to new enterprise.

This time she also looked up her own horoscope, under Gemini.

> A good day for those
> ambitious projects. You
> are highly magnetic today.

It boded well. For Wanda's and Conrad's wedding she had bought everything new: dress, underclothes, purse, shoes. Now, in the new purse she put her toothbrush and toothpaste, a tube of deodorant, a lace handkerchief, and a hundred dollars in cash. Then she sat by the open window and waited for Morris to finish dressing. He was singing at the top of his lungs—"Come you back to old Sorrento! Come you back with the spumoni! Pizza too and minestrone! Buona sera twenty lira!" She listened, and knew absolutely that it was only a matter of which moment he would choose. It happened at the banquet table, after the first toast to the newlyweds. He leaned over to her and said: "Let's cut out of here. Let's drive up to Reno and do it."

They had come out from the mountains and he drove at a steady ninety-five through the desert, which was an intense coral under the fiery sun, like the earth before man. The windows were open and the hot air thundered through the car, drowning conversation, but every now and then Johanna shouted some comment on Wanda's and Conrad's wedding.

"Conrad was strange!" she cried.

"Solemn!" he yelled back.

"It takes everyone differently! Look at you!" And she threw his animated face an approving look.

"Come you back to old Sorrento!" he sang out in his lusty baritone. "Buona sera twenty lira!" The accordion still rang in his ears; the festivities had caught fire in him; he felt manic, wild with a hot liquid delight that poured through all his limbs. He pushed down harder on the gas pedal.

She looked out through the open window. The road extended straight ahead, each flat mile the same as the previous fifty, except that now the desert's brilliance was being swallowed up by an ashy twilight, rose-gray, like smoke or dust. The sagebrush grew indistinct, while the round moon, immense and ruddy, slowly rose from behind the horizon.

An hour later, as Morris drove through Reno's straggling outskirts, he felt a small letdown at the sight of the gas stations, the frosty-freeze stands, and the wedding chapels built in the style of Hansel-and-Gretel cottages or used-car offices. The downtown district was no better: two-story dirty brick buildings interlarded with towering concrete newcomers, a jumble of the seedy, the sleepy, and the glaringly new, all democratically played upon by flashing red and blue neon. He had been here before and had never been affected by the ugliness; but tonight he felt sensitive to everything around him. Well, it didn't matter; he would check them into the best hotel, take her to the best restaurant for dinner. His stomach felt acutely empty . . .

They checked into the El Capitan.

"Can you afford it?" she whispered, looking around the spacious, softly lit lobby.

"If I can't today," he told her jovially, "what's the use of living?"

"I brought some money," she confessed with a smile, "in case you rushed off without any. Oh, and listen, Morrie, don't we need a ring? I don't care, I never wear jewelry, but I think they require one for the ceremony."

"Some flowers, too," he said with spiraling inspiration. He pictured dark red roses, a bunch for each corner of the room, and one for her to carry. He felt prodigal, keenly aesthetic, and was seared by appreciation of her new dress, lime green, of some thin summery material that clung to her figure as though sculpted to it. And her hair, he thought as they followed the bellboy, what color was it? Not black, not brown either, but like burned wood polished to a high gloss. As she walked, it moved, swinging from side to side, alive with grace.

"Like it?" he asked when they were alone in their room; and he began walking around examining everything.

She took in the low bed with its heavy wine-red counterpane, the deep pile of the gold rug, the wall-size window opening onto a balcony with white garden furniture and potted flowers. "It's incredible," she said, dropping her coat and purse on the bed, "it's all incredible." She crossed the room to his outstretched arms, and in place of the words that had not been said on the long thundering journey, they kissed with a groping intensity, as if each were reaching deep into the interior of the other.

They went out on the balcony. Below lay the neon congestion, fading into the sparse lights of the outskirts, which in turn faded into darkness. The night air was warm and motionless.

"Do you want to rest up?" he asked.

"Maybe I'll take a shower, just to get the dust off. No. I won't. Let's leave now."

"You're getting nervous. Go on and take your shower, and I'll have some drinks sent up. I'll order a bottle of champagne."

"Let's wait till afterwards." She took his hand and they went back inside.

"It's a work of art!" she called from the bathroom. "You never want to leave. I may spend the whole night under the shower."

"You better not!" he called back from the other room. "Listen, I'll get those things downstairs—they've got a gift shop down there, maybe a florist's. Meet me at the lobby desk in half an hour, okay?"

"Half an hour."

When she came down at the appointed time he was standing by the desk with a bouquet of dark red roses wrapped in green paper. "It's all incredible," she said again as they found a quiet corner of the lobby. She took the pin from the green paper and put her face into the flowers, as he brought from his pocket a small paper bag and drew out a narrow band set with a blue glass stone. "They didn't have a plain one," he said, handing it to her. "Is this okay?"

"Oh, it's beautiful. It really is. I'll even wear it afterwards."

"Look, sit here in this chair. Wait just a minute. I'll be right back."

"Do you have to get something else?"

"Yeah," he said, and with a momentary hesitation, he swung around and left her.

Thirty minutes passed before she got up and started in the direction he had taken. The hotel was a self-contained city of restaurants, nightclubs, clothes boutiques, beauty salons, all connected by thickly carpeted corridors filled with the muted sounds of swooshing elevators, clicking escalators, and Muzak. Stepping onto an escalator, she descended to a floor where the hotel's final facet was presented to her. There was a roar of voices through which she could hear loudspeakers crackling with announcements, the snapping of fingers over dice, and a steady factory-like clank as slot-machine handles were pulled back and released; and boring through it all a ceaseless strident ringing. Conditioned air, sweet with deodorant, flowed icily through her thin dress. She put her trenchcoat on and, holding the bouquet low, continued her search for Morris' dark blue suit.

"What are you doing here?" she asked, finding him standing at a table, squeezed between an old Filipino woman and a windburned rancher. He glanced at her with an expression of severity and turned back to the game without answering. Through the welter of bodies she caught a glimpse of green felt, fingers, and cards. After a moment he stepped away. "It's the hotel's money," he explained. "They give you ten bucks' worth of chips to hook you in. I thought I might as well play them. Sorry I took so long."

"Did you win?" she asked as they started for the doors.

"Nah—you can't do anything with ten bucks." He stopped in his tracks and stared at the floor. Then he whipped out his wallet and squeezed up to another table.

She stood behind him on the soft red carpet, buffeted by the crowd and deafened by the keen high-pitched ringing sound. The low ceiling was inlaid with mirrors where, glancing up, she saw the tabletop reflected. All the hands, including Morrie's, were deft, like the dealer's: swift, precise, motionless between moves.

After a few minutes someone moved off a stool and Morris plumped himself down, figuratively rolled his sleeves up, and from a platinum blonde in a pink loin-high bunny outfit ordered a cup of black coffee.

Johanna clapped her hands to her ears. "What is that *ringing!*" she cried.

He swung around on the stool and took her hands gently from her ears. "Look baby. Give me a couple hours, that's all. I'm hot."

"Hot? Hot?" she repeated stupidly.

"Go away for a while, please, baby. Don't bad-luck me."

"No! We—"

"See. Now listen. Look. I can grab us something here if I can just have a couple hours. Just an hour or two."

She did not move.

"Look," he said again, patiently, but keeping the corner of his eye on the table, "why do we have to stick to a schedule when there's a chance to get ourselves together financially? I wouldn't do it if I wasn't hot."

He turned back to the table and studied the two cards he had been dealt. A jack and a three. Giving them a quick scrape on the green felt, he was dealt an eight. Beautiful. And he was aware of an oppressive weight removed from the back of his neck. Glancing around, he saw that Johanna was gone. She would go back to the room to wait; he pictured her stepping inside to find the four dozen roses it would now be filled with.

But nursing a painful vacuum in her head, she went to a bar and ordered a whiskey sour, which she left untouched because of the tightness in her throat. She began retracing her first tour of the hotel, lighting one cigarette from another as she wandered through the corridors, carrying the bouquet head-down at her side. In this way two hours were passed. A blister had formed on her heel.

She shoved her way through the casino crowd, using her elbows, but Morris was not at the table where she had left him. She began searching the room, squirming up to every blackjack table, jostling backsides down every row of slot machines. She even paced back and forth in front of the men's room. Finally she returned to the table where she had left him. "Do you know where the man in the dark suit went?" she asked the dealer, going around to her side. "With the dark hair? He was wearing a light blue tie?"

The dealer, a young woman with a deeply tanned, expressionless face, glanced at her without interrupting her dealing. "You can't stand back here."

"I'm asking you. Do you know where he *went?*"

The dealer threw a glance at the pit boss, who strode over.

"You can't stand here, lady," he told her courteously, but with an amused smile at her gaucherie; and she stepped away and simultaneously flung the bouquet to the floor. At that moment she saw Morris come in through the swinging doors from the street.

"Where were you" she asked furiously as she squeezed through the crowd to his side.

"I went to some of the other places," he said in a preoccupied voice.

"What now?" she demanded, staring at him.

"How much money have you got on you?"

"Why do you ask?" she said after a moment.

"Seventy or eighty? Have you got that much?" He took a handkerchief from his pocket and blotted his palms.

"I've got nothing," she said, her voice trailing off in the middle of the sentence.

"You said you brought some cash."

"Nothing!"

"I can pay you back in ten minutes! I'm hot. I can double it right off. I'm asking for a ten-minute loan."

"Shut up!"

"Look, Johanna, sweetness, don't get hysterical. I know you're not used to places like this, but it's just for a while. I can walk away with a thousand—for us." He waited for a response, but there was none. "I can taste it. It'd be a crime to leave now. Look, go back to the room and rest, order some food, some champagne, anything you want. As soon as I'm finished I'll come upstairs and we'll go to the chapel. Or we can go in the morning. We'll be fresh. And afterwards we'll drive to the river—where we camped?—and we'll go swimming and lie in the sun." He paused. "Only I need a stake."

"Not from me," she said bitterly.

"You want me to use my credit card? You want me to dig into my checking account? That's what I'm trying not to do!"

So saying, he lifted her purse from her hand, brought out her wallet, and quickly withdrew the bills it held; then dropping the wallet into the purse and snapping it shut, he pushed it back to her and disappeared into the crowd.

She stood looking at the purse as an iron fatigue crept into her bones. There was no place to sit down—if you sat down you had to play. She went into the casino restroom. All the chairs were occupied. She leaned against the wall. Some of the women nodded off, only to be snapped awake by a reminder from the attendant that no one was allowed to sleep in the lounge. The women, mostly old or middle-aged, looked like barflies or weatherbeaten wives of ranchers; they were like boxers resting against the ropes between rounds, they had an air of dogged perseverance, of unseen cuts and bruises, jarring in all the pink plush.

Finally she went into a booth, lowered the toilet seat, and sat down with a sigh of relief as the pressure was taken off her feet. After a while she realized she was hungry. Her coin purse yielded twenty-two cents, enough for a bag of peanuts, which she craved. Beyond that she did not think. Nor could she feel anything more than a desire to chew something salty. Once, as though to give the night its due, she tried to cry by forcing air up from her lungs, but nothing came of it.

She heard the attendant's voice: "You'll have to get out of there, lady, other people want to get in. Are you sick?"

"No," she said, getting to her feet, "and I'm not a lady." The term offended her; everything offended her. As she opened the door on the casino, she wanted to attack everyone she saw, to wring necks, but most of all to bash into silence that fierce shrill ringing. Walking across the soft carpet, she felt her feet burning inside her shoes; her nose began to run in the air-conditioning. A throbbing headache set in behind her eyes.

At a newspaper-and-candy stand near the lobby she asked for a bag of peanuts, but there was none, and a massive sense of despondency shook her, out of all proportion to the disappointment. Chewing on a Hershey bar instead, she returned to the casino and tried the slot machines, running a nickel up to a dollar and down again. She might have stayed longer, at least as long as the nickel lasted, but the ringing was intolerable here; here was where it came from—a jackpot alarm announcing that a winner must be paid off. Shrieks of triumph would pierce the blanket of noise and an attendant would come running up with a case slung over his shoulder from which he pulled out bills and coins as the ringing abruptly ceased, only to begin a minute later from another machine.

She began a plodding traversal of the burning carpet, always keeping Morris' head in sight, meeting every eye with a wrathful look. After a while her sense of time disappeared. Now and then the room upstairs flashed into her mind and her body begged for sleep; but she was afraid to leave. If Morrie finished his game he must be able to find her immediately or else he would go back to the game and they would never reach their destination. This logic visited her mind several times, and she received it without question. But suddenly it exploded. She stopped in the swarming aisle. There would be no wedding. She could not marry him now, not after this. It was this knowledge that had been clammed up inside her all these hours, and now it broke, an intolerable regret, and an intolerable self-loathing for the regret. Standing immobile, she was jarred by people coming and going. One of them was Morrie. He grabbed her arm.

"How d'you feel?" he asked hurriedly.

She shook her head. In the center of her body, deep in the flesh, was something as real as a hatchet wound.

"Then go upstairs and get some sleep, baby, you look fagged out. I've got to go over to Tahoe, I'll be back in the morning." He glanced at his watch and saw that it was twenty to four. "I'll try to be back before checkout time. Otherwise I'll meet you in the lobby."

She kept standing.

"You need some sleep," he said pleadingly, looking at the door.

Once more she shook her head.

"You come along and you'll be bored," he warned.

"Bored?" The word broke from her throat.

"Okay, let's go," he sighed, pushing into the crowd.

32 He drove over the mountains at top speed, maneuvering curves with jaw-clenched skill, zooming around every infrequent car as if his life depended on it. The radio blared. He wanted no conversation. Something powerful and onrushing was taking its course inside him; words would corrupt it. Now and then he glanced across the seat at Johanna. Her profile looked rigid; only the throat moved, when she swallowed.

In less than an hour he came to a stop in a parking lot the size of an airfield. Motor and radio off, the silence was startling. Under the fluorescent lights row upon row of empty cars were turned a uniform gray, like dirty ice. A paper cup clattered across the ground in the freezing mountain wind. He climbed out, slamming the door behind him.

She followed him as he hurried through the cars toward the casino, his necktie flapping over his shoulder. Inside the doors he waited impatiently for her to catch up. "Here," he said, taking a ten-dollar bill from his wallet, "get yourself something to eat, you must be starved." He touched the side of her face with sudden brief tenderness.

Her eyes never moved to his face. She shook her head.

"That's all you've been doing all night!" he exclaimed, sticking the bill into the pocket of her trenchcoat. "Look, I know everything's screwed up, but I can't stand here arguing!" He clenched his hair at the top of his head with both hands. "Don't stand there making me argue!"

Her eyes followed him with consuming hatred and consuming desire. She knew if she could bear a few more hours of waiting with a minimum show of sulks, she could drive home with him and say nothing as he turned the disaster into an apologetic shoulder shrug, after which she could steer for another, better wedding day; and she knew she could not do it.

He had cashed a check and sat down at a table, his necktie hanging rakishly from his side pocket. The powerful shoulders were hunched, the thick neck tense. She saw the heavy-lidded blue eyes, the soaring nose, the sensuous lips now set in a hard line. Their familiarity was beyond right or wrong, good or bad, they *were*, and were of her. To give them up would be to go against nature, to tear her limbs from her own body. That was the mangled feeling, the bright red terrifying wound.

She saw him order something from a bunny waitress and shoot a pile of chips out before him. He would live to be an active, robust hundred, with or without her.

The shrill ringing bored into her head. Her eyes registered the people around her—different from those in Reno: better dressed, less intense. Fewer of them. Maybe it was the hour, going on five. The darkest hour of the night, even in a room where day and night were the same. She sneezed violently; her throat was raw, her eyes ached. It was good. It formed a kind of film over the wound. She walked over to a waitress and asked about buses, and was directed to a schedule on the wall. A bus for San Francisco left every two hours, the next one at six forty-five. She went into a coffee shop opening off from the casino, and sat down to wait. After a while she ordered a grilled cheese sandwich. When she forced her teeth apart for it, it tasted horribly of cardboard.

Six o'clock. The dead hour. He was drooping, heavy-eyed. All night he had had brilliant winning streaks and long losing ruts, and this losing rut, this deepening chasm, he knew, was the last. Except for a couple hundred dollars in his savings account, he would be wiped out. He accepted it. His tension had left him; he felt unperturbed, fatalistic. Each time the dealer raked in his chips, he replaced them from his dwindling pile with the same careless flick of the wrist. There was only one other player at the table, a corpulent man in his fifties wearing a pale gray, foreign-cut suit over a white turtleneck sweater, who was winning with the same consistency as Morris was losing. Sometimes another player's good luck lit up the table and pulled winnings in for everybody, but sometimes another man's luck sucked its energy from your own—then you had to leave, go to another table. But Morris stayed where he was, taking a growing pleasure in seeing the man amass, without much pleasure, a small fortune of chips. What would he do with it? Buy some more foreign suits and white turtleneck sweaters. Well fed, smartly housed, with a fading wife and three teen-age kids spaced two years apart, and a Mercedes or two in the garage. He felt a sweet powerful surge of self-acceptance as he took in his own wrinkled suit and sweaty shirt. His jaws were bristled, his fingers dirty green. He was a bum, outside the rules of society; he had taken all the money that society had told him to earn and he had not only thrown it away, but with a gesture of good riddance. So much for the rigid future he had imposed upon himself. What was the man? An osteopath? A lawyer? A psychiatrist? Horn-rim glasses. Neatly folded square of handkerchief in his breast pocket. Well-manicured nails, but brittle, dry-looking. How he himself would have eventually looked if he had kept going in the direction he had been pointed in. House mortgages. Vacations at Waikiki. Wife struggling with menopause. Wall-to-wall carpeting. Everything in its place.

He had eight five-dollar chips left. Keeping two, he pushed the rest out. "Don't let me win," he pleaded under his breath. "Don't let me win and have to start all over again." He picked up the two cards he had been dealt: two face cards, a smiling jack and a serious queen. He would win, then.

"Insurance?" came the dealer's voice, and he glanced hopefully at her upturned ace. The other man insured his cards; Morris shook his head in the negative. She turned the card over. A king. He smiled down at the smiling jack, stood up, and brushed his hands off.

"That's it," he said as the dealer swept his chips in. They had been together only a short time, less than two hours, but when you won big or lost big there was always a sense of having shared something intimate. "Donna," he said, looking at her name card and tossing her one of his remaining two chips as a tip, "it was a ball." He paused by the other player and gave his shoulder a pat. "Keep it up, man, you're a winner. At the table."

The subconscious. It always knew what it was doing. It was your true will. Trust it now and forever. It had made him drive like a fiend straight to the heart of the casinos. It had made him keep all but a couple hundred dollars in his checking account. Too much trouble to send his savings book to the bank every payday? Far too much trouble, a lifetime of trouble. Now, in one night, he had freed himself of three thousand dollars, marriage, six years of academic drudgery, and the rest of his life in an iron mold. He cashed his five-dollar chip and put the bill in his wallet. Odd, when you had plenty, five dollars was nothing; and when you had only five, it was a fortune. He would peel part of it off for a breakfast with all the trimmings. He was ravenous.

Johanna.

Where was she? On a bus back? That would be the best. He was too tired for a scene; he would face that when he went to her place to collect his belongings. Odd—and odd how the word "odd" kept coming to his mind; everything was odd; incredibly different from a day ago—odd how normal it seemed to accept the end of Johanna. Painful, but it was a clean, necessary pain, like a cut that made you feel your body's life with every nerve. Odd that he was so alive in his blood and so exhausted in his bones. After eating, he would drive off the highway and find a meadow where he could lie down, close his eyes, and breathe in the sun and grass.

He went into the coffee shop. Immediately in front of him, paying at the cash register, stood Johanna with her back to him. Her hair was half under, half over the collar of her trenchcoat, a tangle of loops and strands. The coat was hiked up in the back, exposing a foot of the lime-green dress. She stood with one foot lifted from her shoe; the stocking adhered stiffly to her heel, where a blister the size of a nickel had broken.

She turned around before he could move, and slowly he put his hands in his pockets as their eyes met.

"The bus fare's nine dollars," she said. "I've only got eight. I need another dollar."

There were bags under her eyes, her nose was red and swollen, her face drawn; only a hint of her beauty existed, as it had the night he had met her. She sneezed, bringing a balled-up lace handkerchief to the inflamed nostrils. He wanted to comfort her in his arms, but since that might undo the conclusion they had come to, a friendly concern was all that he dared risk. "Why the bus? What d'you think the car's for?" he asked with rough cajolery.

"I need a dollar."

She was adamant, then. They stood on two islands. He took the five-dollar bill from his wallet and handed it to her as his stomach rumbled with hunger. But it would sound too petty to ask for four dollars back, also too financially desperate, also callous, since he owed her a hundred. "I owe you a hundred," he stated duly.

"Sixty-five. You've already paid back fifteen and I'll pay for my share of the room in Reno. You can leave me a check. You can come around tomorrow and get your things. Two o'clock. I'll be out." She spoke utterly without expression. Then she walked away, unevenly, her foot still lifted from its shoe.

He was left alone. He listened to the steady ringing of the jackpot bell from the casino. He could not have asked for a cleaner confrontation. Swift. And hollow as a shell. He felt disoriented. As if she had flicked aside their whole year like a piece of lint.

He walked through the casino, past the half-empty tables, and pushed open the doors onto the red-carpeted sidewalk and squinted down the street, feeling his will bear him up; whatever his confused feelings about Johanna, they could not impinge upon the rightness of his decision.

The morning was barely touched by the sun. The white peaks dazzled, but down here all was still shadowed, filled with wind as penetrating as ice water. He turned his collar up. Three blocks away a small crowd was gathered before an orange bus-stop sign, and toward it Johanna was hobbling along with her foot still lifted out of her shoe. The street lay deserted, black and glistening with damp. Behind him, heavy drops of moisture ran down the blue-tinted casino windows. He stood uncertainly, then hurried after her.

Catching up with her, he took her arm, but she jerked away and hobbled on. She looked like a mole. A disgust, a sorrow clenched his throat, and he followed her, afraid to use his hand in a grip, tapping her on the shoulder—like a passerby, he thought, trying to return a dropped glove; grotesque, demeaning.

"Johanna!" He pressed her against a wall and grabbed her jaw; but he could not get her eyes to connect with his; she was staring to the side, from the utmost corners of her eyes, with maniacal strain, and he saw the veins of her throat swelling toward a cry. He felt oddly restored by this extremity; raw, guilty, but somehow whole again. He dropped his hands with a kind of trembling equanimity.

Her eyes, narrowed, wet, finally sliced into his.

"It—it would never have worked out," he said quickly. "The whole trip up here—we both knew it was some kind of crazy joke."

Her face flinched, as if she saw herself back on the desert, speeding toward an idiotic joke under the red moon.

"You never brought up the subject of marriage once on the

whole trip," he pursued. "You knew—you always knew, underneath—how I felt. Look, baby. Marriage, academic degrees, psychiatry—the whole scene, it's passé, it's dead." He pointed to the casino down the street. "The money's gone. I don't regret it. It was a repudiation."

He thought for a moment: all those hard-earned dollars. He began taking two steps in either direction, his hands thrust fiercely into his pockets. "I'm sorry it had to get to this point, I wish I'd brought the whole conflicting mess out into the open . . ."

"You've had other women, too," she said, almost inaudibly, and the skin around her eyes tightened.

As if, he thought, the whole thing boiled down to that. He gave a short nod.

"All along," she said, and she bit her lip with despairing reflection.

"No—not at first when I moved in. I tried it your way. But your way's stifling, Johanna. Nobody in this day and age could stick it. Shit, the others never had anything to do with us! You stress sex like it was the sum total of love."

"Love." She spoke the word with such soft, drawn-out contempt that he felt himself shrivel.

"You want to know something?" he countered intensely. "That room at the El Capitan? If you'd gone back up there like I told you, it was filled with four dozen roses. You never even went back up, you never even saw them!" He glanced suddenly at her hands. "Where's your bouquet?"

Instead of answering, she pulled the ring from her coat pocket and held it out to him in her flat palm.

"No, keep it, keep it, baby," he said, looking away, and remembering the oddly euphoric moment when he had bought it.

She threw it past his head. It landed somewhere in the street with a faint clink that made him wince. He had bought the ring in good faith and he had bought it in a disembodied dream; he had pictured a wedding license on the trip up and he had pictured the green felt of the gambling tables; he had wanted to marry her and he had not wanted to marry her. At what point the wedding had been completely pulverized in his mind he couldn't say; it had been a gradual crumbling through the night, his will working away inside him, grinding down and sifting away the unsuitable life he had planned for himself.

"I wanted to marry you," he said feelingly; and then, afraid that she might construe this as a plea to reconcile, he added in a burst: "But there's a gulf between us. Everything's so *serious* with you. You're a woman without a sense of humor. I can't live like you do. The world's been changing while we were stuck up there in that attic of yours, everything's different, there's been a fantastic breakthrough. I want to be part of it. I can't hang back. I can't do it, not even for you." He stared into her wet eyes. "And that's where it is," he concluded.

"Where!" she cried, suddenly crackling to life. "Is it because marriage is passé or because I don't have a sense of humor? Just for the record. Make up your filthy mind!"

"It's both of them!" he cried back. "And—and, damn it, because you're a gentile!"

"A DP from the dustbowl," she bit out, showing her teeth.

"A gentile! You've never understood, you've never had an inkling—to have the barrier there, the thing in your blood. I could never marry a gentile, it's impossible, it's in the blood—"

"What total rot," she breathed, again with that soft, drawn-out contempt; and in his own ears his words sounded unbearably asinine. If he had ever doubted that he had left his Jewish heritage behind, he would never doubt again. So much for the one unalterable barrier between them.

"All right," he said, "do you want to know the real reason?" He would tell her the one truly selfless motive behind his night's work, though it was the one motive that would hurt her the most. "I don't want to get into the bag where the woman has all the dough."

"Why did you force me to sell, then! I never had any money until you forced me to sell!"

It was exactly what he knew she would ask, and now he took a breath and answered. "Because I wanted you to. You think I'm a saint? You've got this salable talent, I could have leaned back and ridden along on it, and, baby, I wanted to. I'm only human. I forced us to break up tonight so I couldn't do that to you."

"I see," she said quickly, dropping her eyes. She started away.

"Johanna." He drew her back.

"What do you want?"

He shook his head hopelessly. Again she started away, and again he drew her back.

"I guess—I guess I can't stand your coldness," he said.

"You're beyond everything," she said, and he waited with an insane hope for a smile to flicker across her face, not a smile of reconciliation, but of understanding, a smile implying some point in the future where they might meet and try again. But she did not smile. Her eyes consumed him; and for a moment a look of stricken intimacy passed between them. Then simultaneously they turned and went their two ways.

Streaming with moisture, the blue-and-white Greyhound bus had pulled up at the curb. Its door opened with a bustling official thump and the driver sprang out with his clipboard of tickets. Only moderately awake, stifling yawns and stretching in the rapidly brightening air, the crowd formed a loose line and began climbing aboard.

At the corner of the block Morris turned around. He saw her head bend, fly back, and a congested sneeze echoed down the street, a simple human sound that seemed for a moment to rip her from the complex network of their problems and stand her before him, warm flesh, yellow eyes, scuffed sandals, voice saying, "We're out of coffee," or "Let's go up over that hill." The decisive night behind him wavered; he shut his eyes. When he opened them she had disappeared inside the bus. The driver climbed in, the door slammed shut. A moment later the motor started with a deep snarl, thickened, hummed, and the bus moved down the street, gaining speed as it came abreast of him. He turned in a semicircle as it passed, scanning the windows.

She sat low on her spine in one of the rear seats, shielding her eyes from the sun, as from the very roots of her being spread a sensation of being lowered into the earth and covered over.

And as though the sensation were communicated as the bus flashed by, he underwent a moment's perfect stillness in himself, an absence of light.

He was left alone, in a smell of Diesel fumes and exhaust. He stood a moment longer, then, rubbing his tired eyes, he headed for his car and a sleep in some green, renascent meadow.

33

The curtains stirred torpidly at the window, where a fly buzzed against the glass in circles. The room, stuffy in the afternoon heat, lay in the same last-minute disorder that the door had closed on two days ago.

At two o'clock a jangle of keys sounded in the hall, the door was kicked open, and Morris stepped in under a load of empty cardboard boxes. Unshaven, still in his wrinkled white shirt and dark suit trousers—he had spent the night on the Suicide Prevention Bureau couch—he spilled the boxes to the floor and rolled up his sleeves.

He worked noisily, throwing clothes, toilet articles, books into the boxes, stuffing odds and ends into his suitcase and rucksack, and pounding down the stairs with them in half a dozen trips to his car. The desk and TV set he would leave; he meant to travel light. Taking a last look around, he went to the wall and pulled Conrad's sketch of Johanna away from its tacks, folded it into a square, and stuck it in his back pocket. Then, his shirt soaked through, his ears suddenly filled with the silence of his labor's end, he stood in the middle of the room looking at nothing, listening to the drone of the fly. Finally he made out a check for a hundred dollars and laid it on the desk, pulled the house key off his key ring, and placed it on the check.

He went back into the bedroom. Picking up a faded blue half-slip from a chair, he noticed the laundry bag with its red donkey. Some of his dirty clothes inside. No time to sort them out, leave them. The dresser top—bare-looking without his mess of things. Couple of perfume bottles, silver-backed brush, and hand mirror, that was all. The bed, still in morning disarray.

He let the garment slide from his fingers and went slowly out.

Giving him plenty of leeway, Johanna, sneezing and blowing her nose, sat until early evening on her folded trenchcoat in nearby Alamo Square, a box of Kleenex on her lap. She had spent the previous night not in the apartment, which she was loath to re-enter, but on a couch in Aquiline's lofty blue-and-purple parlor.

Aquiline had asked no questions, and had silenced Charles' with a look. The three of them had watched an old Clark Gable movie on television. Johanna felt her heart working like a machine pushed to its ultimate power; it thudded in her ears and all through her body, as if every inch of flesh was embedded with its own pounding heart, and she knew that though she wanted only to sleep, to cease to exist, this furious drumming would never allow her to. At one o'clock, when the movie ended, Charles put on his black coat and, with a reluctant, lingering look at Aquiline, went home. Only then did Johanna sense something wrong between the couple.

"It finishin' up between us," Aquiline stated, unasked, as she made up the couch. She smoothed the frayed edge of the blanket with her long fine-boned fingers. "It got to, so it got to."

"I'm sorry," said Johanna, giving a ferocious sneeze, "I like Charles."

"Who don't like Charles? He good-lookin', too. That don't make any difference."

Johanna wiped her eyes with her hand, glad for the cold's disguise. "It's over between Morris and me, too."

"I figure that when you want to sleep here. Never figure you and Cousin Appendix stickin'. You' not really surprised?"

"But if you really love someone, and really try—Oh Christ, if you want something so much, why can't you have it?"

"You get what you want, that the sad story. I leave thisere light on, you know where the bathroom's at."

It was still hot at six o'clock when she returned from the square and went up the front-yard walk, noticing but not accepting an argyle sock and a box of spilled paper clips in her path. The stairway was tunnel-dark. Then there was sunlight again. She was in her room.

Her brain froze. The whole room emptied of Morrie's anarchy: an austere still-life of check and key on the clean desktop. She stared at the big battered desk. "Why did the bastard saddle me with that?" she asked through her teeth, and her eyes moved up the wall to the four tacks, each with a particle of white paper under it. Had he torn the picture away in anguish? What had he felt? Had he left a note? She began rooting through every room, knowing she would find nothing, but knowing too that it would be easier to come to terms with the rooms' changes if she did it all at once. Bathroom—his toothbrush gone from the glass, half the medicine chest wiped out. Bedroom—the drawers spacious again, rattling with an overlooked sand dollar. Closet—a black gap next to her clothes, the dusty television set still sitting there, the red terrycloth robe hanging forgotten on the back of the door.

She lay down on the bed with her box of Kleenex, which was squashed in the middle and almost empty, balled up a tissue and pressed it to her raw pouring nostrils, and closed her eyes. But the hammering of her heart made her sit up again. The room was filled with amber light. As she watched, it deepened slowly to an intense copper that struck points of fiery light from the things on the dresser top. Then it ebbed away. The room, still hot, grew dark and smaller.

She put her arm out beside her on the bed. Where Morris had been was air. If you got what you wanted, she thought, some part of me must want this; and a sound of utter disbelief broke from her throat. She threw herself on his side of the bed and brought her fists down on his pillow, seized it, and with her teeth tore its slip in two with a long sharp sound; and rolled back, pressing it with her hands against her eyes and mouth.

34

As Morris had expected, he missed his children. The last child he had tested was a slow eight-year-old black girl who suffered from severe curvature of the spine; with hunched shoulders and long spidery arms, she was touching in the way children are who dimly understand that they lack the child's natural allure. The school's slow-moving gears had kept her in the first grade, but now, categorized by his tests, she would be removed to a class for retardees. But, he thought, no matter how limited her potential might be, it had never been given an opportunity to come to light, and never would be, what with the educational system's red tape and lack of funds, not to speak of the child's garbage-strewn homelife. As a psychiatrist, he could have dedicated himself to children like this, and now it seemed a disastrous step away from them that he had taken with his Tahoe decision. He brooded on this as he gave the test, but the one thing he was now sure of was that something bigger, more profound than the patch-up efforts of individuals was needed; the entire machinery of clogged social values had to be overhauled. And so he had taken the child's hand afterward and walked her back to the classroom and stooped down by the door. "Minerva, you stick up for yourself. You're a good girl. And I'll tell you something else—you've got the prettiest eyes in that whole class in there." Minerva screwed up the luminous eyes in a paroxysm of shyness and pleasure. He pressed her hand, opened the door for her, and that was the end of his day and his career.

As for the Board of Education office with its smell of chalk and sulfide, his desk, whose ashtray always greeted him with someone else's damp balled-up Kleenex, and Rhonda with her pointed fingers and broad white bosom, which he had once briefly lain upon—good riddance to it all, he never gave any of it another thought.

Johanna once said that his life had been a calculated effort to avoid risk; but he was giddily unanchored now, his future fundless. If you were going to repudiate the Establishment, you had to do it from the ground up. With everything he owned piled in his car, he peeled off the MAKE LOVE, NOT WAR

217

bumper strip (corny now, there were so many around) and delivered himself into the Haight.

The first day he ran into a familiar figure. She wore a violet tank top and a long black skirt and a pair of granny glasses clamped to the thin bridge of her nose, and she carried an infant in her arms.

"Zaidee, baby," he said uncertainly.

A pause: Then a warm and clearly platonic smile spread across her narrow face.

"It's yours?" he asked, squinting at the infant.

"Her name's Thawn," she said maternally, beaming down at it, "Thawn Olive. After Ollie."

Thawn, he thought. Jesus. But he was filled with a sense of her achievement. In the time since he had seen her last she had created this new bubble-blowing human being. Little old Zaidee with her wide childish mouth and Arkansas drawl.

As they walked along together he found that there was a kind of spiritual largess about her, as if she had almost more wisdom than she knew what to do with. "We are all God, you know," she informed him in the course of conversation, indicating the milling crowds. And she paused and added, with great seriousness, "Even you, Morrie."

"Thanks, Zaidee," he said, suppressing a smile.

"Only I don't know if you'll really dig dropping out," she went on, tutor-like. "You're so hyped up, you know? Like you've got to slow down, Morrie. I mean, that's my advice."

"Right," he said, patting her arm. "Thanks."

She gave him some leads, and he moved into a sanctuary run by the Diggers where you could eat and sleep free. He sold his car and everything in it except his sleeping bag and his rucksack, which held some clothes, his thimble, his sketch of Johanna, and one flawless seashell. He bought an amber pendant and hung it around his neck, and stopped shaving his upper lip, and wandered through the hot streets in his faded Levi's and a net undershirt listening to jugbands and tambourines. And the weeks went by.

His only link with the past was Thursday nights, when he took a bus across town to the Suicide Prevention Bureau. Listening to the same kinds of flat or hysterical voices that he had tried to soothe for three years now, he pressed home new advice: Re-examine society's demands, take chances, live each moment as it came. But gradually the question grew in him:

After that, what then?

On the day of his fortieth birthday, in November, he walked up and down the street, speaking to no one. The Haight was a pinwheel, a glad joke already crumbling at the edges. There were harder facets of the new world—campus rioters, Weathermen—but he was too old for them, stirred by their goals but stricken by their smashed windows and trampled bystanders. He was no hardcore revolutionary; and he was no child who could listen indefinitely to jugbands. Having crawled out from the hardened fist of society, where was he to offer himself?

35

Buy the clothes that will make you look
more stylish. Show you are thoughtful.
Please kin more.

She saw him walking into Roos Atkins and buying a new
shirt, then going home to write chatty letters to his seven
brothers in Brooklyn.

It was a demeaning habit that she could not rid herself of,
like the superstitions—the newel-post tapping and sidewalk-
crack avoiding.

That autumn she avoided many sidewalk cracks. They were
black and sharp in the sun. Around them lay candy wrappers
and cigarette butts of blinding intensity. In the streets the
cable-car tracks blazed, their slots giving off a soft metallic
clatter. She walked everywhere, up bustling Market Street and
down Mission with its Good Will stores and broken wine
bottles, along the Embarcadero's overgrown railroad tracks,
through the tourist crowds of Fisherman's Wharf, and along
the sunny Italian streets of North Beach. Sometimes she even
walked the five miles to the ocean, where, without breaking
her slow pace, she continued along the hazy edge of the water,
always carrying with her the cold, airy amputated feeling at
her side where Morrie had been.

But she usually ended her walks at Aquatic Park, which lay
at the foot of Van Ness Avenue in the heart of the city, and
from the end of the curved stone pier she soberly watched the
bay flow seaward in cheerful haste, pale blue and streaming.
Sometimes she stayed until water and sky were black. A
spangle of lights would come into view, glide by, giving out
a hollow lingering blast; then there was only the small solemn
lapping of stone again, and darkness. With tired legs she
would walk back to shore, passing the Buena Vista Café, which
fed a muted roar into the night, its big windows framing a
merry mashed-together crowd.

In bed she thought of a yellow flower. She climbed into its
center and slept there, deep inside the petals, deep in fra-
grance. But the sleep never lasted; she got up and walked
barefoot through the dark rooms.

One day she passed a place where they made coffins—they were piled up in the factory yard like cords of wood—and then she was overcome by the idea of coffins. When she saw a very tall or very fat person she thought of the kind of coffin they would need. And she began judging people, by their clothes and by their neighborhoods, as to whether they would have a big funeral with hordes of mourners and a costly casket with burnished handles, or whether it would be a pinewood box for them, an old landlady or drinking buddy overseeing everything and comprising the entire congregation at the last rites. For every person in the city there was a coffin waiting: the smart matrons in furs going into I. Magnin's; the children skating out on the avenues; the fresh-faced boy coming out of the library loaded down with books and ambition, whom she bumped into while avoiding a sidewalk crack. All of them. And she thought of the men working in the coffin factory, hammering nails and sanding wood—did they ever stop and wonder? Maybe when they sat down with their lunchpail on a beautiful rosewood job they thought about all that effort and art going down into the earth, and thought the same thing about themselves. She felt clammy and pale in the heat, thinking about coffins; and always that cold, airy amputated feeling at her side where Morrie had been; as though the heat, though she sweated plentifully on these long walks, did not penetrate at all. And she began thinking too: When? That knot of people clustered around a Doggie Diner on Van Ness. Which one of them would go first, which last? You take everyone in Union Square this moment—where she stood now, at noon, the pigeons swooping overhead—how soon before every last person was dead? Give the youngest ones another sixty years. Sixty years and all of them, including herself, would be in their coffins, which were stacked like cords of wood beside the factory. And then she thought of Morrie in his coffin, and put her hand to her face, exultant and grief-stricken.

As she walked along the streets she was sometimes seized by strange irascibilities because of the signs. In a new super-market, a red heart inscribed with: GEE, YOU'RE SWELL! On a bank window: LET US BE OF HELP TO YOU. Whom could they have gotten to print and hang such transparent, embarrassing signs? And she stopped at Woolworth's and bought a tube of Tangee lipstick and went back to the bank and wrote on the window in a trembling hand: EVERY POWER PARADING AS

BENEFICENT. Stepping all over sidewalk cracks as she rushed off before someone caught her.

She thought, too, walking along, that everything was fantastically well coordinated. The city was inset with miles of complicated plumbing; that was a fact; pipes running like metal intestines inside every wall; unseen, unsung pipes, but impressive beyond belief—not to mention the network they emptied into, a vast sewer city beneath the city, contents flowing dutifully to wherever it was they went. Astounding, really. And the heavy manhole covers above, stamped with PGE-CO with a triangle inside the O. Someone had designed those letters and had decided to put the triangle in the O. Much thought went into everything. And the traffic lights, clicking green to red because of some complex mechanism inside. Bus transfers littered the pavement among the twisted candy wrappers and cigarette packages that shone like the windows of Chartres Cathedral, and these transfers—she picked up a pale blue one—were like those microscopic Bibles you saw in novelty shops, the print so small you could hardly read it, dense with schedules and regulations. That was astounding too. And here in a grocery store, the clerk punching a cash register—out pops the drawer, magically—while down the aisle a lady weighs potatoes on a scale and her eyes follow the pointer as it quivers to a stop. Instant recognition. A pound is a pound from sea to shining sea. Astounding, again. Gratitude. And here in a department store—she is at Macy's now—the shoppers all know when it is closing time, because chimes sound at five minutes to five. And everyone leaves. Because the chimes have rung. There is instinct, intelligence, and cooperation here. No one flings himself down and refuses to go. But that is what she would like to do, staring at a counter of colored perfume bottles, amber, rose, pale blue: wonderful, though not really more wonderful than the candy wrappers and cigarette packages that blaze in the sun. She would like to stay here with these wonderful vials —and see how they are arranged, charmingly, each with its tiny price tag, tax included; so are all the counters arranged, with care; imagine the planning behind it all, think of the huge warehouses and the rumbling vans and the storerooms upstairs where people in dust coats stride from bin to box with ledgers and cocked pens . . .

She walks out of the store thinking of the counters and the

manhole covers and plumbing and bus transfers, overwhelmed by their complexity and horrifyingly certain that it will all come apart in one split second.

One day she sat down on a bench next to a woman's magazine that someone had left there. She leafed through it, stopping hopefully at an article entitled "Chase the Blues Away!"

> He who laughs, lasts. But you can't even manage a smile (sob!). Try something new. Eat a fresh orange. Sleep more, or less. Take a long walk. Or treat yourself to some of the nifty new Fall makeup fashions . . .

She threw the magazine aside and started walking again. She would write them and tell them that long walks were not the answer. And she had doubts about fresh oranges, too.

At home she read the newspaper every morning.

SCORPIO

> A good day for those small errands. Be careful of moving vehicles. Plan well.

He took his dirty clothes to the laundromat (a word still charged to its last syllable—pass on) and dropped into a barber shop for a haircut (the springy, fresh-smelling hair dropping to the floor in locks) and bought a frozen steak for dinner (but where did he cook it, where did he live?), keeping an eye on traffic, planning well; and she, sick for the sight of him, walking bodyless at his side.

Passing from the horoscope, she read the rest of the paper minutely, looking for names to amuse her. When she found one she wrote it down on a piece of paper. She would end the list when she had ten names and then she would read them from top to bottom and be amused. She needed only one more name now, and after half an hour she found it on the sports page and wrote it at the bottom of the list. Then she smoothed her hair and read.

> Icy Jean Powell
> Arturo Fucual
> Mrs. R. Canteen
> Mutual Tingle

That one must be a misprint. Still, it had appeared—Mutual Tingle—three times in a legal notice. It was not a misprint. It was a bona fide amusing name.

> Horace Mae Jones
> Tardie Threat
> Acme Wong
> Anna Woman
> Dolly Bongs
> Wladislaw Maniak

She read them again, with concentration, but her lips refused to lift. Then, ashamed of this occupation, she threw the list away and read the paper over again, for serious content.

Black rebellions in Cleveland, in Chicago. Good. There should be no ghettos. It was simple enough. Anti-draft sit-ins in Berkeley. Good again. They had been cretins over there in her day, football and dates during the McCarthy era. A girl without a Saturday night date sat in her sorority house feeling sick to her soul, a leper. Would go out with anyone to avoid that, even someone she couldn't bear. A miserable system, hearts battered with self-doubt and self-contempt. And the boys, all sports and their fathers' businesses afterward. The silent generation, questioning nothing. And she had been no better—worse, in fact, going from her room to her art classes, paint-spattered and introspective. Days so far in the past now, the campus fragrant with spring; but a dead era, the Fifties, she had hated it and kept to herself. And now they were burning draft cards over there and it was unbelievable, but good, for the war should stop. That was simple, too. Yet only the few could see so simply, and no matter what they accomplished, the opaque Many crowded back afterward and undid everything, it had been happening ever since the end of *la grande épopée:* 1830. 1848. And then the two great wars, one noted for trenches, the other for ovens. Downward, darkward, and here was a housewife shot to death on her porch, and here a whole page on industrial spoliation, and here a few lines on the cat starvelings of New York City crammed into euthanasia chambers a thousand a week. And so she puts the paper down and turns to the television set—for she has disinterred it from the closet and set it upon a chair, and sometimes sits for hours in Morris' red terrycloth robe watching whatever the screen sees fit to present—and tonight she sees Philip delivering a news broadcast on what she has just read in the paper, and he looks fine, a little older, but then everyone is growing older, mainly he looks all right, he has survived, and she is glad, and switches to a cowboy serial which has no merit whatsoever except that it dulls her mind almost to extinction.

She had seen Wanda and Conrad soon after her return from Reno (and Closeto's death, such a tiny obscure demise, had nevertheless affixed the official seal to the season) and afterward had stuck her phone under the sofa cushions and tacked the NO ADMITTANCE sign to her door. She felt she had nothing to communicate. Aquiline was the only person she saw, usually in the hallway.

"Why you hit that post?" Aquiline asked.

"What?" Johanna said, flushing. She always tapped the newel post twice when she passed it.

"Gonna tear it down before the wreckers?"

The residents of the building had received a ninety-day notice of demolition. It was a small thing to Johanna, something to be put off and considered at a later date. But it seemed to have made a change in Aquiline, or coincided with a change. She left the house more often, she had new friends, serious surly-looking black men in dark glasses; there was something busy and planning about her; her hair was growing in all directions, released from its former battery of bobby pins, and she had put her pink chenille bathrobe away and wore a pair of black leotards and a smock-like flowered blouse.

"Are you pregnant?" Johanna asked once.

"Only in some ways."

"Oh," said Johanna.

"You ought to wash once in a while," said Aquiline.

Johanna moved off.

"Where you goin'?"

"For a walk."

"You walk all day long?"

Johanna nodded, closing the front door behind her. She began. There, spread out all through the city, were the cracks to be avoided. There, lying everywhere, were ropes of litter shining in the torrent of sunlight, as bright as stained glass, she thought, starting down the sidewalk.

One day she stayed inside and tried to paint. The picture

of the soldier in the blue tunic was still unfinished, but she had no feeling to complete it. She put a blank canvas on the easel, dipped her brush in turpentine, then into umber, and, holding the brush tightly against the canvas, began drawing a scene from the Embarcadero. No sensation moved between her body and the brush. A few rigid strokes were eked out. She pulled back, insulted by what the brush had done, and whipped out some wet slashes that bled to the canvas' bottom edge and dripped to the floor. She looked at the mess. It would do as an action painting, she thought, pulling it from the easel and throwing it aside, but it was a bore. Although it was no more of a bore than the Medieval City, which now hung in some spacious Hillsborough living room whose owner, she had heard, was one of Bing Crosby's closest golfing cronies.

Of what use was a painting, after all? Why should anyone know or care that the seventeenth-century Spanish court had existed? Or that Rembrandt's seamed face under its shapeless toque had existed? Or that the Moulin de la Galette with its summer light and crowds of 1890 had existed? Turn around and you could see it all in front of you, the same old dance to the boneyard; for if art worked with the dance, what it understood was how old and great the boneyard was. Yes, but at least the thing-in-itself? The luminous brush stroke, the glaze of bitumen? Only pigment, stupid as stone. To press wet hog bristles to a square of primed flax and feel your heart race was insanity. To write a line of prose or a note of music was insanity. The thousand-page book lived on in its readers as a poor handful of incidents—a wild peasant dance, a wolf hunt, a boy soldier shot at the stake; the vast canvas of a surrendering army cropped up once or twice in the recollection of the Prado visitor, an image of gracious defeat, a red sash, a horse's rump; the symphony suffered changes already in the departing audience, its complexity abandoned for a few shattering peak moments. What more could the creator expect? But he did, he was like a lover giving himself and being taken on the run. The fool never knew it, but everyone else did. They knew that they had to eat and sleep, to make a living and prepare for death. No more could they take out what the artist had put in than they could fly to the sun. And whether you ended the crime in their streets, or listened to their confessions through a curtain, or taught them sex technique, or removed their cancerous organs, or painted them a picture, it was all the same thing: relief, or solace, or excitement; it was so many stopgaps in the dance to the boneyard, it was so much patching up and promising, a question deferred. And all the serene enlightened talk about the here-and-now, the cowardliness of fearing death (which was, after all, as natural as birth), all such talk was but another stopgap, no different from the peeling surface of the Primavera or the cries from the football stadium on a wet afternoon. And in some distant aeon when the water had repossessed the globe and the globe spun silently through the universe, under its crust would lie the particles of jewelry and pianos and guns and teething rings and canvas and bones that had comprised the now answered question.

Whenever her walk took her down Mission Street she passed the Herald Building. One warm morning in early November she walked into the lobby and hung around watching the people come and go, not sure why she was there. After a while she went into the classified-ads office. She wrote out an ad, asked to have it run in the Personal section every day for a month, and made out a check for ninety-five dollars and twenty-four cents. The ad read:

> On peace march, wearing cloak, pointed
> shoes. Danced, bongos. Call 931–5701.

At home she took the phone out from under the sofa cushions and waited.

The next evening at seven o'clock the phone rang. Her heart leaped into her mouth, but the caller was Wanda, asking what in God's name she was doing with herself, why they never saw her.

"I'll come over soon," she answered, with the certainty that she would, that the next call would somehow release her from her limbo.

The next call came ten minutes later.

"I've got a cape," a woman's voice informed her with alcoholic enthusiasm.

"Yes?" said Johanna uncertainly.

"And I use to teach at Arthur Murray's, two-step, tango, ballroom, and I've got a cape—"

"I'm sorry—"

"You're sorry? Who the hell d'you think you are?"

"I'm sorry," she said again, and hung up.

By the end of the week she had resigned herself to crank callers interspersed by occasional sincere young people who sometimes went on peace marches, sometimes wore cloaks, sometimes danced, but none of whom had been at the little clearing in the Oakland park a year ago. And each time the voice revealed itself as the wrong one her relief was greater than her disappointment; she had no idea what she would say if she found the creature from the glade delivered up to her.

With the reappearance of the phone from under the cushions, her attention was focused on it; the instrument began throbbing with possibility, goading her to use it. Late one Thursday night, with her legs like water—she had to sit down—she dialed the number of the Suicide Prevention Bureau, and held the receiver two feet away from her, as if it would shoot out a white flame. On the first ring a tiny voice spoke into the air. Slowly she brought the receiver closer.

"Hello?" he was saying. "Hello. Hello. Anybody there?"

Soundlessly, inside her throat, she said his name.

"Hello. Hello there?" he was saying.

She was breathing through her nostrils like a bellows. She clamped her hand over her nose.

"Okay, no sweat. I understand. Maybe it's hard to talk. Wait until you feel like it, there's no hurry. We've got all the time in the world."

She heard muted sounds—a cup being set down; the creak of the swivel chair as he leaned his broad back against it. She saw his heavy-lidded eyes patiently gazing across the office as he waited. She thrust the receiver back into the cradle, pressing both her hands on it. Then she picked it up again and dialed another number.

"Will you send a cab to 1405 Webster? No apartment number. I'll be on the porch."

She changed into her lime-green dress, ran a brush through her hair, and walked stiffly downstairs to wait. Sometimes cabs refused to come into the Fillmore at night. She half hoped this one would not show up. But a few minutes later it drew up alongside the rubbled curb.

36 The Buena Vista—darkly paneled, tastefully saloonish—was so groaningly crammed that she was pinned against the door as soon as it closed behind her. She made an effort to move, and her confidence rose as men (never women) stepped aside for her, at least tried, pulling in their stomachs and lifting their drinks high. She began squirming her way to the bar, alert to male glances.

A hand moved its glass aside to give her a scrap of bar space. A stool was magically offered. She looked at the face as she sat down. A callow boy's, snub-nosed, adrift with freckles, something she could never go to bed with.

"Crowded!" he shouted.

She nodded and ordered a straight shot of whiskey. Any kind, she didn't know brands. When it was pushed before her she downed most of it in a single throat-constricting gulp.

"You come here often?"

"What?" she gasped, her eyes swimming.

"Do you come here often?"

"No," she shouted back.

The boy looked at her shot glass with uncertain respect. *"You like it straight like that?"*

"No," she said, and after a moment added: "I've got sinus."

"I can't hear you."

"I've got sinus!"

"It helps sinus?"

"Very much." She began to feel glowingly awash with wisdom, and gave the glass a weighty nod.

"I'll have to tell my roommate."

"What?"

"My roommate's got it!"

"Got what? Never mind!" she cried, and there was a blessed pause in their screaming. Her vocal chords felt raw.

The boy fiddled with a book of matches. *"Say,"* he yelled, *"you care to have a drink somewhere where it's quieter?"*

"No, thank you very much."

"Sure?"

"Yes."

A pleasant if peremptory smile accompanied by a screamed *"Ciao!"* and he moved off. She was sweating from the room's closeness. She turned back to her drink, finding her vision narrowed to the area directly before her eyes, where her cigarettes and shot glass took on the chill clarity of objects under a microscope. Yet there was a haze behind her eyes, and her tongue lay like a heavy bar in her mouth. Now someone was squeezing into the boy's place, someone more likely, heavy-set, dark-haired. Although crew cut. She had not seen a crew cut for a long time. The world's hair was growing, growing like a fertile rain forest. She turned around on the stool, luxuriously at ease, and took in the crowd. Young. Twenty to thirty-five, all abundantly crowned with glossy growing hair, the men as well as the women. All tanned. All talkers. All talking about roommates and sinus. Their clothes were odd—casual, vivid, outré. Broad glaring neckties on patterned shirts, trousers pencil thin or madly flared; the women in shoes with buckles, or old-fashioned boots laced to the knees, skirts stopping at the thigh, embroidered vests, pendants, beads. No more button earrings or pearl necklaces. A girl nearby wore three big rings on one hand, like a Florentine princess. Hand probably took dictation in an insurance office. She had seen these people on her walks through the financial district, strung out among the shuffling Hermans and bouffanted Xerox operators and sober-suited corporation heads, a new and mighty sartorial breed cracking through the standard ranks. And now here they all were, gathered in one room, the crest of fashion somehow having risen from the grimy tunics and torn ponchos of the peace march. Fashions. Ten years ago . . . long skirts, tight hairdos. Hula hoops. Canasta. Mike Todd. Even she, ghosting bespattered across campus, knew who Mike Todd was. It had been Time's very latest moment, fresh, fresh—you hadn't liked it, maybe, but you couldn't question it, it *was*—but how stale Mike Todd and the hula hoops were now—stale and, more than that, the whole era laid open to question—all past eras questioned; so many mistakes along Time's way, Egyptian astronomy, Maeterlinck hailed as the second Shakespeare—and yet, the latest moment in Time, always powerful; this bangled, bespangled crowd; you could feel its delight, its hearty grasp upon the Latest, as if the Latest were life-giving, sustaining, the crest of a wave that could never break—but it always broke, and the staleness set in, the reaction—here were these Sixties; riots, rallies, costumes, oh, shocking, mind-boggling—but the Seventies would find them stale, the Seventies would be different—and yet Time's pendulum knew nothing, it was blind; acting, reacting— blind, for underneath its swings (and they were getting shorter) something had given way—some centrality was gone —for fifty years, rivets wrenched out, a jangling dissolution . . .

"Buy you another?"

She had a distant feeling that the crew-cut man had asked her that several times. She swung around on the stool. *"Sure."* Working hard with her heavy tongue. Philosophy whirled away in a blur, bits flaring bright as they drowned—Maeterlinck, hula hoops, flying rivets . . .

"You'll get smashed," he warned, smiling with lips that were too flat. Nose flat, too. Eyes pebble gray. Nothing like Morrie. She shoved Morrie away. She felt sexually powerful, wanton. She put her chin unsteadily in her hands and smiled at him.

"So," he said expansively, as the bartender set her second drink before her, *"what do you do in beautiful Bagdad by the Bay?"* and even with all the liquor inside her she winced. *"Don't tell me,"* he yelled, his broad earnest face filmed with sweat, *"I'll tell you."* And he put his head back and studied her. *"You're not a stewardess. But maybe you* are *a stewardess. No, wait a minute. You're an actress. Right?"*

She polished off the shot glass with a gasp and delivered a magnificent repartee. "I'm a streetcar conductor."

"A what?"

"No, I'm a walker. I walk around. I don't step on any cracks."

"I can't hear you, honey."

"I'll tell you something. I look at the candy wrappers. And the cigarette packages. On the sidewalk. And they're no more —and no less—impressive—than stained glass." Her voice dropped. "Chartres. I'll tell you something. Everything is undifferentiated." But she had trouble with the word, and said it again, with concentration: "Un-diff-er-en-ti-ated."

He mulled this over. *"You know who you look like? What's-her-name."*

"No I don't."

"That chick, what's-her-name."

"I don't look like her."

He snapped his fingers. *"Maria Montez!"* and he beamed with recollection; then he pulled his flat nose. *"I bet I just gave my age away. You don't remember Maria Montez. Nobody in this room remembers Maria Montez. You want to know how old I am? It's no big secret. I'll tell you how old I am. Thirty-nine years old."*

"That's not so old."

"I can't hear you, honey."

"You've got a few years left."

He compressed his lips and nodded.

She tried to light a cigarette with weaving fingers. He leaned over and helped her. She noticed that there was something strange about his suit. It was too black, it didn't look normal.

"Are you an undertaker?"

"Come again?"

"Are you an undertaker?" Middleman between the casket factory and the earth. Never without business.

"You're soused, honey. Pilot. I'm a pilot."

"And I am a wanton," she said softly, the coffins fading; and she moved her empty shot glass in lazy circles.

"Hey," he said brightly, *"would you care to go up to the Mark or someplace?"*

"Where?"

"The Top of the Mark or someplace?"

"Let's go to my place."

His gray eyes blinked. "Great," he said, clearing his throat.

She pushed off into the crowd, and gathering her cigarettes from the counter in a clumsy sweep, he followed her through the din into the quiet street where she was already waving for a cab.

She led him into the bedroom, where at once she unzipped her dress and stepped out of it.

"Quite a gal," he mumbled, looking around as though for a place to put his hat, although he had no hat.

"I thought pilots were big swingers!" she said, pulling her half-slip off. The wanton of the world, juices seething. An animal pawing the ground.

He sat down in a chair and began unlacing his shoes.

She pulled off her bra and underpants, dropped them to the

floor, and kicked them aside. Blearily she looked up, and saw his two eyes glued to her body, and at that moment all the whiskey in her brain was sucked out as though by a giant syringe.

But now his shyness was behind him; he stepped out of his clothes, rejoicing in a state of obvious readiness. With a look of mingled lust, tenderness, and gratitude, he sprang to her side and folded her in his arms.

He did not smell of fresh air and sun, he smelled of nothing in particular. His shoulders were covered with little offensively curling hairs. He was kissing her. He had been kissing her for a century, lost in this boring activity while she fought down an excruciating urge to stamp on his bare toes. But she had promised herself a fling and by God she would have it, and by God's mercy he was finally getting down to business and sinking onto the mattress with her.

But, like a disease, grossness had settled into her bones; she shifted around on the bedclothes, bumped against him, caught her hair in his watch; but his face was as merry and intent as a jack-o'-lantern's, and when she was finally untangled and unsquirming, he lay on top of her with a lovely familiar heaviness; she felt a spasm of warmth. But suddenly, looking at the round crew-cut head, she burst into a storm of tears.

His head jerked up. "What's wrong!" he whispered.

"Nothing," she wept. "Just go ahead!"

He hesitated, then lowered his head again. She laid her hands on his broad back and kept crying, filled with an infinite, fathomless loneliness.

"Christ, honey," he moaned, rocking back on his haunches, "what's wrong with you?"

She took a deep breath and held it. "Nothing!" she gasped. "Don't pay any attention!"

He looked at her irresolutely, then began caressing her shoulder gingerly.

"I can't!" She tore away from him and sat in a lump, racked by loud wet sobs, her fist in her mouth. He was looking at her with round eyes. Then he jumped off the mattress and began dressing hastily.

"Is there something I could do?" he asked in a strained voice a few minutes later, tie in hand, shoelaces undone.

She shook her head, still sobbing.

With a nod he hurried to the front door.

"I'm sorry!" she cried after him, pulling her wet fist from her mouth; and she got up and went to him, cringing in her nakedness. "Do you want some coffee?" she asked through the streaming, humiliating tears.

"No no, no no, it's all right."

He brushed her cheek with his lips. The door closed. She heard him walk quickly down the stairs, tripping once on his shoelaces.

She crept back to bed. After a while the crying ebbed away. She turned her head to her clothes on the floor. "Some wanton," she said.

But at least some things were still differentiated.

37

Wanda and Conrad had tried to see Johanna often, but she always seemed to be out. They got her now and then on the phone, but her conversations were unsatisfactory—muted, preoccupied. When they invited her for Thanksgiving and she declined, they drove around to her building, knowing she was in, and knocked unremittingly on the door. Wanda carried the day's newspaper under her arm.

At last Johanna answered.

They had not seen her for almost two months; she was thin, the soft curves of her cheeks were gone, and her yellow eyes were large in her face, bright, as if she had a fever. She was amazingly dressed. They had expected to find her in slothful jeans and sweatshirt, but she wore black suede boots, a pale blue microskirt, and an embroidered maroon Indian vest over a white silk blouse. Price tags hung everywhere. Her hands and neck were gray with want of washing.

"Well," she said, her restless eyes jumping away from them, "come in."

In the center of the room a television set stood on a chair; around it on the floor lay a pool of disorder—clogged ashtrays, dirty plates, a soiled red terrycloth robe. Everything else in the room was neat, unused, covered with a layer of dust.

"Well, don't you look mod," Wanda said at last. "That's a smashing outfit."

"Oh. Well. I bought some clothes. I don't like them." She bent down, unzipped the boots, and kicked them off. "Do you want them?" she asked Wanda. "Do you want the vest?" She pulled that off, too.

"No, you keep them. They look good on you."

"You look like you're starving to death, don't you eat?" asked Conrad, sitting down on the sofa next to a five-pound box of See's chocolates.

"Do you want those chocolates? I don't want them."

Johanna saw her two friends exchange a look. "I went on a buying spree," she said impatiently. "Haven't you ever gone on a buying spree?"

"What else did you get?" asked Conrad, pointing to a crate on the floor.

"A stereo."

"Why don't you open it?"

"I haven't gotten around to it."

Wanda moved the chocolates and sat down next to Conrad. Like a jury, Johanna thõught, wiping her damp palms on her microskirt. She sat down stiffly and lit a cigarette, narrowing her eyes at them through the smoke. For the first time, she noticed that Wanda's hair was in a braid over her shoulder, and that she was shockingly thin.

"What about *her?*" she bit out to Conrad. "*Who's* starving to death?"

"Well, I'm not really starving to death, I'm pregnant," Wanda said with a smile.

"Oh," said Johanna. She tried to feel something deep at this news, but it struck her as commonplace. "Why have you braided your hair?" she asked.

"Oh, it's so greasy. Hormones."

Johanna nodded. "I thought women got fat when they got pregnant. You've gotten thin."

"The first stage. Sometimes you get thin. Especially if you throw up everything you eat."

"Are you going to quit work when it's born?" Johanna asked.

"Oh, no. At least, I don't know—we're going to have to work something out. Maybe we'll hire a nurse. Connie's getting commissions like crazy, did you know that?"

"No, she doesn't know that," Conrad said. "How could she know that? She's the man on the moon."

"Tell me about it," Johanna said dutifully.

"Oh, I did some posters for this beauty salon that wanted a psychedelic image. Bring in a new clientele. It just caught fire."

"He's a psychedelic wonder," put in Wanda. "He just throbs and undulates all over the place—like wow, as they say."

"And so you're getting a lot of commissions," said Johanna.

"I keep busy."

"Well, that's fine," she said, stubbing out her cigarette, but there was something wrong with the conversation; there had been an empty spot along the way that should have been filled. She thought back, and said to them both: "About the baby—how nice. I'm very glad for you."

The stilted words produced a moment of embarrassment. And then, as though grabbing the awkward moment by the horns, Wanda took the newspaper from under her arm and looked down at it as she spoke: "You know, for a couple of weeks we've been seeing this weird ad in the personals. We never noticed the telephone number, but for some reason it jumped out at me today. It seems to be yours." She looked up, worriedly.

Johanna said nothing. She lit another cigarette.

"Well, what's it about?" Wanda asked.

"Nothing."

"Excuse me," said Conrad, "I've got to use the bathroom."

Johanna followed him with her eyes as he went out of the room. Prearranged, no doubt. Thinking that it would be easier for her to talk to one of them alone. He would be in there for twenty minutes. And when he came out Wanda would suddenly depart for a protracted stomach ache. They were very concerned and very transparent and she wished they had not come.

"It must cost the earth to run," Wanda was probing.

"I suppose."

"Don't you get all sorts of crank calls?"

As though on cue, the phone rang. Johanna answered, listened for three seconds to a smooth unfurling of obscenities, and hung up.

"What *is* it all about, Johanna? It's the peace march in Oakland that we went on, isn't it?"

"We haven't been on any others, have we? Dedicated sloths that we are."

"Speak for yourself, dearie. We've been on them all."

Johanna's eyebrows knitted angrily as Wanda went on.

"This—person. Did you meet him that day on the march? I mean, did you talk with him or something?"

"No."

"Then—"

"I want to find him, that's all!"

The words slipped out from Wanda's mouth: "Oh, Johanna, you ought to see a psychiatrist."

"No doubt, no doubt," she muttered; and her restless eyes suddenly fixed themselves on her friend's face. "Let me assure you that if you find me strange, I find myself much more than that—I find myself repellent."

"Oh, but you're always so extreme," said Wanda, not

knowing how to manage this unexpected confession. "Look, you were in love with Morris, though God knows why, and now you're going through a bad time. Don't condemn yourself. God, you always sound like you're trying to uphold the Categorical Imperative."

"Of course," said Johanna, again looking restlessly around the room.

"Of course? To act as if everything you did were to become a universal law? Who can do it?"

"Who can afford not to?" She lit a new cigarette from the one in her mouth.

"It's unrealistic."

"It never used to be for me."

"Only since about a year ago?" Wanda said, lifting her eyebrows significantly.

"Do you—" Johanna pushed back her lank hair with an abrupt movement. "I don't suppose you ever hear from Zaidee?"

"Zaidee? No. Oh, look, Johanna, you broke with him. It's finished."

"Finished?" Johanna murmured. "Yesterday I heard a fatal car crash announced on the TV news broadcast. I wanted so badly to hear his name given as the victim's." She glanced at Wanda, who was observing her unhappily. "It could be finished that way, maybe. It would finish me, too, though."

"Oh, Johanna—" said Wanda, feelingly, but with impatience.

"Don't you understand?" said Johanna with much greater impatience. "You say it's over, but it's like taking a sack of salt and a sack of pepper and mixing them together and then saying, all right, the salt goes back into its sack and the pepper back into its."

"I don't think Morris had any trouble doing it," said Wanda as Conrad came back and sat down.

Johanna flashed her an aggrieved look.

The conversation took a trivial, desultory course, and then, as Johanna expected, Wanda got to her feet. "I feel queasy," she complained.

"Why don't you go on, sweet?" said Conrad. "Take the car and go on home to bed. I'll walk."

"Yes, do that," Johanna told her. "But don't fall asleep, because you and your husband will want to exchange impressions when he gets back."

"Touché—we stand exposed. But I'm going anyway." She lifted her friend's gray hand, pressed it, and went out the door.

"All right," said Conrad pointedly.

"You can't come in here like an interlocutor," she warned him.

"Can't I? What's this incommunicado bit, and that crazy ad, and buying things you don't want?"

"A nervous breakdown, I suppose. Your wife suggested I see a psychiatrist."

"Wife? Husband? Why do you put up this wall?"

"Because I'm ashamed. I don't want to be on intimate terms because what I am shames me." Her eyes, always moving around, now wandered to the ceiling. "It shames me to be so futile."

"Okay, everybody feels futile at times. You have in the past. But you never made an issue of it, you never turned away from your friends."

"I didn't know what real futility was then. I didn't realize what it had to offer. It has finality. It's the ultimate pain-killer." She stopped speaking abruptly.

"Go on," he said.

"You wouldn't understand," she said, getting up and walking around in her bare feet, which were as gray as her hands and neck.

"Try me," he said.

"You wouldn't understand!"

"Well, fine, then—snow me under. You can't lose anything."

She stopped walking. "My grandparents."

"What about them?"

"You couldn't understand."

"That refrain's getting to be wearing."

"You know I was raised by them?"

"I know that."

"You know what they were like, I've told you. And you've seen his portrait."

He nodded.

"All right, then, they weren't my grandparents, they were no relatives of mine. They were neighbors who took me in. My parents I hardly knew, I don't think they were ever married. We migrated out here in a truck from Oklahoma during the Depression. She had a round brown face and a

239

crimped permanent and she died young in the county hospital. He was an alcoholic with a whine and a mean temper. He disappeared, thank God.''

Conrad was rubbing his forehead. ''That's an odd story.'' He looked up at her. ''Why didn't you ever mention them?''

''I should think it was clear enough. I didn't approve of them, I decided they hadn't existed.''

''Well, okay, you disowned them, you liked these other people better. Where does all this fit in with what we were talking about?''

''Where does it fit in? I told you you wouldn't understand!'' And with a savage downward look at her whole body, she said: ''It fits in with the nature of the mongrel, with sloth and squalidness of the spirit. Von Kaulbach chose the highest common denominators of life, he chose honor and beauty and order. Maybe it was easier in his day—you can't use those words now without a smile. They're too big. They're like big out-of-date furniture. But I believed in his choice, I believed in those things for myself. But it seems now that I was holding them in place like a bad graft, it seems that the first time I ever opened up completely to another person I came apart like a piece of wet paper.''

''Morris wasn't just another person—''

''You don't have to tell me that! His face was like—I don't know—a perfectly resolved chord. He thrilled my soul, he moved me— Oh, I know, I'll have to smile now!''

''No, you don't have to smile. But I meant that, whatever else he was, he was also your exact opposite number.''

''And the opposite number won.''

''Won? I don't see love in terms of a pitched battle.''

''Ours was.''

''Then why do you want it back? And you do—I can tell.''

''I don't want him back. I do. I don't know.'' She sank into a chair, twisting a button on her blouse. ''You see, I've lost my old confidence.''

''Confidence? An iron-clad, self-determined ethic. Sometimes terrifying to behold—''

''I don't want to talk about myself anymore,'' she broke in. ''Why should you interrogate me? I don't probe your private feelings.''

''You can ask anything you want.''

''I don't want to ask anything.'' She dug into a carton of

240

cigarettes, broke open a new package, and lit up again. Her fingers were deeply nicotined, grading from copper to yellow into the gray of her hands. Her face was closed, the eyes moving with shallow darts around the room.

"I wish you would ask something," he said helplessly.

"How is everything with you?" she inquired, complying.

"Well," he said with a smile, "it's odd, getting to be a father at this age."

"You're glad about it."

"Oh, yes, I'm glad about it."

"You don't look overjoyed."

"Oh, I suppose I will in time. It's just that I'm still—you know. About Closeto." He glanced away; he seemed self-conscious. "Have you ever sat indoors and looked out the window and you can see the wind but you can't hear it? There's a feeling of stillness. It's always like that with me now, underneath. It's a good thing, I guess. It's peaceful. It's limited. Well, it makes happiness different. It makes it steadier, but it makes it smaller." He said brusquely: "I know I cut a laughable figure, going through a period of protracted mourning for a cat."

"Why? You're supposed to mourn a year for a person, a month for a dog, and a week for a cat? Where do these ideas come from? What does anyone know about anyone else's feelings?"

"Not half enough, Johanna," he said meaningfully.

But she was busy stabbing out her half-smoked cigarette and lighting another.

"You're smoking a lot."

"Apparently."

After a silence, he said: "You didn't mention to us that you had to move."

"How do you know that?"

"There's a notice tacked up downstairs."

"Oh, yes."

"Have you been looking for another place?"

"No. I've still got a month. I'll start looking when I feel like it. I don't feel like it now."

"Just don't wait so long that you wind up on the street."

The phone rang. She got up and answered it. He heard her say: "Yes? . . . What kind of shoes? . . . Headgear? . . . I'm sorry . . ."

"That ad!" he exclaimed, striking the newspaper which Wanda had left. "What in—"

"Conrad, my head's breaking!" she cried, clamping her fingers into her hair. "It's kind—kind of you, but please stop!"

"Won't you come and stay with us for a while?" he asked, getting up.

"No."

"I don't know what to do," he said, slowly shaking his head and going to the door.

"Thank you for coming."

He stood at the door looking at her for a moment. "Good night," he said at last, and went out.

She turned on the television set and sat down on the red robe. When the screen went white at one A.M. she had fallen asleep in front of it.

38

In the weeks that followed his birthday, Morris had grown more and more dissatisfied with his situation. Zaidee and Thor had departed for a commune in Big Sur—the Haight was getting "spooked up" and they wanted safer surroundings for their baby—and finally, in the beginning of the new year, Morris followed them, hitchhiking south with his hair a mass of corkscrew curls and his ragged walrus mustache lifting in the wind.

Holy Mountain, the commune, wasn't much to his liking, but he sat the winter out there and hoped that spring would bring him some direction. Then he began hearing miraculous things about a human-potential center in the area called Esalen, where the approach to the personality was original, unstructured, where the academic sludge was sliced through and the here-and-now was believed in, and where the results were as immediate as the philosophy. He decided to look into it.

There he slept not in one of the motel-like rooms provided at high cost, but in a canyon, where every night he threw his sleeping bag down under a different tree and gazed for hours at the star-thick sky, listening to the wind in the towering pines. At dawn, none the worse for lack of sleep, he was up and off for the Esalen kitchens, where he paid for his classes by peeling potatoes and washing dishes.

At first it was impossible for him to expose his deepest feelings in front of other people. Herb, his group leader, was the soul of patience, but even he had finally heaved a sigh at such recalcitrance. And then, suddenly, Morris brought his thoughts to bear on his father, his strongest and saddest memory, and he had managed to pump up a horrible gush of despair: tears spun off his turbulent face, his eye sockets and nostrils burned, and with each new outburst he saw his father's old face weeping too, more and more, and being joined, one by one, by other faces, a long line of people whom Morris had insulted and injured, all weeping bitterly. Quiet at last, he sat with his head in his hands and felt a strong taste of cheap theatrics; but arms were going around his body and cheeks were pressed against his head.

From then on he had no trouble baring his soul. He strangled pillows that symbolized his self-deceptions, he wept shamelessly in the arms of a girl who represented all the women he had mistreated; he confessed his hunger for success, for youth; nothing was left out—the tarnished thimble, his wife's Biography of Zero, the nickel-sized blister on Johanna's heel; even, God help him, his tutti-frutti-and-TV stupors, for, as he had always known, it was the petty disgraces that cut the deepest. But in this clean windy place hung between sky and sea there was no disgrace. Supported by a ring of faces as vulnerably human as his own, he found his pain almost enjoyable.

And yet one night in his sleeping bag he had said suddenly into the stillness: "I don't see any of it nationalizing Standard Oil," and he knew that the old worm, perhaps only an undernourished threadworm, had nevertheless begun nibbling at the rose.

Still, there were changes in him that buoyed him along: less interest in food, a reduced sexual urge. In any other environment his quieted loins would have terrified him, but here he basked in the release from their tyranny. Here it was the accepted path to spiritual growth. Any kind of gluttony was regarded with pity.

Sometimes he took a day off and hiked over the Holy Mountain for a visit, wandering among the tents and shacks where he too had grown vegetables and carried water from a stream, but where, unlike Thor and Zaidee, he had felt life slipping by. The young couple thrived. Zaidee was pregnant again, her first baby still tied to her chest with a fringed shawl. Thor was busy calking their shack, his hair hanging to his shoulders in gold ringlets, his skin the fresh pink of his not quite seventeen years. Morris felt inexpressibly world-stained around him, yet in an odd way he felt younger than the boy. Thor and Zaidee had pooled their simpleness in a bid for the more staid joys; there would be no new paths in their lives, no flash of the miraculous. He pictured them standing eternally in the door of their shack, their faces aging with the seasons, a gaggle of children growing at their side.

No longer involved with Zaidee, he felt his affection for her deepening. He was touched by her pride in her small family, by her pleasure in belonging. And he realized that he was thankful for her happiness not just because he was fond of her, but because her happiness reassured him that no one died of a broken heart. Often he thought of Johanna standing in line to board the Greyhound bus, and he would pass his hand slowly over his face. But then his spirits lifted as a certainty skimmed through his mind like a breeze: that they would meet again someday, in a better future.

And hiking back down the mountain, with the wildflowers blazing in the long grass and the air alive with bird cries, he would stop in his tracks, dazzled by the blue fragments of sea shining through the trees.

As spring progressed he met a woman who had no immediate impact on him, but whom he found pleasantly vivid and together. Her name was Dorothy, she was in her late forties, with a brisk manner and a deeply tanned, deeply scored face. Her features were large and generous, the eyes an electric green; she wore arty earrings, peasant skirts, and bright red lipstick, like a bohemian from the Fifties, but she was very much up-to-date, with three ex-husbands and a thrown-over career as a child psychiatrist. She had come to Esalen to study massage.

Dorothy's enthusiasm counterbalanced the doubts Morris had begun to feel. "The trouble with revolutions in the past," she said, "was that they were always grafted onto the same old psychological makeup. But we're changing people from the inside." And he would nod hopefully. "Massage, for instance," she went on, "heals psychic wounds and releases life energies—"

He couldn't go along with this; it sounded dangerously close to osteopathy and cultism. But he would have to make some bread when he left, and though squeezing sore muscles wasn't his idea of a brilliant career, he took a class in massage. It was humble work, but he was good at it, and it soothed his growing restlessness.

In the meantime he settled into an affair with Dorothy, spending a couple of nights a week in the small anonymous room she rented on the Esalen grounds. She was sensual, vital, and comfortable; he liked her very much, but he was afraid that her feelings might run deeper than his. He began hinting that theirs was only a temporary liaison.

"I'm taking off pretty soon," he told her one evening, as they lay on her bed. "There's not one damn thing I haven't vomited up in that group. I'm tired of it. I'm tired of massage. I'm through."

"Oh, hang on and ride it out," she said, patting his shoulder.

The dark square of the window was silently traversed by the twin lights of a distant jet. Morris' eyes followed them as a nameless longing spread through his chest.

"Yeah, I'm through," he said again.

"Oh, don't go yet," she said, putting her arms around him. He pulled slightly away. "What is it?" she asked.

"Look, I've got to be honest, Dorothy—the vibes I get are that you're in deeper than I am—"

"Oh," she said, and astonished him by giving a good-humored smile. "You're all wrong, Morris. I like you. I'd be sorry to see you go, sure, but only because going to bed with you is a friendly, enjoyable thing." And she gave him an amused glance of her bright green eyes. "I can tell that your past is littered with broken hearts, and that's how you think it ought to be."

He shook his head in denial, but could not keep his eyes from falling on her worst point, the deep furrow that ran from between her eyebrows to the middle of her forehead. She had no right to be so flip, so certain. She was old. She had never comprehended his generosity, he who was nine years younger and involved with so leathery a face. And he felt that not only he but his entire sex was being ill-used.

She seemed to follow his thoughts.

"If you're unhappy with anything, then please split, Morris. Don't turn something nice into a hassle. I don't have time for all that." She turned around and switched on the lamp by the bed. And it was as though nothing had happened; she looked at him as warmly and cheerfully as ever. "I think it's dinner-time—if you'll excuse me for being so practical."

"Not at all," he said, relieved, stretching in the restored atmosphere of goodwill. "Practicality's a charming quality, one with which I am also blessed, if you've noticed. Let's go eat."

"Sometimes you come out with a phrase right from the last century," she said, swinging her legs over the side of the bed.

"Oh?" he murmured, lying back for a moment. "Must be a hangover from this girl I used to know. She had a way of talking all her own. Like she used to call me—" and he paused —"Despairovitch."

39 | All during that preceding autumn, Johanna's NO ADMITTANCE sign hung on her door. Ignoring it, Aquiline sometimes wandered into the studio where Johanna was trying to paint. Johanna made no objection; there was no concentration that stood to be broken.

"Do you think this is good?" she would ask indifferently, pointing at what she was doing.

"No," Aquiline would say. Her hair had grown into a natural, and she had discarded her leotards and blouse in favor of a long batik gown.

"What do you know about painting?" Johanna asked her.

"Nothin'. But I know that ain't good."

"You're right." She showed her an old painting, the portrait of Herr von Kaulbach, but did not look at it herself. "Do you think this is good?"

Aquiline nodded. "He got a pair of eyes there."

Johanna put the painting away, still not looking at it. "Have you decided where you'll go when the place is torn down?" she asked.

"Oakland," said Aquiline firmly.

"What will you do there, anything special?"

"I got something lined up, don't you worry."

"Oh, really? What?"

"That my business."

"You're a big bag of secrets."

"That my right."

"And Charles, I suppose he'll finally have to give you up if you move to Oakland."

"Yeah. You see him comin' round and comin' round, drive me crazy? He got a tender heart and now it hurtin' and he don't know how to stop it. I tell him it stop hurtin' if he don't see me."

"I don't know if that works," said Johanna.

"Gonna bust him on the head next time, always hangin' in the hall like the CIA. Try to make me sorry. He know I like to keep him, he the best man I ever had."

"Why don't you?"

"That my business," she said shortly. "Where *you* goin' when they tear this mess down?"

"I don't know."

Wanda and Conrad were still after her to get with it—it was now two weeks into December. Conrad had taken on a gentle, humorous tone. Today he had said on the phone, "Here, this will make your day. Josh asked about you and I told him you had to move, and he said, 'Tell her I have a cottage on my grounds, tell her she can have it free of charge.' "

"You know what he can do with his cottage," she had said.

"I realize that."

"Then why mention it?"

"Well, first of all, I thought you might be amused. I'd forgotten that you no longer have a sense of humor. And secondly, love, to keep your mind on the subject. You've only got two weeks left."

She wiped her hands on a rag now and said to Aquiline, "I guess I'll wind up somewhere."

"You look like you wind up in the mortuary."

"Thank you."

"You look like you from another world. You got these big holes in your cheeks. You don't connect no more, you' eyes they just go right through everything like it was air."

"Well, I'm seeing you, Aquiline," she said, looking at the dark probing eyes and smiling.

"No, I don't think you see nothin'. And I don't care. That you' problem. Why don't you get you' ass movin'? You got dust piled up in the other room a mile high. And you' neck is dirty. You ain't even got the energy to wash you' neck?"

"What good does it do to wash your neck?"

"What good it do not to?"

"Sometimes you make me very impatient, Aquiline."

"I'm goin', don't worry. You' no company for anybody."
Their visits usually went along these lines.

One gray foggy afternoon Charles came to Johanna's door, sweating very hard under his black suit, which was badly wrinkled. He leaned unsteadily against the doorjamb and, looking at her with bloodshot eyes, asked if he could come in.

"You know what it's all about with Aquiline?" he asked with a thickness to his hollow voice, sinking into a chair. "She comes into the hall and she *kicks* me. Then she locks her door and she hears me pounding and she won't open up."

Before Johanna could speak Aquiline came banging through the door. "You come up here and shoot you' mouth off about us!" she yelled. "We are private! You come on out of here!"

But Charles dug himself into the chair, eyeing her with desperate hope.

"This Johanna's house, she don't want you here!"

Johanna opened her mouth to protest, but Aquiline brought her foot down thunderously on the floor. "You hang around and hang around like I was never finished and I tell you I *am* finished! What I have to do?"

"You're so hard," he said mournfully, and he said again, into the air, "Kicked me."

"I didn't *want* to kick you!"

His eyes spread out over his wrinkled suit and trembling fingers. "Look at me, Reverend Charles Mackay, he's drunk in the sight of the Lord. Never touched it in his life, now he's been full of beer for weeks."

"It only beer," Aquiline said impatiently.

"Never touched it before."

"I tole you I was a bad influence. Now you see for you'self."

But his eyes warmed and he shook his head. "No, sweetheart, we always got along good—"

But this tremulous appeal seemed to set her afire.

"I don't *want* to get along good! Get along good with you, like everybody you know get along good, sittin' and prayin' and lovin'—not me, man, not me! I don't want love, I want change! *You* never change in a million years, you and you' kind been hangin' doin' nothin' forever, like you been hangin' in that hall with you' big sad eyes. You a useless nigger, Charles!"

He had risen unsteadily toward the end of her speech, and he stood before her with his shoulders rounded, a look of bitter concentration on his face. "Those are not things to say here," he said, and walked stiffly across the room to the door.

Aquiline followed, slamming the door shut.

Johanna went to her window and pulled the dusty lace aside. A minute later she heard the street door opening, and a few final shreds of words; then Charles walked down the brambled front walk into the foggy afternoon. The telephone began ringing behind her, but she could not take her eyes from the tall figure, super-erect in its effort not to weave, making its way along the rubble-bordered sidewalk. She dropped the curtain and answered the phone on the sixth ring.

"Calling about your ad," said an indistinct voice at the other end.

"Yes," she said, and explained in the words that had by now become a formula: "I'm trying to locate a person I saw on one of the peace marches."

"Why?"

The voice was bodyless, a faint scraping of sound.

"I have certain things I want to discuss," she said with the deep sense of pointlessness that always overcame her during these conversations.

"Speak about what?"

"Let me compare notes with you," she went on. "This person was wearing a cloak."

"Right," the dim voice said.

"What color?"

"Black."

"What kind of shoes do you wear with it?"

"Cloth."

She paused for a moment. "And headgear?"

"Hide," came the faint reply.

She felt a prickling of sweat along her hairline; when she spoke her voice sounded forced. "You were on the first peace march?"

"Right."

"Can you tell me where it ended?"

"Some park in West Oakland."

"Can you tell me about a clearing?"

"Clearing? Yeah, there was a clearing with some guys on bongos. Late, when I was there, I danced for a while . . ." The voice faded away.

Her mind was furiously empty. She was staring at the looped cord of the receiver. "I'm sorry to ask so many questions," was all she could think of to say.

Silence.

"I've gotten so many crank calls, I've had to try to weed out the—"

"What you got in mind?" the voice broke in softly.

"It's hard to put into words," she said, trying frantically to clear her mind, "I can't tell you in just a few words . . ."

"Where you located?"

250

"Where am I located?"

She did not answer; she was on the brink of hanging up.

"This some joke, it's okay with me."

"No," she protested, pressing her nails into her palm. "I'm in the Fillmore. 1405 Webster."

"Right, then," the voice murmured; indifferently, it seemed.

"When—when would you come by?"

"Tonight," it said, almost inaudibly.

"Then, about eight? I'll be downstairs to let you in."

The receiver at the other end was replaced with a delicate click.

She dropped into a chair and threw her head back. The conversation had drained her; she was blankly unequal to whatever might follow it.

40

Outside, through the window, the day was closing in fog. She looked out over the waste of rubble across the street; the solitary chimney and bare staircase stood faintly outlined in the gloom. The streetlights went on, dimly, as if under smoked glass.

Eight o'clock came and passed. She began to breathe more easily. Nine. Nine thirty. Nothing. At ten, deeply, blankly tired, thawed in her bones that he had not come, she undressed and crawled into bed.

A distant sound—a dry sifting stony sound that somehow oppressed her; half awake, she tried to push it from her ears, but it endured, unplaceable and troubling. She climbed sleepily from under the blankets and, crossing her arms in the chill, went to the window. Only the dark fog, palely bruised by the streetlights. Then gradually she became aware of a dark voluminous blur progressing up the sidewalk with a slow sidewinding movement, dragging something along the pavement behind it. Her head snapped back from the pane; she blundered to the night table and grabbed the clock up to her eyes in the dark. Past one. A name sliced idiotically through her mind: Wladislaw Maniak. The outside door should be locked at nightfall, but often it wasn't. Often it wasn't, she thought, pressing the clock back down and hurrying again to the window. The figure flowed up the front walk onto the porch and was lost from sight.

She rubbed her arms fiercely in the cold. Small sounds from the entranceway below. Sounds on the stairway. Finally the hall floorboards gave a single creak like a rifle shot, and a soft knock sounded on her door.

Drowsiness flooded back; she yawned blindingly and held her face in her hands, urging the moment to pass and deliver her back to bed. Yet, moving her hands from her face to the red robe, she struggled into it. She stepped soundlessly into the other room. The knock came again. A stupor of indecision. Suddenly she turned on a lamp, crossed the rug, and slid the bolt back.

The cloak filled the doorway—black, webbed with silver moisture. She shot her eyes to the gap between the wings of the high collar and saw a strip of faintly Mongol face, male, young. The skullcap was of some scraped animal skin, dented, discolored, glistening with wet. The figure moved past her dragging a heavy burlap sack, and with a long bare arm noiselessly closed the door.

She flung her head rigidly to the bedroom door. "My husband is asleep in there!"

He crossed the rug, the cloak trailing damply, and stood by the lamp. Behind the narrow slot the eyes drifted around the amber-lit room; they were narrow deep-set eyes; the nose below was fine, curved; the lips thin. She dropped her eyes to the damp sack on the rug, to the feet protruding from under the cloak, clad in muddy burlap-like material stiffened with something waxy, the toes excessively long and pointed, angling upward. The feet moved; he sank to the arm of a chair like a great bat half settling. He was looking at her now, with a kind of animal mindlessness, a sleepy indifference to her poise for flight—one hand at the lapels of her robe, the other on the doorknob. In the silence she heard the hollow, distant yawn of a foghorn. She was keenly aware of the coolness of the doorknob, she anticipated the twisting movement of her wrist; yet the hand remained motionless.

"Right," he said at length, in the windy blurred voice from the phone; and she could hear now that it derived from some flaw in the larynx. "What do you want?" he asked.

"*I don't want*—" She stopped, and tried to control her voice. "I don't want to see anyone this late. I didn't expect you so—so late."

"How long you been looking for me?" he asked in a lax tone of curiosity, his eyes drifting away from her.

"A while."

"How long a while?" he asked, his eyes settling on her again.

"Six weeks," she told him, and gave her head a dazed shake. Six weeks, over two hundred dollars, merely to see this damp unappetizing creature step out of its cloak?

She moved across the room, slowly, her hands groping into her pockets and working inside them. Her nostrils breathed in an odor of damp cloth, mixed with some musky earth smell. An empty place, she thought, a wet field, muddy burlap, old moldering rags like black underbrush, a dark, sweetly rotting smell . . .

"It's past one o'clock," she heard herself saying, sharply.
"I don't see no time . . ."

"Can't you speak up?" she asked, clutching her hips
through the pockets.

"You come close, you can hear good enough."

"My husband will be stepping out of that room any minute," she whispered threateningly, and in spite of her tension
her lips trembled with amusement at the ridiculous words.

There was no amusement on the strip of face before her,
no capacity for amusement. It was a withdrawn, dully ob-
servant visage.

"I—suppose you're on drugs?" she said, and again her
words struck her as ludicrous, and her lips trembled.

". . . You suppose?" he asked with a smile, and she saw
small silvery teeth, thin, translucent.

"I don't know why I asked you here." She broke out with,
"There's no point—I'm sorry—"

"Sorry . . ." he echoed.

"I have to sleep, I have to sleep." She stared past his face
at the wall of etched landscapes; the clearing in the park,
she thought, shafts of sunlight pouring low through the trees,
how he had danced, his cloak swirling, saturated with light,
how she had wanted to know, so badly, if the light penetrated . . .

"I want you to dance," she said, her hands sliding up
around her face.

He got to his feet. He seemed to be sleeping, swaying
imperceptibly inside his voluminous garment. A moment
went by. Then he began with small groping movements
of his burlaped feet to move around the rug. He began
whirling, with dizzying intensity, the cloak flared with a soft
flap, washed gold by the lamplight. He flew in circles, bending
double, then shooting backward, catching himself with a deft
wrench and crouching again, the long burlap toes darting
soundlessly over the rug.

"I want you to take off the cloak," she said, taking a slow
step back.

Still dancing, he began undoing the clasps, one by one. He
pulled the garment from his shoulders and dropped it to his
wheeling feet, then scraped the skullcap off and threw it
down. Erratically, he came to a stop, feet apart, breathing
normally, as if he had not moved at all. His torso was bare

except for a short vest of animal hide, gray, the fur worn to the quick. Against his smooth chest lay the usual web of beads and pendants. He wore a pair of soiled black pinstripe trousers tied at the hips with a cord. The face, released from the wings of the collar, was broad, smooth-skinned, the color of honey. The Mongol look resided there, in the complexion and in the deep-set eyes, but the hair was an Anglo-Saxon dirty blond; from a ragged center part it hung down to either ear in uneven hanks, through which she caught the gleam of an earring. He was very young, twenty, twenty-two. The thin nose and lips gave him a look of premature wear.

"You like my dance," he said in his distant, cloudy voice. His slim muscular body, lightly filmed with sweat, shone in the lamplight. "You dance," he said, sitting down on the floor with a quick folding movement, like an animal dropping.

"No," she said.

He seemed to fall asleep in an instant, half sitting, his head bent to his knees.

"Don't go to sleep," she said. "You have to go."

He slept on, half sitting. She dared not touch him, somehow. She heard the foghorn again. Drops of water pinged to the ground from the eaves. She sat down and waited for him to wake.

41

A shattering blast of rock music woke her. The room was pearl gray with early morning, damp. The throw rugs were still in disarray, the cloak still lay on the floor. Coming out from the kitchen, a transistor radio blaring from a pocket, his skullcap pulled down to his eyes, her visitor came shuffling in with his fingers snapping. He said something through a mouthful of white bread and began putting his cloak on. He seemed unaware of the noise, which now flowed out from under the great garment. He leaned over and tried to kiss her, but was easily turned aside. He seemed unaware of being turned aside. His fingers snapped softly.

"Do you have a name?" she asked.

"Clovis," he said, taking the sack by its neck.

"And you saw the ad only yesterday?" she asked, trying to detain him.

"I don't read the papers," he said, going to the door, pulling the sack behind him. He stopped. Whether he had merely come to one of his odd standstills or was waiting for her, she did not know, but she went into the bedroom and, without combing her hair or washing, pulled off her pajamas and robe and got into the nearest clothes at hand, her paint-stiffened Levi's and an old sweatshirt. Grabbing her trench-coat, feeling groggy and foul-breathed, she went back to him and they walked out into the foggy morning.

Half an hour later they arrived at Aquatic Park. The beach was wet, a handful of gulls hopped alongside the muddy surf. They came to the curved gray pier, but Clovis turned onto a smaller wooden pier that lay parallel to it, ducked under a chain, and proceeded along the splintered planks, which echoed hollowly under their feet. At the tip of the pier sat a square stucco building the size of one large room and the color of a scuffed canvas shoe. Old crates and sodden cardboard boxes littered its approach, where pigeons and gulls scrounged in the windblown drizzle. A maroon hearse was parked by the building's side.

Clovis dragged his sack through the rubble and knocked on the door, where a handwritten notice fluttered from a nail, its inked words faded to an indecipherable rust.

256

No one answered. He tried the knob and pushed the door open. A gust of wet wind blew in with them, then the door slammed shut and Johanna was aware of intolerable heat and the smell of burning dust. The place was dark, but her companion swept to a window and sent a shade up. The room filled with gray light, it was a kind of storehouse-cum-studio; armor, stacks of crockery, and a score of birdcages stood cheek-by-jowl with tables of chisels, mallets, a large sanding machine, and stones of all sizes ranging up to waist-high boulders. On the floor, which was covered with stone dust and stone chips, three electric heaters glowed. Two people were getting to their feet from a mattress, a stocky middle-aged man with a pronged red beard, and a girl of striking paleness emphasized by elaborately darkened eyes and a black velvet robe.

Clovis stepped out of his cloak, turned off the heaters, and went to a small but modern buff-colored kitchen unit behind a cluster of birdcages and lost himself in some dish-clattering activity.

"The room gets so hot," the bearded man said to Johanna, his pale blue eyes sparkling with astonishment, "because we fall asleep with the heaters on."

She absorbed the information, wondering what it was about her that caused him such astonishment.

"How are you, Jane?" he asked, turning to the pale girl, and his eyes bore her the same look of delighted amazement.

"I'm fine."

"I'm so glad."

He smoothed out the two prongs of his beard and beamed around him. His hair was long and auburn, his face ruddy, with sandy eyebrows and lashes. He wore black Levi's covered with stone dust, a heavy, ribbed blue sweater, and a chain holding a flat smooth gray stone. He rubbed his hands together, then strode into what was apparently the bathroom.

The girl disappeared around the birdcages and a moment later emerged with a plate of glazed doughnuts, which she handed to Johanna with heavily beringed fingers. Then she lit a thin brown cigarette. Johanna's sandaled feet, coated with stone dust, were icy now and she sat down with the doughnuts on a pile of old rags and tucked her feet under her. The cigarette was offered to her. The smoke she inhaled was harsh, but she inhaled deeply and held her breath, which

257

she had heard was the proper way.

Clovis came soundlessly from behind the birdcages, wiping his lips. "You better buy more hamburger," he said in his thin voice.

"He eats hamburger raw," the girl told Johanna in a full-bodied matter-of-fact tone. Johanna saw that the edges of her blackened eyelids were stuck with tiny jewels.

"You guys driving to Marin?" Clovis asked.

"That mattress gives me a backache," the girl complained, putting her dead-white hand to the small of her back.

"Stand up and sleep, then," said Clovis, exposing his translucent teeth.

"He stands up when he sleeps," the girl told Johanna.

"He slept at my place last night and he didn't stand up," Johanna replied, uncertainly.

"Were you awake all night?" the girl asked.

"No."

"Then how do you know? He gets up, and he stands, and he's asleep." She spoke forcefully, yet without a grain of approval.

The bathroom door opened and the bearded man approached, again rubbing his square red hands. "Well, Clovis," he said heartily, "what have we got there?"

Clovis crouched by the sack and began working from its interior an old-fashioned green birdcage with a round top.

"Oh, very lovely," murmured the man, rocking back and forth on his heels. Setting the cage down, Clovis reached farther into the sack and brought out two stones, each the size of a man's head, of an ordinary gray color.

"There you are, Scotty," he said in his whisper, getting to his feet with a dull jangle of beads.

"You've got an eye for shape. Hasn't he got an eye for shape, my dear?" Scotty asked, beaming Jane his jolly astonished look and pulling a wallet from his pocket.

"They're round," she agreed.

"Yes!" As if her remark were intensely original.

"You're a sculptor?" asked Johanna.

"I am," he said, handing Clovis a five-dollar bill.

"I used to work at the Antigone Galleries," she told him.

"Is that so? Josh Gillingsby is one of my oldest friends, he's given me tremendous encouragement. Hasn't he, Jane?"

"He's very helpful to struggling artists," Johanna said,

pausing to test herself for some reaction to the cigarette. All she felt was a voracious hunger, and she bit a doughnut in two.

"Scotty isn't struggling," Jane said assertively, "he knows what he's doing, he's conquered his material."

"I meant struggling in terms of recognition."

"Fuck that," said Jane.

Scotty was following the exchange with hearty amazement, his eyes jumping back and forth between the two faces.

"You going to Marin?" asked Clovis, taking a green tablet from the pocket of his pinstripe trousers and swallowing it.

"Marin?" Scotty asked, as if he had never heard the name before.

"We've got to get another mattress," Jane told him, and suddenly the room was set on its end by rock music as Clovis brought out his transistor and turned it on. Just then a couple came through the door in ponchos and sandals, a girl and boy of no more than eighteen, both with dark wavy long hair parted in the center, a style which suited the pink demure face of the girl, but which made the boy look like George Eliot.

A few drowned words were exchanged, then it seemed to Johanna that time came to a stop. For the first time since she had broken up with Morris the horrifying restlessness was routed; she was not content, but she was not discontented either; rather, she seemed to have found a pocket of existence where neither state was important, and where the lack of their importance was not important either. Everything around her—music, faces, objects—was continually being fed into this pocket and continually consumed, a circular, never-ending, and somehow satisfying process. She was now acutely hungry, though she had eaten all the doughnuts. With no sense of impoliteness she went into the kitchen and opened the buff-colored refrigerator. She took out a wedge of Monterey jack cheese and a turkey leg and consumed them, leaning on the shining counter where a band of cockroaches marched beneath her nose. She looked at the clock over the stove—it was past four o'clock.

When she walked back around the birdcages, the others were leaving, as if they had forgotten her existence. Scotty, in an ankle-length gray plastic raincoat, was carrying a large stone that had been chipped and polished in such a way that smooth surfaces alternated with pocked declivities. She looked at the rest of his artifacts; some of the stones were simply sanded along their natural lines, others had been punctured with deep holes or were grooved with wavy lines like the cancellation mark on a postage stamp. She wandered back to the doorway, where Clovis was lifting the hem of his cloak and wringing it out. His movements were extraordinarily precise, as if he were involved in a ritual, and his lips moved without sound. His eyes seemed not to focus. Jane locked the door and the little group climbed into the maroon hearse, whose back section was outfitted with car cushions. Scotty drove, Jane beside him. Clovis lay on his back on the floor, staring at the curved ceiling, his lips still moving. The boy who looked like George Eliot had been given the stone to carry, and he and the rosy-cheeked girl held hands over it. The vehicle, a capsule of fragrant smoke and whining rock music, rumbled down the wooden pier, stopped while Scotty jumped out to draw the chain back, and then proceeded with hearseful elegance into the dark afternoon.

Johanna looked through the lozenge-shaped windows at the wet buildings, at the orange cables of the Golden Gate Bridge, at a dense wall of trees; then a blast of cold air filled the interior and they were climbing out in a carport attached to a low-slung house of rain-darkened wood, strung almost to death with blue and white Christmas lights.

"I'll take it," said Scotty, lifting the stone from the boy's arms. "Turn off the music, Clovis," and he led the group into the house. A woman was standing by the fireplace, painting. She had apparently heard them, but had not moved, only lowered her brush. She had a small square of board on a metal tripod easel, and was, Johanna saw as they came abreast of her, rendering a beribboned kitten in acrylics.

"Hi, Mom," said George Eliot, kissing her cheek.

She put the brush down now and removed her pink spotless smock. She was a woman in her fifties, neat, colorless, in a gray wool dress with a pearl necklace at her throat. The room, a showplace of Scandinavian modern, was dominated by a white Christmas tree hung with pale blue ornaments. Behind her, the mantelpiece was decorated with white candles and loops and rosettes of blue satin ribbon.

"This is my wife," Scotty told Johanna with merry surprise.

The wife gave them all a polite, uneasy smile which curdled slightly at Clovis. "How are you, Scotty?" she asked.

"Here," he boomed, holding out the stone to her.

"It's too heavy," she murmured with an embarrassed nod. "Could you put it out on the porch?"

"I'll show you something, my dear," he smiled at Johanna, and led her out to an open porch overlooking the darkening ocean, where a long row of his stones lay on the floor against the railing. He set the latest one down and straightened up briskly. "I think it's lovely here."

"Yes," she agreed, looking over the side to the beach far below. It was there, she was sure, that she and Morrie had hiked that first day, after their night on Mount Tamalpais, and the red sun had gone down and reappeared behind them as the moon, silver and cool. The moon rose in her memory, only to disappear through the top of her skull.

They joined the others, where the wife was busy putting more logs in the fireplace, as if needing something normal to do. Her son got up to help her and she handed him a log silently, with a long look.

"You have beautiful hair, Mrs. Kirk," commented the young girl with a tender smile.

Mrs. Kirk touched her brown hair with an awkward gesture.

"And you have a beautiful home," the girl went on softly. "I think you're a beautiful human being."

"She is a beautiful human being," echoed Jane, closing her jewel-studded eyes.

Clovis sat hunched on a footstool, a pool of darkness.

"Mrs. Kirk is a beautiful human being," the girl announced feelingly to Johanna and Scotty.

"Oh, shut up, Susan," George Eliot muttered.

Susan smiled more tenderly still. "She created you. That was the most beautiful thing of all."

"What about me?" boomed Scotty. "Don't I get any credit?"

"They need a mattress," the boy said shortly, not meeting his mother's eyes.

"There's one in the playroom," she said. "I'll help you with it, Michael."

So his name was not George Eliot, but Michael. Of course it would be. Every male under the age of twenty was named Michael, just as every female under the age of twenty was named Susan. Poor souls, growing up with names no better than so many overworked numbers, wouldn't you think they would change them for something fresh and fitting—as she had changed Fayette for Johanna? And her name, Johanna, floated through her head and, like the moon, disappeared through the roof of her skull. She swung around and tried to find it, staring up at the smooth white ceiling. Then the need passed; what she wanted was more food. She wandered into the kitchen, all yellow, splashed with yellow curtains, yellow potholders, yellow daisies. Susan was already there, helping herself to a bowl of potato salad. Johanna dug a spoon in, and once more time came to a standstill.

She was sitting, now, at the kitchen table with its yellow cloth. The others were there, too, eating and talking desultorily. Outside it was dark, with the blackness that indicates night, not early evening. The mattress lay on the floor with Clovis at its center like a great bat, chewing a sandwich through the slot in his collar. Mrs. Kirk sat next to her husband, who, with his arm around her, now and then planted a warm kiss on her cheek, at which she gave him a strained but not unkind smile. Jane, who was working over an astrological chart which she carried around in her bag, raised a pair of unperturbed eyes at the sound of the smack.

"I think it's getting late," Michael said, only a moment after they had all assembled, it seemed to Johanna.

"It *is* close to twelve," Mrs. Kirk agreed; and a look of worry crossed her face, as if she were afraid they would all stay over.

"What a nice time we've had!" Scotty said. "Thank you, my dear! It's always a pleasure to visit you!"

"Thank you, Scotty," she said in her turn, lowering her eyes from the pronged beard.

"And what have you discovered?" he asked Jane, pointing to her chart; then he pointed to Clovis. "Get off the mattress, my boy, we're going!"

They trailed through the house, Scotty and Michael carrying the mattress. Mrs. Kirk opened the door for them; she flinched as Clovis' cloak trailed over her shoes, but bade them all a courteous farewell, hugging herself in the cold, her eyes lingering on her son.

"How do you like my house?" Scotty asked Johanna as the mattress was thrown into the hearse.

"I like where it is, above the beach."

"I think it's a lovely house. I had it built to specifications.

Ruth likes it very much, she likes rattling around doing little things. Did you notice the decorations? Ruth is awfully good at that. I'm going to come home for Christmas. She always makes a very nice Christmas for me. Hop in, everybody.''

Somewhere along the route, with the sea sounding in their ears, Clovis was released into the night.

''Where has he gone?'' Johanna asked, but no one bothered to answer.

And she did not mind; she was content to sit and watch the dark shapes fly by the windows. Abruptly the hearse stopped again, and the young couple got out. Then they were back at the pierhouse, and she was curled up on the old mattress. She heard the sound of lovemaking and turned her back, dreaming of stone gargoyles flying through the night sky.

42

When she awakened, the small room was over-heated, reverberating with the usual electric guitar music, a sound which since yesterday seemed built squarely into the universe. Looking through the stringy hair over her eyes, she picked up a roach at her side and lit it, sucked on it.

She spent the day smoking hashish and listening to rock. At one point Clovis reappeared and she felt a small quickening of interest. She breathed deeply of his musky odor and said to Jane: "He smells of something."

"He rubs himself with sheepfat and rosewater," Jane said.

"Why?"

"Because he wants to."

And it occurred to Johanna that Jane could tell her every-thing.

"Where does he come from?" she asked, glancing at him as he took off the cloak and dropped to the floor.

"He comes from the earth," said Jane.

"You must explain that to me," said Johanna.

"Your vibes are lousy," Jane muttered. "I want some quiet."

"Quiet?" murmured Johanna, lifting her head in the racket. And she said suddenly: "How did he lose his voice?"

"A ram kicked him in the throat. Stop talking."

And she felt that she was indeed talking too much. Life was not to be questioned, but lived, and she was living well at this moment, in a warmth of drifting time.

So the better part of a week passed. There was a constant coming and going; people wandered in, rolled out sleeping bags, stayed a day or two, then disappeared, to be replaced by others. There was a long evening at Michael's and Susan's Haight pad with weird lights playing on the wall; there was a rock-gathering trip in the hearse; but mostly there was smoking, dozing, and the thin mattress under her bones at night, and the stifling heat gathering and pressing down.

In the back of her head was something she had to attend to. She tried to ignore it, but it finally nagged itself forward. "My apartment's going to be torn down," she said aloud,

"I've got to move by the end of the week." And she thought of all the things to be packed and moved somewhere else. She would store them, and remain here at the pierhouse.

"Get in touch with Josh Gillingsby!" boomed Scotty, clapping his big hands free of stone dust. "He knows everybody. He helps everybody."

There was no invitation to stay.

"I don't want to take favors from Josh," Johanna said, after a pause.

"Why not?" Scotty asked, grabbing up a chisel and a mallet.

"Why not?" she echoed, searching her mind. She had had a reason once, but she could no longer locate it. And the overhanging problem of moving slowly dissolved as she contemplated the simplicity of what she would do. She would call Josh; she would call the Bekins moving company; they would do everything.

A note had been stuck under her door when she got back to her apartment. It was from Conrad, asking her to call him.

"Where have you been?" he asked when she got him.

"Around," she said.

"Your friend downstairs said she hadn't seen you for—"

"Where is Aquiline?" Aquiline's door had stood open, the lofty blue-and-purple interior was bare.

"I don't know," he said. "She was moving out when I saw her yesterday."

It came to Johanna that the building was silent. They had all moved. She wondered if she would ever see Aquiline again, and was dimly sorry that they had not said goodbye.

"I was going to call the police if you hadn't gotten in touch today," Conrad said severely.

"Why?" she asked with sullen annoyance.

"That ad—is that it, you found that guy?"

"No," she lied.

"Then, what? Where've you been?"

She thought for a moment. "With Scotty Kirk," she said. Scotty was warm and kind, no one could object to him.

"Scotty Kirk?"

"I suppose you know him, he knows Josh."

"Sure I know him. He used to be a business associate of Josh's."

"Now he works with stones," she informed him.

"I know. The man's non compos."

"I suppose so," she murmured, as the fact dawned on her.

"What are you doing with him? This is a guy who could be certified."

"Like an accountant?"

He ignored the remark. "Like a madman. He's harmless, of course, his wife gives him an allowance and he floats around. But what the hell are you doing with him?"

"I don't know. I met him and some of his friends."

"Johanna—"

"Listen, you'll be glad. I'm moving into Josh's place."

He responded to this with silence.

"Are you there?" she asked.

"Why are you moving there?"

"The cottage is there. Why shouldn't I have it?"

"Because you didn't want it."

"I want it. And I just called him, and he's going to clear some people out and it'll be ready in a couple of days. And I'm going to call Bekins. They'll do everything. I can just sit back."

She waited for him to compliment her on her good management, on her decisiveness after such long procrastination, but he said:

"Sit back and do *what?* For three months you've just been—"

"I'd appreciate if you stopped hounding me, Conrad," she said, and hung up.

Josh's property, one of those densely wooded half-acres that dot the incline between Russian Hill and North Beach, lay along a shaded quiet street so vertical that stone steps took the place of a sidewalk. On the other side towered a high-rise apartment building whose concrete foundation, shaped like a streamlined pagoda, was in itself three stories high. But once inside Josh's blue gate, which had a heart carved out in its center, you were in leafy isolation. His house, rambling through overhanging green boughs, was mostly glass; on its cathedral-like door hung a wreath of holly draped with broad red ribbon. A flagstone path ran from the gate to the house, through tiers of tree-choked flower beds where a gardener in a white pith helmet was working. Next to the garage, backing into the tall hedge that separated the grounds from the street, stood the cottage, made of granite blocks, with a quaint peaked roof painted blue. Trees grew so closely around the building that it was almost lost from sight.

Standing inside the blue gate in her trenchcoat, Johanna watched the Bekins movers carry her possessions in from the van, which stood at a frightening angle on the sheer street. She glanced up as a figure hurried down the flagstone path to greet her; it was Josh, in his black chinos and black sweater, Antigone clinging precariously to his shoulder. His pink face, under its monk-like fringe of blond hair, was beaming. She watched him uncertainly, recalling the fury his presence had once set off in her.

"Hello," she said, touching the extended hand and looking into the face, which was like any other face.

43

The walls of the cottage were of granite blocks fitted together, the floor of rough planking. There was a large rustic fireplace, and overhead ran heavy wooden ceiling beams painted blue. The deep-set windows looked out on dense trees that admitted no light, and the room was dim, the small bedroom black. But the kitchen and bathroom were modernized and lit with fluorescent bars. Josh had stocked the freezer with food and outfitted the spruce Nile-green bathroom with his best monogrammed towels.

When the movers left, Johanna did not bother to put things in place; furniture and boxes stood crammed together hugger-mugger in the limited space. She had gotten rid of Morris' desk, his television set, and his red terrycloth robe; she meant to forget him, to start fresh in this place.

When it grew late she decided against the claustrophobic bedroom and dragged her mattress and blankets up to the attic. Looking out the window under the eaves, she saw lights everywhere in the garden. The garage apparently held an upstairs apartment, from which lights shone; another light flickered through the leaves from a small structure that she had thought was a toolshed. Josh's house itself was brilliantly lit and alive with people. She lay down on the mattress and pulled the blankets over her head, but all night she heard cars coming and going, the blue gate creaking, and voices echoing from the flagstone path. Only as she was dozing off did she realize it was Christmas Eve.

This party turned out to be no less than Josh's way of life, a never-ending open house. She made no effort to join it, but stayed inside her own four walls waiting for something to happen from within her. One entire afternoon she spent setting up her painting equipment, stretching canvases and cleaning brushes. Another day she uncrated her new hi-fi set, studied the instructions, and installed the machine in a corner, though she did not play anything on it. She found herself poking through the boxes of books and pulling out favorite volumes, piling them on the floor to be read when the mood sprang.

And then a face peered through one of the windows. It was Scotty's.

"Orphans of the storm," he told her, bursting through the door as she opened it, and staring at her with his usual amazement.

"The place burned down," Jane stated, trodding behind him. "Fucking electric heaters. He lost all his crap."

"All those things," Johanna sympathized.

"He'll get more. We barely got out with our skins. We're holed up at Josh's."

"Oh my!" Scotty cried, tenderly feeling the stones of the wall. "Oh my!" And he pulled ecstatically at the two prongs of his beard.

They stayed the day, returning to Josh's to sleep. The next day they were back; and that night they slept in the small bedroom.

Once more Johanna sat with a brown wrinkled cigarette in her fingers; she was buying them now, from Jane, who was a shrewd business woman despite her horoscoping and jeweled eyelids. Jane said hash hit everyone differently; she herself apparently felt almost no effects, but Johanna was like blotting paper, she soaked it right in, glassy-eyed in a flash.

She sat in her cramped heap of belongings, with her books standing in piles on the floor. There were books in her lap, unread, used as some kind of hopeful ballast. Her fingers stroked their covers, and she tried to draw Scotty and Jane into arguments.

"You have to read," she said, "you have to . . ."

"Words," said Jane. "Words are shit."

"Why?"

Jane couldn't say why, it was apparently some instinctive thing.

But Scotty said, "Words lie. What lies better than words?" And looked startled, delighted.

"Oh, but beauty . . ." But her mind was faltering as it had in the pierhouse, skidding from thought to thought. "I could tell you things," she went on dimly, looking down at the books in her lap, thin volumes of poetry she had grabbed up from the floor, Shakespeare's sonnets . . . *Since brass, nor stone, nor earth, nor boundless sea* . . . how did it go? . . . and Stephen Crane, that poem she had always liked, about a creature, its heart, a bitter taste . . . she couldn't remember that either . . . And Rilke, Frost, Edith Sitwell . . . a poem of Sitwell's about dying that had broken through her like

pieces of glass . . . she couldn't remember that one either
. . . and anyway, she could not speak about any of these
things here, in this room. Instead, she said, "Edith Sitwell's
father invented a musical toothbrush," which was true.

Jane looked at her with an amused, slightly disgusted smile,
as though to say: That's what you learn from your books.

"And then," Johanna went on sullenly, "there was Jenny
Lind, the great singer; she was engaged to a man who was a
count. Count Puke was his name." And she thought: This is
black humor, I'm doing black humor and the imbecile doesn't
realize it.

"Count Puke," Jane said, with disgusted good humor.

"Count Puke," Johanna repeated, closing her eyes, her
mind already skipping on, for some reason, to a horse with
a human expression . . . horses were known for having no
expression at all, just two eyes going off in opposite directions
above a foot of hide-covered cartilage . . . fine for a horse,
a horse did wonders with it, but horrible to see such a face
somehow human, partly human, would-be human . . . "I'm
a horse head," she mumbled.

"Horse ass, you mean," corrected Jane.

With the lamps burning all day, the fire blazing, rain pouring down outside, they sat in their dark bower; rock albums
accumulated from nowhere—possibly from Josh's—and the
hi-fi set went day and night; Scotty was knee deep in new
stones, birdcages, armor, stuffing the already crowded room to
its limit; his sanding machine shook the rafters, and the
stone dust gathered. People wandered in and stayed for days,
sleeping on the stairs, in the kitchen, crammed among the
furniture. On the bark door of the cottage Scotty now tacked
a legible replica of the lines that had hung on the pierhouse
door. With mild curiosity Johanna looked over his shoulder
as he pushed the tacks in.

"There are some guys who use words who *don't* lie," he
boomed triumphantly, his pale blue eyes alight. Written with
a ballpoint pen in his jerky hand, the verse read:

> But you, children of space, you restless in rest, . . .
> Your house shall not be an anchor but a mast . . .
> a mansion of the sky, . . .
> *The Prophet*—KAHLIL GIBRAN

She felt an urge to flee the cottage, which bore the stamp not of the esoteric, not even of the deracinated, but of the banal. Immediately she swatted the urge like a fly. You could judge nothing fairly from literary taste. Besides, the verse was actually not bad; only it had no right to hang on that particular door. That cottage a mast? Night songs and silences? The scrap of paper was all cheek, delusion, and witlessness.

No matter, she thought, turning away, the ink would fade in the rain.

Clovis was often in her mind, but when she mentioned him her friends responded as if he had been a stranger.

"Clovis?" asked Scotty. "Who is Clovis?"

"The guy in the cape," Jane told him.

"But you knew him well," Johanna said.

"A long time ago," said Jane.

"Only a month ago." Yet to Johanna, too, it seemed long ago.

"Maybe he's dead?" suggested Scotty, chipping at a stone with immense energy. "I remember him, I think maybe he's dead. Raw meat's not healthy."

"He's not dead," Johanna said sharply, "I don't believe that."

"Why do you care, do you want to sleep with him?" Jane asked in her matter-of-fact voice. And narrowing her jeweled eyes neither with endorsement nor with opprobrium, she said, "You should, he's absolutely something else."

"We both slept with him once," Scotty informed Johanna over his chipping, "and he—"

She broke in: "You shared a bed with him? Or you—"

Jane was looking at her with a contemptuous smile that made her feel a fool. True, she, Johanna, was not personally acquainted with the variations on the basic sexual theme, but she had always known these variations existed; why should she be shocked just because the abstract had been made concrete? The capacity to be shocked, she thought, gazing at Jane's practical face under its white powder, and Scotty's happy, beaming features, was a stale leftover of the cloistered personality. "And?" she said languidly. "Go on."

"And he cried!" boomed Scotty.

"He cried?"

"I tell you, he cried. Didn't he cry, Jane? He cried like nothing on earth, without a noise and without anything at all in his face. And his tears, my dear, his tears were ice cold."

"Well, did he enjoy himself?" Johanna asked after a silence.

"Oh, yes, very much."

"How do you know?"

"How does he know?" interjected Jane. "How does he know anything? He doesn't know anything. And neither does anybody else. What does it matter?"

"Then why," asked Johanna, "do you work out astrological destinies, if you don't want to know anything?"

"It passes the time," Scotty answered her. "Doesn't it pass the time, Jane?" And he added, amazed: "I'm the only one who knows how to live in time." He lifted aloft the stone he was working on, and studied it happily, crunching back and forth on the stone dust.

A fine film of stone dust covered Johanna's possessions. She walked through the clutter, wiping surfaces with her hand. She looked through her albums to see if dust had penetrated them, and drew out the Thomas Mann recording. Removing a thundering Jefferson Airplane disc, she put the other on and stood back.

Five or six people were in the kitchen. "Shut up!" she cried, and crouched by the phonograph. The long-silent voice that rose from the machine sounded uneven; she snatched the record off and checked it, but it wasn't warped, there was no dust on it. Yet when she replaced it the voice continued to drag oddly. Wondering if the acoustics of the room were at fault, she pulled the set to another spot and tried again; then to another; but nothing availed the strangeness of the sound. She called Jane over. "Do you hear how this record sounds?"

"Yeah," said Jane, screwing up her face to listen. "I can't understand what the guy's saying."

"He's speaking another language—"

"So what're you listening for?"

"I understand it."

"So what's your problem?"

"It sounds wrong. Does it sound wrong to you?"

"Yeah, I want to hear Chinese I'll go down to Chinatown."

"It's German."

"I want to hear German I'll go to Germany."

"It sounds odd. It never sounded that way before."

"Put the music back on, I don't like this guy's vibes."

"I don't even feel them," said Johanna with bewilderment. "There must be something wrong with the phonograph."

But Jane put the Jefferson Airplane back on and it was obvious that nothing was wrong with the phonograph.

44 | Under the trees, leaves covered the ground in a wet purplish mulch. Fallen branches, beetle black, decayed among patches of acid-green moss; mushrooms sprouted overnight; worms the color of coral lay in rings. Ruffles of fungus grew low on the damp trunks, crumbling at the prod of her tennis shoe. When people came down the wet flagstone path she stepped deeper into the gloom. But one day a figure appeared whom she did not avoid; it was a long-awaited highlight, she took him into the cottage.

He removed his cloak and skullcap and leaned into the warmth of the fire, his dark blond hair falling forward, beads swinging. The fingers of his extended hands were grimy with soil.

He turned to her and said something.

She lowered the ear-splitting volume of the hi-fi.

"Where do you sleep?" he asked in his flawed voice.

"In the attic."

"Alone?" And his fingers touched her arm.

"Alone," she said, drawing back.

He dropped his hand. The broad plain of his face was golden in the firelight, the thin features too meager for it; a badly put-together face, not ugly, merely odd, haphazard.

"Where were you?" she asked him.

"Somewhere," he murmured, sitting down before the fire and closing his eyes. The momentous occasion faded into the stone dust lying thick on every object. There was only one fact that she knew about Clovis: that he was on acid. And she wondered if that was the only fact about him, if he was only a human-size green tablet.

Jane, who looked neither surprised, pleased, nor annoyed to see Clovis back, turned the phonograph up again. The noise no longer reached Johanna's consciousness; it was a lulling, blotting background, and when it ceased she felt lost in the silence. The density inside the cottage—the noise, the people—had become a necessity for her; alone, she felt informed by a dark, pure unintelligence.

Sometimes, not often, there were conversations around her; shreds of conversations. The Bird of Paradise was spoken of, the Major Arcana, and God's eye, and the twelfth dimension; centeredness and inner freedom, cusps and houses and aura goggles. She listened and tried to understand, but more often than not was visited by her own visions: the quintessential coffin, ebony, standing upright; or the horse's long half-human face. They were not intense visions, they passed by her rather than through her, but they were frightening when she was alone.

The cottage was her world. From time to time a newspaper worked its way into the clutter, and then she got wind of the larger world; afterward she would dream of cinderblocks and data processing, technical surveillance, industrial spoilheaps— the stinging sulfuric afterglow of some earlier grace. And then newspapers could pop up for days in a row and she would not look at them.

Once Jane asked her if she wanted her to work out her astrological destiny.

"How much does it cost?" Johanna asked.

"Ten bucks."

It occurred to Johanna that she might ask Jane to do Morris'; then she remembered that she did not want to know Morris' destiny, she wanted to forget him; and she remembered also that she didn't believe in astrological destinies.

Scotty cried out over the music: "Let her work out your mystery!" And he informed everyone in the room; some were laying out tarot cards, others were sitting immobile, trancelike. "Mystery is wonderful! Mystery is everywhere! Do you realize that!"

"Oh, he's going off on a tangent," Jane muttered.

"Does he do that?" Johanna asked.

"Every three months. It's a cycle."

"Mystery!" He was squeezing a stone ecstatically. "Mystery!" His eyes popped out at the figures around him. "But you just pass time!"

"*Tan-gent!*" Jane yelled warningly, sing-song, grabbing a jewel that rolled from her eyelid.

"Mystery! Oh mystery!"

Johanna thought, in the slippery way that her mind worked, as if the brain were coated with grease: Mystery . . . a single gem in a velvet box . . . to work long with some single mystery like an old diary you found . . . to eke out its soul bit by bit, to stand in light at the end . . . time, time to do that in . . . but no sense of time with newspapers pointing out that you suffer from high cholesterol, from sibling rivalry, from pollution . . . no time with faces on television laying down the law, our world consists of politics, of food chemicals . . . with such loud traffic of advice, such probing, scraping, collecting, itemizing, urging . . . the machinery of hell . . . with such traffic . . . "The solitary gem is lost," she said aloud.

"I found it," said Jane, feeling around her black velvet folds.

"I meant . . ." But she could not remember what it was that she had been thinking about, that had led her to comment on a gem.

With a vengeance Scotty turned on his sanding machine and grinned over it, like a god whipping his steeds through the heavens.

For a long while Johanna had been ravenous, but now she had no appetite to speak of. Nor did she sleep much, lying open-eyed under the wet night sky of the attic window. She began allowing people to share the attic with her, to spread out their blankets and sleeping bags and make the long nights less solitary. There were nights when she made love with anyone similarly inclined; as if the feel of a body would somehow cut a notch into the day that had floated by. Waking in the morning, seeing the man's face next to hers, she would roll a little away and close her eyes again, indifferent. But one morning she was confronted by a crop of shiny cream-colored pustules at the corner of her sleeping partner's mouth; his whole face was ravaged by adolescent pimples and boils; and she had kissed it, kissed the mouth. She gagged, horrified; but a moment later the sores fell into perspective, and she saw that they were no different from dust and grime and body odor, a natural part of life; and she turned over and went back to sleep.

Every morning her ears were forced to acknowledge the rich blare of the taxicab as Josh drove off to the gallery; and every evening the same clarion call announced his return. Whenever she used his now very dirty monogrammed towels she was aware of his presence, and outside she was aware of it too; it was on his sufferance that the heart-punctured blue gate swung back and forth, that the Porsches and panel trucks lined the steep curb, that the gardener poked ineffectively in the mulch (he being the backward boy in the red beret, now given over to a rainworthy pith helmet). Now and then she saw her protector in the flesh; he was friendly but did not detain her, and he quickly slipped back into a disembodied presence. She wished dimly to keep him that way, and never went with the others to his house. But she dreaded the nights when she was left alone in the cottage, and it was inevitable that she finally accompanied them.

The house was audially very similar to the cottage; visually it was similar to the gallery, with a geometric pop effect. The drapes were bone white, the rugs black, the sparse bulky furniture yellow and purple, sharply delineated under the snowy glare of metal bullet lights.

Johanna felt everything ooze through the corridors of her brain and sink into the gray democratic limbo of all existence.

Someone spoke loudly over the rock music. "Nice to see you again, Miss Kaulbach. How are you?"

It was Cobbledock, extending his hand, the narrow swarthy wrist like a twig sticking out from an enormous violet shirt-cuff. He wore a loose wide-lapeled Clyde Barrow suit with a broad yellow tie, and his thin face was now crushed between two black sideburns that bristled solidly down into the pockets of his cheeks. She felt her hand being shaken and wondered if he would say anything about her appearance—snarled fishnet stockings, a soiled pajama top stuffed into her micro skirt. She had not combed her hair for a long time. She could think of nothing to say.

Nor could he, apparently, for a moment later he had drifted away.

A Filipino houseboy in white duck pants and a black shirt open to the waist was serving drinks. Ten or fifteen people wandered around eating, drinking, talking. In a corner an elderly frail-looking black man stood on his head meditating, his gray natural smashed flat.

She saw Antigone. Sitting in an air-filled transparent plastic chair was the boy in the pith helmet, still wearing the clothes he had worn the day of the happening—loafers, white gym socks, the gray overcoat with big padded shoulders. He was sunk very low in the chair, his knees higher than his head. He was holding Antigone to his chest. The rat was trembling violently. Johanna stepped closer.

"I think she's dying," the boy shouted nervously over the music.

"Why?"

"I think it's the noise."

"I should think she was used to it by now," Johanna said, and she tried to focus her thoughts. *"Can't you take her where it's quieter?"* she cried.

"Josh says I'm not supposed to move out of this chair."

"Where is he?" she asked, looking around.

"At some fund-raising thing. He won't be back till late."

"And you can't move till he gets back?"

He gave a resolute nod.

She thought a while longer. *"What if you have to go to the bathroom?"*

Consternation filled his face. *"I don't know, I have to stay here!"* he yelled.

"Can't you turn the music off?"

"He wants it on."

"But he's not here."

"It doesn't matter."

Scotty and the others came by with pizza pies, tomato red and mustard yellow in the snowy glare. *"She's sick,"* Johanna shouted to them, *"she doesn't like the music."*

Scotty shoved a red wedge through his beard and chewed vigorously, his eyes wide; then he followed the others to a small aquarium where three baby alligators sat immobile on the wet rocks.

Johanna's palms had begun to sweat. The gray-brown ooze in her brain was drying and cracking. A judgment was about to be made; and once judgment arrived it was likely to keep marching, firing cannons and planting flags; a stupefying prospect, for the terrain was dark.

"I can't help you," she cried through the noise, and just then the creature began biting its own side in a frenzy. Johanna stooped down and grabbed the rat to her chest and ran to the door with the boy at her heels.

The door slammed behind them. His hands dove for the rat.

"Don't grab her!" Johanna cried.

His hands fell back, fidgeting wildly at his sides.

She struck off for the cottage, but she saw people going inside and she knew the phonograph would shatter the air in a moment. "We can go to your tool shed," she told him, "it's quiet there." But she dreaded the quiet.

Inside, he reached up and pulled a string. The bulb shed a weak yellow light through the room, which was cluttered with tools and hoses; in a small cleared space stood an unmade cot.

"Let me have her back, please," he said, almost in tears, "she's my responsibility."

"No, you'll take her back there." She sat down on the cot. Her face was pebbled with sweat; she felt nauseated. The rat's body was very cold, rigid; its red eyes stared straight ahead.

"Poor Antigone," she murmured; and the boy stared over her shoulder. His eyes were the soft brown of a dog's eyes. From what she could see under the pith helmet, the lobeless ears grew at an angle from the head.

"My God, it's so quiet!" And she began asking him questions, to make the silence less frightening. "Where did you meet Josh?"

He responded with the quickness of someone used to obeying orders, though his eyes never left Antigone. "I went into his gallery."

"Where did you go after you drove his taxi into a ditch?"

"Langley Porter Clinic."

"That's not a medical clinic, is it?"

"No."

"Then what did you do?"

"I come back here."

"Do you like Josh?"

"I love him."

"Why?"

"I don't know. Because he helps me out. He lets me stay."

"How old are you?"

"Twenty-nine."

He looked seventeen, with soft pink lips and downy cheeks that had never felt a razor. She tried to think of more questions.

"Who are the others that live out here? Over the garage?"

"I don't know. Some sculptors. They make things out of metal."

"What kinds of things?"

"I don't know. Shapes."

"What kind of shapes?"

"I don't know."

The sweat was trickling down her face; she had not spoken so many sequential sentences for weeks. She stroked the sick animal, whose body was still rigid, but whose eyes had closed. She moved her fingers under the chest, where she could feel the heart hammering erratically.

And they waited.

They must both have dozed off eventually. Josh was leaning down and taking the rat from her lap. The boy jumped up, his face white. "She made me leave, Josh! She grabbed Antigone and come down here!"

"Don't worry," Josh soothed him, cupping the rat to his chest.

"I couldn't help it!" the boy cried tearfully.

"It doesn't matter." He turned to Johanna. "I'm so glad you visited my house at last, Miss Kaulbach. I hope we'll be seeing more of you."

She felt the nausea again, a dull pressure of rage.

"You're sweating," he said, and touched her forehead.

She shut her eyes. His fingers trailed up her forehead, through her hair; then he turned and went out the door, the boy staring bleakly after him. Johanna hurried back to the cottage, which was raucous with music and newcomers.

The next morning she saw Josh walking to the garage with Antigone riding his shoulder as usual. The rat looked quite perky. It was smelling the fresh early air, pointing its rosy nose in every direction.

45 Every week Morris had set himself a date of departure, then passed it by because he couldn't decide where to go or what to do. He told the group about his indecision, and Herb began working with him on it.

"Cut it," Herb said one night.

Morris looked at the piece of string on the floor in front of him, took his jackknife from his pocket, and cut it in two.

It was a symbolic act, cutting the bonds that kept him from leaving.

"What's the string made of?" Herb asked.

"I'm not sure—" He looked around the ring of faces. "I guess everything—this room, the ocean, the canyon."

"Throw it away. Say goodbye to it."

Morris threw the string aside. "Goodbye," he said.

"Listen to how you say goodbye," Herb said, lifting his hand to his ear.

"Weakly," Morris said.

"Weakly. You've never been able to leave anything completely. You've got partially hacked-off stumps still sprouting shoots inside, nothing's cut off cleanly. You're like a sink clogged up with unfinished business."

Morris nodded.

Herb looked searchingly into his face. "Your father—you've never worked through that relationship to autonomy. That's the first and biggest frayed end."

"You're right," Morris said, but he wondered what there was left in the relationship that he had not already turned inside out.

"Okay," said Herb, picking up a styrofoam cup of coffee and taking a sip, "are you ready to work?"

Morris straightened up and nodded again.

"He died when you were how old?"

"Eleven," Morris said, after a pause.

"You're eleven—no, don't turn yourself off, Levinsky; you turn yourself off so that this key point and all the rest won't add up to a pile of shit." And putting the cup down, he went on quietly but firmly. "You're eleven years old, still in short pants—"

"Long pants. Corduroy, dark gray—"

"Are you stalling? Or are you trying to create an authentic mood for yourself?"

"I don't know," Morris said tightly.

"It's hard. Who said it wasn't hard? But this is where it's at, at your father's funeral, and you've got to work through it."

"I didn't go to the funeral."

"You're mindfucking," Herb said suspiciously.

"No, I'm not. I came down with measles that day."

"Okay, forget the funeral. Take the time you saw him last." Morris was silent.

"Are you willing to work?" Herb asked.

"Yeah," Morris said.

"All right. The time you saw him last."

"That was," he began, and cleared his throat. "That was in the hospital."

"All right, we're not going to talk anymore. You're going to say goodbye to him again. A final goodbye." Herb moved farther in from the circle and folded his hands in his lap. With his face impassive except for the gently encouraging eyes, he sat very still, wearing the dead man's identity with respect. "Say goodbye to me," he commanded softly.

Time passed. From the circle of figures Morris breathed in the strong, supportive patience. People lay stretched out on the floor or sat in groups of two or three, leaning against each other, arms around each other; now and then a pair of hands began gently massaging the neck or shoulders of a neighbor, or a match was unobtrusively struck under a cigarette: small surface movements like ripples on a deep pool.

He felt his heart being finely shredded. That face, sunken, swarthy, it seemed to grow swarthier as the illness progressed, the pillow blinding white . . . Morris always got to the room thirty seconds before the others, hurrying ahead of them through the corridors, "Dummy, germs you breathe on his face," from his mother pushing the door open behind him, and his father pressing his hand with conspiratorial patience, who would have thought he had the strength? Now all around the bed swarmed his mother and older brothers and their wives, breathing and whispering and floor-creaking for the following half hour. . . . His father seldom spoke, but once he turned to Morris with effort—such massive pain inside such wasted bones—and said, and he not given to puffed-up phrases, "Treasure your life, Moishe," neither of them aware of the others, the two of them always separate from the others . . . and so the visits had passed for more than a week, and at the end of one visit, the last visit, which seemed no different from the preceding ones, his father gave Morris his goodbye nod with a look of such piercing and final tenderness that Morris held on to him, heaving like a bellows, and he was pulled away, soothed and scolded by his eldest brother . . . in the crowded doorway he twisted madly around and lifted his hand, his father lifting his from the blanket, the hand cold twelve hours later.

His face had gone knotted and wet; the faces around him were quiet, compassionate, ennobled by their willingness to share his old sorrow. Herb sat with head bowed and hands crossed in his lap, a humble, patient man. Herb's cigarette had burned out in the ashtray, next to his cup of coffee. A ballpoint pen was clipped to the pocket of his dungarees. And these seemingly neutral objects grew indecent as Morris stared at them, the indecency spreading into all the faces and into the very air of the room, until a hot wave of nausea boiled up in his chest. He got to his feet.

"It belongs to me," he said, and threaded his way through the group to the door.

In the canyon he unrolled his sleeping bag in the sharp night smell of bark and leaves, and lay down, looking up to the stars. He saw not the infinite but the finite; about endless space he knew nothing, he could only see as far as the stars and a little beyond. And inside himself he could only see as far as that sink of unfinished business, as Herb had put it. He would never get past it, if getting past it meant allowing strangers to share it in the light of a natural phenomenon. Of course it was a natural phenomenon—his father had been old, it had been time for him to go. Natural enough, but hard, death was hard, that moment was hard, and it was his and his father's alone. You could peel yourself so far, then you came to this sink of twisted roots and ever fresh farewell. He had a feeling that those secret, soul-battering memories were man's natural condition, they constituted whatever muddled richness he possessed, and he was being dispossessed of it by a well-meaning world of good works. And he was more confused than ever, because he believed in progress and healing. But at the center of his confusion he stood by his action of tonight. It was the long solitary nights in the canyon, the dark sky overhead, that had been preparing him to know things differently, and now he knew. Nothing in his life would ever become easier, different; he would probably never see a miracle, or discover a wholly new road, because he was he, with a familiar and permanent soul.

He closed his eyes. He felt entirely alone in the ravine. He was keenly aware of the sleeping bag's cool fabric under his hands, of the hard earth under his body. The ground was dry, burned by weeks of sun. In the fall it would be too wet to sleep out, but he would be long gone by then.

46

Josh was giving a bash at his house. The occasion was his birthday, his forty-seventh, he was quick to admit, with a mildly stoic and humorous look. He walked amiably, smiling, through the crowd with Antigone on his shoulder, directing the houseboy and the help that had been hired for the night, shaking hands and pressing shoulders as he went, sometimes mouthing a greeting through the roar. His own rock band, the Corduroy Nephew Corp., was blasting away in the center of the living area; guests spilled in and out the sliding glass doors to the floodlit garden; it was late April and freakishly warm. He had rolled up his sleeves and the blond fringe of hair on his forehead was damp. The contingent from the cottage had not yet arrived; maybe they were too stoned to move, or they had forgotten. It was past midnight.

A hand touched his arm. He turned and saw Conrad and his wife. He had never met Conrad's wife. A big girl to begin with, a Maillol, and plus that, ready to give birth any minute, maybe to triplets. Overwhelmingly *there*, not the wisp he had expected of Conrad, nor the frump: long blond braid, well-cut paisley floor-length gown. But sharp irritated eyes. Not used to big parties. Conrad, holding her around the waist like a piece of china. A very old father-to-be, filled with the miracle of life. Filled too with the miracle of new commissions. A late flowering. And a flower in his buttonhole. Red carnation, picked from the crop outside the door as they rang the bell. Wife's touch. A loving, doting pair, true newlyweds—who would have thought it of old Conrad? If only he would stop yelling. Didn't he know it wasn't expected of him to converse?

He leaned forward like a good host.

"*Johanna?*" Conrad shouted.

"I don't know," he said, casting the door a glance. And with a nod he passed on to greet Cobbledock and the museum people.

"*Why don't we go down there, where she lives?*" Wanda asked.

"*Let's wait.*"

"*You don't really want to see her, do you?*"

285

"I don't know. I do, but—"

"We should have come a long time ago, Connie."

"It wouldn't have done any good. I don't think it'll do any good tonight."

"You're probably right—but—oh, screw this noise! How are you supposed to think!" She grabbed a meatball from a precariously passing tray and tossed it irritably into her mouth, but she forgot to chew; she was staring across the room. Conrad followed her gaze.

Through the large cathedral-like door had come something in an enormous black cloak, an animal-skin skullcap on its head.

"Is that him?" Wanda asked nervously, swallowing her meatball. "The one she advertised for?"

Conrad couldn't hear her; anyway, his eyes had passed from the apparition to the figure beside it, a woman whose hair was cropped short as a boy's, but whom he could not mistake. He gave a bitter inward groan of shame for her. She was in a dirty pajama top and dirtier skirt, the laces of her tennis shoes dragged, her black fishnet stockings were snagged all over, the flesh showing through in holes the size of dimes and nickels. The face, the lovely cameo face, was all cheekbones and hollows now, sallow; she finally looked her age, older, in the cold white light. She moved with a kind of stupid ease, a fluid dullness, at the side of her theatrical monstrosity. Behind her loped Scotty Kirk, his kindly, crazy eyes starting from his head; then came a girl in black velvet whose face was coated with flour paste; then a handful of standard hippies. They all flowed into the crowd and disappeared from sight.

With his legs like iron, Conrad took Wanda's hand and started in the direction Johanna and her bat-like escort had gone in.

He found them ten minutes later near the alligator aquarium, sitting together on the black rug in a thicket of moving legs. Glancing up and seeing him, Johanna lifted her hand, either in welcome or in rejection, maybe in surprise, he could not tell. A smile or a grimace crossed her face. He got down on one knee and nervously took her hand. It was nervously withdrawn. He tried to stake the claim of his presence by catching and holding her eyes, which were moving restlessly around, with discomfort, as if pieces of abrasive grit were caught under the lids. He took a look at her companion's strip of face: a pair of dark deep-set eyes gazed expressionlessly past him at the forest of legs. *"Conrad,"* he announced aggressively to the strip, thrusting out his hand. The overture either did not register or was ignored; the creature would not be drawn into the normality of handshakes and exchanged names. Conrad looked back at Johanna. *"Wanda's here,"* he shouted, hoping for some response. The moving eyes rested briefly on his. *"Up there,"* he smiled, pointing up at Wanda's face. *"She can't sit down or she couldn't get up again."*

Like a dutiful but morbidly shy child, Johanna stood up. Again the grimace-like smile and the wandering eyes. Wanda, standing behind the great melon of her stomach, felt lost. But she moved in, nevertheless, laying her hands on Johanna's upper arms. "How are you?" she asked, forgetting to shout, searching the gaunt face with open concern.

"How are you?" Johanna said flatly, holding herself in under Wanda's hands.

"All right," said Wanda. After an uncomfortable silence, she shouted, *"You've cut your hair."*

Johanna's dirty nicotined fingers touched the short hairs at her neck. Her head looked small and fragile, her neck reed-like.

"How come?" Wanda asked, her face beginning to show the strain. Johanna's face had broken out in perspiration.

Instead of answering, Johanna leaned down and grabbed her companion's shoulder. She pulled him off into the crowd, throwing a mumbled apology over her shoulder.

"We're going to take her home," Conrad told Wanda.

"How?"

"I don't know. We'll talk to Josh."

Johanna had hurried into the garden. The confrontation with Conrad and Wanda had sent streaks of pain through her head and limbs—a searing pain like that of atrophied muscles suddenly put to use. Oddly enough, she had fully expected to see them; she had expected to see them every day since she moved into the cottage. It was a vague, dull dread, and it grew duller every day, but tonight she had been sure they would be present at the party. And yet she had come. And here she was a mass of shooting pain; large drops of sweat rolled down her face, her hands pulled at each other's fingers. Clovis walked calmly at her side.

"Can't we go somewhere else?" she said, stopping in front of the cottage. Wanda and Conrad would come there.

Clovis was putting one of his green tablets on his tongue. He flicked the tongue back to the black cavern of his throat, and the thin lips met. He went into the cottage and came out a moment later with Scotty's car keys.

"Give me one of those," she said. "One of your pills."

He reached inside his cloak and brought one out, breaking it in half.

"Stingy," she said, laughing and furious.

"You don't know anything," he said in his empty voice.

She took the half he held out, and swallowed it with a gulp of air.

It was strange, oddly disheartening to see Clovis do anything so mundane as drive a car, even if it was a hearse, and even if he drove with a unique style. He did everything in slow motion; he would probably not be able to step quickly on the brake if he had to. And he would probably have to, because the hearse was going very fast. He was so slow and the car was so fast. She pondered this while waiting for the pill to take effect. Luckily, every stoplight they came to was green and they sailed through without mishap. He seemed asleep at the wheel. The pill was not doing anything for her. "Give me the other half," she demanded, but he did not hear, or would not hear. His burlap shoe looked ridiculous on the gas pedal.

"I want to get out," she said. But she would probably be killed if she opened the door. She thought about this, still waiting for the pill to bring her peace, bring her something. She thought of the thick chopped-up air over the mud and entrails of Verdun.

"Why?" she asked herself aloud. "It's presumptuous. I feel ashamed. I feel ashamed."

They were on the approach to the Golden Gate Bridge. He slowed the hearse down while carefully he dug into his pocket under the cloak for his fare. The man at the tollgate was middle-aged, stooped, tired-looking. The hearse with Clovis in it seemed too much for him. Grimly picking the coins from the extended palm as if they were thick with germs, he lifted his lip like an old, aggravated dog.

"Peace, old cock." Clovis smiled, driving on.

"Nobody is ever happy to see you," Johanna said.

"But they *see* me," he whispered.

"Oh, what did you give me, an aspirin? I don't feel anything. Except that I feel worse and worse. I feel like that old man back there."

"You're talking too much."

"One word is too much talk for you. You don't know how to talk. None of you do. Where's your transistor?"

"Forgot it."

"Isn't there a radio in this thing?"

"Dead people don't need a radio."

"Then go faster. I want to get there."

"Where?"

"I don't know. Don't *you* know?"

"Yeah, I know."

They drove off the bridge into Marin County and she dimly recalled the journey to Scotty's wife's house. They had set Clovis off somewhere on the way back, near the water. That must be where they were going now. They had turned off the highway and were driving along dark blue overgrown roads, very fast, the velvety motor humming. If they bumped into something, she thought, it would be a velvet bump, it would be like having a dark blue velvet box click you softly inside it. But now they were out in the open, without anything to bump into. He eased the hearse to a stop by a barbed-wire fence and got out. A field of dark blue grass ran down to a cliff; beyond it stretched the ocean, dark blue, too, with a shimmer of moonlight along its surface. Wrapping his cloak tightly around him, Clovis climbed between the barbed wires and held them apart for her. They squished through the grass, which was still wet from weeks of rain, Clovis leading the way, his cloak trailing behind him. At the cliff's edge they turned and followed a path. "There are lights," she said, looking at the long coastline of towering cliffs.

"Campfires. Caves."

He led her into a barren shallow scoop of land where the earth was muddy and slippery. Halfway up the incline, obliquely facing the ocean, was a black hole. Gracefully, without using his hands, he climbed up and disappeared into the hole. She followed, digging her fingers into the clammy earth.

He had lit a stump of candle and stuck it in the clay. His body took up almost all the space. She squeezed in beside him; they were pressed together from shoulder to ankle. She smelled the wax from the candle, and the damp earth, and the sickly sweet odor of Clovis. The top of the cave pressed down on her head. It was all dark brown clay, with fibrous roots hanging from the ceiling. A square of burlap was pressed into the floor. One side of the round entrance held the charred remains of a campfire.

"It's where I live," he said in his whisper.

Then, she thought to herself, this is where it ends, in this hole.

"See," he said, removing his skullcap as though in obeisance, and he nodded his strip of face at the shimmering ocean.

"Yes, there's that. Can you climb down to it?"

"You'd kill yourself."

"You don't swim there."

He shook his head.

"You don't walk in the surf. I can hear the surf. But you don't walk in it."

He closed his eyes. His fingers drew long grooves in the damp clay.

"You don't take a boat into it."

"I told you, you can't get down."

"You only look at it."

"You ought to see how it looks."

"I see how it looks."

"No you don't. Not yet."

"I see how it looks." It looked calm, calmly beautiful, distant. As she watched, a new smell worked its way into her nostrils, a cold smell of urine and feces. "Do you use this place as a lavatory?" she asked, wondering if she was sitting on a pile.

"Other people. They come here sometimes when I'm gone. I throw the crap out, but the piss sinks in. It bother you?"

"No," she said. All smells had ceased to bother her months ago. "I just don't want to sit on it."

"Kiss me, Johanna." He pushed the enormous collar wings down with his long muddy fingers.

"You come here and make love alone," she murmured.

He pressed his cheek to the damp earth of the wall. "So?" he asked, and sat forward, facing her in the candlelight. "Kiss me, Johanna."

Kiss*me*, it sounded like, kiss*me*, through the thin teeth. His eyes were closed. She brushed back the lank blond hair and kissed his forehead, feeling neither repulsed nor attracted. "Kiss*me*," with the chin tilted upward, the eyes still closed. She brought her face forward again and laid her mouth on his. The lips were soft, unmoving; between them she felt the edges of the brittle teeth like shavings of metal. The smell of his mouth was sweet. He seemed not to breathe. Two tears were rolling down his broad face. She touched one with her fingertip. It was ice cold. His eyes were open now, watching her, but from a great distance.

"Are you happy?" she asked.

"I think so! I think so!" And he stared out at the ocean as the tears poured from him without movement of his chest or throat, soundlessly, and fell from his jaws.

Her heart had begun beating very fast, skipping. She felt strange. There was an air bubble in the back of her head. Clovis slid down the slope and began dancing, his long arms making circular motions at the shimmering ocean. She climbed down after him, and followed him as he ran up the path along the cliff, watching with cold detachment as he flung himself dangerously near the edge, his arms extended to the moon. How silly he is, she thought, as he turned into the field of grass and ran ahead with his arms still upraised. She felt ripples all over her body, like caterpillars squirming under the skin. Her mind was very clear. She crawled through the barbed wire and got into the hearse beside him. The interior of the hearse looked warped, very long and bulging. Her nose was ice cold and stopped up and she felt mildly nauseated. She was astonished to find the hearse driving back across the Golden Gate Bridge only a minute after Clovis had started the motor. "Stop," she heard herself say, staring past his profile at the lights of the city, "please stop." She thought she would die if she could not stare unimpeded at the lights.

"Wait," said Clovis. They went through the tollgate—this time she didn't notice who took the fare—and he drove into the wooded Presidio and stopped the car on a hill. She threw the door open and jumped out. It was the larger buildings that struck her, those clustered on hills. They were of towering complexity, cube upon cube within cube, in exquisite shades of gray-blue and rose, hung throughout with silver lights like hot ice. Above them the sky was violet, pricked all over with trembling stars. She looked behind her at the bridge, a long line of vibrating gold lights like a string of bumble-bees. She was filled with serene delight and no longer surprised at anything. She saw two ships coming into the bay, and they had great sails like Nile barges, and they moved at an immense speed, like arrows shot from a bow.

"Do you see these things?" she asked Clovis, who was looking from the car window.

"Never anything but."

"Then it's not so bad that . . . " She wanted to say that it wasn't so bad that he made love alone in a cave, because his eyes could probably see things that ordinary eyes could not. But she could not arrange the words in her mind. She got back into the car. Clovis had lit one of his brown cigarettes.

"You drop acid and smoke hash too," she commented. "Your trip must be twenty times stronger than mine." But she was not envious. She regarded the cigarette with detached interest. "Let me see that," she said as he began to drive, and she took the cigarette from his fingers and studied the tip. She could see through the casing of white ash to the ember, which was like a red asparagus tip, its flattened jewel-like pellets glued one upon the other, with deep black fissures between. She broke into laughter. The cigarette had gone out by the time they parked at the bottom of Josh's street. There was no parking space farther up. The party was still in progress.

47 | The cottage was empty. She went into the kitchen and turned on the light. Her eyes felt too wide, light kept pouring into them like water into holes, and she began laughing because the room was so high and her head was up under the ceiling. Going back into the other room, she sat down, closing her eyes, and the laughter increased as a fish swam into view —of an ecstatic color, the iridescent blue-green of a peacock feather, but almost deeper and brighter than she could bear. It gleamed apart into gems bound by twisted ropes of gold. She opened her eyes and everything vanished, her laughter faded. Quickly she closed them again, she was on a tropical beach where a man in a helmet of woven palm fronds pulled her down as the waves, pale green and warm, washed over them. She was brilliant with sexuality, like a flame, and she felt his hand—broad, scattered across the back with dark hair; Morrie's hand. She stroked the fingers and kissed them.

Her eyes opened. It was Clovis' hand, she realized without surprise. With his other, he turned on his transistor, and Judy Garland was singing "Over the Rainbow," bathing the room in the glory of a celestial choir. Again she closed her eyes and now she stood in a sunny meadow, Morrie was walking there, she saw a smile on his face, then the smile was on the face of Morrie as a child. He was happy, he was at the beginning of his life, and she felt the presence of goodness as palpably as sunlight.

Suddenly she stood up. She wanted to be clean. In the bathroom she filled the Nile-green tub with water and emptied a bottle of bubblebath under the tap. Mountains of foam rose up, icebergs with the ocean showing through in green fissures and pools. She began laughing at this and looked at herself in the mirror, seeing a face cheese white except for a bright red nose. The pores, in the dead white cheeks and flaming nose, were deep as craters. The eyes—dilated and glassy— were squeezed inside two fleshy mounds. The minute hairs around the mouth were like wires. She backed out of the room, and the face faded from her mind.

She must have been away for a long while; Clovis lay asleep or in a trance on the floor; the sounds from the big house had ceased. She went out into the garden, which shimmered under a soft gray velvet sky. Morrie's voice spoke in the trees and drifted on; she followed the sound; it was saying, "Ten questions, chapter one," and she was sitting in the old apartment with him, his textbook on his knees and his face against hers; she could feel the bristles. The apartment was dark, there were shapes everywhere, lying on chairs, on the floor. She passed a bright kitchen where people were drinking and talking. She passed the alligator aquarium, and paused to look at the sleeping little reptiles, which were encrusted with dark gems. She passed on, from dim room to dim room, until she found him asleep on a round bed, lying on his side on a shiny quilted spread. Pale light shone in from a window. There was a squat purple night table by the bed. It held a little leather matchbox with an enamel crest, and a round orange sand candle. She extracted a match and lit the wick, which gave forth an icy coral light that foamed in her ears. Down in the candle's crater there were pale waxen rivulets rushing like water, and waxen cliffs standing in complicated tiers; the crater deepened, the cliffs crumbled before her eyes, the rivulets became waterfalls that plunged deep into boiling pools. Suddenly one side of the candle collapsed; bits of black sand, each sharply defined, zoomed in an elegant avalanche down into the flaring center. The wick became a brilliant blue, grew smaller and smaller, and went out with a pop, pulling the darkness of the room into its expiration.

Josh had been watching her for more than an hour. He was suffering a hangover, but he muffled his belches and wiped his brow surreptitiously, concentrating on the rapt profile in the candlelight. Now the light was sputtering out, the room was dim again, and she turned her face to him. Her eyes were closed. Holding his sour breath, he extended his hand.

Her mind was very clear. She touched the dark springy hair. She ran her fingers across his lips and his large arrogant nose. Slowly she pulled off her clothes, and now he was naked too; his skin filled her nostrils with fresh air and sunlight. The ecstasy came in pools of pale green water, one lying below the other like the descending pools beneath a waterfall; she sank from one into another, turning as though in the air, smiling with this unending joy, until it did end, gently, the pale water ebbing away and dry light taking its place. Her eyes were open and she was looking at a white sunlit ceiling.

294

She dropped her eyes to an elaborate blue wicker cage. Antigone lay peacefully inside. Her eyes traveled to her own body, legs flung out by two other legs, bony, fuzzed with blond hair; at their groin drooped a spent organ. Her eyes faltered, then moved up to the face.

Josh's hangover had vanished. Every aching bone, every tendril of nausea was replaced with brightness. If he were given to hysteria, he would claim to be made of hammered gold—he had sucked on her hatred for him, he burned with it, he was heavy and real with it, and when he walked, his feet would ring solidly on the ground. Bit by bit he had poked the crumbling edges of her volition, and tonight he had had the whole golden meal in one ravishing gulp. There was nothing left. It was not an image he would care to promulgate, but everyone took his nourishment in his own way; one had to eat or be blown away like a shell. But his daily fare, of smaller, less succulent wills, had not prepared him for this fullness. He was sleepy, heavy-eyed; yet he watched the posthumous face with the last of his long fascination. The face stared, that was all. Then one arm was quickly lifted to cover the breasts.

"I didn't know it was you—I was tripped out—" Her face was white as paper.

He smiled. "No matter."

"I did—I did know." And she knew that if it was possible for a human being to be loathsome, as a crunched beetle is loathsome, or pile of slimy garbage, she was.

"Of course you knew," he said. "No matter."

Then she vomited on the black rug.

"You'd better leave," he said, turning his head from the bitter odor. He was blissfully sleepy.

Racked by dry heaves, she pulled on her clothes and swung open a door, barging not into the next room but into a storeroom that held a faint musty smell like old onions, and she saw that among the boxes and filing cases stood a large cage with four glossy white rats inside. She stood bent over, still heaving, yet somewhere inside her feeling a puzzlement, remembering Antigone shivering on her lap in the tool shed. She leaned against the cage, wiping her mouth. A long string of Antigones, each one succumbing to nerve damage? Each one replaced? Her hand dropped to the latch and opened the cage door. The creatures nibbled and nudged her fingers, but they would not come out. She stood a while longer, until the heaving had passed, then she went back into the bedroom.

"Don't you think I'll tell about those rats?" she asked, and the horror in her words was partly for the exquisite triviality of his fraud.

"Tell what?" He was lying on his back with his eyes closed. "That I keep playmates for Antigone?"

"I'll tell the SPCA."

"Tell what?" he repeated.

The cage was clean, well stocked with food and water. The Antigones, like everyone else he kept, were neither starved nor beaten.

She sucked her mouth for some spittle, but it was dry as a bone.

His eyes remained closed. The hands lay long and crossed on his stomach, which rose and fell evenly.

She bent down, picked up the blue cage, and went to another door.

The Filipino houseboy had pulled the drapes back and was piling stale ashtrays and dirty glasses onto a tea wagon. A transistor radio hung around his neck, softly giving forth a rug-clearance commercial as the leftover guests yawned to their feet and plodded to bathroom and kitchen. In a corner, sprinkled with butts and ashes, an hors d'oeuvre ground into his shoulder, the boy in the pith helmet lay curled up, asleep. She crouched down and shook him. "Go into Josh's bedroom," she said, but he was dead to the world, he stank of liquor. She pulled one eyelid up with her finger; the eye, bloodshot and dull, stared straight ahead, then the iris slid out of sight, leaving only the veinous white. She let go of him, and passing the frail old black man with the bush of gray hair, who was picking out the raisins from a piece of bread and eating them one by one, she went outside, through the garden, and into the street.

And now, where? And what did it matter? She started walking up the steps in the sidewalk, holding the cage in her arms.

Her vision was normal again; everything around her looked natural, perhaps slightly fresher than usual. She felt no lingering effects of the drug, only her dry mouth and a vestigial quality of detachment. She had heard that people felt paranoid as they came off an acid trip, but she was lucky; she had been lucky during the trip, too; if you were shaky to begin with, you easily cracked, saw monstrous things. Except in the bathroom, all she had seen was beauty. It had been a beautiful trip, except that during it she had destroyed herself.

For a cheap hallucinatory thrill. No, for that alone—to conjure Morrie from someone else's body—anyone would have done: Clovis, any of the guests on the floor. It was Josh she had chosen, to make her jelly-soft jelly-dark pocket of existence absolute. Which it now was.

At the top of the hill was a small park. She walked into it and sat down on a bench. It was a quiet morning, holding only the sound of foghorns, more than she had ever before heard all at once, each in a different key, like the faint notes of a flute blown at random. Then gradually they faded as the fog burned off the bay. The morning grew fuller. Other people were out in it—a young couple with tennis rackets, an old man with a newspaper under his arm.

She sat in the spacious silence, the cage by her feet. Her neck was chilly. She had cut her hair because her scalp had itched and her comb broke when she tried to use it. She put her two hands on her cold neck, then laid them in her lap, one hand holding the other. She twined the fingers. In death too—her next logical step—your hands were together; on your chest; on all that you would take home with you in the dark.

Only the silence, and the hands in her lap; olive-skinned hands, pale blue veins just under the surface, an old white thread-like scar on the right thumb, the ten fingernails like smiling faces—she had thought that as a child. She lifted them up before her as the old man seated himself at the other end of the bench, opened his newspaper, and frowned at her—seeing a demented creature with a rat in a cage, holding her hands in the air.

Palms printed with images going back to her Berkeley days, back to Herr von Kaulbach, back to the old truck bouncing over the Oklahoma potholes, layer under layer under layer of imprints. She could take all these things home with her in the dark, they were not shameful, not even the old truck was shameful. But she would have to include last night in the final reckoning, she would have to include all these last months, the whole last year with its deepening crack. The nausea rose in her chest again, and she thought: to be as foul as she, corroded, was to be beyond help. She had done it all herself, no one had forced her to do anything; she had treated herself foully. And how could she treat herself differently, how could she bring respect to something that gave no cause for respect?

She dropped her hands.

The old man glanced over at her from his paper. Wherever you went nowadays there were young people giving off odors and mumbling to themselves. But it was his morning bench and he would stay put.

It was impossible to forgive herself, because it was impossible to find a spark of liking where there was only loathsomeness. It was like asking the dark to give off light.

"I don't know," she said aloud.

The old man pursed his lips, but kept reading.

Nothing. Only two hands in her lap, with dark skin and blue veins and an old scar thin as a thread. From some summer month of 1940 when she had run off from Clarrie for a hike, scratched herself along the way, she remembered sucking the hand as she walked in the acrid smell of the underbrush. Good hands, deft, the way they clamped from branch to branch— slap, slap—making swift passage up a tree and pushing into the leaves on top to part them for the sky . . .

"Ask them to forgive—"

"Do and be done with it," the old man muttered, addressing himself to the paper which he rattled in his lap.

A while later he glanced up. Thank goodness she was going, standing up, God help us, in a pajama top and a scrap of skirt, both flaking off pieces of dried mud. What was it all coming to, this world, this little park? But at least, having finally noticed him, she had the decency to look ashamed of her existence. It was not such a young face after all; and it looked strained, ill; but was summoning some concentration, some life to its features.

"It's a nice morning," she said tentatively.

"That's a matter of opinion," he replied; but something in the way she stood, as though unsteadily trying to absorb the sun, the smell of the grass, the color of the sky—all the things that meant so much to him and, after all, belonged to everyone —made him add, not without stiffness: "Nice enough."

She picked up her rat cage. He watched her go down the path until she was out of sight. Then, instead of reading, he laid his head back under the warm morning sun.

48 Johanna moved from room to room hammering, painting, and varnishing. The flat was in reasonably good shape, but she took a long time with it, oiling door hinges, polishing each old brass doorknob, absorbed in her labor. She kept Antigone on the back porch for the time being, where the smell of the paint would not bother her, though she herself liked it: smartingly fresh.

The flat was in the heart of North Beach, among small stores and Italian restaurants, near St. Peter and Paul's Church, whose white baroque towers overlooked Washington Square, where old men lined the benches with their elbows on their knees and argued in Tuscan dialect. In the late afternoon she would stop her work and walk through the neighborhood or sit in the square as the spires and towers of the cathedral grew whiter against the evening. The streetlights went on, and quivered, luminous, in the plum-blue air. A permanent joy in streetlights was one of the things the acid trip had left her with; what else she had been left with she did not ponder; an instinct for self-mending made her lead a totally physical life, working hard on the flat, and falling into bed exhausted at night.

She had gone back to the cottage once, to have her furniture moved. She felt a shock when she saw how she had misused her possessions, letting them stand pushed together collecting dust, scuffmarks, rings where glasses had been set. No one queried her appearance—kerchief around her hacked-off hair, laundered trenchcoat—or her decision to move. She stood listening to the splintering grind of the sanding machine and the thunder of the hi-fi (the noise of the hi-fi ceased a moment later when the Bekins men carried it out) and knelt by Clovis, who was stretched out on the floor, his glassy eyes fixed on the blue beams of the ceiling where a haze of smoke hung. "Are you seeing good things, Clovis?" she asked, but he never responded when he was like that. She wrote her name and her new address on a scrap of paper and stuffed it in his pocket and went to the door. She seemed already to have been forgotten by her old roommates: an interchangeable cog, except perhaps in Clovis' eyes when they were functioning. She waved to Scotty, who gave an eye-popping smile over his machine and waved back, and went out the door where the bleached poem fluttered in the breeze.

Now the flat was finished, and she walked through it satisfied. The walls were pale yellow, the doors and trim dark varnished wood. The rug was laid, the furnishings repaired and arranged, her paintings hung—one wall was given solely to Herr von Kaulbach's portrait. Everything smelled of fresh paint, furniture polish, and sun. The windows were open to an unseasonably hot May in which the old cream-white buildings of North Beach stood drenched and glaring like a Casablanca. She picked up the phone and asked Conrad and Wanda to a housewarming. She had seen them frequently these last weeks, in fact had stayed with them when she first left the cottage, and the friendship was working its way back to normal, though it had suffered a long serious gap. One of the things that had helped bridge the gap was the story about the rats (she had not given the particulars surrounding her arrival in the storeroom), which had united them all as animal lovers. The SPCA was called (nothing could be done) and Conrad had gone to Josh in the gallery. There was nothing from Josh except an incredulous smile, a fine glossy Antigone perched by his ear as always. Conrad never went back.

She also asked her downstairs neighbor to her housewarming, a young ophthamologist named Alan. And a couple who ran a neighborhood bookstore, and a few hippies she knew from the square. The Mediterranean community disapproved of the hippies, the *capelloni*, but was unruffled by them; it ignored Grant Avenue, once the home of the Beats and now resurging with the seedy-ornate look of the Haight, as it ignored Broadway with its night hordes of tourists, its topless clubs and elbow-grabbing barkers. It was an indestructibly provincial neighborhood, and as though bowing to its laws, all the *capelloni* ever did there was sun bathe on the grass or arc their frisbies through the air. Nevertheless, they were not appreciated.

Everyone liked the flat, and Conrad and Wanda were especially impressed by the harmony of the old and the new. Set in a format of bright paint and interspersed with new white wicker furniture, the heirlooms were no longer concentrated on one rich island lapped by dust and dim light, but shed their mellowness evenly throughout the room, whose windows were hung with the old lace curtains, but carefully handwashed, several shades lighter.

She has actually done it, thought Conrad, sitting down on the new wicker love seat, she has really come through, and even looks herself again—at least no longer gaunt, drawn; but no longer freakishly young either. The cheeks slightly convex, faint lines under the eyes, a reflective set to the mouth. A simple flowered dress, brief, more stylish than her old taste— she meant to have some of the good things. And she said she no longer had compunctions about selling her work (once she began painting again), for she wanted to be free from scrounging through life with pointless jobs. She would not charge as much as Josh had—the prices had been outrageous —she wasn't interested in making a fortune. And who knew, maybe in a different kind of gallery, with prices that did not turn aside all but the wealthy Cobbledock clique, she would find an audience that was more honestly in tune with her work. Again, thought Conrad, the harmony between her old idealism and a new and healthy concern with her physical well-being. He felt that when she began painting again her palette would be more luminous, her subjects broader, a new dimension of understanding would grow beneath her brush. And his thoughts went to his own work. Which he had never returned to. Which, guiltily, he realized he did not miss. He was now a designer of posters, an artisan for eight hours a day, a husband for the rest, and soon to be a father, and it was a way of life as old as the Bible, somehow powerful, somehow fulfilling. Those periods at the easel in his old room, those mute, rapt twelve-hour stretches with Closeto sitting beside him—those long hours seemed now like an immersion in the lonely, nervous juices of some unnatural need . . . now he had woven himself into a different fabric of life, and a new bond was being woven daily, this child, to be Claire or William, this human being who already filled him with not exactly joy, no, but tenderness, and some strange near-panic at times . . . a panic which his wife did not seem to share . . . she was young, took everything in her stride . . . sitting down next to him now, heavily, carefully, radiating capability, though she had had some bad times . . . he put his arm around her broad waist.

His concern was boundless, his empathy touched her. During those first months she had felt the cavities of her body aslosh with a staleness like old sink water, her mouth was coated with a cloying bubblegum taste, her throat convulsed with half-digested upheavals; and the thought of lovemaking was often repugnant to her, as was the smell of Connie's morning coffee, and on occasion even his kindness, which set her teeth on edge. In her gray vomity vertigo she had had to force her mind back to the day she had found out, a day of absolute flying joy, and believe in that and not in the nausea . . . and finally the nausea had gone away, and now she felt better than ever before in her life . . . doing natural-childbirth exercises because it seemed the only right way of bringing your child into life (besides, the excruciating pains of ordinary labor terrified her, why did people think big tall women were heroes?) . . . there was a flush in her cheeks, she felt it all the time, Connie said she was beautiful though she rather doubted that; still she was sometimes given to visions of the beauty of motherhood, oh very romantic, she would be the kind of mother always there with comforting hands and a soft lap; in a rush she saw a gray afternoon, a fire in the hearth, sitting rocking her infant in her arms . . . sentimental, but maybe the world needed sentiment, it was a world of paying bills, defrosting meals, and trusting the spawn to Sesame Street and the school psychologists . . . but despite her visions of the hearth, she would be a working mother, they would have to hire someone at first to take care of it, later it would go to a nursery . . . and she felt horribly callous, wrenched with guilt . . . and yet she had worked too hard to throw her career over, she loved her work . . . was it selfish, even unnatural, to want her work as much as a child? . . . And yet the men in her office—Connie, for that matter—no one ever suggested that a man did not love his child because he was not prepared to spend his entire life taking care of it . . . strange traditions, strange apportionings of duties, no one ever questioned them . . . almost the whole female population of the country worked, but there was a feeling that this was somehow unfortunate, an economic necessity that left the children rootless, morally skimpy, and she had to admit there was truth to it, and yet the old way was not just, not fair . . . so many nuances, so many things to think about . . . well, let anyone criticize her, she knew she loved the child, beyond words or reason, as she loved Connie . . . and here was Johanna with a plate of sandwiches,

302

asking if she wanted a pillow . . . everyone was so thoughtful when you were as enormous as she was now . . . yes, she
would like a pillow, and Johanna went to get one . . . and
she thought how simple Johanna's life was, fixing up her
new flat, arranging her painting equipment, probably opening up by pleasant degrees to the idea of a new lover; no
awesome biological bond growing inside her day by day . . .
and now the other guests had all arrived, one was a young
eye doctor from downstairs named Alan; maybe this would
be the one to take Morris' place in Johanna's affections . . .
and Wanda addressed herself to this possibility, looking for
hints of interest in their glances and words . . . yet, after
all, it was of no great concern to her, it belonged to a different, more youthful, and essentially uninteresting realm
of existence . . . what was real was the dragging weight
of her belly, a weight that moved her to weariness yet filled
her with a pervading sense of rightness, of completion . . .

After her guests had gone Johanna straightened up the
flat and went into the studio. Everything stood in readiness:
new brushes, new tubes of paint, a dozen stretched canvases.
But though the next morning she rose at five, dipped herself
in cold water, and put on her paint-stiffened jeans, she spent
the whole morning pacing before the empty canvas. The next
morning was the same, and the next, until a week passed. She
was not ready yet, she was still knitting together inside; and
closing the door on the studio, she patiently continued to wait.

There are hundreds of lakes in the area of the Russo-Finnish
border, like splinters of ice among the firs. The largest of
these—the largest lake in Europe, in fact—is Lake Ladoga,
whose northern perimeter lies frozen all winter, and even in
midsummer thaws only on the surface, leaving a block of ice
below, and below that, dark currents that never see light. In
the winter of 1940 Finnish troops were massed on one side
of a Ladoga inlet, Russian troops on the other. Early in the
morning, while it was still dark, the Russians muffled their
horses' hooves with sacking and began an advance across the
ice. But, hearing them, the Finns sent up flares and bombarded the ice with artillery. Within minutes the Russian
troops had sunk from sight. To this day, in the summer,
guides will row you out and point down: there, below the
shallow surface water, below the ice, you can see the dark

massed shadows of a thousand men and horses. The peasants will not come near. They say at night you can hear the horses neighing.

Johanna heard this story one night at a Grant Avenue coffee house called the Outasite, a place of straw flowers and candle stumps stuck in Cinzano bottles, tie-dyed tablecloths, and walls patterned with the usual fluorescent posters, some of them Conrad's. The café throbbed by day, but by late evening, when it was Johanna's habit to drop in for a baklava, it was quiet and worn down; a good place to sit on warm evenings, eating a baklava, being part of things, yet not part of things. Besides, she liked the counterman, she liked the way he kept a cigar in the corner of his mouth, like Edward G. Robinson, though he was more cheerful-looking than Edward G. Robinson, and much younger, in his mid-twenties, broad-chested, dark, with heavy-lidded eyes. He was leaning on the counter now, a towel over his shoulder, listening to the long-haired youth who was addressing his tale to two girls in micro-dresses and ankle bells. The counterman almost never spoke, but seemed to listen a good deal. Johanna, at a nearby table, was listening too.

"How do you know that's true?" one of the girls asked the youth.

"I was there."

"Man, in *1940*?"

"Last summer," he said, with a look for her stupidity. "This guide took me out in a rowboat."

And as she listened, Johanna saw the flares pop and blossom in the darkness, then float gracefully down, shedding a magnesium brilliance that blanched everything around her bone-white, while silence hung like a delicately tipped pail. A blast of artillery overturned it, the air flew with ice splinters like hail raining upward, as below ran a wildly complex sensation of the earth disengaging, losing its connective tissues in a thousand places; suddenly, with a surf-like roar, acres of ice and men shot downward; what had been whiteness was a massive wound of black; and heeling over in an avalanche of horseflesh and leather and flailing arms, she was inside the wound, plummeting, deafened, her mouth flowing with water.

She stood up from the table, leaving her baklava uneaten, and walked home.

At four A.M. she finished the picture of the soldier in the blue tunic, and went up to the roof of the building to stand in the cool air. So, whatever new tissues had formed, whatever balance and amenity she had achieved on the surface, her visions were the same, would always be the same; she was essentially someone who stood alone on a roof at night and saw armies drowning. It was neither good nor bad, it was she; and she remembered the poem of Stephen Crane's, which she felt she had always understood, not with her mind but with her blood, a poem about a creature

> Who, squatting upon the ground,
> Held his heart in his hands,
> And ate of it.
> I said, "Is it good, friend?"
> "It is bitter—bitter," he answered.
> "But I like it
> Because it is bitter,
> And because it is my heart."

Rising at five every morning, she painted into the afternoon. Then she put on her bikini under her clothes and walked down to Aquatic Park. There was a sign on the beach saying POLLUTED—SWIM AT YOUR OWN RISK, but the waves were clear and green as glass, and braved by a score of fanatic water lovers like herself. The water was electrifyingly cold, and she gasped and vowed never to set foot in it again, but within minutes she was propelled through the waves by a sense of tingling well-being. She felt no ill effects from the pollution, but in a year or two the water would cloud with scummy yellow, the froth on the beach would stink, people would be forced back from the beach to the lawn. And she was glad that at least she had this summer.

She would stretch out afterward on the hot sand, eyes closed. From under the mossy pilings where the sand lay in shadow, cool and pungent, the dark water slapped with a faint sound. There were other sounds—voices, drifting, as voices always drifted on beaches; the distant rattle and clang of a cable car; the ceaseless soft beat of bongos spreading from a knot of crouched youths. And lying there, she was visited by an old pain, not exactly for Morris himself, but for the times they had spent together—the long hikes through the Marin hills; one hike in particular, when he had plowed the car jeep-like through brambles and bushes until he could go no farther, and she had jumped out to survey the bay below, a polished green puzzle-piece inserted into the foot of the hills, with the orange bridge suspended high above it, light and air filling the lofty spaces between its pillars. She turned to find Morris sitting on an outcropping of rock, his shirt snapping madly in the wind, one side of his figure like gold foil in the late sun. She was rocked, mad with joy, and scrambled up after him, and there on the hard stone, in the sight of all the seedling cars on the bridge, they had made love.

It was as if something had grown up next to them, something with a life of its own, a tapestry of sights and sounds and scents which, even after all this time, refused to die.

49

She heard that he sang at an operatic café called the Bella Voce, the counterman with the cigar, and one Saturday night she made a point of going there, bringing her downstairs neighbor Alan along as an escort. Broadway heaved with banjos, rock music, and gunned motors, while overhead in a brightly lit glass cage a girl clad only in a fringed G-string did the twist from eight P.M. till two A.M. with decreasing vigor, and searchlights swept the heavens in celebration of a new go-go club.

Inside the Bella Voce, at a grand piano heaped with dog-eared music scores, a fat man in a brown suit was playing a Chopin polonaise, while the three entertainers on the platform looked on. The counterman wore black trousers, a wide red sash, and a loose satin blouse, and under the yellow spotlight his face was sharply defined—large-nosed, the dark eyes heavy-lidded, the hair straight, blue-black, with narrow sideburns like a flamenco dancer's. When he smiled he flashed a mouthful of gold inlays.

She sat down at a table with her escort, and he ordered drinks. Before they came she had tried to give him a couple of dollars to pay for her drinks, but she felt she had somehow made an unladylike gesture that had put him in a sour mood. "I suppose they're no good or they wouldn't be here," he complained now, as the polonaise ended and the counterman bounded to his feet.

"An' now, leddies, gen-e-teel-e-men," the counterman announced, flinging his arms out, "our lowvly Miss—Miss Soprano—she sing for you '*O don fatale*' dal *Don Carlo*."

No wonder she had never heard him speak at the Outasite; he was a recent immigrant. She foresaw a communication barrier, but supposed the international language might overcome it; and she smiled at this romantic thought. At the Outasite, romance belonged to the past; clothing might harken nostalgically back to the Roaring Twenties or even the Gay Nineties, but eyes met and locked—if they did—with a sense of cool encounter. The thought of anyone clutching his heart and bursting into song there was ludicrous.

Miss Soprano had risen coyly from her chair and looked at

the audience with an arch smoldering smile. Then the mouth unhinged, and from its vast circumference an unmoored and strident voice cut through the air.

"God," said Alan, putting his hands to his face.

Johanna forced herself not to grimace, though the high notes set her eardrums ringing as though from a pneumatic drill. The voice bleated on and on while the false eyelashes batted provocatively and the old hands—she saw that they were quite old—busied themselves with mannered gestures. The eyes were still smoldering as she neared the end of her song, but they smoldered now with a kind of self-hatred, and at last, with an ear-splitting shriek, she gave a simpering bow, coy to the end, except for the eyes.

There was a polite spate of applause. The accordionist began *"La Tarantella,"* swinging his head around and beaming, as someone called up to him, "Ciao, Arcangelo!" Everyone seemed to know everyone, everyone spoke Italian. The counterman grabbed a red gourd and shook it in exuberant tempo.

"Christ, you don't really want to stay," Alan told her.

Her eyes were on the counterman. "Of course I do," she said.

"He's pretty young for you, isn't he?" Alan asked, following her gaze.

"Around your age. You're not exactly rolling a hoop."

He flushed and said nothing.

"Why don't you go home?" she asked, glancing at him. "I thought I needed an escort, but it's not that kind of place. Go home if you're not enjoying yourself. I don't care."

But his expression was one of dutiful forbearance. When *"La Tarantella"* came to an end and Miss Soprano stood up, he gave a long glum sigh.

"And now, ladies and gentlemen," she announced roguishly, "our fine tenor, Mr. Sergio Guidi, will sing for you *'Questa o quella'* from *Rigoletto.*"

Sergio Guidi leaped to his feet. He planted himself with legs apart as the piano and accordion ran through the rousing prelude; then lifting his arms and throwing his head back, he poured from his swelling throat a voice so rich and authoritative that Johanna could not believe she was hearing this sound in a café. She leaned forward on her elbow, rapt, moved by the manliness of the voice; it embodied everything that was strong, spirited, heartfelt, and she felt not only its beauty, but a deep sexual appreciation of the male.

The audience was entranced; obviously Guidi was the café's drawing card. Arcangelo was smiling with measureless pride, with almost pained delight, as though he himself had given birth to the singer. But Miss Soprano, in repose, looked haggard and melancholy; yet judgmental, appreciative. Johanna sensed that she was guided by inflexible rules, absolute standards, as cruel as those on any opera-house stage; all such severity apparently having come to nothing for herself. It gave the café, suddenly, a forlornness. Along the walls, under soft lights, hung scenes from *Aïda, Bohème, Elisir d'Amore* —the great peaks to be scaled; while glasses clattered indifferently from the bar and street noises rolled in with the customers.

Sergio Guidi sang on sublimely undisturbed, one hand across his breast, and finished the aria to a storm of bravos and stamped feet. He bowed, and bowed again, arms upflung, teeth bared in a grin of undisguised pleasure, and with a flare of showmanship, picked up his wineglass and toasted the audience.

The fat pianist flung himself into another polonaise, and Arcangelo stood up and declared an intermission. He and the singers came down from the stage to join friends at their tables, and as Guidi passed, Johanna smiled. The singer paused, and Alan was obliged to offer him a chair. He sat down and beamed at them, wiping his brow.

"I enjoyed your singing," Johanna told him.

"Cosa?"

"Your singing—it was beautiful."

"Ah, my plaisure, my plaisure," he assured her.

"This is Alan," she said. "My name is Johanna."

He shook hands with both of them. "Giovanna." He smiled. "My plaisure, Miss. You stody, you sing?"

"Oh, no, only listen."

"Cosa?"

"Listen?" she said, cupping her ear.

He nodded uncertainly.

"I think we know each other from the Outasite," she told him.

"Ah, the Outasite! Sì. Lavoro là. L'ho vista là qualche volta."

"How long have you been over here?" Alan inquired, speaking for the first time.

"Cosa?"

"How many months," Alan enunciated, holding up his fingers, "in the United States?"

"Ah," he said, brightening, and held out eight fingers. "Otto anni."

"Eight *years?*"

The counterman gave a cheerful shrug. "Non parlo molto bene la sua lingua. Sono troppo pigro del impararla. Learn speak, no. Lazy."

"You can't be all that lazy if you're a singer," Johanna said.

"Cosa?" he said again, shaking his head. "Non ho capito. Mi scusi."

Alan threw her a look of mingled exasperation and satisfaction.

"To sing," she explained, ignoring Alan, "much work. Much—efforto? Laboro?"

"Ah, lavoro!" He nodded, grasping her meaning. And shrugged again. "Not more. Mi son dato per vinto. Si deve soffrire troppo per riuscire. No good, you push-push, push-push, so? No good to get there, La Scala, Metropolitano. Here, okay. Good time. Basta così."

She nodded reflectively. Here was a man of ability, content to match his vocal cords with the clatter from the bar. Perhaps even Miss Soprano regretted no more than the aching back that came from working till two A.M. She was disappointed, and said: "It explains the cigar. Serious singers don't smoke."

"Cosa?" he inquired, the strain of the conversation beginning to show on his face.

"The cigar." She put two fingers to her lips. Gallantly, he withdrew a cigarette from her pack, gave it to her, and lit it with a flourish. "My plaisure. Now, I go." He shook hands with them again, his hand lingering in hers, and stood up.

"You request?" he asked her suddenly.

"Pardon?"

"To sing? I?" He touched his chest.

"Ah! I'm afraid I don't know opera that well. I don't know the tenor arias."

"Cosa?"

"No," she said, shaking her head. "Thank you."

"Tenk you."

"Thank you," she murmured.

"Tenk you."

With a friendly wave he returned to the platform.

Alan followed him with his eyes. "Isn't there an old saying: Dumb, dumber, tenor?"

"He doesn't speak English, that's all."

"Why not, after eight years?"

"Why don't you leave? I'd like to enjoy myself."

"You'll look like a pick-up."

She stood up, overcome by intense dislike for him. He stood too, with relief, but she stepped over to an empty table and sat down. For a moment he seemed not to know what to do; then he joined her. Again she got up and went to another table. This time he stayed where he was, his lips compressed. Arcangelo and the singers had reassembled on the platform, where they now broke into "*Ciribiribin.*" Johanna felt Guidi's eyes on hers; his broad smile was directed at her.

By the time he came down to her table at the next intermission Alan had gone.

50

Sergio Guidi had lived for eight years in two rooms that he rented from a cousin in an alley around the corner from St. Peter and Paul's Church. His rooms were nothing much, but satisfactory: he had a radio on which he listened to the *Italian Hour,* and a cheap phonograph, his collection of opera records being his only extravagance. A few Italian James Bond paperbacks stood on the table, and on the wall hung an oval gold-framed photograph of his family in Lucca.

As soon as he arrived from Lucca he had gotten a job at the Ghirardelli chocolate factory, and here he had stayed for seven and a half years. At night he studied voice. It was a gift, his voice, and it had always excited everybody; but he was not excited, though he loved to sing. The thought of agents, managers, taxes, tours, crowds, not to speak of jealousy and temperament, all this bored him to death . . .

Coming to the United States was his family's idea. "Italy is filled with fine talents who can't scrape two lire together and thus wither away in the very vineyard of opera," said his father, who was poetic. So he had come, and for years he had studied hard because his voice was a gift, but he would rather have played boccie or strolled through the streets looking at girls. He began to wish for marriage. He had a weakness for children, and for the pleasures of the bed. But the young ladies he took out were Italian and as untouchable as their sisters in Lucca, and the girls he bedded down with were *capellone* who did much staring and mumbling and sometimes left a louse between his sheets. Still, he was not unhappy, and never had been.

Then one day his old voice teacher fell over dead. Sergio was heartbroken, but he was also free, and he bought a cigar, which he had coveted for years. He found the Outasite job in order to enjoy the daytime, and he began appearing at the Bella Voce on Saturday nights, a place that perfectly fulfilled his love of singing. Everything at the Bella Voce was a pleasure except for the soprano, whose long German name he could not pronounce. She was a vocal monster, tenth-rate to her soles, but he respected her for her tragedy. It was Miss Soprano who was most pained by his cavalier attitude toward his voice, and one day when she saw him on the street with his cigar she almost wept.

He thought: Either she should have my art, or I should have her drive, then one of us would go down in history. "You would take the pleasures from my life," he chaffed her in Italian.

"È vero," she agreed without humor.

He bowed and she passed on, perhaps sixty, perhaps more, a bakery clerk who taught a few beginning students in the evening, and whom he had noticed long before the Bella Voce, squashed season after season in the standing room of the opera house, eyes alight, fingers moving with the music.

Well, life was filled with injustices. He had this voice, she had that soul. His father had poetry, but no face, most of it blown off in Libya. War, Sergio believed, should be fought in an open field by those who liked it, and he rejoiced in a deficient kidney which would keep him from all fields of battle. Not that he couldn't be fierce—sometimes he had to throw people out of the Outasite, which he did with spirit and efficiency. Nevertheless, he was well liked there. They thought he stood in lasting agreement with them, when the fact was that he understood nothing of what they said. Così è la vita.

To find an Outasite patron at the Bella Voce was amazing, and he had looked twice—but yes, it was the baklava lover, usually in jeans and an old shirt, not exactly a *capellona,* a little older, and ate with neatness. *Carina.* He might have passed her a look along with her baklava, but he never felt moved to make overtures in the cool bewildering Outasite. Tonight she looked completely different; she wore a delicious dress high above the knees, her eyes were bright, and she smiled at him. Unfortunately, she was with a man.

"L'uomo con te, chi era?" he asked when they left together at two A.M. He had offered to walk her home. "De guy?"

"Oh, just a friend. Amigo. Amico?"

"He was a-hungry at you."

"Hungry? Oh, angry. Oh, no, we're just like cousins."

"Cosa?"

"Like a cousin. A figlio—di fratello—di mi padre?" she fumbled.

"Ah, cugino!" He smiled, with seventeen in San Francisco alone, not to mention the hordes in Lucca. So she had cousins, too, but strange ones.

The street mobs had thinned, the girl in the glass cage was tiredly winding up her dance. He always enjoyed watching her, but it was no place for a human being, not even a *puttana*. And he wondered what this Giovanna was—not a whore, not a *capellona*, not a tourist lady, the only kinds of American women he came across. Well, whatever she was, her eyes had warm promising things in them—though they gleamed through a layer of reserve, which he found titillating. At her door he pressed her hand to his lips in the best continental manner, and departed in good spirits.

The following nights she came to the Outasite and he walked her home when he was finished. He put his arm through hers (holding hands being an American custom which he found childish) and they conversed in their obscure fashion, and lingered on her doorstep. On Saturday night she arrived at the Bella Voce alone, without the unfortunate cousin, who was as sour as an old sock, and she sat near the stage and applauded until her palms must have stung. Two weeks passed this way until one warm, clear evening the growing promise was at last fulfilled.

"And so," said Wanda a few days later, "you've finally gotten over Morris. Good."

"Except," Johanna corrected her, "he reminds me of Morris."

"He sounds so different."

They spoke with long pauses between, with a kind of languor.

"Oh, it's the face. It's human nature, don't you think?"

"I suppose so."

Wanda lay on the bed in her housecoat. It was early evening and the room was darkening. A peacefulness pervaded the room, and the conversation seemed to concern some other, distant world. The nightstand, in the deepening gray light, gleamed with baby bottles, balls of cotton, and other strange things. The baby lay in its crib in a corner, three days old, abandoned to sleep. That was the corner the stillness emanated from.

"You know," Wanda said, "it's odd. I don't know how to explain it, part of me is living over in the corner, but it's in me too."

314

"I know what you mean—I felt that way about Morris."

"Oh, I know what you mean—but it's different, I think."

Johanna was sitting on the end of the bed. She looked at Wanda. "You're very glad, aren't you?"

"Infinitely." And she added, after a moment, "Only it's odd. It makes you nervous."

"Because he's so small, maybe."

"He's not small, Johanna," Wanda laughed. "Ten and a half pounds?"

A mewling sound rose from the crib; then with a snuffle it left off, and the room was silent again.

"What was it like," Johanna asked, curious, "to bear him?"

"You sound like Thomas Hardy. Bear him."

"What should I say—whelp him?"

"I don't know." And she was silent for a while. "It was rotten."

"I'm really sorry I didn't get back until today. I'd have come to the hospital."

"You were carousing with your Caruso," Wanda smiled, as if she were past such trifling occupations, yet indulgent.

"He had some vacation time coming, so we went over to Bolinas—he's got a cousin who's got a shack there. He's a great swimmer—Sergio, I mean. But I wouldn't have gone if I thought it was going to happen then."

"I didn't know either. Two weeks early. He gave me a time."

"What about the exercises?"

"I guess they'd have worked except that it was a breech birth. I was in labor forever."

"And it was really painful? Even with the drugs and everything?"

"Even with the drugs and everything."

"Was there a feeling of—it must sound naïve, but—well, greatness? In spite of the pain? You hear that."

"You hear a lot of things. Mostly from doctors and male novelists. I wanted to claw myself free. I'd have clawed anybody to pieces. Connie, even."

"And yet you wanted to be conscious."

"Listen, as soon as something goes wrong all your fine ideas about Chinese peasant women and nature being simple and good go down the drain, and all you want is drugs, but they won't give you enough. Don't tell me about nature, nature mostly goes wrong and fouls things up. I hate pompous pretty stories.''

''Well, are you going to have your tubes tied or something?''

''No. I'll probably go through with it again someday.''

''They say you forget about it later. And it's as though it never was.''

''I remember how it was having a wisdom tooth pulled, why shouldn't I remember this?''

''But you *are* glad,'' Johanna insisted, feeling that the small creature in the corner was being slandered.

''Of course I am,'' Wanda said, sitting up and carefully putting her legs over the side of the bed. She turned the bed lamp on. Her face was tired, but it wore a look of deep, pleasant anticipation as she got to her feet and went toward the crib, a look completely at odds with her words of a moment before; and Johanna sensed that this pleasure was as real and strong as her denunciation of pain, and that the two things somehow existed side by side.

''Should you be walking?'' she asked.

''Oh, yes,'' Wanda said absently. She went to the side of the crib and arranged the coverlet.

''Can I help with something?'' Johanna asked.

''Oh, no, I'm just looking.'' And she stood entranced, with her hands behind her back. ''Newborn babies are all supposed to look like little wrinkled old men,'' she said.

''He does, doesn't he?'' Johanna agreed.

''Well, I don't think he does, that's the point. I think he's an exception—I mean, objectively, I do think so.''

Johanna nodded. ''He's got a nice round head.''

Wanda passed her hand over the small head and lightly smoothed the coverlet. ''I think he'll sleep another hour.''

''Maybe you should try to sleep, too.''

''You're like a Jewish mother, my dear,'' she smiled, but she went back to bed.

''Isn't it funny?'' she said after a while. ''A few years ago you'd have thought Connie and I were prime candidates for zero reproduction. Me with my job and him in his crazy little room.''

''And here you are, Mama and Papa.''

''And Mama still has her job.'' She looked across the room at the crib. ''I don't want him to grow up alone on cold TV dinners.''

316

"But Conrad will be home during the day, won't he?"

"Oh, he's out running around town conferring with people. And besides, he's got to get a studio pretty soon, there's not enough space in the dining room. He's spreading out all over the place. Poor Connie, he's becoming a success."

"Well, don't worry about it now. Get some rest."

Wanda closed her eyes.

From the corner of the room came the little mewling sound again, then there was stillness. Outside the wind wove through the dark geranium bushes, ruffling the leaves.

51 Someone up on Holy Mountain had tried to burn
his mother in effigy and had reduced the commune to ashes instead. The next day a sooty Thor
and Zaidee stumbled into Esalen looking for
Morris, having nowhere else to go. Dorothy took
over. She found clothes for Thawn, who had been snatched
away without a stitch, began feeding her pregnant mother
iron pills, and invited the young couple to drive north with
her and Morris. A few days later the lot of them drove off
from Esalen for Sausalito, where Dorothy owned a large
brown-shingled house on a wooded hill overlooking the bay.

While Thor and Zaidee camped out in the backyard until
they decided what to do next, Dorothy outfitted the living
room with massage tables and a pile of Ravi Shankar records,
established herself and Morris at the San Francisco Esalen
Center, and began building up a private clientele.

Life was full. The August sun shone every day. Each
morning at seven Dorothy tugged on her black one-piece bathing suit, grabbed a towel, and strode down the path to the
narrow shale beach for an astringent dip. Then, turning,
gazing up at the fine old house whose windows blazed red in
the early sun, and where Morris could sometimes be seen
stretching mightily, she rubbed herself down and started
back with a zestful step.

And so, thought Morris, watching the haze burn off the bay,
here he was. Doing honest work, making good money, in touch
with kindred spirits. The view was superb and his sex life was
smooth. Dorothy put no holds on him, and made it clear that
she wanted none. For a woman of no physical attractiveness,
she had a surprisingly sustained effect on men, and ex-lovers
and ex-husbands were always dropping in for a day or two, at
which times Morris moved out of the bedroom. As for himself, his sex drive had been permanently lowered, along with
all his other drives. A dimension of himself had closed down
that night in the canyon—probably twenty years past due.
He felt a dryness, an acceptance. Not that he led an austere
life : girls shared his bed (at these times it was Dorothy who
moved out) but there was less compulsion in his invitations
than nostalgic habit. At one time women had somehow formed
a ladder to the sun ; but his spiritual deceleration had robbed

him of this heady climb, this one great shaking experience he was capable of. He remained horizontal.

He was not happy. He was not unhappy. He watched Dorothy climbing up the path with long strides, and looked past her to the glittering water and the hot blue endless sky.

Sometimes in San Francisco he wandered around visiting his old haunts. In the Haight you could smell the sweet decay. The flower children were debilitated by malnutrition, hepatitis, gonorrhea, and lived in a rash of bizarre assassinations peculiar to the drug trade. Tourists were as thick as ever, but they looked wary, as if exploring a Port Said side street. He saw no one he knew.

One day he walked to the apartment building he had lived in; he wondered if the old gal with the Cuban heels still ran the place, and remembered how she had chased him down the hall as he was dragging out his big battered desk. A long time ago. Now, spray-painted along the white stucco wall were the standard obscenities. The entrance had been fitted out with an iron grilling.

Another day, strolling down Van Ness at five o'clock, he turned his steps toward the Board of Education building to watch his old co-workers come out. He caught a glimpse of his boss, his bald head shining as always, but now set off by two bristling sideburns. And then he saw big Rhonda tripping down the steps in a sleeveless summer dress, her white pointed fingers like little hard white carrots busily searching her pink plastic purse for bus fare. Off to her ceramic class, no doubt, after a quick bite at Foster's cafeteria. She glanced up with her sugary smile, but didn't recognize him, all hair and mustache, old Levi's, and forty pounds slimmer.

"Hey there," he said, extending his hand in greeting.

She put a quarter in his palm.

He looked up from the coin. "Thanks," he said.

"Shanti." She smiled, going on.

Lord, even Rhonda.

And then finally one day, toward evening, he went to the Fillmore to look at the old place. But it had disappeared from the face of the earth; he thought he was losing his mind until he realized that, of course, it had been torn down. It was the same old lot he stood at, but the front walk ended in grass already grown high, rippling in the evening wind, silent as a country cemetery.

Her name was not in the phone book.

The following week he found himself at the gallery looking covertly through the window. Another girl was at the receptionist's desk, so he went inside. Josh was out in the patio, half lost in a mountain of sailcloth that bulked from wall to wall. He was looking for the edge of the material, crawling and poking, the white rat clinging to his shoulder. A few people looked on from the entrance.

"Where's Johanna?" Morris asked. "She doesn't work here anymore?"

Josh glanced around, but didn't interrupt his search. "No," he said.

"When did she quit?"

"About a year ago."

And again Morris felt that sense of silence. A year.

"Where is she now?"

"No idea," said Josh, finally finding the edge. When he had fitted it with clamps and ropes he meant to hang it across a ravine somewhere.

Morris went back outside, thinking that he might walk over to Conrad's and Wanda's place; but his steps slowed. He wondered about Johanna, yes, but he wasn't quite ready to find her. Besides, Conrad and Wanda would slam the door in his face, they had never approved of him: Conrad and Wanda and Closeto, a smug little trinity of poetic love and loyalty. No, if he and Johanna were to meet again, it would be in the fullness of time. And he said the phrase over; it had a natural sound to it, like the wind blowing or the waves rolling.

52 The idea of marriage began to glow like a candle in Sergio's mind. True, Giovanna was different from other women, peculiar, she cared too much about her paintings, which were crazy and complicated, but she had beautiful eyes the color of honey, and a smile that pierced his heart. At the Outasite, leaning on the counter with his towel over his shoulder, his mind swam with words like "luce" and "rosa" and "amorosa," filling him with pleasure and tenderness and lust while he chewed more and abstractedly on his cigar.

"Io ti amo," he told her one night, taking her face gently between his hands.

But though she responded to his kiss, his words were not returned.

"I'm glad you found your golden tenor. I haven't seen you look so good for years; he seems to stick to your ribs."

"You make him sound like a plate of antipasto," said Johanna.

Conrad was in the neighborhood to see his printers. His fringe of gray hair hung to his collar, but was trimmed by the barber, and his hands were clean, scrubbed in deference to the outside world. They were drinking coffee in the living room, where the sun sprayed through the lace at the windows and made patterns on the worn blue arabesques of the rug. Antigone scuttled across the rug and ran up a table, where she disappeared into a blue china bowl in which she kept broom straws and bits of chewed newspaper and a domino counter or two. Conrad glanced at his watch, unconsciously describing a man whose time is of value. "No," he said, "I'm sure he's more than that; but every love affair should have its antipasto."

"You know," she said, "he wants to marry me. He proposed the other day."

"And?"

"Oh, what can you say when you can't explain anything? I tried to tell him that I don't want to be married, even though I care for him. But how can you draw the distinction between 'caring for' and 'loving' when you don't know the language?

321

I said 'affetto,' but he knows better than that—I feel more than affection for him. But it isn't love, either, not the kind he has in mind.''

''Why don't you marry him, Johanna?''

''I just told you why.''

''He's a nice guy—''

''Yes, but he's an Italian, after all. He wants someone who'll cook and have babies. He thinks my work is some eccentricity that will go away when I have less time on my hands. And there's his singing—I can't help it, but it bothers me that he's wasting his gift. I'd make his life miserable over his voice. But it isn't even that. It's the X quality that's missing. The thing I felt for Morris.''

''But that's not what you get married for. That's the worst thing to build a marriage on.''

''Maybe. But it's the only thing I'd ever marry for.''

''You haven't changed as much as I thought you had,'' he said reflectively.

''Why do you look so long-faced?'' she asked, looking at him over the rim of her coffee cup. ''Is it Morris? You think I'm going to go out looking for him and start the whole thing all over again? Don't worry—he's tarnished beyond hope.''

''Good—that clown.''

Her eyes suddenly flashed up to his. ''Not to me!''

''You've lost me,'' he said suspiciously.

''I said he's tarnished. I didn't say he was a clown.'' She was quiet for a moment. ''And for that matter, I had plenty of faults, too. I had plenty of ambiguities. I still hate him for that night in Reno, but we're all fallible.''

''I see trouble ahead,'' Conrad murmured.

''Well, you needn't. Besides, what I felt for him only happens once. It burns itself out.'' She set her cup down and lit a cigarette. ''That's the X quality, God help it. It usually happens to seventeen-year-olds blind with hormones and spring. And that's when it should happen, when you've got a lifetime to recover in.''

''Hear, hear,'' he said quietly, with the shadow of his old, tender look. ''It takes its toll on us ancients.''

''So it does,'' she agreed, meeting the look with understanding.

''Unfortunately,'' she went on after a silence, ''here is Sergio. Stomping on his good sense, losing his head more every day. And how can I just say, 'All right, let's end this'? It's not that simple, there's too much involved. I care about him very much. You can't just slice something like that off with one stroke. I don't know, it's a kind of mess." She paused with a sigh. "I can certainly pick them. The one Jew in the world who gambles, and the one Italian in the world who's faithful."

"Well, what are you going to do about him, besides hinting in bad Italian?"

"Bide my time. He'll come to realize how I feel . . ."

"But he won't. How did he take your rejection of his proposal?"

"He's persuaded himself that no woman ever accepts the first time. She's too swept off her feet."

"Well, there you are," he said, glancing at his watch again. "I've got to go," he said reluctantly, getting to his feet.

"And Billy?" she asked, putting her arm through his as they went downstairs to the door.

"Old Billy? He's the sun up in the sky, he's the apple of his Daddy's eye. I think that's an old song, so I can quote it without embarrassment."

But she could see that he was embarrassed; or not embarrassed, exactly, but, as always, keenly aware of the thinness of his skin. He had been born without an outer layer, she realized. A word, a gesture could go straight to his heart as though through butter. Which made him frown now, disgustedly. "He never stops yowling, the little bastard. We're up all night with him."

"How's the sitter working out?"

"Okay, except Wanda's jealous of her. Swoops home from work like a dragon to reclaim her infant. And it'll be worse now that I've got a studio."

"Conrad, you never tell me anything, you're always so busy pumping me. Have you got a studio?"

"Near the Embarcadero," he said, opening the door and going down the steps. "Big as a skating rink."

"And are you painting?" she asked, following him to the sidewalk. "I don't mean poster work."

"Some—" he called back.

"How much?"

"Some—" he said again, and threw his hand up through the air, partly in a wave, partly in a gesture of something else;

and strode quickly down the street in the direction of the printer's shop.

As he turned the corner someone came around it whom she felt she knew, a young man of nineteen or twenty, dressed in a striped seersucker suit with a navy-blue shirt and broad yellow necktie. It was George Eliot, she saw as he drew nearer, shorn of his long tresses.

"Hey," he said, strolling over.

"Hello, Michael," she said, half inclined to turn away, though she had nothing against him.

"Hey, you're looking good."

"So are you."

"How about that?" he said, self-consciously, giving his trousers a swipe of his hand. "Yeah, went back to school. Hey, we got married, Susan and me."

"Congratulations," she said, surprised.

"Yeah, we're living with my mom till we find a place. Like Susan's expecting?"

Time whipping by, George Eliot clean as a whistle, student and father-to-be, living in that impeccable house. His mother must be beside herself with relief. "Congratulations," she said again. "And Scotty? How's Scotty?"

"Fuzz got him. He tried to rip off an urn in Golden Gate Park. Like he wanted the pedestal? And he bashed one of the cops in the head. They sent him up to Napa for treatment."

"Poor Scotty, without his workshop."

"I brought him some of his small stones. They won't let him have the big ones. They're still in the cottage."

"Who's in the cottage now?" she asked.

"Bunch of weirdos. Into the Black Mass."

"And Clovis?"

He shrugged. "Dunno. He took off somewhere."

"I gave him my address. He never came."

"Clovis was a stone weirdo."

"And where's Jane?"

Again he shrugged.

Time, scattering everyone.

Michael smoothed his forelock back, looking very much the young man about town. "Listen, I've got to split. Take care, hey?" And he walked off as Sergio arrived with a "Hey, mia passerotta!" It meant "little sparrow," but he grabbed her robustly around the waist and flung the departing youth a

324

look of jealous disdain.

Upstairs, she saw that he was annoyed because of Michael. Antigone didn't help, peering at them from her bowl of valuables; though he was courteous to the creature, he never warmed to it; it was another of her eccentricities.

"Sergio—cantare for me?" she asked, since his voice always smoothed out the little ruffles in their life.

But he pointed contemptuously to the floor. Alan habitually grabbed a broom and pounded the ceiling with its handle when the voice burst out overhead.

"He's out—lavoro," she said.

"Bene! Cugino stupido!" he muttered, for she had never been able to get it through his head that the man wasn't her cousin. And suddenly "Santa Lucia" filled the air, and she sat entranced by the sounds, as always; and, as always, she was sorry that this voice would eventually lose its mastery.

"Beautiful!" she said when he was done.

"Bella!" he agreed. He always spoke freely of his gift, without conceit, as if it were an external phenomenon like the sun or the moon.

"It's a shame," she could not keep from adding, softly.

"Cosa?" he asked cheerfully.

"A pity. Pitissimo." But it was just as well that he didn't understand her Italian, she thought, looking at his beaming face.

53

All the while Morris was cloistered at Big Sur the world had been waiting outside unchanged. It was a world where morning came with the damp thud of a newspaper, and night with a blaze of electric lights; where time was measured by clocks and calendars, where not owning a car was a gross impracticality, and massaging backs the puniest of all occupations. Every day this old world trod more heavily on his heels, and every night pressed closer to his side. Once again past and future seemed like two book ends pushed together with nothing in between.

It was time for a change. He began investigating alternatives. He helped out in a health-food store and gathered information on the growing of macrobiotic products; he peddled an underground newspaper with the thought of starting his own sheet; he watched the street peddlers and wondered if he should become a craftsman. But none of these things appealed to him any more than massage did, and in that field he was going rapidly downhill. Dorothy was worried. She said his touch was gone. He agreed, and told her he was going to split.

"Oh, Morrie!" she protested. "Just when everything was going so great. We've got this lovely house, we've got a good clientele, and we've got each other."

"I notice you put that last," he observed.

"Don't you?"

He had to admit that he did.

"Well then," she said.

"I don't know. It's all middle ground with you and me. We work fine together and we have fun together."

"It's not so bad, is it?" she asked, taking both his hands.

"No, it's not so bad," he said, pressing the hands. "But I'm splitting."

"Well, I'm sorry, Morrie," she sighed. "I'm sorrier than I can say."

"I guess we won't die over it."

"Oh, no, I don't intend to die over it."

He would leave as soon as Dorothy found a new co-therapist. He felt better having made his decision, and discovered that he enjoyed his massage work now that it had taken on a temporary cast. Everything looked brighter. He had even pointed Thor and Zaidee in the right direction, thanks to a street peddler he knew who had good things to say about a commune down by Hetch Hetchy Dam and was going to give the young couple a lift there this coming Saturday.

On Saturday Thor and Zaidee stood ready, their belongings strapped up—pots, pans, blankets, and enough iron pills from Dorothy to last five months. Morris was to hitchhike with them over to San Francisco and meet the peddler in front of the Cannery, a fashionable brick shopping complex given over to expensive imports and tourist crowds, where folk singers, flutists, and even a harpsichordist performed in various corners of the courtyard, their hats collecting pennies at their feet.

It was late afternoon, sweltering, the October air salted with fish smells from the wharf and overlaid with exhaust fumes. They arrived hot and sticky and began looking for their man on the clogged sidewalk where youths and girls sat on outspread blankets surrounded by leather, embroidery, and jewelry; suddenly a banjo broke through the noise with "Dixie," and a young tapdancer in a top hat and star-spangled cutaway began clattering his very soul into the pavement.

Zaidee's ears pricked up. "Isn't he cute!" she cried, lapsing into a distant vernacular, and she hurried with Thawn in her arms to watch. Morris wandered after her and joined the crowd gathering around the boy. The boy was good; he was certainly energetic, and Morris threw a quarter into the cigar box on the sidewalk. Zaidee's sandaled foot was tapping away, she was jouncing the baby in her arms, her eyes shining with pleasure. Yet, Morris noticed, the pleasure seemed to be mixed with and finally overcome by some other, strange emotion, something virulent.

"That's what Ollie wanted, she broke out with, spitting the words at the boy's feet, "only nobody gave a fuck for tapdancers then. They'd never come and watch. How come he couldn't be around now! Look at this one!" Her underlip protruded stiffly, her eyes were vicious. He had never before seen such an ugly look on her face, and he was sure he never would again; it was one of those rare moments when the dead are so abruptly brought back to life and reburied that

327

the whole soul strikes out at the source of this blow. Only, look further, Zaidee, he said to himself: put the feeling where it belongs. But politics was too abstract; the sound of the metal cleats was as far as she could go, and she hated them. But now she was recovering herself, the moment was passing; once more the tattoo brought forth only nostalgia, and her toes began moving in their sandals again, restrained. When the boy finished and swept his top hat off with a grand and grinning flourish, she gave him a shy smile and put a dime in the box. Morris encircled her with his arm and they walked back up the sidewalk in search of the peddler. He was closing shop, rolling up his leather purses and belts in his blanket and securing it with a strap. Morris introduced everyone, various bundles were adjusted on backs, and they followed the peddler down the street to the parking lot where his ancient panel truck stood, throbbing with fluorescent designs in the sun.

"Where you going, man?" he asked Morris.

"Back to Sausalito."

"Take you down to Van Ness and Lombard."

"Great, man." And he climbed in beside Thor, whose eagerness to be off had set him to drumming his fingers on his knees. Zaidee got into the back with Thawn, who had begun to cry.

"Hey, baby," she soothed, "we're going down to Hetch Hetchy. Hetch *Hetchy*. Come on, sweety—" And in her Arkansas drawl she began to croon, "Hetch Hetchy here we come, oh baby's on her way, Hetch Hetchy . . ."

And then it happened, as they drove out the exit and Morris glanced through the side window at the pedestrians who had stopped for them to pass.

Johanna's heart went white. The clatter of the passing truck, Sergio's voice at her side, both disappeared into a roaring silence. The face in the window stared, then the truck turned into the street and disappeared around a corner.

"Cosa hai?" asked Sergio.

Perhaps five seconds had passed. Her mouth was ice cold.

The bush of hair, the huge mustache—it could have been anyone under all that. But the eyes!

"Stai attenta!"

She had plowed into someone in front of her. She apologized and wiped her hand across her brow. She was as flushed now as she had been cold a moment before. The city seemed to blaze and dazzle around her.

"Let me out here!" Morris cried as they turned the corner.

"Can't stop here, man. Next block."

"Is something wrong, Morrie?" Zaidee asked from the back.

"No," he said shortly.

He jumped out at the next corner, slammed the door shut, and thrust his arm back through the open window to shake hands with Thor. "Hey, you guys take care," he said as Zaidee crawled with Thawn into the front seat.

"Thanks for everything, Morrie," she told him, squeezing his fingers.

"No sweat. So long, baby. You got all those pills?"

She nodded. "You sure nothing's wrong? You look sort of crappy. Pale."

He shook his head, staring down the street.

"Listen, take care," he said again, touching Thawn's head, and stepped quickly away.

"We won't be back this time!" Thor yelled cheerfully from inside, and the truck lurched off in a cloud of exhaust. Morris was already halfway down the street. His heart hammering in his throat, he returned to the parking-lot exit and pushed on through the crowds, checking every female face he passed. But the streets were dense, it was Saturday; and he condemned all Saturdays as he forced his way through the sauntering bodies. Twenty minutes later he had covered every teeming street in the area. Was she looking for him too? Or had she hurried into the back of a store to avoid him? Had it even been her? The hair was shorter, the face older; and the glance had lasted only a second or two. He came to a stop and stood battered by the crowd. Then he began retracing his steps.

At that moment she was four blocks away, walking as slowly as was humanly possible, while her eyes flicked from one face, one vehicle to another. Everything around her was dazzling. She felt torn up by the roots to leave this area, which had suddenly passed into some new significance. Lagging and dawdling behind Sergio, she found the sleek dark back of his head suddenly intolerable; his face, as he turned questioningly around, made her furious. She pulled sharply away from his hand and followed him sullenly.

But gradually the last half hour began to seem unreal,

deranged. First of all, it had not been Morris, and even if it had been, that chapter was closed. When she saw the face she had been startled, that was all; she had temporarily lost her bearings. Sergio was Sergio again. He was hurt by her sudden hostility and covering it up with anger, berating her in Italian; she caught the word "Americana"—spoiled, no doubt, self-centered, unnatural. "What'sa wrong wi' you?" he demanded.

"Scusa," she said, finally speaking. "Scusa."

"What'sa wrong?" he demanded again.

"I don't know. Oh, Sergio, I'm sorry. Really I am. Scusa, please scusa."

He put his hands on his hips and studied her. "Hokay," he said at last, gruffly, and they walked on. By the time they reached her flat, peace had been more or less restored, but the odd dazzle of the streets flared in and out of her mind like the stars of a hammerblow.

Morris had finally given up the search and started back. Passing Aquatic Park, he turned and walked down the green lawns to the beach. The sun was low, smoldering, dusty; everything around him had gone red and orange and gold; the air was as still and warm and promising as midsummer. He walked along the waves, listening to their slow wash. There was a distant joyous clanging of bells as a cable car racketed over the hills. He stood still, the long afternoon kindling up inside him; the fullness of time had come.

54 "Well, you certainly seem in great spirits these days," Dorothy told him the following Monday as he accompanied her down the path for a morning dip. "You're just bubbling over with togetherness. You ought to decide to leave more often."

It was true that he felt much closer to her since he knew he would soon be parted from her. At times he almost felt like staying on.

"Well," he said, pounding down into the glassy water with an immense splash that shattered the early morning calm, "well," he said, surfacing and whipping his wet hair back, "I like you, baby. You've always been a shot in the arm."

"You would be too, if you didn't jab so hard," she said, striding in up to her waist and splashing the cold water onto her chest and shoulders with a stoic grimace. "You're a man of fits and starts. Style you ain't got, Morrie."

He watched her push off with a firm sidestroke, her brown muscular shoulder flashing. The nicer he grew, the more critical she became. Just as well. It doused his little flames of irresolution about leaving when they cropped up. He dove under and emerged with a smooth powerful crawl, passed the brilliant green eyes with a cheerful smile, and left her behind. The hazed morning sky was clearing and deepening; the pastels of Tiburon and Angel Island were turning flaxen and lush jungle green. It would be another fine day. He had plans for it.

He got to the gallery just before noon and found it in a turmoil. A truck and two buses stood at the curb, traffic was snarled, a crowd had gathered. Workmen were carrying the colossal sailcloth from the front door as Josh directed them in his calm, subdued voice, which was blanketed out by the noise.

"Hey, man, you sure you don't know her whereabouts? Johanna?" Morris asked, having elbowed through the crowd to Josh's side. A boy in a pith helmet, apparently acting as a bodyguard, stepped closer to Josh and shouted: "Don't interrupt Mr. Gillingsby!"

"Hey, Josh, I'm talking to you!"

The boy, in a big gray overcoat despite the heat, folded up under the shout and slouched back.

Josh said something, his eyes never leaving the sailcloth, which was rolled up like a cumbersome rug and seemingly a mile long as it kept disgorging from the doorway.

"I can't hear you!" Morris said.

"I told you I don't know."

"Okay, then tell me what's the name of that guy Conrad," he shouted. It was good Johanna wasn't there to hear him ask, since it would only prove that he had paid so little attention to her friends that he hadn't even absorbed their last names.

"I'm busy," Josh stated, stepping away.

"Just give me his last name!" he insisted, following him. Antigone, in a state of either terror or ecstasy, was trembling on the black shoulder, her red eyes squeezed shut.

"He's busy," the boy growled nervously, as if afraid Morris would strike him.

"You know a guy named Conrad?" he asked the boy.

The boy's face grew bright with importance. "No," he said reluctantly.

"A girl named Johanna?"

Again the brightness; and the sorry reply. "Uh-uh."

Morris stood a moment longer. "What's he going to do with that thing?"

"It's no thing. It's no thing! It's a monument. We're taking it up to a mountain!"

"Get me a cup of coffee, will you please?" Josh said, turning.

The boy's eyes widened with confusion. "Where?"

"At a coffee shop, I would think."

The boy hurried off.

"Look, Josh—" Morris tried again.

"Get the siding off that truck!" Josh called out, threading his way to the curb. Morris curled his lip and walked off. There were other galleries, after all, where Conrad might be known; Johanna, for that matter. He stepped into one a few doors down. No, they knew of Johanna Kaulbach's work, but she hadn't exhibited for a long time. They knew Conrad, too— bald fellow, did lots of Renoir things—but only by the name Conrad. But at the third gallery the owner was a friend of Conrad's, and gave him the last name. As he came out the door he saw Josh drive by in the truck, followed by the buses, a couple of cars, and the taxicab, with a thin black man in a gray natural behind the wheel. The boy in the pith helmet was rushing back down the street, his eyes glued to the sloshing paper cup in his hand.

Conrad's name was in the phone book. He dialed the number and an elderly female voice answered.

"Is this—"

"The baby-sitter," she said curtly.

"The baby-sitter?" he said, at a loss. "You mean—for Closeto?"

"Who?" The voice was rudely impatient.

"They've got a baby?" he queried, hearing an exasperated sigh at the question. A whole year. More than a year. Incomprehensible. "Let me talk to Conrad," he said.

"He won't be in till tonight." She hung up.

He hitchhiked back home, and at six o'clock he took the phone into the bedroom and closed the door.

This time a man answered. A baby was squalling in the background.

"Conrad—Morris Levinsky," he said, wincing, expecting to be hung up on.

"Yes?" said Conrad, after a moment.

Good, he thought with relief. Now he should probably ask how they were. But he couldn't, because it would be and would sound phony; he plunged. "I'm interested in knowing where Johanna is."

"I don't think she'd be interested in your knowing."

"I've been away all year—I just got back." As if Conrad gave a damn; but he didn't know what to say, and he was afraid that if he allowed a silence his listener would hang up in it. "I've been away," he repeated, stalling. "Look, if she doesn't want to see me, give me her number and she can tell me herself."

"No soap, Morris."

"She's an adult. Let her make her own decisions."

"She has made her decision."

The finality of the voice. Suddenly he squinted accusingly at the receiver. "You're not even going to tell her I called, are you?"

"I don't know that there'd be much point in it."

The loyal friend. The self-appointed censor. "You're not doing her a favor, Conrad. She has a right to—"

"To be free of someone like you."

"Don't take that pompous tone with me, baby," he warned, breathing into the mouthpiece.

"I'll take a more pompous tone. Baby. I think you're about as shoddy an article as I've run across, and I've known some rare turds in my—"

"All right, all right," he broke in. The lousy judgmental prick. He took a deep breath through his nostrils and exhaled. "I dig how you see things, I dig your loyalty. But you're an outsider, everything's black and white to you. I'll lay you odds you've got more hard feelings than she does."

There was no reply. Conrad had hung up.

The next day he went to the San Francisco main library and looked in the city directory. Nothing. Next to the directory were ranged all the phone books from the Bay Area; he began plowing through them. One solitary Kaulbach, a Jimmy Kaulbach in San Lorenzo. He went to a phone booth and called the number. A nasal-voiced construction worker originally from St. Louis, no relatives in the area that he knew of.

He went to the Suicide Prevention Bureau to see if she had ever called and left a message for him. He phoned Rhonda and, breaking through her happy exclamations, asked her the same thing. Then he tore the art-gallery yellow pages from the phone book and began assiduously to check each one out.

Conrad debated with Wanda about mentioning the call to Johanna. It seemed underhanded not to. So the next time Johanna called, he said casually, "Listen, I had a call the other day from Morris."

Silence.

A blow to the solar plexus. The room rocked around her.

"From Morris?" she asked at last, faintly; then, clearing her throat, she said with ringing contempt: "What did *he* want?"

"To get in touch with you. I didn't tell him anything." He paused. "You didn't want me to, did you?"

"No, of course not!"

She had to bite her tongue not to ask questions. Where had he called from? What was he doing? What exactly had he said? She made the only neutral inquiry open to her. "When did he call?"

"I don't know. Monday."

Two days after the panel-truck incident. It had been him, then. And the moment flashed through her again.

"Well. I hope he won't start pestering you," she said dryly, so weak she had to sit down.

"I don't think he'll call back."

"Good. Well, how are things with you?"

55

No sooner had Conrad settled into his Embarcadero studio than he felt cut off from his family. For two weeks he struggled to get used to the isolation, then he sublet the place to a sculptor and returned to the small dining room (so large two years ago, after his old room) and was once again hogtied by lack of space and distracted by the sound of crying. Billy was a large sturdy blond baby, a replica of his mother except for the voice, which was so small and plaintive that it broke his father's heart several times a day. Each of these times he set his work carefully down and went in to see what was going on. The sitter complained that he got in the way. They had a stunning lack of rapport. They ate breakfast together and lunch together in absolute silence; she read a movie magazine as she chewed, and, as a non-smoker, turned broadly sideways when he lit a cigarette over his coffee; she did not like his too-long hair either, which she sometimes squinted at pointedly; and she had once inquired how many years older he was than his wife. She was thrilled to see him go off on his errands, and greeted his return like a housewife opening the door on a bill collector. It had been a relief for both of them when he got the studio and was gone all day. But then he was back again, sheepishly dragging in all the paraphernalia he had just moved out.

He told Wanda they would have to work out a different system. She was obviously as displeased as he with things as they were.

She agreed. But, she thought, no matter how close people were, they always diverged at some point. Words, eyes, touch could never fill the gap; could merely express the wish to understand. This wish was a bridge of sorts, a footbridge swaying high in the wind—perhaps the only connection that really mattered; yet the individual's labyrinthian non-design, with its endless hues and shadings, woven from every brainwave and heartbeat since birth—this was your own alone.

She could not, for instance, understand what had made Connie turn from his green parks and happy nudes, when for so many years he had slept and cooked among them; drunk his coffee from a mug layered with thumbprints of Naples

336

yellow and terre-verte; had actually drunk his colors, had worn them, dreamed in them. Now he never felt the urge to leap from bed at three A.M. to paint. He did his posters from eight till five, he was a craftsman, a man of responsibilities. It was a change in him so deep that she could never hope to plumb it. When he spoke of it he said he had a latent domestic streak, that he had found in her what he had once made from paint. But the explanation was pat, it threw no light on the process of change itself, on the relinquishment of three decades, the thousand nuances of feeling that must have stirred and overlapped and fought at the juncture. Times since he must have felt like a man in a boat being borne away from a familiar shore. She wondered how much of this change had been caused by male pride, unknown even to himself: the need not to contribute less than the wife. After all his fine talk about being beyond such things. Layers under layers under layers. And how much regret, really, somewhere among those layers? Especially now, drawn back to the unsuitable dining room for Billy's sake, while she had not been drawn away from her work.

He didn't understand why she had not yet asked for a reduction of hours at work. And she was at a loss to clearly communicate the reason.

She had never had any feeling of kinship for other women. If anything, she had not liked women very much, because she was plainer than most and early in life she had been shouldered into the sidelines by men, from which spot she had watched her comelier sisters first with resentment and then with contempt. But time—and possibly Johanna—had broadened her vision, and she had learned to look beyond pretty faces. Still, she could hardly call this belated act of human acknowledgment kinship. It was only when she became pregnant that she had felt a nebulous bond with others of her sex, knowing that they too underwent this sloshing deadwater misery; and the bond increased tenfold in labor, as though she were giving birth to both a child and a new consciousness of her species; and it had grown still greater with the job-child conflict.

The job had never been a job but a calling. And since Billy's birth, as she considered cutting down her hours, the job began swelling with symbolic value. If she enfeebled her dedication to her work, it would seem as though she were corrupting the empathy she now had with her sex. Like herself, millions of women had followed the dictates of their nature—to achieve something in the world—but when they allowed for domestic incursions, they were assumed to be career dilettantes after all, corroborators of biological destiny. It was the injustice of this situation that tied her in a knot. She was as angry at society as she had been at nature during childbirth. And when she tried to put her confused feelings into words, she sounded inflated, as if she viewed herself as a Principle Incarnate.

"I don't see why the world should rush in to make a judgment on womankind just because you decided to cut down your working hours," Connie would say.

And this made her all the more determined to give no quarter. But the scales were tipping; already she had missed the first four months of Billy's life, she did not want to miss the rest. She was prepared to admit defeat, though to Connie it would only be an honorable compromise. It was where the gap between them lay. He saw her hurry in to Billy every night, and that was as far as he could see, for all his desire to understand.

He would not understand the significance of her words if she were to say, "I'll ask for part-time status." But she said them now.

His face broke into a smile. He began telling her what he had been thinking about. They should move to an outlying area where the rents were not so high, and find a house big enough so that he could work at home; he would try to schedule his work so that all his business errands were channeled into two afternoons a week. They would divide the care of Billy evenly. It would mean a cut in pay for her and less production time for him; on the other hand, they would not be paying for a studio, or for a sitter except on occasion.

"I think we ought to try it," he said.

"I think so," she agreed, in a tone of creeping relaxation. Now that she had promised to take the step, a burden was falling from her shoulders. She allowed herself to imagine what it would be like to spend whole afternoons with Billy and Connie. The rosy sentimental hearth leaped up before her like a vision that had been waiting in the wings. The truth was, she thought, that she had been upholding the principle of freedom at the cost of refusing it to herself. And only if you served your own nature honestly did you have freedom.

Only a private pocket of freedom in an imperfect world, that was all; but it was all she could manage.

The next Saturday they drove across the city to Potrero Hill, a high gusty mélange of the rural and the creepingly suburban. Here were beige or avocado ranch-style homes spread out behind tinkling wind chimes and motorboats on blocks; and there an old frame house peacefully collapsing at the edge of an open field. Something in between was what they wanted, and eventually they found it, a stucco bungalow from the Twenties which had been built onto at various times by various tenants, the result being wildly eclectic—a stucco nucleus with outcroppings of painted and unpainted wood, of brick and shingle; reminiscent, in its small homely way, of those great cathedrals built over the centuries, workers adding a wall here, a stairway there, and disappearing into the mists like the anonymous craftsmen they were. The studio would be the room overhead, whose author had provided it not only with an abundance of odd-size windows but with a door that opened onto thin air. Conrad at once planned to build a balcony there.

He stood in the backyard of the flat wearing an overcoat and muffler. It was the end of November, a wet silvery afternoon. The benches, the pre-Columbian statues, the paper lantern and potted plants were gone; overhead the window was curtainless. Out front Wanda and Billy waited in the car.

The geraniums were still in bloom, even this late in the year; a hardy plant, a good plant, he said to himself, sitting down on his knees. He looked at the dark soil under the bushes, smoothed it with his hand. A raindrop pinged off his bald head. Presently his back and shoulders began to spot. He reached up and broke off one of the large umbrella-shaped leaves and carefully tore it in two, burying one half, and placing the other in his overcoat pocket. Then he got stiffly to his feet and went out the alley gate.

56

Sergio was growing impatient. On New Year's Eve he had brought Giovanna to a family party; all seventeen of his cousins were there, with all their children, and there were aunts, great-aunts, uncles; all happy, all eating good food and drinking good wine and having a good time; and Johanna had enjoyed herself, had even danced with Uncle Attilio the nitwit, who did a ferocious tresca. But afterward she had shown no sign that she understood all this could be hers. Well, not all; he believed in birth control. And in case she was afraid of living in his family's pocket, he assured her, "Non dovresti frequentarli troppo." But he never knew how much she understood. For instance, one of his cousins had offered him a rent-free apartment if he would manage the building. But Giovanna did not seem to understand what this could mean for them. He had recourse to his Italian-English dictionary, to make it clear to her.

"I take to us in let the appartamento of my cousin."

"Cosa?" she asked.

He spent another minute with the dictionary.

"We marry, poi we inhabit."

"Oh," she said after a moment. "But I'm not preparato to marry, Sergio. I think non mai . . ."

He studied her face. Non mai. Never. It was a manner of speaking. So deep was she into her painting just now—she had a show coming up in April—that she could not see her way clear. But after April . . . ? He dared not probe further. He slapped the dictionary shut.

And he moved into the apartment, to get it while the getting was good. She did not mention if she understood the reason for his move.

February came and went in a downpour, now March poured down. Sometimes she did not show up at the Bella Voce on Saturday night, but painted into the morning instead. This made his heart sink. His singing no longer moved her. She thought his voice was slipping. She wanted glory for him, as everyone else did. He thought a great deal about this problem.

"The voice—you like for it more claps?" he asked her

340

finally, and went on before she could answer: "Hokay, I take again i miei studi." He faced her resolutely. He had made up his mind. It was against his principles to resume his lessons, but it would flame up her interest in his voice.

"No," she said.

She seemed angry. He could not fathom her.

"Sì!" he insisted, and smiled, to show that he was happy about the decision, that he was not forcing himself.

"That's not what *you* want! I don't want a sacrifice. You non capisco me."

"Ah, mia passerotta," he said, smiling more broadly, and bunching her hair at the back—it had grown long now—"you got bad Italian."

"No, you're not bad. You're good."

He shook his head. Two sentences and they were lost.

"You come hear Sergio sabato sera?" he asked.

"I'll be there. I love Saturday night."

"You love Sergio."

She put her face to his, but that was not what he wanted.

She did go to the Bella Voce the following Saturday night, but she arrived very late. Just before dressing she had taken in the evening paper and glanced through it. Her eye was stopped by an item on the back page.

SKELETON FOUND

A human skeleton was found Thursday by fishermen three miles south of Stinson Beach. Estimated as that of an 18–25-year-old male, it had been exposed for as long as a year, according to the coroner's report. Remains of a blanket and fur vest were also found. Death may have been caused by a fall from a cliff.

She felt behind her and sat down.

She read the paragraph again, with the same feeling of impact without understanding. She read it a third time, then lowered the paper and stared into the space before her.

But they didn't mention the pinstriped trousers. Or the burlap shoes. Or the beads. It was someone else.

But it said remains. Just a few shreds. Everything had rotted but the hide vest. The string around his neck had rotted, the beads been blown by the wind and covered by sand; the aimless face crusted with salt, eaten away.

It was close to eleven o'clock when she got up at last and left for the Bella Voce. The night sifted with fine rain. She opened her umbrella and crossed the square to Columbus Avenue. So he had finally whirled off the edge, into the moonlight.

A dazzling heart-swelling sound enveloped her as she pushed open the door—the pianist, in the middle of a Chopin ballade. Gulls ate anything, probably. She sat down at a table and ordered her usual sherry. His soiled fingers and drifting eyes, the lithe golden body—oh Lord, how unhappy he would have been to hear his flowing cloak described as a blanket. She finished her sherry and ordered another, and thought that all those months she had wondered when he would appear at her door, he had been down there turning to bone.

No, she would rather go home to bed alone, solo, she said. They were walking home under her umbrella.

Sergio tightened his lips. She had come late and had not listened, and she had drunk much, and now she wanted to go home alone.

"Perchè?" he asked shortly.

"I don't feel good." She stopped and turned to him. "It's not you, Sergio. I'm not in the mood, I feel like being by myself."

He understood nothing of it. "Hai preso quattro bevende," he paid her back in his own language. "Cosa hai?"

"Non capisco," she said with a preoccupied sigh, moving on.

"You're hungry at me."

"No."

"Sì! You drink, no look at me—"

"I looked at you, I was thinking of something else—"

"Speak to be understand!"

His intensity tired her. A distracted look, a less than radiant smile—it meant she was angry, unloving. That she could be upset by something that had no bearing on him never crossed his mind. His blind subjectivity. The blind subjectivity of love. How tiring it was when you were on the other side.

She tried to explain. "I had some bad news tonight. An amico—" She searched for the words. "Mortale—finito—" She drew her finger across her throat. "Amico. In the giornale.

I regarde the giornale avanti the Bella Voce. It is triste, I am triste."

"Ah," he murmured, his face softening. "O mi dispiace," he said sympathetically. He took her arm again and they walked on in silence.

She was not cold with him, then; she had had a blow, but she had come to the Bella Voce anyway. It was loving and good of her. He kindled with compassion and understanding; he would leave her chastely at her doorstep, as she wished.

But he could not help asking, "Un' uomo?"

She nodded.

"Chi?" he asked, looking sideways at her face.

"Nobody."

"Eh?"

"He was only an amico, not an amore."

But he wondered. Two sherries for a friend, yes. Even three. But four?

"How happen è morto?" he asked, circling around this faceless lover.

"He fell from a cliff," she said tonelessly. "Montagna."

A mountain climber. Iron muscles and glory.

"Young guy?"

"What does it matter?" she asked, with a strain in her voice.

Her heart was breaking for a mountain climber while they passed his big lonely apartment which he had only moved into so they could live there together, and crossed the square where he never tried to pick up *capellone* anymore because she had killed his desire for them, and approached the steps to her house, which always electrified his soles because they led to her, to Giovanna. And none of these things meant anything to her in her preoccupation with a dead lover. And how long had they been lovers? Perhaps—and he felt the ground sway under him—she had been seeing him secretly all the time.

Suddenly he grabbed the umbrella and dashed it to the ground, leaving them free for a confrontation.

He shook her roughly by the arms, trying to force what he wanted from her—not words, she sensed that through the turbulence, but an ardent statement of her eyes that would cut through all the uncertainties and disappointments he had endured for her sake; a request that stunned her with its perversity, as if a man while feeling his bruises demanded assurance that they were not there. He was acting from a realm of emotion so different from what she felt for him, so much greater, that she hung her head with exhaustion.

He left off abruptly. She went up the front stairs, thinking of Clovis, of all things that were not bad in themselves but ended cruelly.

Grabbing the bent umbrella, he followed her. "Giovanna, scusa," he muttered as she opened the door.

"Don't come in, please, Sergio. It's finished."

He looked regretfully at her arm.

"No, it isn't that. It's just finished. Finito."

"Cosa hai?" he asked. His voice was calm, but she knew that under his shirt his heart was pounding; she remembered the feeling well enough.

"Because it has to be," she said.

"You want never see Sergio no more?" he asked scoffingly, and gave her a knowing look. "Non è vero, Giovanna."

"Yes, but you want all of me," she said almost inaudibly, "I only want part of you."

"Cosa?"

She shook her head.

"But we make the matrimonio," he said, as if she had lost her senses. "Perchè no?" he cried, grabbing her wrist.

"Because it's no good, can't you see that? You and I?" She disengaged her wrist.

"Is good. Is good!"

"What you feel for me is good, what I feel for you is good, but they're not the same thing. Together they're bad. They degrade each other. And don't say cosa. Don't say anything, please!" She closed the door quickly, locked it, and ran up the stairs. The next morning she found her umbrella leaning against the front door, bent carefully back into shape.

Often in the days that followed he returned and rang the bell, but she would not answer, and after a couple of weeks he stopped trying. Her work helped her to weather the break, but she missed him badly, and once she went so far as to buy a cheap blond wig, and taking the bus all the way to Potrero Hill to borrow a coat from Wanda that he would not recognize, she slipped into the Bella Voce to hear him sing. He was in good voice, not as exuberant as usual, but not visibly morose. It made her feel better, and though she continued to miss him, the keen edge of the parting began to blunt. She became very much involved in the preparations for her show.

344

57

There were no galleries in the city that she had any feeling for or desire to deal with. Those that were not given to pop or minimal art, but reached calmly back to the traditional, exuded the hushed money-heavy smell of a Rothschild's inner chamber. The rest, though they handled some excellent work, invariably padded their walls if not with leopards on black velvet, then with bright sketchy bullfighters and clowns, painfully naïve bowls of flowers, and pink portraits of the famous done from photographs. There was an artists' co-operative, but its work was also uneven. She felt that while unevenness was democratic, so was tooth decay.

In the fall she had looked into a newly formed cooperative in Berkeley. This was housed in a converted drygoods store in a rundown section of town, and was run on wonderfully casual lines except for its selectivity—dazzlingly merciless. It was here that her show was going to be.

On every wall was the evidence of ruthless sieving. Down the drain had gone the pigment journalists and housewife daubers, the visual punsters and stripe manufacturers, all that was merely expected or merely unexpected, all academic craftsmanship for its own sake, and, conversely, all holy cathartic splats. She felt she had blundered into the kind of perfection reserved for fantasies.

At night in bed, Sergio would talk about Giovanna as though to a third party who agreed with all he said. "How would you like to have a rat crawl up your leg while you ate? Do you suppose it was agreeable? And always painting—and, frankly, they were not intelligent pictures. Think of a chandelier hanging in the sky and an animal hanging in the chandelier and tell me what you make of that. But she was possessed. How could a sensible man have been so blind? To expect someone like that to become normal? Not that she was not wonderful—not that she was not wonderful—" And he would fall silent in the dark.

He began taking the *capellone* to bed again, and was low-powered and mechanical, like a defective pump. Every Saturday night he looked into the dark audience for her; and Arcangelo, trying to be kind, offered him Tums and spoke of a raise and gave him tickets to a dogshow. Even Uncle Attilio was affected by his misfortune, and reminisced about his wife who had run off with a captain in Garibaldi's army, though Uncle Attilio was born well after Garibaldi's death and had never been married. Sergio was ashamed of having a misfortune that everyone knew about, and he began putting on a gayer front, and as time passed he found the soreness growing smaller, although the seed remained—he knew that was there for life—and the time came when he could actually pass an art gallery and think of Giovanna working in her studio and wish her well.

But Johanna's show was a failure. It was not reviewed in San Francisco except for one small maverick newspaper that gave it a glowing commendation but probably reached a non-existent audience. By the end of the month only three paintings had been sold, their moderate prices totaling less than eight hundred dollars, part of which went back into the co-operative. At this rate she would have to exhibit every other month if she was not to starve when her savings had been exhausted, a point she expected to reach inside a year. Starve, or return to the pale green lunchrooms.

She was not unduly worried. The cooperative was less than six months old, it needed time to build up its name. Not that its small handful of members had much talent for or interest in publicity, and not that they hadn't cut off a substantial number of contacts in the art community by their exclusiveness. The drygoods store was a long spacious building, but its ample wall space was sparingly utilized. A PR man who had come around to sell his services advised them that wall space was their stock in trade, and that they were like a farmer with twenty acres who only cultivated ten square feet. He left his card, which subsequently found its way into the wastepaper basket.

The soldier in the blue tunic was one of the canvases that had been sold. She missed that particular painting, but at least it had found a good home. A militant young black couple from Oakland had bought it—or were in the process of buying it. The woman worked in an outpatient clinic in the ghetto, the man—Johanna was not sure what the man did, but according to gallery rumor they were both involved with the Black Panthers. It was a few days after Martin Luther

King's assassination when they came in; they had immediately been drawn to the painting, had brought it the rapt living exploration that is balm to the painter's soul. It was clear that they identified not with the trampled soldier but with the riders, which was as valid a viewpoint as any. They had asked without much expectancy if they could buy it on time, and she had surprised them by agreeing. With a down payment of fifty dollars, they would send her ten dollars a month for ten months. Whether or not she ever saw the first installment—for the couple was obviously scraping along—she didn't really care. But in May a check for ten dollars arrived, with a note.

A friend of ours, Aquiline Adams, saw your painting and recognized it. She said you used to live in the same building, and says to tell you hello. Regards—

June Jackson
Bob Travis

"Guess what?" she exclaimed, and it was a moment before she remembered she was not in the old Fillmore apartment with Morrie studying in his chair.

She telephoned the couple that evening and asked if she could have Aquiline's number. But apparently Aquiline had no telephone. What was she doing? Oh, things. Was she well? The children? Fine. All fine. Then silence. Well, tell her I return her hello; and she put the receiver down.

Aquiline flooded back from the past—the dry humor and disinclined kindness, the hard secret center. For all her poses, Johanna could well believe that she had worked herself deep into the same dark activities as this tight-lipped pair. And again there shot through her the impulse to share this news with Morris, even now, when their shared past was so distant, and when even the panel truck and Conrad's call were things that had happened a long while ago. Weeks had turned to months, months to half a year, and there had been no third incident. Nothing. Yet still when the telephone rang, between the moment she lifted the receiver and the moment she heard the voice at the other end, she underwent a white scribble of panic.

58

"Now see, Clarence, it's like a comic strip except the squares are all mixed up. What I want you to do is spread them out and look at them, and then put them in the right order. Okay?"

Morris sat back with his stopwatch.

Although he wore slacks and a sport jacket, the times had changed in his favor; his walrus mustache and bush of hair were still in luxuriant evidence and a pair of thong sandals were on his feet. Around his waist he wore a belt carved with designs of breasts and phalluses which no one, to his delight, had yet picked up on. Thus outfitted, he felt less depressed to be back at his old job. He had also bought a motorcycle, striking a decent note between necessity and air pollution. This purchase had also made him less depressed; in fact, he had been buoyant the first few weeks; it gave him a fine feeling not to have to climb inside something and close a door behind him, but merely jump up and be off with the wind in his face. He deplored noise pollution, but again he struck a balance by at least not punching holes in the exhaust pipe for additional volume, which a lot of cyclists did.

He lived in a couple of nondescript furnished rooms close to the Haight but not in it. The sketch of Johanna—dirty and frayed along the creases where it had been folded—was pinned to the wall over his bed; his rucksack stood thrown in a corner; everything he owned was contained by a couple of dresser drawers. His only new possession besides some clothes and the motorcycle was a cheap plastic briefcase.

Macrobiotic farming, running an underground newspaper, making leathercraft—they had not intrigued him in the first place, and as soon as he turned a practical eye on them they had dissolved. And he was tired of the unknown.

He had called his old office for an appointment.

"Him's so *thin!*" Rhonda cried when he came in, impressed, yet already worried over his health. He felt her breath all over him.

"Your quarter didn't get me into a chophouse," he told her, glancing around.

"I don't dig you, Morrie."

The argot was dismally wrong for her.

She was beaming, as delighted as he was cast down. In his

348

nostrils, the faint smell of dust and sulfur. His boss strode over, sideburns to his jawline, lilac shirt, huge tie, hand extended.

Changes. Not just sideburns, but meaty changes, he discovered as he listened. The IQ tests were limited, useless for the culturally deprived (he could have told them that—he *had* told them that); the tests had become more elaborate, diagnostic technique was more sophisticated. They wanted a comprehensive picture, they wanted the Gestalt. He had missed the internecine warfare, but it had been bloody, and a whole faction of unyielding, habit-starched psychometrists had finally been thrown out. The days of narrow application were over.

This was the only possible good news he could have heard in his old chamber of horrors. It took a good part of the sting out of his return. So did his desk when he strolled over to it —no balled-up Kleenex in the ashtray; either his faceless colleague had been one of the liquidated, or his or her perennial cold had finally dried up.

He asked if there was an opening in the Hunter's Point district, the black housing-project ghetto overlooking the Navy Yard. He wanted to sink his teeth in and accomplish something.

So every morning he strapped his briefcase to his motorcycle and sped south through the city to the huge decaying project on the bald hill overlooking the cranes and gray warships. IQ testing might change, but apparently war would not. He did his testing as usual in a storeroom where space had been cleared, and after some initial hostility from the children—the previous psychometrist had been black—he settled down to his work, partly comforted by the new methods, partly by his symbol of freedom outside. The motorcycle also helped diminish barriers; the kids liked motorcycles and didn't associate them with teachers. He was somewhat unplaceable, they felt a certain freedom with him.

He clicked his stopwatch. "Okay, Clarence."

He looked at what the boy had done and marked his score on the sheet. Not very good for a nine-year-old. He was sullen, a loner, at the rock bottom of his class.

Morris had thrown his coat over the back of his chair. The boy was looking at his belt. "What you got on you' belt?" he asked in an undertone.

"Designs, man," Morris said. "Circles and lines."

"Look like boobs and pricks," the boy said after a pause.

"Well, that's interesting. I never thought of that."

"Yeah, look at 'em."

Morris peered down at his middle. "Hey, you're right, they do at that. You've got sharp eyes."

The boy nodded.

"Let's take a breather," Morris said, sitting back. "What would you like to be doing right now, if you could do anything you wanted?"

"Ahhh, not be here, I guess."

"Here? Hunter's Point?"

"*Here.*" He grimaced at the tests.

"You don't like school, do you?"

"Sheeit," he muttered.

"What would you like to be when you grow up, if you could be anything you wanted?"

"Fireman."

"All kids say that. Tell me something different."

The boy thought for a moment, looking bored. "I like to get me a motorsackle, I guess."

"Okay, what else?"

"Don't guess no else."

"Just ride around on a motorcycle all day?"

"An' all night."

"You'd have to eat."

"Pick me up somethin' on the way."

"With what?"

"*Money,*" he said, squinting at Morris' stupidity.

"Okay, never mind. Well, tell me, where would you go on your motorcycle?"

"Okinawa."

"Okinawa?"

"What wrong with Okinawa?"

"Nothing's wrong with it. Why do you want to go there?"

" 'Cause it sound good, the sound."

"Yeah? For some reason it doesn't grab me, the sound. What does it sound like to you?"

"I don' know," he said, closing off.

"Where'd you hear about Okinawa?"

"I don' know."

"You realize there's some water you'd have to cross?"

"I *know* it a Pacific island." He indicated the window with his head. "I put my motorsackle on the Navy ship down there. Then I take it off in Okinawa."

"Doesn't sound like a bad idea; nice vacation. How long you intend to stay?"

"Maybe three months. Depend on how I like it."

"But you know, we've still got to eat."

"I'm not takin' you along, man."

"Well, *you've* still got to eat. You need money to eat. How are you going to get money for food?"

He picked at his lips, reluctantly. "Guess I sell coconuts."

"Seems to me those people on the island would pick their own coconuts, Clarence."

"Hey, I don' have to sell 'em, I just eat 'em!"

"You'd get sick of nothing but coconuts for three months. They're pretty tasteless."

Clarence was twisting his mouth in thought. "Fuck coconuts, I get me invited to dinner with the natives, they dive for oysters. Like they good to eat, oysters." Suddenly he clapped his hand to his forehead. "Hey! Man, *I* gonna dive for oysters. You know they got pearls inside? It a piece of sand first and it get rubbed up into a pearl—nobody know how they do it, it a secret process—"

"Process?"

"Yeah, like when somethin' happen. Well, I sell them pearls and I got plenty money for everything."

"Great. I guess you'd send some of the money back to your family?"

"Yeah, sure, if I get plenty."

"You wouldn't want to take your family with you?"

"Sheeit. No way."

Morris shuffled through the next test. "You think you might be interested in a book on the Pacific islands, with pictures of the oyster divers?"

"Might."

"I'll see if I can bring you one. We'd better get back to work now—use some elbow grease this time, man."

"What that?"

"Concentration. It shouldn't be too hard, you've got brains."

"I know," the boy said coolly. "Don' need nobody tell me that."

Morris felt exhilarated afterward. There was nothing new

in his talking off the cuff with a child and discovering qualities
at odds with the tests, but these personal forays no longer
had to be wasted; his judgment counted, he could go ahead
now and work more elaborately with this boy, and it was very
likely that Clarence would find himself moved from his class
not into a group of slow learners but into an advanced class.
His decision to return to the Board of Education was absolutely the right one, he felt, as he roared back into the city,
and he recalled his massage work with increased impatience.
Parking by the main library, that imposing gray structure
topped by robed statues of the Greeks, which he had only once
before entered in search of the city directory, he hurried up
the great fern-hung staircase into the big card-catalogue room
with its glittering chandelier, and began his quest for the
islands of the Pacific, thinking of Johanna. The library's
beauty was not matched by its organization, he was over an
hour searching, and when he finally found the book he realized
he had no card. Zooming off again, he tried to think of how to
scare up a card, stopped to phone Rhonda—yes, she had one,
but it was at home; waited till five and gave her a ride home
on the back of the motorcycle, probably the high point of her
life, got the card and returned; and as he finally checked out
the book, the sense of Johanna which the place exuded from
every corner culminated in a sunburst of inspiration. She had
always had a library card. She must still have it. His heart
banged once, twice against his ribs. He hurried to the application counter, his mind a spiraling miracle of the impromptu, and whispered to the woman there, "I'm doing a
paper on Pistowitz—"

"You don't have to whisper," she informed him, glancing up.

He began again, in a gentle, scholarly voice. "I'm doing a
paper on Pistowitz, the Austrian ornithologist? Late eight-
eenth century, drowned in the great Danube flood?"

"This is just the registration office—"

"If you'll just bear with me for half a moment. I used to
know a woman, Kaulbach was her name, Johanna Kaulbach; a
little Viennese lady, up in her eighties, but a very fine scholar,
and a great user of your library. And I wonder if you could
be so extremely kind as to take a peek in your files and see if
she still has a card and if so if you could give me her address.
She's an authority on Pistowitz, you see, and if—"

"We don't keep a file like that," she broke in impatiently.

His face fell.

"There are people behind you, please," she told him, as if addressing one of the elderly nuts who wandered around with fistfuls of yellowed notes mumbling to themselves.

"Ignatz Pistowitz," he stated loudly, shooting his head forward, "discovered the giant night loon!" And she stepped back.

As he walked outside he could still feel the slip of paper between his fingers—the expectation of it, a slip of paper with an address written across it, black on white, securely between thumb and forefinger, oh fantastic moment! And instead, the void again.

Clarence said, "Thanks, man," in the brief grudging way he had; but he held the book with an unmistakably proprietary grip, though he refused to glance at it in Morris' presence.

This time they had a very long conversation, about earthquakes, shooting stars, deep-sea monsters, life on other planets ("They the same as us," said Clarence, "only they completely backassward, they eat they dessert first and they drive they motorsackles sittin' backwards, only they got this special radar in they head, and they get born old and when they reach baby age they die"), and finally the nature and use of a shiv (Morris could contribute nothing here). The testing went better this time.

But the following week when he sent for Clarence, the boy's teacher told him he had been gone for four days. A school official had inquired at the boy's home and was told by the man the mother had been living with that she had suddenly packed up and headed back for Detroit with her children. A neighbor down the hall corroborated this, adding that she had had a broken nose when she left.

"Shit!" he said under his breath. "Did she leave a forwarding address with this guy she lived with?"

"Are you joking, Mr. Levinsky? He broke her nose."

He wandered back to the storeroom and sat down at the desk where he had laid out Clarence's tests, gathered them together, and put them in his briefcase. The vanished book would cost him a fifteen-dollar library fee, but he would gladly pay twice that just to know that the book had accompanied the boy. But it was probably lying in a corner of the room where the fist had smashed the nose and so much more.

"And so what the hell good is it," he said later at the

monthly staff meeting, getting to his feet in order to express himself more volubly, "to work with a kid with a homelife like that? I don't have to meet his mother and her old man, I know them—behind them there's a shack in the South or an Eastern tenement, in front of them a bunch of barracks built in 1942 to last a couple of years. You don't expect people who live in these rotting pens to sit down and help their kids with their homework. Besides, let me ask you, what homework? Those kids aren't getting an education, they're getting a monitoring service to keep them off the streets. The buildings are lousy, the teachers are hangdog—what do they do with kids whose vocabulary and experience are completely alien to teaching methods? You and I get the dumb ones and the bright ones, but what about the ones in between? They're the majority and they're ignored. And okay, take the bright ones. We put them into special classes where six hours a day they're worked with, and then they go home to a place where there's no rapport with any of it, where life's immediate: food, clothes, shelter, and some violence for distraction. You can't educate kids as long as their environment stays the same; and you can't change their environment, even with new housing, unless you change the adults; and you can't change the adults unless you find them employment, and you can't do that because they've already missed an education. It's a vicious circle, and don't tell me about Black Studies programs and the OEO and all the rest—they're like monkey wrenches poked into a huge machine that just keeps grinding on anyway, with maybe a few new jerks and some extra noises . . ."

He stopped speaking, aware that it was futile to go on about a vicious circle, that he sounded rhetorical and naïve, and that his colleagues, who had given nods of agreement but who were anxious to return to the problems within their province, were hardly the ones to lay this unanswerable complaint on. He sat down and was silent for the remainder of the meeting.

59 During the summer the cooperative folded, wobbling for a month or two and then collapsing all at once in the space of a week. There was some talk among the members of using one of their homes to show their work in, but the idea was too unprofessional, even for them, and the group disbanded and that was that.

It came as a blow to Johanna, but she understood what had happened. The group was simply too small; its selectivity had turned it into a gallery version of one of those little magazines whose sole contributors are the editors; as business enterprises these journals always fail unless the editors are independently wealthy, though as artistic creations they are sometimes found thirty years later in bound editions in university archives, with some particular issue recently ripped out by a fanatic student who wanted for himself the once obscure, now fabled germ of some movement or school. But a gallery was different; once abandoned, there remained no concrete evidence of it. And it seemed that in these days there was not even a collective spirit to preserve memories as though in amber, as there had been in the past.

Who, even now, did not know of the Paris salons? The official Salon de Paris with its Bouguereaus and Cabanels, and the Salon des Réfusés, where Manet's "Lunch on the Grass" was copiously spat on and would have been torn to bits had it not been roped off from the crowd; and later, the outlaw Independent Salon, where there was no jury at all, where anyone could exhibit (but it was before the days of hobby shops and disposable palettes and art as a national pastime on a par with sending in boxtop coupons) and where Rousseau's first puzzled lion had peered forth and puzzled Alice B. Toklas; and then the Autumn Salon in the Petit Palais, where the cream of these outlaws was invited to show, bringing the public out in droves and exciting another bombardment of spittle, this time for Matisse. These exhibitions were events of great moment that permeated the whole city and reverberated through the world; they became fables in their own time, were passed on through conversation, memoirs, were still fact today though the salons had long since crumbled. But now, for all the popularity of art, the Art History courses, and inexpensive reprints, there was no boiling interest, no antagonism, no public honing itself on painters or painters honing themselves on the public or on each other; the new art was the official art, it had not even had time to look ferocious before it was eagerly adapted by interior decoration and clothes design, and had now passed into a region of hoax and happenstance so all-permissive and clueless, so indistinguishable from life itself—a saw hanging from a nail, a hole dug in a park—that there was no nerve line of intent to stamp on. Always supposing anyone cared enough to stamp, which no one did; whatever happened to art in the future would happen through attrition. And in the meantime the once-incendiary Matisses sat in the vaults of investors.

So much for the expectation that an obscure, short-lived gallery might be locked in the amber of a collective awareness. Awareness had diffused, it flashed around and around, like a lawn spray.

And such philosophizing was all well and good, but the effect of the cooperative's collapse was an immediate and personal one. She felt a cool wave of fear as she contemplated her future. Even if she were to try one of the other galleries, she realized that her success at Josh's had been the result of the Gillingsby-Cobbledock influence. She saw the pale green lunchrooms floating in the distance.

60 The whole year, as though to make up for the year before, had been cold and wet; now in the summer the rain ended and the fog settled in. On weekends Morris put his swimming trunks on under his old clothes and roared off on his motorcycle in search of better weather. Sometimes he drove south along the coast route, through billows of mist that rolled across the highway, the hills and ocean both gray as pavement. Then all at once the fog would clear, he was jolted by color: gold-white hills, ultramarine sea, orange patches of poppies flashing by, swathes of yellow mustardseed. At Santa Cruz he stripped to his trunks and swam and baked in the sand for an hour; then he was off again, along the byways of those dense green Santa Cruz Mountains that seemed to stretch as far and remote as the Great Smokies. The roads were like dark green tunnels; his handlebars would flash in a stripe of light, then again he was in semi-darkness, twisting and climbing, until suddenly he found himself high in the open with enormous valleys below him, lying blue and shimmering under the heatwaves.

Night came slowly, blueing the air until his headlight cut through pitch; then he came down into the sprawling outskirts of San Jose and stopped to eat at a steak house. Driving on, he took any direction that didn't lead back to San Francisco. Late at night he would check into a highway motel, rising early the next morning and setting out again.

He explored desert-like flatlands, and green deltas where wild boar were said to still roam, and the dry hill country that stretched all the way to Oakland, a vast unpopulated area dominated by Mount Diablo, which you could see from San Francisco and yet when you got there seemed to belong to a world where cities had not been dreamed of, the mountain rising from a chain of dry foothills and scrub oak giving off the heat-dazed metallic ring of cicadas.

He sped up the simmering road, passing a pair of red-faced bicycle riders panting over their handlebars, and arriving at the peak, he recalled having read in the papers a long time ago that Josh had hung his canvas on Mount Diablo. He gazed down the slopes, and there it was, or at least something that

357

looked like a giant soiled towel stretched between two ridges, flapping a little.

He drove back down, turning onto a dirt road and stopping. He got off the bike and sat down on the dry grass. The metallic ring of the cicadas was always in the same key, in the middle of the register, a blind sound. It would break off—resume; break off—resume; always in the same key, desolate. He lay back and closed his eyes. When he woke his face was aflame with sunburn, his nostrils caked with dust, and he thought of the first time he had ever hiked with Johanna, the day after their night-long vigil on Mount Tam, when they had climbed down through the dusty underbrush to the ocean lying green and glassy as a mirror. Once more he was up and off in a cloud of dust, pointed toward the Carquinez Bridge and Solano County; why, he didn't know until he crossed into Napa County and found himself climbing into the hills where she had grown up, La Faye Yokum, or whatever, with a couple of starched old Prussian exiles—an odd situation, he might have shown more interest at the time; he remembered how hurt she was when he showed no interest; and now he was making an actual trip to see her homeland, if only she could know that. He curved the motorcycle through a Mediterranean landscape of vineyards and warm red soil, rolling hills of fruit orchards, everything green and pleasant, with trees trailing down Spanish moss, climbed upward through dry grass and scrub oak and regiments of eucalyptus trees, and finally stopped, looking out over thick green forests that covered the mountains as far as he could see; they were peculiarly pointed mountains, like the pictures of mountains in a child's picture book; like an ocean in storm struck motionless. He was sticky, parched, and suddenly happy, and the air was warm and yellow, like plum juice. He kicked the motorcycle zestfully into action and sped off, taking the hairpin curves with such exhilarated speed that he scared himself, but he was well out of the hills and on a simple straight road into Santa Rosa when he lost control on a patch of gravel and lifted himself from a ditch with two broken fingers and one side of his face like ground meat.

Fourteen days later, the motorcycle repaired, a couple of big plasters still on his face, his damaged fingers in a splint, he resumed his weekends.

He never took a girl along, though he could have. He didn't

358

have a great number of them, but they nevertheless merged into each other, all Haight Street pick-ups with long hair and long dresses and bare feet. They were all very young, but there was nothing naïve about them; even back in his Berkeley days he had noticed this oldness, this bland evenness of temper under the bizarre clothes and wild hair; crowds and music could break it, nothing else; alone in his room they were silent and apathetic, gentle and affectionate in that bland knowing way they had. If one of them showed an inclination to hang on, he told her his straight middle-class wife and four kids were moving back in with him, and that did the trick.

But one morning late in the summer he had a woman sitting behind him on the cycle. He had kept desultorily in touch with Dorothy, and one day she had called to say she wanted to know how her two protégés and their new baby were getting along and suggested a drive down to Hetch Hetchy. When she learned that he had a motorcycle, she insisted that they drive down on that because she had never been on a motor-cycle.

"Bring a helmet," he told her.

She came to his place with a big white helmet that made her look like a weathered traffic cop.

"Where's yours?" she asked.

"I don't use one."

"What're you trying to do, get yourself killed?" she asked, in a practical, comradely tone that put his fears to rest. He had been afraid that she might want to resume their affair.

She was a good trooper, never complaining in the furnace-like heat south of Modesto, and not taking him to task when they reached Yosemite and he got lost three times before finally jolting over the dry ruts into the commune. It was another Holy Mountain, disorganized, smelly, and they found Thor and Zaidee's shack off in the woods by itself. Zaidee greeted them with astonishment, then hung on their necks and kissed them resoundingly. Whatever shyness she had once had seemed to have been burned away with her childish ap-pearance; she had the brown stringy look of her dirtfarmer forebears, and her hair was once more pulled back from her long neck, in a knot. Thawn, a brown two-year-old, was play-ing in the dirt, naked except for a straw hat. Amazing, Morris thought, picking her up, that they grew so fast; she probably had her own private thoughts now (and she did, struggling to get down) when only a couple of years ago she had not even existed. She was even an older sister already (though it gave her no power, for now Dorothy was picking her up), and he felt bowled over by Time, and was glad that he had no children because they were the most blazing measuring sticks of all.

"And has she got a sister or a brother?" Dorothy asked.

"A sister, come see," said Zaidee, leading them into the shack, where an infant lay asleep on a blanket.

"What's her name?" asked Morris.

"Tosha," said Zaidee fondly.

It sounded like a French poodle. Names must be Zaidee's one luxury, he thought, a leftover from the days when she collected ceramic ballerinas from Woolworth's.

She led them back outside and seated them on a patch of cool grass. Thor was down in the valley selling jewelry to the tourists. It brought a little bread in, she said, but mainly they depended on what they grew and what Thor trapped or fished. Winter was terrible, it snowed like it snowed back in Arkansas, but when spring came it really came, like it broke you up, so winter was worth it. The commune was shitty, they were going to move on alone. They had picked a place three miles back in the hills with no road to it, and Thor had already cleared it and built a shack. They would move in September when the tourist trade in the valley fizzled out.

"But, Zaidee," Dorothy said worriedly, "what about bears? And if the kids get sick?"

Zaidee was very serene and practical. "There aren't any bears around here, they're farther up. And the kids are healthy. And three miles isn't thirty miles. And it's where we want to be and where we're going."

"Well, you tell us the directions so we can visit you," said Dorothy, unconvinced, and Zaidee drew her a map on a paper bag.

"Well, now tell me everything that's with *you*," Zaidee exclaimed.

"Well," said Dorothy, "I'm still in the old place, and the work's coming along fine. I've got a new co-therapist—Morrie moved back to San Francisco."

"What are you doing now?" Zaidee asked him.

"I've got my old job back."

"You mean with the school?" she said with surprise. "Man, I thought you hated it. What made you go back *there?*"

His lips tightened slightly before he answered. "It's different now. It's opened up."

She nodded her lean head. "I guess I'm not too surprised, I never really figured you for one of us—remember I said so when you first showed up in the Haight? You're probably better off back with your job."

If she had lost her shyness, she had lost none of her social ineptitude. He tried to see the remark in the light of her limitations, but felt a need to defend himself—not because his own work couldn't hold its own with growing your own beans and making jewelry, but because he could not bear to be thought of as a man who had drifted back to an old job because everything else had failed.

"It's not the way it was," he explained. "The whole testing system's been changed, it's a completely new scene. It's challenging, there's autonomy. It's where I want to be."

"I'm glad," Zaidee said with such friendly enthusiasm that he cringed. Sitting between these two women, both old girlfriends who had gone through his hands without a lasting mark, who felt neither searing ill will toward him nor lingering ardor, he felt faced by fleshly monuments of his whole life's invalidity. He had an overwhelming urge to get away from them. "I'll take a tour of your estate," he said with a forced smile, and managed to push the darkening mood aside as he walked through the trees.

They stayed until dusk, and had a short visit with Thor, who returned as they were leaving. He was full-bearded now, a broad powerful young man of eighteen with crow's feet at his eyes, his mop of gold curls pulled back under a sweat-stained kerchief like that of an immigrant day laborer.

When Morris and Dorothy started down the path, the young couple waved goodbye from the doorway of the shack, Thawn standing beside them, and the baby in Zaidee's arms—very much as Morris had once predicted: their faces aging with the seasons, a gaggle of children growing at their side. He lingered at the bend in the path, looking back; they struck him as a strangely handsome sight.

It was late at night, cold, foggy, when they reached San Francisco. He parked before his building and they dismounted, dust-caked, bent over with soreness.

"I'm going home to soak in a hot bath for twelve hours," said Dorothy, smacking a sisterly kiss on his cheek. "It was lovely, Morrie, I enjoyed every minute of it. Thanks so much."

He walked over to her car with her. "So long then, Dorothy. And everything's okay with you? Everything's going good?"

"Oh, very good," she said, opening the door. "Of course, I miss you."

It was like balm to his heart.

She pulled off her helmet and vigorously started the motor. With a cheerful wave, she shot the car into the street and was gone.

In September he ended his summer-school work and started the new school year. The good weather began, and although he no longer needed to leave town to find the sun, he continued to go away every weekend, driving farther afield each time, sometimes to Los Angeles and back, or he crossed into the Nevada desert, or hit the Oregon border before turning around, driving all night as well as all day, crouched immobile over the handlebars with his teeth clenched against the jarring, while the miles flashed by and the stubble of his beard grew. Monday morning, his jaw shaved and his teeth aching, he would strap his briefcase to the dirt-caked motorcycle and drive soberly in the direction of his storeroom.

61

"What do we want?"
"Peace!"
"When?"
"Now!"
"When?"
"Now!"
"When?"

The march, unattended by television cameras or curbside crowds, tramping in the heat down Van Ness to the gates of the Presidio Army Base, was divided as usual into contingents— the blacks with their casual, fractious glances, their fabulous naturals like dusky barrel lids from the back; the bell-shaking Hare Krishnas in orange sheets, Caucasian pigtails hanging from pink shaven heads; the sexual-freedom zealots, whose leader's middle name, legally changed to Fuck, was proclaimed from a bobbing sign; a new group, the Women's Liberation, six strong (seven if you counted Conrad); and the Viet veterans, one being pushed along in a wheelchair, the others carrying a black plywood coffin; and among these loosely strung units, the vivid, motley street people, the ragged carnival, beating tambourines, blowing a trumpet, generously sharing a jug of cider up and down the perspiring lines with such as firm-stepped Dorothy in her peasant blouse and walking shoes, and old Uncle Attilio, who always fell in with a parade for at least two blocks before stepping aside with a crisp Garibaldian salute.

Conrad felt no embarrassment as the only male walking behind the WOMEN'S LIBERATION FOR PEACE sign, which was carried by a brogue-shod woman with humorous and determined green eyes, dressed in the arty-peasantry style of the Fifties with the addition of peace buttons—an old updated bohemian like himself; the rest of the fledgling group being younger, some, like Wanda, with babies in canvas carriers on their backs.

He felt that though he and Wanda had solved her career-v-family problem, they should do what they could to help decalcify the system; and so here he was, even if he did harbor some questionably traditional attitudes: the painter's undemocratic appreciation of female beauty in repose; an almost shameful, orphan-like delight in Gemütlichkeit, in cozy evenings and warm kitchen smells; and an inability to comprehend Wanda's strong emotional bond with these marching women. Well, you couldn't share everything (she, for instance, could not understand why he no longer painted), but the two of them lived in love, warmth, and pleasure, and more than that no one could wish.

He wished the same for Johanna, who was walking to his right but outside the group, as befitted a non-joiner. He wished that she had married her Italian and had someone to look out for her. She had placed some paintings in what she considered the less offensive galleries, but they were not moving, and in a few months—it was early November now—she would have to give up her pleasant flat for a couple of rooms and turn back into a file clerk. She presented a stoic face, but he could see the disappointment underneath.

"You wouldn't think of having a go at what I'm doing?" he asked suddenly, turning to her and lifting his voice over the noise. "I'd do what I could to get you started."

"For me, worse than filing," she shouted back, rudely enough, though adding: "Thanks anyway."

Still the purist, he thought to himself. To modulate into a minor key, an associate art—oh, no, better to stay untainted and die slowly in the corner of an office. An implicit criticism of himself, of course. She never mentioned his abandonment of the easel, not since she discovered that he wasn't wrestling with demons, that he was happy—as if she had absolute faith in his happiness. But he knew his metamorphosis left her at sea, alone.

"What I'm thinking," she said, "is that I'll become a mailman. They're hiring women mailmen now, you know. I'm a good walker and I like the outdoors and there wouldn't be any green lunchrooms."

"You're serious?" he asked.

"Oh, well, I suppose so. I just thought of it. All these tramping feet." She raised an eyebrow. "Or I should say dancing feet?" She made no bones about her attitude toward the peace marches, it had not changed in three years. "I guess the gesture's worth something," she allowed, "but it should be a cleaner gesture." And she stared through the tinkling, chanting, ridiculous-looking Hare Krishnas at the metal gleam of the veteran's wheelchair.

It will never be your way, Johanna, he thought, it isn't in life.

They turned off Van Ness onto Lombard Street, and Conrad lifted the orange canvas carrier from Wanda's back and hung it over his own. She put her hand in his, and he felt the pleasant heavy sleeping weight of Billy's head against his spine, and a little blossom of drool pressed into the hot fabric of his shirt.

Twenty minutes later the marchers poured off Lombard into the street that ran alongside the Presidio wall; they bottlenecked, flowed up over the sidewalks and onto the steps of private homes, crowded onto the hoods of parked cars, and climbed up trees, where they lined the branches, jugs and sandaled feet dangling. On the speakers' stand erected before the wall, a gray-haired woman in a mumu was singing with hoarse vigor into the sputtering microphone:

> Little boxes on the hillside,
> Little boxes made of ticky-tacky,
> Little boxes on the hillside,
> Little boxes all the same.

Pinned immobile in the crowd, which heaved first one way and then the next like a solid mass shifting in a container, Johanna lost sight of the Women's Lib sign; it was not in the sea of weaving, bobbing signs, it must be behind her, but she couldn't squeeze around to look. Wanda and Conrad were lost, too. The sun pounded into her hair and eyes like a steady downward blast of oven heat. She worked her arm free and shaded her eyes with her hand, the flesh glistering like the skin of citrus, the small hairs along her wrist burning gold. The microphone on the speakers' stand shot forth a blinding glare behind which the seated figures were watery, unreal.

The song ended; she caught the name of a radical young lawyer much in the newspapers; the glare was adjusted to his height—flashing down, up—and through the electronic crackling, through the crying of babies, the noise of the crowd, and the distant detached voices of the military police who had been stationed at the gate in case of eruption, he began to speak.

"One of the leading scientists in the development of napalm recently stated, 'It is not my business to deal with moral questions.' I ask you—" The microphone went dead, and the voice continued tiny and naked, and stopped. Someone hurried to fix the instrument, the glare flashing up and down, hollow thumps, squawks; a final adjustment, and the speaker continued. "I ask you if man's inhumanity to man is not—" Again the microphone went dead. More adjustments, the sound of chairs scraping on the platform, the growing murmur of the crowd.

Johanna's eyes watered in the glare; she dropped them to the shoulders and hair she was pressed against, hair like an undone scouring pad, maybe the very same girl who had so impressed her three years ago on the first march (but no, the face, turning, revealed itself as a man's), and she thought of Clovis, nowhere recreated in the crowd, for although there were Clovis types everywhere, none were so mad as to wear their heaviest raiment on such a stifling day. Only Clovis would have been so mad. She remembered him flinging himself around the sunny glade, the long pointed toes flashing from under the black hem . . . she remembered everything that had happened in that hot dusty significant little glade, and suddenly she began trying to force her way out of the crowd, using her shoulder as a wedge and squeezing through sideways, face flattened, feet catching and jamming between shins and calves, pushed on by fear. As she labored, worming and prodding, the lawyer took up his speech again, his words now indecipherable through the microphone's crackling.

Yet he finished to a round of applause, which increased as the second speaker was introduced, a young veteran in Levi's and a fatigue jacket. He began talking in a nervous, unpublic voice, was nudged closer to the microphone, and again the metallic crackling drowned out the words. A groan of protest went up from the audience.

Gradually she began to feel less pressure among the bodies; gaps appeared; she was standing free in the fringes. The microphone had been turned off, and the youth was using his own voice, which was so faint as to be inaudible. Under the incoherence and the relentless sun the crowd began breaking up. She hurried ahead of the flow, passing a knot of bereted blacks leaning against a car, a familiar face among them. Wearing a gray patterned summer dress, her natural enormous now, Aquiline was hard to reconcile with the pink chenille bathrobe and raft of bobbypins; but the face was the same— and when she caught sight of Johanna, who lifted her hand in greeting and paused, she responded with a smile of recognition; but it was not a smile of welcome, and the neat heart-shaped face was already turning away, inward, opaque. Johanna went on.

At the street corner she turned around and gave the crowd a last quick scan. This time she saw the Women's Lib sign halfway down the block. The woman in the peasant blouse who was holding the sign was talking with a bushy head, but Conrad and Wanda were nowhere in sight. She was prepared to go on home, it was useless to look for them; maybe they had gone on home themselves. But before turning the corner she glanced back at the bushy head—one of so many unpruned tangled clumps, yet held at a familiar angle, though the man's figure, which she caught a brief glimpse of through the crowd—seeing also a white arm sling—was not of familiar bulkiness. Still, she stood where she was, buffeted by the straggling crowd as the youth in the fatigue jacket spoke dumbly into the noise and heat of the afternoon.

62

"Compound and *comminuted?*" Dorothy yelled over the din. "What's comminuted?"

"Ground to powder, more or less," Morris yelled back.

"God, you really did a job of it, didn't you, idiot? What do they do with an arm like that?"

"Fill it with steel pins, aluminum pins, I don't know what they are. It's my left arm, no sweat."

"Next time it'll be your left head. Why don't you act your age and go back to cars? I mean, I loved our joyride, Morrie, but you're going overboard."

"How've you been, Dorothy?"

"I can't complain," she shouted cheerfully.

"Is it safe to stand here?" he asked, indicating her sign. "Or is my scalp in danger?"

"Listen, a woman who's been married three times may have her problems with men, but, for good or for bad, they're her métier. Where would I be if they were all scalped?" She gave a laugh, then looked at him threateningly. "And speaking of scalps, are you finally going to invest in a helmet now? Or better yet, maybe the arm'll keep you from driving?"

"Nah, the wrist's immobile, that's all."

"What are you trying to do, Morrie?"

"There's somebody waving at you."

She looked around. "We're all scattered—I've got to see if I can get us together. Take care, Morrie. I mean it." With a wave she moved into the crowd. A loud squawk turned his head back to the speakers' stand; there was more work being done on the microphone, people were on their knees scrabbling around with the wires, the vet had stopped speaking and stood with his arms self-consciously crossed. But this time when the instrument was replaced the youth's hesitant, earnest voice came across clearly, without a trace of interference. The half-dispersed, milling crowd drifted back and coalesced, its noise fading; and as Morris glanced down the street at the stragglers, his eyes were arrested by a figure standing alone on the corner, shimmering and weaving in the glare like a figure in water; yet he was filled with a sense of its absolute immobility, as if it were rooted to the pavement, its attention

boring a groove through everyone and everything else, directly
to him. Male or female he could not tell at this distance and
with the sun in his eyes; it seemed, oddly, to have a broad
pale band wrapped around its middle, the rest dark. As soon
as he moved, its immobility broke and it took one long step
back; but there it remained as he walked toward it, the
band resolving itself into an exposed midriff between dark
blue hiphuggers and a burgundy shirt knotted just below the
breasts. The face he did not raise his eyes to, certain that it
belonged to some acid head whose trip it was to stand like a
statue, staring, seeing God knew what; the city crawled
with them and this was one, with brown eyes, long nose,
frizzy hair—features he steeled himself to meet in another
moment, but for this moment allowing himself the joy of a
minuscular possibility.

Pale amber eyes finely edged in black.

He felt a physical jar, a moment of rapid horizontal
vibration behind his eyes, an overwhelming weakness that
prevented him from moving his lips, even to smile.

He saw that her lips were bitten in, clamped, as if in grief;
and in a thinner, slightly older face than he had left; fine lines
extended from the outer corners of her eyes, the cheekbones
were more prominent, almost Indian—she could have Indian
blood, she was from Oklahoma; such irrelevant thoughts glided
through his mind like the tails of comets—the buttons on her
burgundy shirt, not round but triangular—as if he hung in
that moment before sleep when images pass silently through
the mind as though on a movie screen, and everything, great
and small, is of equal value. The brows, drawn at a painful
angle from the eyes, which shone wet; hair pinned up haphazardly against the heat, burnished by the sun; the exposed
neck damp, the throat as warm and salty as those days on
their long sultry hikes when he had pressed his mouth
there . . .

Even from a distance his mop of hair gave off a delicate
grayish sheen and now she saw the individual white hairs
subtly interwoven through the dark locks framing the face,
which—a swift impression of blue eyes, then the huge
mustache, disappointing, an obfuscation where his lips had
curved. A sense of his body having changed, still stocky,
broad, but compact, legs in grease-stained Levi's, one arm
bare, brown, sunlit, faded shirtsleeve rolled high—in the V

of his collar black hairs glistening with sweat. A sling, ragged
edge of a cast protruding from it, limp fingers curved—bones
shattering, some time past; knitting now, his bones, Morrie's,
inside Morrie's flesh—Morrie's face again, the rough high-
colored features more integrated now, as if her vision had been
shot through with blind spaces and was now cohering; the
crease between his eyes deeper than in the past, a black
crayon stroke, and a net of intricate lines beneath each eye;
and for all its changes, the only face: the eyes under their
heavy lids as blue as the sky.

She felt his face against her throat—the bristles of his
mustache, the damp perspiring contact of his cheek; then his
mouth was on hers, the fresh sunny smell of his skin in her
nostrils. He felt her arms going around him, tightening, as if
to embed their two bodies in each other. Sensations whirling
within sensations, and one of these, hardly glimpsed before
whirling off, yet for that moment impaled in both ther minds
—the scorching white of the pavement, the salt air sweltering
in from the bay; midsummer, when the days stop turning like
the leaves of a book; when the sun stands transfixed and all
time with it, warm, still, deathless.

She loosened her arms, and then she turned and walked
away from him.

For a moment he didn't think to call or pursue her, he was
aware only that he felt air where she had stood. Then recovering himself, he went around the corner for her, the
smile that had been drained from his face now shining
radiantly, despite this amazing retreat; because her embrace
meant more than her flight, the flight was doubt, nerves, pride,
any of a dozen things, none as strong as the impulse that had
flung her arms around him.

"Johanna!"

The first time in two years that she had heard his voice; as
immediately a familiar sound as if they had spoken yesterday,
as if they had never been apart. His hand was laid on her
upper arm.

"I'm going to the bus stop," she said in a thick voice.

His smile faded by degrees, its brilliance disappearing into
the mustache, but there, she sensed, remaining as something
tender and tentative.

"Why?" he asked.

He saw her face shade from one expression to another as

she struggled with an answer, her mouth forming a word only to decide against it, then forming another, the eyebrows straining; brow wrinkling, smoothing, wrinkling; sad expressions all, a bitter project. His chest grew heavy. A knot of street people passed by, shooting water pistols at each other; Morris' heart leaped up automatically at the feel of the cool spray on his burning arm, then sank again. Suddenly she gave a tremulous sigh, staring down at the pavement. "I can't put my words together."

"Don't talk now," he urged her softly. "We'll go someplace and sit down."

"When I saw you in the crowd I should have walked away. But to just walk off—" She was silent for a moment. "But I should have. It's worse this way." She looked up at him. "This is all there's going to be."

"You want that?" he asked, unbelieving, remembering her embrace.

"I have to want it."

"Have to?" And biting abstractedly on his mustache, he looked at her face for a melancholy moment. "You're involved with another guy?" he asked in a voice that came out frail.

"No," she said, "not at the moment."

"Then—"

"Do you really think I could allow myself to—"

"Allow yourself— Christ! Just because we had some rough spots—"

"Rough spots!"

"—because there were some rough spots, you're going to opt out."

"I'm not going to opt out. I'm open—"

"Then—" he said again.

"But not with you, Morrie."

He was silent. "I've changed," he offered at last, passing his fingers over the hand at her side, trying to show in his gesture and in his eyes all that the statement left undescribed.

"So have I," she said stubbornly, and with a look of bitter concentration, she pulled his fingers from her hand; and once more she walked on.

"*I still have your sketch,*" he cried, following her, his voice rising with the need to bring sense between them. A block down the glaring street, lined with white stucco apartment houses and beds of blazing red curbside flowers, he saw a trolley bus stop and go on. "Christ, can't we stop and talk like friends? I want to tell you what I've been doing. I want to know what's happened to you. Two years!"

"I guess," she said, not looking at him, "those two years have been directed to this moment."

"Don't talk in circles. Where do you live, what are you doing? Are you happy?"

She didn't speak for a moment. "Not particularly."

"Can't we talk about it?"

"There's no point."

"How can you be so cold! Ask me something! Morrie, how are you?"

"No," she said, not coldly; not coldly at all, but with effort, disconsolately.

"I went up to your mountains once, in Napa, because I couldn't stand not knowing where you were. Look at me. Please."

She would not look; but he saw two tears slip down her face.

"We saw each other that time at the parking lot," he said quietly.

She wiped her sleeve across her face and gave a short nod.

"Did Conrad ever tell you that I phoned him?"

Again she nodded, with a shaky sigh.

"They've got a kid now? Poor old Closeto."

"He was killed," she said nasally.

"Ah, too bad. Poor old Conrad. How is he? How's Wanda?"

"Fine."

"I went back to the old place once, it was torn down, grass all over. Did you ever go back?"

"No."

"Rhonda always asks about you. You remember Rhonda, at the office? I'm back there now, got my old job back."

She threw him a surprised, still-wet glance. "I thought you dropped out."

"No, I went back. I made my bed and I'm laying in it. I told you I've changed."

But she was taking a coin purse from her pocket; he looked around them and saw that they had arrived at the bus zone.

"You're not really getting on that bus?" he asked, astonished; the wet eyes, the quiet conversation having built up his hopes again. And as he watched her take a quarter out, and saw that his time with her was telescoped into a few more brief moments, he was finally at a total loss, and gazed

372

somberly at the hot pavement, his mind as blank as its surface. And then a new spark of hope shot through him: on Sundays didn't fewer buses run, with as long as half an hour between? A reprieve, a limitless span of time. Renewed, he plunged his fingers through his hair and straightened up, but simultaneously he saw and heard a fuming, overloaded trolley bus lumber up to their side—a clap as the folding doors swung back, an explosion of voices, feet thumping down to the pavement—and in the space of a second, without a word or glance at him, Johanna was at the door, squeezing herself in among the passengers on the step. He blundered after her, his hand outthrust, and felt it collide with a hot gritty surface as the sides of the door heaved back together across her back, catching a piece of the burgundy shirt between them. The furnace blast of the motor enveloped him, blowing his hair, and with a lurch the scrap of burgundy moved off down the street. He took a useless step after it and stood there squinting in the glare of the sun, shading his eyes with his hand.

Low and heavy with cargo, listing to one side like an old freighter, the bus rumbled down the street with surprising speed, and he thought, why, when buses were notoriously slow on Sundays, couldn't this one have been slow? Why when half an hour more, just half an hour, might have sealed the terrible gap; and a golden seal passed through his mind, very large, richly embossed with various emblems of love, honor, glory—he was growing soft-headed, he felt fatigued, sick; and as he stood there trickling with sweat, his eyes straining after the diminishing vehicle, he saw it veer around a corner, and —unbelievably, unbelievably—it was no more.

"Don't turn," Johanna had commanded herself as Morrie's hand thumped against the door and the bus roared off. It was the bright red terrifying wound all over again, something torn out from her center, and she told herself: Think of a year from now, ten years from now—it will all be in the past— But this made no impression on her, and she pushed away from the vulnerable door and squeezed up the step, deeper into the clamorous, swaying crowd, where she stood hemmed in, immobile, the floor lurching under her feet.

Think, think of a hundred years from now it won't be anything at all. And she tried to comfort herself with this terrible thought as the bus, leaving the street with Morrie, swung around a corner, heaving the crowd first to one side and then to the other, as a collective cry went up.

About the Author

Ella Leffland grew up in Martinez, California, and graduated from San Jose State College. She is the author of three highly acclaimed novels and a collection of short stories (including the title story "Last Courtesies," which shared first prize in the 1977 O. Henry Collection). Her stories have appeared in such periodicals as Harper's Magazine, Atlantic Monthly, The New Yorker, *and* Cosmopolitan.